Down Dog
BILLIONAIRE

LUCY EDGE

Edge Street Press

ALSO BY LUCY EDGE

*'A hilarious search for a more meaningful life
turns into a joyous discovery of India'*

—THE TIMES

'A hilarious, hapless and desperate quest'
—CHRIS STEWART,
author of Driving Over Lemons

*'Lucy Edge, a former London advertising
executive goes in search of spiritual riches (and
the perfect headstand) in India. Neither boringly
cynical nor stupidly gullible, she's open minded,
warm and funny; even – though she'd be the
last person to claim this – rather wise'*
—INDEPENDENT, Books of the Year

First published by Edge Street Press, 2015

ISBN: 978-0-9933341-0-8

Cover and interior design by Domini Dragoone
Cover illustrations by Solène Debiès
Author photograph by Leah Giorno

Serene we swam
Bold silvered shoal
A bubbling brooking quest

Deep down the stream
A pearly gleam
Beyond the cygnets' nest

Far would we go
The high, the low
The joy of it unbound

Through reeds and weeds
Our moon backs wove
All treasure to be found.

'Trust me'

I left my body at 16:08 precisely. I know this because I had a bird's eye view of Pat's over-sized watch. It was, as ever, placed purposefully in front of her – time management being her biggest thing. I floated silently amongst the speckled ceiling tiles, looking down on her brittle hair, doing my best to escape that thin, reedy voice of hers.

On she went, justifying herself from behind that big desk, the first to be inset with a sunshine yellow panel designed to boost optimism – her idea. The colour was reflected in the hollows of her face, giving her a pallid deathbed look, at odds with the studiedly upbeat disposition. She was in her stride now, 'Disappointing I know … consensus view … more to prove … next year …'

I stared gloomily at the decaying froth on her skinny decaff cappuccino (a cappuccino without point as far as I was concerned), a coffee I'd bought in a different lifetime – a lifetime in which I believed that people keep their word. I thought back to this time last year, when I'd told my best friend Becks that she needn't worry, that the promotion would be 'a dead cert' next time round, that the company she called 'Con World' couldn't possibly screw me over again.

Pat paused a moment, her head cocked to one side, now adopting the role of confidante. She was asking me to believe that she was my 'number one fan' but, oh pity her for finding herself in this position, she was 'a lone voice in the wilderness'. She was probably right about that. I was beginning to doubt anyone knew I existed. I'd operated under cover since the day she arrived – her personal property, chained to her desk. Whatever she wanted – another market report or competitive review – I delivered. Becks used to joke about it – when it was still funny – asking me what her last slave had died of. Actually, the last slave had been reborn as a nurse – apparently a night shift at the Royal Berkshire was a lot less stress than a day on Pat's detail.

I thought longingly of Becks' kitchen, of a glass of wine and a hug, but I knew what her first words would be: 'Did you stand up for yourself?' She'd asked me the same question last time around and when I'd told her that I hadn't said much, that I'd just have to work harder to prove myself, all hell had broken loose. I'd got the whole nine yards on my willingness to over-work and how it stemmed from believing I wasn't good enough. That I hid behind 'mild manners' and 'people pleasing'.

I attempted a deep breath, feeling nothing but the knot in my stomach, and took to the witness stand. I outlined the past year's achievements, trying to keep the emotion out of my voice, still hoping, somehow, that reason would win the day. I made sure I mentioned all the successful BOGOF's – the buy one get one free promotions that were the centre of my universe, and of course my reworking of the numbers to show that Pat's pet project, a competition, had not been a disaster after all, but in fact a great success, achieving press coverage in excess of the half a million the company had lost in prize money. Then I reminded her of the one idea that really excited me, the one I'd worked on every weekend for a year, hoping it would shoot to the front of the product pipeline, with me attached.

That idea was Chocolate Therapy. I'd presented it to her a month ago – a new brand of chocolate that would match every conceivable emotional need state to a soft healing centre of fruits, flowers or herbs. Milk chocolate and soothing lavender for inner peace and calm, dark chocolate and pink rose petals to feel loved, mint and essence of eucalyptus to refresh, lemon and lime for clarity, an intense burst of orange for an instant hit of happiness.

I'd thought it all through, right down to the packaging. The pretty red box tied with ribbon – a little self-gifting at the checkout. The twelve jewel-bright twists of cellophane and foil – like upmarket Quality Street. The context-driven social media strategy – tweeting inner peace to mums on the first day of the school holidays, making workers smile on gloomy Monday mornings, sending love to all the lonely on Valentine's Day.

I'd taken Pat through my financial projections, projections that were based on the proven emotional need states of ten thousand women, and I'd explained the brand values. Values that would fill all the gaps in our current brand equity, especially when people found out that ten percent of profits were being donated to a basket of mental health charities. I'd done my research; cause-related marketing could add many millions to the bottom line *and* it would make us seem more personal, less manufactured. We'd be a brand that made a difference, desirable, aspirational; a good citizen of the world, again.

'It'll be a feel good brand in every way,' I'd said, finishing my presentation with a final flourish, an animated graphic of the pink ribbon wrapping around the red box. It'd taken me days to put it together but I'd imagined it would be worth it – it could play behind me on the big screen as Pat announced my promotion to Team Leader.

At first, she'd seemed to get it – agreeing that the brand values were absolutely right – that they'd make us more personal, more upscale. 'It's about creating desirability, and aspiration,' she'd repeated, sniffing the rose petals, letting them float like confetti through her fingers.

'Of course, I have considerations,' she'd added quickly. 'The ribbon is probably an unnecessary expense, the twelve need states might be over-done,' but she felt the basic idea was strong – one she could 'take forward, with confidence'. With that she'd looked purposefully at her watch and snapped her laptop shut, telling me we'd meet again in a month, when she'd had time to 'digest and discuss'.

And now here she was, giving me 'feedback from on high', feedback she claimed to consider 'invaluable'. Down she counted on those ringless fingers. Number one – no to the 'too fancy' cellophane. Number two – no to the ribbon – 'think Tesco shelf-stackers'. Number three – no to the twelve different need states – 'far too many, far too complicated'. Number four – no to giving to charity – 'impossible in the current economic climate'. Number five – 'make it pay back inside a year'.

'Big issues Megan,' she said, shaking her head sorrowfully, 'I'm sure you agree.'

She did concede that the social media strategy was 'probably a good supplement', but that my fondness for 'twits', as she liked to call them, wouldn't be enough. 'This needs big budgets – TV, cinema, posters – a classic Confectionery World launch.' In other words, a formulaic campaign – probably starring a girl luxuriating on a sofa, or in a bath.

'No one argues that you've worked hard Megan,' she said, sounding so incredibly reasonable, 'it's just that you're still too much in your head – a little prone to academia. We need someone more experienced, more practical, with more gravitas, to take charge. Someone who can make it happen.' The words were coming out super-syrupy now. 'Surely you understand that? The need to put the project first?'

I stared at her speechless, still stuck at 'too much in my head'. At least I occupied my head. At least I spent time thinking. At least I didn't mistake a brainstorm, a flip chart or a wall of Post-it notes, the scribbles of half-formed 'thought starters,' for an idea. I started my thoughts, and I finished them. I took responsibility. What was wrong with that? Really. I wanted to kill her – strangle her with one of her marathon medal ribbons.

She paused, choosing her words carefully, oh so conciliatory. 'I know this is hard for you Megan, but can you rise above it? Feel flattered that the project is getting such high quality attention? See it as compliment? Let someone senior take it from here?'

'But I would be senior, if you'd promote me,' I replied, feeling the first prick of tears.

This was met with a disapproving silence; it was a widely known fact that her 'open invitation to speak freely' only went one way.

'So who is going to look after it?' I asked evenly, remembering the image I'd carried into the meeting – of the Managing Director striding across the floor, congratulating me on my idea, looking askance at my little grey cubicle as he told me I was needed in New York.

'It'll be a big team,' she said, focusing on a ceiling tile not far from where I was floating. She explained that 'everyone' was in agreement that she should be Project Champion, and that there'd be several others reporting into her – me included, 'of course'.

Then she was off again, burbling on about how this was actually a great opportunity – one that would give her the 'evidence' to really build my 'case.' She emphasised the word, shooting her cuffs, play-acting the courtroom lawyer. This was utter rubbish; there was plenty of evidence – she just wasn't prepared to share it with anyone. Becks had said it time and time again; why hadn't I listened? The plain truth was I made Pat look good and, as long as I was her gofer, her dogsbody, she wasn't going to let me go anywhere, let alone desert my little grey cubicle.

Finally, she came to a halt. 'I know this company Megan, I know what it can take, and when. Just give it time.'

'But I've given it three years,' I said, my voice wobbling.

'Don't give up now,' she said firmly, smoothing down a sleeve, 'not after all your hard work. You're a valued member of the team – work with us, help us put this plan into play.'

'But it's *my* plan,' I said, trying not to sound like a bleating five year old.

'There's no need to be *negative* Megan,' she replied sharply, kicking the word away as if it might be contagious.

Opening her office door, conscious that she now had an audience, she caught herself, and swiftly reverted to her favourite role – the part of benevolent employer. There she stood, waiting patiently, a picture of empathy, as I peeled myself slowly off the ceiling.

'You'll make it Megan,' she said, her smile as fake as her Louis Vuitton handbag. 'Trust me.'

Conventionally, people who've had an out-of-the-body experience make a full comeback. Not me. I'd left some not-so-small part of me behind – forever stuck to the sound-proof, mould-proof, fire-proof tiles.

I took what remained of me to the stationery cupboard and quietly closed the door. Grabbing the steps, wheeling them into the darkest corner, I sank into my misery.

Usually, my tears were done in a few minutes. I'd wipe my eyes and smooth down my skirt and walk out as if nothing had happened, determinedly back on track. I'd pick up a coffee and escape into an ExCel spreadsheet – emerging a couple of hours later with a file full of neat numbers – back in the driving seat.

But this day was different. I hung my head, massaged my throbbing temples, no longer able to ignore the fact that I was twenty-nine and going nowhere – well past the age when people pat you on the back and say 'Never mind; there's plenty of time yet.' What had happened to the Grand Plan, the one I made the day I graduated?

1. Big career in brands – love it so much it doesn't feel like work
2. Make money and do good – best of both worlds
3. Own office – with a view, ideally of the Gherkin
4. Calm, modern, spacious flat – with taupe tones
5. Loving husband – respects my independence
6. Friends – remaining true to self and others
7. Baby – best of both of us, but if not that, then normal

Okay, looking back it was all a bit Bridget Jones, but the heart of it was right, and it was still the dream. While Becks was now working her way back up the list, having accidentally started at point seven, my Grand Plan had stalled at point one.

I thought back to the glory days of the grad recruitment fairs – when the world was my oyster. Would things have been any different if I'd joined John Lewis? They'd seemed such a principled company, what with all that employee co-ownership, and the Partners' Dining Room, and those country estates where everyone went to play tennis. 'And even if they aren't,' reasoned mum, 'at least we'll get bargain bed linen.'

I'd got through to the last round there, but then the letter landed inviting me to an interview at Hinshaw's. The letterhead announced 'Chocolate makers since 1850' in old-fashioned curlicue script – the hand of Bob Hinshaw himself.

Like John Lewis, Hinshaw's was known then as a fantastic place to work. It had been ever since Mr. Hinshaw gave his factory workers a free school, a library, a doctor's surgery, a subsidised grocery store and even a pension plan. Over a hundred and fifty years later employees (interviewed for *The Sunday Times*' 'Best Companies' feature) were still rhapsodising about the shared sense of purpose, the like-minded people, the matching of opportunity to talent, the free food – breakfast, lunch, and chocolate.

And Hinshaw's didn't just look after the people at home. They took their developing world responsibilities seriously, earning themselves a Fairtrade accreditation. My favourite idea of theirs was the twinning of cocoa farmers with Hinshaw employees – the farmer got someone on the inside who had the power to help, and the employee got to understand the grassroots issues.

As if all that wasn't enough, Hinshaw's was also home to some of the nation's best-loved brands. Some of them had been around since those early days and still made 'Ad of the Year', as voted by viewers. These were brands I'd loved since I was a kid, when I wished I could climb inside the TV and be the pretty girl skipping alongside the Pop-it puppets, or picnicking in the woods with Hinney the Bear.

The Head of Marketing at that time was the world-renowned brand guru Graham Lovatt. Whilst all my other interviews had lasted two days and involved lots of group work and role play in which the goal seemed to be total humiliation, he sat me down, looked me in the eye, and asked me what I'd got.

Pausing only to admire the feats of German engineering that stretched for miles in the car park below, I pulled a colour-coded dossier out of my bag.

Exhibit A. Chocolate for students, targeted by need state. Brain-food chocolate. Alcohol flavoured chocolate. Detox chocolate.

Exhibit B. Brand Ambassadors, walking the street armed with free chocolate fixes. Swooping down on people stuck in a queue, or caught in the rain.

Exhibit C was my favourite. Becks had given me the idea. She'd spent her summer holidays working for NGOs in India, Africa and South America and she'd seen lots of women escape unreliable men by selling door-to-door. She said it worked because there were no start up costs and the women used their own extended networks to sell. I told him it'd be like Avon ladies, except my 'Lakshmi Ladies' would be women in need of a new start, and a fridge – which would need to be big for all that chocolate.

'Well,' he said, suppressing a wry smile, 'you certainly have no shortage of ideas.'

A week later I got the letter.

There was one downside, but I wouldn't always be in Slough. I'd be taking the fast train to London a lot – seeing research companies and the ad agency, and afterwards we'd have dinner in happening restaurants stuffed with handsome waiters and statement flowers. I figured that when I'd got some experience under my belt I'd travel further afield – to see our partners in New York and Sydney, swapping Slough for a SoHo loft or a harbour side penthouse. Eventually, I'd settle down with a younger version of Graham, and set up the first Hinshaw's crèche, and once I'd made Marketing Director I'd get shares and buy me, mum and dad, and Becks (if there was money enough) the houses we'd always wanted.

The first five years had gone pretty much according to plan; every day filled with as much excitement as that first day – when I couldn't believe I could stuff my pockets with chocolate and call it corporate pride, not stealing.

On the bus to work, I'd soak up my books on marketing theory and all those company directives – making sure I wasn't missing anything, that I was in the loop. I'd skip across the temperature-controlled, light-filled atrium that promoted Hinshaw's as a global force, picking up a coffee (two shots), jabbing at the button for the lift, bounding down the corridors of automatically watered palms and humming light fittings, as enthusiastic as Tigger. I'd arrive at cubicle 03.26 with my coat off and my sleeves rolled up, fully mobilised for another day fighting Mars and Cadbury on the shelves of Tesco.

I loved being on the road even more than I loved my desk. The graduate training programme had yet to be cut back when I joined; it was still an old school immersion in all aspects of company life. Graham had put it in place and it involved a lot of days out – supermarkets for shopping psychology, our lawyers for patent applications, NGO's for fair trade, and creative immersion days at our ad agency. But despite the drinks at the end of the advertising day, the marble loos and model-turned-receptionists, our Swindon factory was my favourite place.

I still remember my first visit. The aircraft sized hangar, the donning of gloves, hairnets, and rubber shoes. The vast silver vats and the ridged rollers, the seven metre long cooling tunnels, the drums coating cherries with sugar, the smell of milk and vanilla. All the other grads moaned but I loved the lessons in chocolate viscosity, the thrill of watching a new brand of chocolate come off the quivering conveyer belt for the first time, the million gold bars stacked and ready for shipping, a chocolate heist. I saw myself as part of this perfectly attuned machine – a little cog that could play its part in delighting customers, in creating overtime for hard working families, a little cog that would one day make a big difference.

I got promoted from Marketing Trainee to Manager when the Brand Ambassador programme took off and then to Senior Marketing Manager when, with more than a little help from Graham, Lakshmi Ladies went into the field.

And then, just as I was about to be promoted to Team Leader – only two levels below Marketing Director, Hinshaw's became Confectionery World. It was, to put it mildly, a hostile takeover.

The new American CEO stood behind a lectern, reassuring us that our jobs were secure and that nothing would change.

Six months later everything had.

The photos of our smiling founders, the ones that had lined the boardroom for all eternity, were ousted in favour of giant images of fit looking types abseiling over rocks in some display suggestive of what – marketing prowess? Bob Hinshaw's own signature was replaced by a new logo – three triangles in a circle. Within six months twenty percent of the staff had been made redundant, the award-winning ad agency who'd worked with us since the second world war had been replaced by a multi-national famous only for its size and cut-price rates of commission, the VP for Social Change had been fired, Bob Hinshaw's beloved school and library had been sold to a property developer and pretty much all the NGO contracts had been cancelled, including Lakshmi Ladies.

Graham left.

Pat arrived.

My little cog ground to a halt.

Everything, it seemed, was on fast track, except me. New products had to succeed in four weeks or they were pulled, the old directors did whatever it took to achieve their year end bonus and left, and the new directors spent meetings monitoring the company share price or surfing Prime Location for riverside frontage in 'exclusive family-friendly havens'.

Meanwhile, I went home to a flat above a launderette. (You'd think, what with all that washing powder, the flat would smell clean, but somehow other people's old socks, liberated from a week in a laundry bag, always won out.) It did, however, have 'excellent transport links' (estate agent speak for being sandwiched between a bus stop and a railway station, and under a flight path).

After several flatmates of the *Single White Female* variety, including a girl who spent her entire life mainlining my Walkers' Sensations in front of the telly, I opted to live alone. Consequently, most of my money went on rent. Buying a Mars Bar might've been my first purchase as a kid, bringing with it my first taste of freedom; those colourful wrappers and whimsical names – Curly Wurly, Rolo, Kit Kat – promising a life beyond our Reading semi, but I hadn't had a pay rise since the takeover.

Before Con World, when I'd imagined that life would always be sweet, I'd not made the wisest investments, treating myself to an eclectic array of high-end kitchen equipment that never got used – partly because I was always at work, and partly because I was rubbish at cooking. I'd also splashed out thousands on an Italian designer sofa. A factory mix up had resulted in the delivery of a four-seater and, imagining the nights of unbridled passion to come (this was several lifetimes ago), or at least nights spent hosting the local book group, I thought I might as well keep it. Now it sat accusingly – a vast thing like a beached whale taking up the whole sitting room, willing me to tell the world it was witness only to ready meals for one.

I fished a chocolate bar out of my pocket. That was another problem with this place; there was temptation everywhere, a basketful of shiny wrappers on every desk, the only remaining legacy of the Hinshaw years. It was like a harvest festival of chocolate, except that the opportunity to feast in praise of our factory's abundance wasn't limited to autumn. Not good news for me. While other working women carried the weight of the world on their shoulders, I carried it on my size fourteen hips and thighs. I went to take another bite and found I'd demolished the entire thing. I hadn't even noticed myself eating it. Perhaps we'd reduced the size of it? That happened a lot these days.

I unwrapped another bar, finally acknowledging, as strawberry and milk chocolate melted together, what not-so-small part of me had been left behind on those sound-proof, mould-proof, fire-proof ceiling tiles.

Hope.

As long as Pat was in charge I wasn't going anywhere. I could give her all the ideas in the world and it would never be enough. She'd always find something lacking in my ability, some reason to knock me back, some reason to keep me wrapped in grey burlap. Slowly, I wheeled the steps back into position and stood wearily against the wall, flattening hot muscles against the cool bricks, turning my head from side to side, trying to release my neck. All I could see, wherever I looked, were vast shelves heaving with flip charts, Post-its and calculators; Con World's weapons of mass destruction. It was at this point I realised that, unless I did something about it, there was a strong chance I'd die in here, my body discovered by someone hunting for file dividers. Perhaps they'd rename the cupboard in memoriam: Stationary not Stationery.

'Stick or twist'

CHAPTER TWO

'Aunty Meg!' screamed a small voice, 'Stick 'em up!'

The pink clad fairy was in her tree house, her water pistol trained on me.

Slowly, I raised my arms, a hostage for the second time that day. 'Your gun for chocolate?'

Peering over the top of the parapet, she inspected my handful of colourful wrappers.

She checked the catch on her pistol. 'No dice.'

Normally, I would've clambered up there after her, happy to stake out Southcote's fir, fruit and plane trees, just like her mum and I had done at her age. Not on this day.

I raged up the ragged garden path, barging through the back door like the Terminator.

'Bad day at the office?' said Becks, looking up from a stack of marking.

I nodded curtly, staring down the framed Barack Obama 'Hope' poster - he didn't know Pat.

Clearing me a space among the piles of exercise books, she emptied the remnants of several packets of biscuits onto a plate, dusty crumbs falling on the floor where they were swiftly eaten by J.R., a rescued mongrel named for his voracious appetites. With a steady hand she filled her trusty kettle. I swear that woman could stave off the end of the world with a packet of PG Tips.

We settled on either side of the table. Her in her beloved purple 'OM' t-shirt and yoga pants, me in my best suit. She pushed the biscuit plate towards me, expectant.

'"More to prove",' I said, imitating that thin voice, my shoulders slumped. I pointed two fingers against my head. 'I'm a moron.'

'You're working for a hostile,' she said, grabbing my hand, forcing it back to the table. 'She's the moron.'

'I spend all my time working on brands that promise happiness,' I said, staring unseeing into my mug, 'and all I am is miserable.'

We sat in silence for a moment, contemplating this newly acknowledged fact.

'What now?' I asked, quietly.

'Two options.'

'And they are?'

'Stick or twist.'

'Well, I can't risk a tombstone that reads "Here rests Meg Rogers. She gave good BOGOF."'

Becks laughed and began an extended hunt for more biscuits while I stared out of the window, to the clothes gusting on the line, wondering whether the world would always think 'buy one get one free' was the only promotion in my reach. 'Maybe I should've joined John Lewis, or M&S – perhaps I'd have got somewhere by now.'

Becks snorted in disbelief. 'M&S couldn't even get their knickers right back then.'

'Well,' I shrugged, 'I can't do it anymore.'

She looked at me thoughtfully. I hoped I wasn't heading for another session on her couch. Thankfully, she went the other way, ploughing another well-furrowed path.

'Personally, I think you should take my backpack and take off. Climb Machu Picchu, trek the Himalaya, have some fun.'

It was Becks' dream, not mine. The bugs and bites, the heat and dust, the long and crowded bus rides – I couldn't think of anything worse. Her craving to be a good citizen of the world had been barely satiated by the university holidays she'd spent teaching kids in Bihar and digging wells in Kampala – summers I spent working in The Body Shop. I'd always known, beyond all doubt, that I would be a lot more use raising money for good causes in a shop that smelled of strawberries and coconuts than building latrines in Cambodia.

'There's no way I'm going to drop out. I want to achieve something, do something with my life, prove that a Rogers can make it big.'

'What are you talking about?' said Becks, staring at me as if I was mad. 'Your dad was an *accountant*.' She said it like he'd been Finance Director of a major corporation instead of a one-man band working out of a converted garden shed. 'And your mum was huge – she was the Don Corleone of Reading.'

Being a florist, mum knew everything about everyone – every birth, death and marriage – but I had always wanted more for her. She could've opened more shops, done bigger events – god knows she had the talent, but she always wanted to get home to make us dinner, and rehearse her dance routines with dad. And now it was too late, she and dad had retired to Barnstaple, repatriating the previous owners' 'garden office' as a potting shed.

'It's not always about money Meg,' said Becks, flicking a biscuit crumb at me. 'But if you're that desperate to "make it big" set up a business of your own. Work from home to start with – convert that big cupboard of yours into an office.'

Whilst dad always waxed lyrical about the time saved commuting from the bedroom to the shed, about the lack of politics, being his own boss, the idea had always filled me with dread. On the rare days I worked from home, I'd got cabin fever by lunchtime. I needed to be with people, to bounce ideas around – or at least to have the theoretical possibility of bouncing ideas around. And what about the money? Where would it come from? It wasn't as if I had some big network of potential clients yanking my skirt. Dad had spent years building up his business – his clients were mainly one-man bands just like him – and yet he still had dips and troughs. I could still remember the early nineties recession, when I was six or seven; there had been milk but no cream – camping holidays in the rain (long before glamping), a car that had seen better days, talk of moving to a smaller house. I knew I wouldn't be able to deal with all that on my own.

I reminded her of the Grand Plan – of that Gherkin view, of making money and making a difference. These things were only going to come with working for a corporate.

Mere mention of the 'c' word triggered a diatribe on 'exploitative structures' that ended with a demand that I would not allow myself to be 'subjugated' again.

Then she moved on to her other favourite idea; that I should work for a charity. 'You should do some more campaigning – you're brilliant at it.'

I smiled at the memory of Becks, our newly crowned Student Union Welfare Officer, jumping victorious into the campus fountain. 'You would've made it anyway, without my help.'

'What about your homeless charity? They love you.'

I groaned. Once a year, around Christmas, was enough. 'You wouldn't believe the politics involved in handing out soup.'

'At least it'd be shorter hours; give you time to find a man.'

'I don't want a man.'

'Of course you do.'

It was my turn to flick a crumb across the table. 'I'm quite happy on the shelf – except when I worry I might break it. Actually, I'm thinking I might take a leaf out of your book; "Practice non…?"'

'"Non attachment",' she said, patiently.

This was otherwise known as 'love 'em and leave 'em' – a policy she'd implemented after she split with Susie's dad. Becks liked to model herself on Katharine Hepburn – doing what she wanted on her terms, not afraid to be alone. This didn't mean a life of celibacy. Far from it. Becks had strong appetites and fast turnarounds, and having a child had done nothing to dent her enthusiasm – though she only ever indulged in a sleepover when Susie was on a sleepover, and she never introduced any of them to her friends, not even me.

'Any new victims?' I asked, watching the mistress of covert operations duck her head into the fridge. She emerged a full minute later with a bottle of wine and a fervently expressed desire to spend the rest of the evening workshopping my taste in men, again.

Richard was the last serious one, and that relationship ended six years ago. We'd met on a Market Research Society training course; I was a couple of years in, still living the Hinshaw dream, and he was working for one of our competitors.

He was a bit older, 'seasoned', as he liked to call himself. Imagining myself as Carey Mulligan in *An Education*, in the hands of a sophisticated, cultured, man – someone with experience; successful and sorted, I spent my weekends working through his shelves of 'important' novels, foreign films and jazz greats, always with a glass in hand.

He said all the right things. He wanted to work with the UN to improve the lot of female farmers, he wanted to halve production-generated greenhouse gases, but his eyes were a faraway place with no direct flights, and Becks never trusted him. She kept asking why he didn't like going out, why he hadn't introduced me to his friends, why he didn't have a sense of humour, and why, if he really was Mr Big, I'd met him on a junior-level course. I kept making excuses until one fateful day, a year later, I went round to his house to leave a surprise present for his return from a weekend away (an obscure recording he'd been after) and there he was, in bed with another girl.

I'd had a few flings since then; a geek more passionate about building his *Guitar Heroes* website than he was about me, one of Beck's Buddhist friends who was only interested in replenishing his yang vitality and finally, a battle re-enactment enthusiast. It only took one day in an itchy brown dress, pretending to be a serving wench, for me to throw in the bar towel.

Becks, as usual, had plenty to say about all of them – each one further evidence of my own 'distance from myself' and a certain 'lack of self-knowledge'.

'The only relationship I have is with chocolate,' I said, slumping into my chair.

'And me.'

'And you,' I replied, shivering at the thought of leaving her warm kitchen, taking the train back to Slough.

Before I left, she told me to take this latest Con World stitch up as 'an opportunity'. She wanted me to 'turn it around' – create a new future for myself, one rooted in 'self-knowledge and self-expression'. This 'self-knowledge and self-expression' could be in any direction, as long as it didn't involve Con World.

I promised.

A couple of days later I pulled a sickie and headed to London. The first headhunter on my list (a round-faced, bouncy-haired woman) told me cheerfully that potential employers would be concerned I'd become 'institutionalised'. Apparently, eight years in one company, especially at my age, spoke of 'a certain lack of drive'. The second called Con World a 'dinosaur' – said my lack of recent digital experience would be 'a total roadblock'. The third couldn't understand why I'd want to leave – thought Pat was great, that Confectionery World was the promised land.

The next morning, a glorious day, the curtains stayed closed. I sat at my kitchen table, opened my laptop, determined that I would not leave my flat until I had found something. Something, anything, that would get me as far away from Slough as it was possible to be.

By six o'clock, I'd made ten applications – one to each of Con World's rivals, and the rest to other FMCG companies. Another 'fast moving consumer goods' company would surely be the fastest ticket out. Though none of them felt right, anything was better than where I was right then. I closed my laptop, turned on Saturday night TV and hit the bottle.

Sunday morning, I lay in bed listening to the sound of spinning washing machines down below as I gloomily checked my Twitter feed. All the usual suspects – 'three signs your marketing is wrong', 'five reasons to change agency' and this, from Brand Republic #marketingjobs:

> 'Into brands? Ambitious? Super-luxe yoga spa goes
> global @Shine. #RiseAndShine'

I spent several minutes glued to their homepage, obsessing over the attention to detail – the images, the social media integration, the golden lotus flower logo. I thought about Con World and the doomed quest to bring positive meaning to three triangles in a circle – a logo that would forever remind me of a radiation warning.

It was a slam-dunk; Shine would be the perfect antidote to a life in moulded chocolate. Born in California, it now had fifteen centres up and down the West and East Coast and, in what was clearly a plan to take over the world, it was about to open in London. Founded by a seriously ambitious ex-City guy called Max Walcott, Shine combined Silicon Valley smarts – think intuitive, personalised user experiences – with buckets (or should that be vitality pools?) of Asia-Pacific style.

Back at Hinshaw's, I'd always felt a disconnect between what we stood for – making the world a better place – and what we did – make people fat. Shine, on the other hand, was all about transformation and healthy living – it's values and purpose a seamless whole. It'd only been in business three years and, while I'd slid slowly under my Con World desk, its fortunes had soared. No surprises there – it really was marketing genius; it put advocacy above advertising, it was open and authentic, and it was all about co-creation – everyone tweeting everything from motivational messages ('In it together #CrushIt') to the café ('In love with a wheatgrass muffin @Shine').

At the heart of all that transformation was the spa. I'd treated Becks to a weekend at Champney's when I was last promoted. We'd spent our days having massages and manicures and our evenings in the bar, drinking champagne to oxygenate our blood. But thanks to my pay freeze and Becks' teacher's salary, we had to learn to content ourselves with Tesco's Finest bubble bath. Perhaps, if I ever got the job, this would change. I imagined emerging 'dusted with a golden glow' from a two-hour, four-handed massage called a 'Maharani', and wondered whether a maharani had ever got a train home to Slough.

There was no getting away from it; the Shine brand was all about perfection. The women on the website were slender, sculpted, golden types; Doutzen Kroes, Kate Hudson, Gigi Hadid types. Not very 'me' types.

I had, one New Year, mistaken myself for a girl who jogged at dawn. I duly became the proud owner of a bright red Nike tracksuit. It'd sat ever since in my drawer – gathering dust besides my date-night knickers. Nowadays my exercise routine consisted of walking from my cubicle to the Con World coffee machine (a distance of ten paces) and unwrapping chocolate bars. I did it every day, with great discipline – sometimes five times a day.

There was hope on at least one count – Max Walcott had

once been a bit of a porker too. I didn't have to do much digging; surprisingly it was all out in public – it seemed he liked to tell the story as testimony to the power of Shine – and, of course, from a brand point of view, all that openness gave the transformation platform plenty of authenticity. Out in Hong Kong, his deals were fuelled by cocaine and celebrated with champagne – a £400 bottle was for wimps. He'd buy six magnums at a time – they'd arrive in a blaze of glory – with sparklers in the corks, lighting up his table with fizzy promise. The cocaine, if not the champagne, had apparently stopped when he'd discovered yoga, putting an end to the premature paunch and the lifestyle that created it. My self-medicating had been limited to chocolate – surely my reformation would be easier?

I read on, trawling through the website. Words such as 'detox', 'portion control', 'exercise' and 'yoga' flitted before my eyes. They all made me nervous, especially the 'yoga' word.

My one and only yoga experience had been with Nate.

Don't get me wrong; he was a lovely guy, a real salt of the earth type, and quite good looking if he'd only make an effort, but his teaching was Becks' thing not mine. All that 'breathe, relax, observe', all that life in the slow lane. After two hours (his shortest class), I'd wanted to run for the hills, though I'd settled for the nearest bar.

At least I wouldn't have to go far for a drink. Every Shine spa had a champagne bar – staffed by the male version of the California Goddesses – also slender, also golden, also sculpted. Apparently the presence of alcohol was all part of the 'balance culture' – a culture I felt ready to embrace.

Delving deeper, it seemed Shine's yoga might be served up with the same balanced approach – at least that had to be my hope. It wasn't a straight line from the old Indian sages, the way Nate taught it, complete with temple incense, bells and chanting – it was always done in combination with another exercise, like

Ju-Jitsu, or boxing. While I could see the downside of this might be faster classes requiring more effort, there were upsides. Judging by the Yo-Jitsu videos on the website, there was no sitting around learning to breathe – they were big classes, full of energy and always to music. Perhaps I could think of it as dancing on a much smaller dance floor – a yoga mat. I could deal with that – especially as no class ever lasted more than an hour.

So, there was just the small matter of getting the interview. I was going to need help. Serious help. I'd been so boxed in at Con World I hadn't built any kind of network but, there was one person I could always rely on; Graham. We'd stayed in touch over the years – nothing major, just updates around Christmas, but discovering on LinkedIn that he had a connection to Max Walcott was a gift. It looked like they'd met at a TED conference. What had it been? Seth Godin on 'How to get your ideas to spread' or perhaps Malcolm Gladwell on 'Choice, happiness and spaghetti sauce'. I fired Graham an email. The response was immediate. He wasn't sure Max would be my thing but he'd put in a word, with pleasure.

'The prettiest feet I've ever seen'

By Friday afternoon of the same week, I was ringing Max Walcott's freshly polished doorbell. I couldn't believe that I was going to meet the man himself. As I was applying for the lowly position of Brand Manager, I'd expected to get passed down the line, but the email had said that Mr Walcott took a personal interest in all his staff – especially the brand people – and wanted to meet me himself. What had Graham told him? It must've been quite the recommendation.

Getting in the lift, I pressed the button for the top floor, inhaling the distinctive smell of Brasso as the whirr and rattle of the engine seemed to echo the lurch in my stomach. Travelling ever upwards, I checked my reflection in the ornate gilt mirror. Mouse-blonde, out-of-control corkscrew curls. Beaky nose. A new spot. Doutzen Kroes? Not so much. I polished my front teeth with my index finger, practicing my smile, praying that my dry mouth wouldn't make it impossible to speak. Turning to face the worn brass gates, I wiped my sweaty palms on my skirt and took a couple of deep breaths, listening for the 'bing' of the bell that meant access to a different world.

'Meg Rogers,' I said, marching forward, hand extended, expecting Max.

'Camilla,' replied the coltish woman in a white trouser suit and bare feet, offering no further explanation as she looked down her rather long nose at me.

As I tried to get my bearings in the dazzling light, she suggested that I might like to remove my shoes.

'Great idea,' I said, holding on to the cupboard door with one hand as I levered them off, while inside I cried. I'd bought them to go with the jersey wrap-dress, to spice it up a little, to lengthen my legs. Without them, I felt provincial; I really was Slough Girl, completely devoid of the sassy chutzpah I'd spent days rehearsing. Next, she spirited away my coat and bag, acting like she'd prefer to put all of me in the cupboard.

She was right – I wasn't a natural fit. I felt like I was stepping into the pages of *World of Interiors*; everything newly purchased, co-ordinated by some supreme all-seeing eye. The Mah Jong set on the side table was made of the same wood as the timber-framed arch windows – teak? The lampshades matched the chairs that matched the rugs that matched the abstract prints – fifty shades of grey? I managed a wry smile.

I padded up the stairs behind her, wondering whether a bottom that small made sitting an ordeal. The room was vast – it must've been fifteen hundred square feet, the whole of the outside wall made up of floor to ceiling glass. A balcony of stainless steel balustrades extended the empire. The Gherkin and several cranes gleamed in the near distance.

Leading me towards a long, low-level sofa, Camilla poured a glass of water and placed it on a white lacquer wood coffee table, firmly marking the spot where I should sit. Once she was satisfied I was in position, she gave me a look as cold as the water and disappeared.

Max was at his desk, on the phone – sitting beneath a large oil painting of a matador fighting a bull. The animal was dying but ready for a final charge of glory; clods of red paint glooped from its neck, the matador a tiny reflection in his blaze-of-fury eyes. Max had the kind of charged presence normally reserved for matinee idols: the luxurious flop of straight black hair, the strong brow, the olive skin, the brown eyes, the deep diamond shaped crevice that ran from his nose to the firmest of chins, framed by the faintest of dimples. He made me think of dark chocolate. I'd always preferred milk.

I curled my toes into the depths of the wool carpet, resisting the urge to run straight back to Con World – it was, at least, a world I knew. Two things kept me there – one was the thought of living with myself if I walked out, the other was Max.

He looked up and smiled apologetically, rolling his eyes and holding up his index finger. Then he leaned back in his chair. It was a slow but decisive movement that created a tantalising opportunity to admire what lay beneath his Gucci jacket; the flash of red lining, the buttoned waistcoat, the curl of hair above the open necked shirt, the threads on his wrist – were they Kabbalah or Buddhist, or plain old fashion?

Trying not to stare, I busied myself with the collection of wall-mounted, ebony-framed, black and white photographs; many of their subjects familiar from my late night crawls around the Shine website. There he was, his arms round a mother and daughter celebrity pair, the three of them of them radiating white teeth, health, and Hollywood Hills happiness. He was even more handsome in the flesh.

I tried to settle into the unforgiving sofa, and waited for him to finish the call – a protracted discussion about a crate that had been impounded by Customs. Watching him made me think of old JFK footage – he had the same commanding presence, an easy smoothness, and an absolute expectation of compliance. He was clear that he would win the argument; it was simply a matter of time. He spoke quietly, almost whispering – an act that seemed to hint at intimacy. Listening required my full attention and I found myself leaning in, wanting to get closer but, at the same time, feeling a distance – there was a sense of being kept out, controlled. The effect was disorientating.

I tried to centre myself by leafing through one of the press files. The first cutting featured a smiling Deepak Chopra and Oprah alongside a headline proclaiming them 'King and Queen of the Spiritual Rich List'. The article, prettily offset by a picture of a bare-footed, cross-legged Max, placed Mr Walcott at number twenty. The journalist had made Max his 'tip for the top', pointing out that he had a way of spinning money out of money. He'd already turned the eight million he'd made in tech stock into a turnover ten times that and he planned on a centre in every major city within five years.

It was with some effort that I ended the daydream; the two of us pictured in next year's Rich List surrounded by grinning children from the Indian orphanage we'd built together. I could see the by-line now – 'the Guru in Gucci meets his match'. Now afraid to meet his eye, I stared at the floor – but that was no good either; his bare feet were clearly something of a trademark, and they were the prettiest feet I'd ever seen. They were large but hairless, tanned and smooth, topped by crescent moon nails with a pink sheen – buffed to perfection.

Finally, he finished persuading the official of the error of his ways. Apologising for keeping me waiting, calling for Camilla to bring some coffee for me and a Diet Coke, he offered me his hand; his grip was firm, his gaze unstinting, sweeping over me like a searchlight, scrutinising me, while he remained entirely inscrutable.

Who did I think I was? I tried to smile but my lips stuck to my teeth. I ignored the glass of water because my hands were shaking and seized the first thing that came into my mind – it happened to be his collection of James Bond first editions, anything to divert his attention.

'Other kids wanted to be train drivers,' he confessed, 'I wanted to be Bond.' There was a pause, then 'How am I doing?'

Something in his manner suggested he thought he might be doing rather well. 'Not bad,' I risked, gesturing in the direction of Camilla, 'you do have a Miss Moneypenny.' As Becks would say, the man clearly suffered from high self-esteem, though actually, he did have the look of an early Bond – a sixties Sean Connery type.

He gave me an easy but impenetrable smile and, perhaps sensing the need to break my palpable tension, commanded me to follow to the plinth by the window. Tucking in behind, I absorbed his height and the way he moved – the broad T of his shoulders, the muscular legs. I found myself pulling my own shoulders back, sucking in my stomach, trying to walk tall in my stocking feet – feeling like a duckling following a drake.

The open topped model was a scaled down version of the new London centre, and came complete with tiny model fountains and painted people. We stooped over it as Max described how the hundred thousand square feet of space – four floors of wood, glass and steel – would work. The fourteenth floor would house the reception and café, the champagne bar and shop, the fifteenth floor would contain the changing rooms, lockers and all the office space, the top two floors – the ones with the best views – would host the beauty and blow-dry bars, the exercise studios and treatment rooms. 'It'll be the biggest spa in Europe,' he concluded, adjusting the folds in a miniature screen, placing it precisely a centimetre from the wall of the top floor studio. I noticed how steady his hands were, and how his perfectly manicured fingers matched his toes.

He asked me which Shine location was my favourite. 'Perhaps Santa Barbara, or maybe the Upper East Side?' I mumbled something about it being impossible to choose, that they all looked great – but he'd already moved seamlessly on, explaining that they shared the same 'design vernacular' but that each one had its own quirks, designed to fit the local character. I chuckled knowledgeably, recounting the sorry tale of Con World's ill-fated attempt to sell their bog-standard chocolate bar to young Chinese women – women with an insatiable desire for luxury. Then, fearing that the story might, by association, suggest complete incompetence on my part, I moved to abort – diving headlong into a complete review of the global spa market, and Shine's fit within it.

'And breathe,' said Max, smiling gently. 'We come in peace.'

Wishing I could disappear into Camilla's cupboard, I took that breath. 'Yoga may have come to the West as part of the sixties counterculture but your mission is to make it palatable to corporate culture. That's what you're focused on here – everything you do is designed to meet the needs of urban professionals – your spas are located in the business hubs of cities, your classes are no more than an hour because that's all they have time for, and you give them every comfort – from valeted yoga mats to eucalyptus-scented towels.'

'Exactly,' he said, picking up the thread. 'None of them want to attain enlightenment, none of them want to walk on water, and none of them want to merge their consciousness with the universe. They want to de-stress so they can perform better at work, realise their potential mentally, physically, and materially. They want a hot body and, of course, eternal youth.'

'I can relate to that,' I laughed, embracing the release. 'I'd love to realise my potential, and of course eternal youth would be nice.' I stopped suddenly, conscious that I was gushing again.

He apologised for 'dragging' me over to his place, telling me that he wanted to meet me on site but that Shine was still a hardhat zone, despite the fact that it was opening in a week. I agreed it was a shame, though nothing could've been further from the truth; I wouldn't have missed this flat for the world.

He took a sip of Coke and frowned, clearly frustrated by the delay. 'And ideally I'd have introduced you to Zoffany – but she's away again on another scouting mission. Who knew Tibetan tree bark could be so hard to find?'

'It will be worth it,' I replied, smiling reflexively at the image imprinted on my mind. Zoffany was a fashion icon, a permanent fixture in the glossies – a woman whose trademark was superglam-Boho. The vintage dresses, the over-sized bags and bug-eyed sunglasses, the huge gold jewellery, the tousled beach-blonde tresses, thick eyelashes and honey tan – the giddy collision of Studio 54 and Saint Tropez – it was unmistakable. It was hard to imagine that she really existed, and even harder to believe that I'd meet her, if I got the job.

'"Modern ethnic luxe" – isn't that her signature style?' I offered, quoting from one of many interviews. Becks didn't call me a 'girly swot' for nothing.

He looked amused.

I skated on, seizing another opportunity to demonstrate the thoroughness of my research – knowing that I was being over the top but powerless to stop myself. Was I hoping for a gold star? 'She uses "local traditions and organic materials as signifiers of a natural world, synthesizing them with the best of modern tech."'

'Full marks,' he said, smiling again, 'though we don't always use modern tech.' He picked up a miniature cushion from the fourteenth floor and placed it in the palm of my hand, dropping his voice to an almost whisper. 'This one is handmade in India, by a maharajah's weavers.'

'It's beautiful,' I replied, turning it over in my hand, running my fingers over the vermilion fabric and the fine golden thread – hoping that my sweaty palms wouldn't mark it.

'And I'm assuming there's a Buddha in there somewhere?' I joked awkwardly, pretending to peer in through the windows. 'One in every spa, and all that.'

Swiftly he took the cushion out of my hand, placing it carefully back on the fourteenth floor. 'We're a deity-free zone Meg; that means no mantras, no chanting, no incense, and no shrine to anyone; not Shiva, not Ganesh, not Buddha.'

'Don't worry,' I said hastily, blushing at the thought that he might mistake me for a Nate blow-in. 'I'm much more interested in singing along to Beyoncé than Buddha.' Where was I getting these lines? I sounded ridiculous.

Giving me a quizzical look, he took a final swig from his can of Diet Coke and tossed it in the bin. How long before I followed it?

He paused a moment, perching on the edge of his desk as he seemed to scan my CV, perhaps buying himself some time as he wondered why he was wasting a precious half hour on a complete airhead. I waited anxiously – trying to calm myself, trying to breathe.

Eventually, he looked up; smile restored. 'Graham spoke very highly of you, said he'd have hired you all over again if he hadn't decided on early retirement, said you should've been well on your way to the Board by now, said Confectionery World is an asset-stripping disaster and your Marketing Director, Pat Someone, is a complete waste of time – no imagination, no creativity, complete control-freak. Ring any bells?'

There are moments when all that's required is a smile.

I smiled, broadly.

He refilled my coffee cup; it appeared we would now be getting down to business.

He told me that when he first started Shine he thought he'd need to staff the whole place with 'serious yogis'. I nodded sagely, telling him I understood – that this would be important from a brand authenticity point of view. 'But,' he said, 'it turns out they don't have a business brain cell between them – they do it because they love yoga, not because they understand the first thing about making money.'

'I know people like that,' I said, eager to demonstrate my first-hand understanding of the central issue, drawing on my knowledge of Nate's operation. 'They only have one studio and most of them don't sell anything beyond classes – no teacher training, no books or clothes, no food or drink, no spa or even a treatment room – they get by on their sense of community, on their personal touch, but they're never going to make it big.'

'There's plenty of money out there for people who know how to attract it,' chimed Max, telling me what I already knew – that *The Wall Street Journal* had forecast the global spa market would double in the next five years. 'I want a minimum ten percent slice of that pie,' he said, making a gesture that looked more like thirty percent. 'I want to be bigger than Bazu.'

I recognised the name. A patrician Indian who'd developed his own brand of yoga – 'where power meets precision' was the line. He was in the top ten on that Spiritual Rich List; pictured on the steps of his Westchester County Old Colonial, his regal wife, three preppy teenagers and a sleek chestnut dog – apparently an Egyptian Pharaoh Hound – lined up beside him.

Max spoke carefully, as if he was sharing a confidence with me. 'As you've clearly identified, it's a high fixed cost business – the only way to make money is by creating a global brand so we're expanding into China, Hong Kong, Taiwan, Singapore, Australia – even India.'

I laughed. 'I read about that – it made me smile; like selling coals to Newcastle.'

He grinned, relaxing. 'India is a primary market for us. The middle classes currently have to content themselves with ashrams and sadhus, which are all well and good if you can disappear for a while – go on retreat – but who's got the time? Delhi and Bangalore professionals certainly don't. After a long hard day in media or IT they need somewhere easy, somewhere comfortable, where they can work out, get pampered, meet their friends.'

I assured him that I'd done a lot of research in developing markets. 'Last time I was watching research groups in Bangalore,' I said, leaving out the fact that I'd been watching the groups in a Slough conference room via webcam, 'I realised that Indians really like having things brought to them – in their own homes. I think that's why Swami Ramdev is so popular – he's on TV every morning between five and seven, demonstrating breathing exercises, meditation and simple yoga postures for everything from acne to obesity.' I paused a moment for dramatic impact, 'he's got an audience of twenty million.'

Max raised an eyebrow. It was my masterstroke – I knew he wouldn't have heard of him. The truth was, I hadn't either – until Becks told me about him. She and Nate had spent time with him in India and they were both huge fans. Now that she'd consumed all the saffron one's DVDs, she chased down new classes on YouTube.

'Of course, Ramdev wouldn't be right for Shine,' I said quickly, thinking Max might be imagining a Bollywood hottie. 'What he does is really slow – for the pot-bellied, just like him – not very on-brand. No, I was thinking you should put all your classes online. It would work for India, and of course there's already an established market in the West.'

He opened another Diet Coke enthusiastically, seeming to find new energy. 'Absolutely right Meg – it was a no-brainer for us. Huge opportunity. We're in development right now – making sure we do it our way.' Perhaps it was the talk of tech; he was off, leaning forward, talking fast. 'Yoga's so fragmented – two hundred million students, a million teachers, quarter of a million studios, but no one's pulling it together – creating scale – owning it. So that's what we're going to do. Own it.'

'The Google of yoga?'

'Exactly – everything searchable, everything in one place – our classes, our music, our downloads, our clothes, our books, our retreats, all our people, all our members.'

'It's perfect,' I said, feeling entirely vindicated. This was exactly what I'd been saying to Pat for years – that Con World should be a one stop shop for all things chocolate, to give us a direct line to our customers, and their data. But of course she could only see the cost, not the value.

'And I assume there's an app for that?'

'It's also in dev.; it's more focused on location – helping members find a class near them, or in the city they're visiting.'

'"Shine anywhere",' I suggested, grinning.

Max grabbed a pen.

Enjoying an adrenalin rush I hadn't felt since Graham left, I excitedly threw him another pile of ideas. The glossy tomes piled up in front of me inspired one of them. I suggested a practice book featuring all Shine's teachers, and maybe their best students. 'It'd be a coffee table book packed with beautiful shots of beautiful people doing incredible postures in amazing locations. Call it *Shine World*. Nice and simple.'

He nodded enthusiastically, telling me it was already in production as an app, handing me his iPad to show me the wireframes. As I pretended to be absorbed by all those images of beautiful people doing incredible postures in amazing locations, I gave myself a good kicking. It was the same idea, except that his version was made for the 21st century, for selfies and Instagram. Perhaps that headhunter had been right; maybe I'd spent so long on BOGOFs the modern world had left me for dust. I quickly sieved through my remaining ideas for the ones that sounded most current. 'What about a range of Zoffany designed home accessories? You could spread the word on Pinterest and do a partnership with a high street brand for broader distribution. It'd be a great way to connect with your audience, involve them in your brand.'

He wrinkled his nose – as if he'd smelt something really offensive. 'Not the high street Meg – definitely not the high street.'

'Of course,' I said hurriedly. 'Maybe you should partner with one of the European brands – with Roche Bobois or Natuzzi?'

I was thinking of that glossy Italian showroom where I'd been persuaded my dreams would only become reality with one of their sofas. I checked Max's face again – better, but still not completely convinced. 'Or, you could open your own furniture stores.'

'Of course – our own stores.' Now he was nodding, happily.

'And there's lots more opportunities in branded content,' I said, rattling on, my sentences rushing into each other in my eagerness to keep that smile on his face. I gestured towards the framed photos on the wall, 'have you thought about *Celebrity Raw?*'

The smile grew, 'and *Celebrity Raw* is…?'

'A through the keyhole look at the domestic kitchens of the celebriyogi – what they eat when they're home and off duty – Miranda Kerr's superfoods for supermodels, Gwyneth Paltrow's detox secrets, Jennifer Aniston on foods that keep you hot over forty…'

He laughed and nodded, raising his can of Coke to me.

I beamed, exhausted but resuscitated; the heavy-calved girl replaced by a woman with the world at her feet.

When he asked if I had any other thoughts, I grabbed my chance. I told him Zoffany's 'local traditions' and 'organic materials' would be a natural fit with a fair trade policy. That it had worked brilliantly at Hinshaw's, for our reputation as well as our farmers. I marched into some well-rehearsed territory – a position I'd honed over many a late evening debate with Becks. She always argued, with a holier-than-thou stridency, that charities ruined themselves when they associated with so-called 'fat cats' and that corporates should be what she called 'true altruists', not expecting anything in return for their good behaviour. She hated it when I made the commercial case – that all the analysis showed both sides getting a big financial payback. I seized a chance to make the case again, uninterrupted.

'I'm always happy to follow the money,' said Max, pausing for a moment before launching into some well-rehearsed territory of his own. He was soon in full flow. 'The politicians and the charities focus on the under classes, the developing world, but the middle classes, the people in our own backyard, suffer in their own way – under pressure, over worked, lonely; they're left to fend for themselves. That's why I set up Shine – to help stressed-out workers get healthy, get fit, so they can get the best out of themselves. Corporates, like your very own Confectionery World, claim they're all about work-life balance but they're sweatshops too. I'm not saying they're anything like the ones in Bangladesh – but employers here couldn't give a toss either, as long as everyone's working fourteen hours a day. Am I right?'

'You are,' I replied, clapping my hands together decisively, though not entirely certain where we'd got to. I decided to let it slide, for the time being. I was anxious to voice my next consideration – what might be considered the elephant in the room. I took a deep breath, trying to keep my voice strong and confident, as if I was asking how important it was that I'd mastered PowerPoint or Excel, a small detail, no big deal. 'I'm no stranger to spa and beauty treatments,' I told him, wondering if own-brand bubble bath really counted in his book, 'but I do prefer massage to exercise.' I made an open gesture. 'As you might've guessed.'

'Don't worry,' he said warmly, admiring his buffed fingernails, 'I might demand perfection from myself, and our front of house staff, but it's not a requirement. I'm more interested in your brain, not that you have any worries in the looks department.'

He regarded me thoughtfully, and lowered his voice again, as if sharing a secret, 'Having said that, perhaps all you need is the right teacher. I wasn't into it either, not until I met Jed. He's a real "everything's possible" guy.'

I thought about my half-hearted attempts to get fit over the years and quickly concluded that he'd have to be superhuman to get me going, but I was willing to give it a try. 'Actually, I have already made a start. I gave up chocolate last Friday,' I said, not feeling the need to tell him the exact circumstances of the sudden alienation from my lifelong companion, 'I know I'll get into all of it – given the right environment.'

Agreeing that I would, he pulled the ring on his next Diet Coke, embarking on another speech he'd clearly given before – this one was about focus. 'At Shine, we don't believe in sitting about contemplating our navels, embarking on some kind of esoteric journey with no end in sight – we get on our mat and we get moving; we work hard and then we play hard, we relax a while, but then we get back to the real world, ready to get on with it. It's about empowering ourselves to be the best people we can be.'

It was very hard to imagine this meticulous man, this vision of hard-edged controlled perfection, contemplating a navel of any size, but perhaps that was why he was so anti-Buddha. It was an impressive transformation.

I sat forward on that uncomfortable sofa. 'Did you change your diet?'

He laughed, 'It takes a lot of pink sushi to look this good.'

I smiled. 'But you haven't always been into healthy living, have you?'

'I did a lot of self-medicating in Hong Kong but, as Keith Richards might've said, "I always bought quality" and that's what saved me. So now I make sure that everything we offer at Shine, whether it's green tea or a cappuccino, is the best it can be.'

'No high-grade cocaine then?' I sat back astonished, flushed with embarrassment.

He laughed ruefully. 'Diet Coke is the last of my self-medicating habits, though I'm not fanatical – I still like a glass of champagne, or two.'

'So if all else fails I can wash the sushi down with Moet?'

'Only if it's vintage,' he said, looking at his watch, appearing to reach a decision. 'Meg,' he said, 'It's been a pleasure to meet you but, I'm not going to give you the job.'

'Oh.'

'All the major brand work is run out of L.A. – the boys over at Bloomstein Silverday do a grand job, so the UK Brand Manager role is just admin really; you'd be implementing their work, dealing with executions, not very challenging really.'

'I understand,' I said, picking my bag off the floor and with it my heart, wondering how I could get out of his flat without seeing the dreaded Camilla. 'There's no need to explain. Thank you for your time.'

'Slow down Meg,' he replied, motioning for me to sit. 'You're an ideas person right?'

I nodded, now feeling the full extent of my exhaustion. I didn't want his career advice, or to be parcelled off to someone else he knew. I was clear. I wanted to work for Shine and, more specifically, I wanted to work for Max.

I zoned out while he went on about my 'commercial instincts', my 'clear need for more autonomy' and 'the opportunity to put ideas into play'. I was reminded of the 'it's no one's fault, we just want different things' speech that I'd given to close down those stupid flings.

I nodded again, not really listening. My mind had already fast-forwarded to next Monday, to another Con World status meeting, to another round of BOGOFs, to yet another session in the stationery cupboard; it was too much to bear.

'So, Ms. Rogers, how does 'Director of Brand Experience' sound?'

He had me as 'Director.'

Truthfully, I wasn't exactly sure what a Brand Experience Director did but there was no point in asking; I would've cleaned the loos if it had got me in the door. Fortunately, it turned out not to require a dab hand with a brush; it required the ability, in Max's words 'to rove'. I was to have 'a roving brief' across all aspects of the brand/customer experience – I'd come up with new product ideas, but I'd also work with the 'commercially-challenged' P.R. girls on the launch party, keep the local wunderkind agency on brand, and, most terrifying of all, help Zoffany. I wasn't sure how I was going to 'keep our Design Chief on the straight and narrow' but I was prepared to give it my best shot.

And suddenly it was over. 'So,' he said, hopping off his desk, walking me to the door, 'when can you start?'

'Yo-Bollocks'

'This isn't real yoga,' Becks said finally, chucking my iPad on the table, crossing her arms and leaning back in her chair – preparing to repeat an oft-told lesson. 'Do you remember your visit to Nate's place?'

'To Enema-thingy?'

'Ekatman,' she corrected. 'Meaning "one soul". What yoga's *supposed* to be all about.'

I nodded, resisting the temptation to remind her of marketing rule 101 – the importance of brand name memorability.

On she went, reciting her favourite mantra. How yoga was about 'stripping away the layers of ego, revealing the true self, uniting mind, body and breath, and uniting with all beings, at a soul level'.

She looked at me expectantly. 'Capisce?'

I nodded again. It was always easier to agree, and wait my turn.

'This "Yo-Bollocks" – it's all about ego. Even the name "Shine" – it's all about rising above everyone else. There's no breathing regulation, there's no meditation, and there's definitely no internal journey. They're all "Shanti Bunnies" – it's just about looking good.'

There followed a rant about projected body image that made her sound like Naomi Wolf on *The Beauty Myth*. I pointed out that they were healthy looking women – not stick insects, but this just led to harrumphing around 'the coercion of women' and 'the reduction of the female form to formulaic images of perfection'.

I told her that this 'Yo-Bollocks' had worked for Max; that he'd transformed from City porker to buff-bodied yogapreneur.

'Didn't I read that he was a drug addict?'

'More an ex-pat bon viveur.'

'A drug addict and a City boy? What a combination. Are you sure he wasn't an M.P. in a previous life? Does he have a duck house?'

I risked a joke about 'not so fat cats.'

Unfortunately, this led to another diatribe – on fat cats. I tried reasoning with her – surely it was better that Max did something positive with his money, that had lots of health benefits for lots of people, than light up the bars of Hong Kong?

This drew more talk of 'tainted money' and 'the poisoning of an ancient tradition' with 'the wages of sin'. 'Yoga is a discipline,' she said primly, 'a discipline that's been honed over several thousand years, passed down from adept to adept.'

'Well, maybe Max is a modern-day adept. Have you thought of that?'

'You, Meg,' she said, boring into me as if I was an under-performing pupil, 'are not a superficial person.'

'Who gets my copy of *Grazia* when I'm done?' I asked, still trying to coax a smile.

'That's just to stay in touch,' she said prudishly, straightening her t-shirt, returning Che Guevara to full prominence.

I waited to see the familiar glint in her eye but it didn't come. 'This,' she said, giving the discarded iPad a good shove, 'is a complete waste of time.'

I talked up the spa, telling her it was a self-styled 'temple of wellbeing' designed to help wrung-out workers just like us, that it looked like 'heaven on earth' – full of impossibly beautiful therapists wafting about in white, dispensing lotus flowers to the needy.

'Can they bring the dead back to life?' she said, gesturing towards a huge pile of schoolbooks.

'Becks, I was six feet under when I went for my interview. Now look at me.' I smoothed down my hair, gave a little shimmy: '"Brand Experience Director".'

'I'm sorry,' she said, taking a breath. 'I didn't mean to rain on your parade. I just want to make sure you see it for what it is. I don't want you getting sucked in.'

I assured her that I could see, if his nails were anything to go by, that Max had plenty of hidden shallows, but that my eyes were wide open. Then I drew her attention to the significant upsides. The endless supply of freebies, which, of course, I'd be sharing with my best friend. The turmeric and honey facials, the papaya and mango massages, the melon and black sesame body scrubs, the coconut and rose oil hair treatments, the ylang ylang candles.

The detox diet was a bit more of a sticking point. The Shine signature dish was pink sushi. Becks read out the recipe; it wasn't really sushi at all, but beetroot mashed with avocado, carrot, cucumber and sprouts, wrapped up tight in a sheet of Nori seaweed. In the end, we agreed that pink sushi was certainly a long way from our usual comfort food, but perhaps that was the point.

One thing was certain, we both needed a change from the usual. She had dark shadows under her eyes and her skin was pale and blotchy.

'Paperwork, feckless parents, wasted kids – the unholy trinity,' she said, by way of explanation.

'Not quite the *Dead Poets' Society*?'

She grimaced. 'The bullying is the worst of it. Last week I had to rescue a girl who'd been smeared with makeup and hung in a basket between coat rails for two hours, and the week before a kid's school bag got smeared in shit. Where were we, the teachers? In the staff room, having another bloody meeting about student discipline.'

It was ironic really. Despite Becks' three-year campaign to break me out of my Con World chains, she was just as trapped. Instead of inspiring teens to the joys of *A Clockwork Orange* and *Brighton Rock*, she spent most of her life ticking boxes, grading and doing something called 'work sampling' which, we'd long ago agreed, was a glorified way of sneaking on your colleagues.

There she sat, all caved in. It was a pitiful sight. I asked her what she was going to do. I got the usual considerations – that she was tied to Reading, that Susie was happy at school, that she couldn't possibly move away from the place her parents were buried, or the house where she grew up. Buoyed up by my recent leap, I suggested she make one too, to the private school up the road. 'Forty acres of grounds, a mahogany lined library and double the salary – what's not to love?'

'It's not that easy for me,' she said, flushing. 'I have principles–'

'And I don't?'

'Not relating to your work, not in the same–'

'*Seriously*? My principles – my loyalty and my commitment – are what kept me a slave for three years.'

'That's not what I meant,' she said, starting a favourite polemic on private education.

I was saved by the pink fairy, who had downed her weapons for the day and was ready for bed. I volunteered to do the honours, jumping up a little faster than normal. Taking her upstairs, running her a bath, reading her a story, always had a soothing effect on me and, by the time we got to 'and they all lived happily ever after', I was yawning. I sat in the old nursing chair, watching the steady rise and fall of the duvet as she fell asleep. Picking up her favourite Barbie, placing it carefully on her bedside table so it'd be the first thing she saw when she woke up, I smiled. Some might think it weird that Becks hadn't banned the doll as a bad role model, but actually, she'd never impose her politics on her daughter. I was very glad about that – especially as I was the one supplying the Barbies.

'Truce?' I asked, giving Becks' shoulder a tentative squeeze, putting on my coat.

'Truce,' she said, abandoning the pile of marking, wrapping my scarf around my neck. 'Where is it by the way?' she asked, handing me my coat. 'Which glamorous hotspot will I be frequenting for my many massages and facials?'

I explained that 'Shine City' was taking the top four floors of a downsizing bank on Bishopsgate, just up from Liverpool Street station. I'd been to look at the building before my interview – it rose up like a sword, floor after floor of tubular steel and angular glass, its lines as sharp as a City suit.

A dark shadow passed across her face. 'But isn't that quite near Nate?'

'About twenty minutes walk but it's a different planet,' I said, turning the door handle. 'It's all expensive wine bars and silk shirt shops. There's no way there'll be any cannibalisation. Don't worry about it.'

'Cannibalisation?' She looked horrified.

'Meaning they won't steal each other's business,' I said quickly. 'Ekatma-thingy is the polar opposite of Shine.'

She leaned against the door, seeming to sink into herself. 'This is going to kill him.'

'I really wouldn't worry Becks,' I said brightly, releasing the door handle. 'Shine is appealing to a completely different market; there's no spiritual stuff, no chanting, and absolutely no hippies.' I was very clear in my mind – the two could not be more different. Our people were *Times* readers; Nate's were *Guardian* readers. Our people were taxi addicts, lawyers and bankers, corporate high-flyers. Nate's were cycling fanatics, social workers and academics, poets and dreamers.

There was no way his customers would want to emerge from a massage 'dusted with a golden glow' – they were far too egalitarian for that, and there was no way they'd be into the champagne bar – they were far too keen on twiggy tea. He would be fine.

I reassured her that Shine was only interested in the urban professional. How the centres opened at five in the morning, so that city traders and corporate basket cases could get a class in before they started their day, how they didn't close until midnight – catering to those working across time zones. How all that superficiality – the state-of-the-art studios with their expansive city views, the hotel-style welcome desks manned by resting models, the valeted yoga mats, rainforest showers, spa lockers stocked with designer paper knickers, embroidered slippers and amenity kits, the beauty bar, blow-dry bar, and, of course, the champagne bar – was hardly going to appeal to yoga purists.

'Poor Nate,' she said, appearing not to have heard me, 'he's worked so hard – making the world a better place, all that community work, all those donation only classes–'

'I know, and he's a brilliant human for doing it,' I said. 'The fact he's kept the place going all these years is a miracle.'

'You know, his mum used to ship her guru in from Rishikesh,' she said, wistfully. 'Chrissie was such an idealist, a genuine hippy.'

'And that idealism lives on Becks,' I said, affectionately pinching her cheek. It was true – I may not have liked the yoga but the old shutters, the shrine to Ganesh, the peace – it really was a special place. 'He's local, he's authentic, he has genuine provenance, good brand values – everybody loves all that stuff. It's just like mum and her florist shop. His people go for the community spirit, the chat, and because they love him. I'm sure it'll still be "omming" away in another thirty years.'

Did this go someway to reassuring her? I wasn't sure, but I thought I saw a faint twinkle in her eye when she asked if we had a business concierge.

'Complete with personal assistants in immaculately tailored white dresses,' I replied, nodding happily.

'Personal workstations?'

'Check. Complete with treadmill.'

'I guess not too many of us "hippies" will be interested in that,' she said, managing a half smile.

'What we need is a BOGOF'

The big day finally arrived. I pressed the button for the fourteenth floor and seconds later emerged in a vast atrium of light that smelt of spicy jasmine. I hugged my files to my chest and stood completely still, taking it all in. Several skylights framed the deep blue sky, throwing vast parallelograms of sunshine across the gleaming white floor. Peruvian alpaca rugs and floor cushions, just like the miniature one Max had shown me, were scattered to the side of three concentric ponds, white lotus flowers floating on the dark water. Pebble walkways snaked amongst them, towards a lush bamboo garden and beyond that to a terrace, steam rising from a hot tub into the crisp September air.

Tracing my hand along the curved glass wall, peering in at the suspended lotus flowers, preserved forever like prehistoric beetles in amber, I could see Max's high tech touches everywhere. In the noise-cancelling sound system that gave the atrium the muffled buzz of an art gallery, in the freshly ionized, bacteria-busting air, in the tiny headset worn by every member of staff – white trimmed with gold and contoured to follow the shape of the ear, like a piece of Egyptian jewellery. In the huge bank of screens displaying Shine's Twitter feed – each one an endless stream of messages aimed at turning intentions into actions, '@BentleyBoy you rock,' 'Way to go @CityGirl47,' '@YoJitsees

#Hydrate' and all the replies – '#NailedIt @Shine,' 'Awesome @ParadiseJed,' and my favourite, 'Drink @ShineBar @FitHead @CindyC 8pm.'

There was a white flash and then, written across all of the screens, in giant letters:

'Shine welcomes Meg Rogers. Happy first day Meg!'

'Face recognition,' said the languorously beautiful Japanese creature gliding towards me in an ankle length, white silk jersey dress. It clung to her fat free body in all the right places. I wouldn't have been able to get it over my thighs.

'Pleased to meet you,' I said, holding out my hand expectantly, but she pressed her palms together in apparent prayer, and bowed in return. I stuffed the offending hand back in my pocket, wondering if it was a hygiene thing like the ionized air, and followed her up the stairs. 'Stairs' didn't really cover it. This was a double waterfall staircase with a golden handrail and white steps – the kind you see in old Hollywood movies – where girls clad in tiny satin shorts and heels dance and preen with huge feather fans that finally peel back to reveal Fred Astaire. Except the preening dancing girls had been replaced by preening yoga girls, all of them clad in tiny white shorts. Would they peel back their yoga mats to reveal a smiling Max? They were laughing, leaning into each other, ring-fenced by bottles of water and this season's handbags. Had they just done a class? There wasn't a hair out of place.

The languorously beautiful Japanese creature was explaining that Max had instructed her to bring me straight to the P.R. meeting. I smiled and nodded but this was bad news. The meeting was supposed to have been in the afternoon and I'd been looking forward to having a few hours to settle in, to review my notes, to find the kettle, and the nearest loo. Actually, I really needed the loo; news of a meeting was doing nothing to calm my nerves. Perhaps they were hidden behind all the

Tibetan tree bark. There was no way I was asking her – she didn't look like she'd ever used one.

By the time we reached the top of the stairs, I was sporting a sweaty glow. I tried to make a joke about it, along the lines that I was shining already, but she'd obviously lost her sense of humour around the same time she'd lost the use of her hand. I followed her down the softly lit corridor, vases of fresh flowers on every windowsill. It was about as far from Con World as it was possible to get. My tired grey cubicle always had the static, stale air of a long-haul flight – the kind that makes it impossible to summon the energy to do anything more than watch *Friends*. No wonder the lights used to turn off when I'd been in there a few hours – they were movement sensitive.

The languorously beautiful Japanese creature opened the door to the meeting room, standing well back to one side – perhaps so I might make my entrance, or perhaps she didn't think I'd fit through the door otherwise. 'Would you like a green tea Meg, or perhaps a skinny cappuccino?' I'd had my usual double shot espresso on the way so I managed to say I'd take the green tea, hoping it wouldn't taste like poison.

Three gorgeous girls were clustered around that month's hottest mobile, scrutinising some photos. The colour-block dresses, the matching lipstick, the slick ponytailed hair, gave them the look of a catwalk caterpillar; one body, one mind, six arms and legs. The oldest one, an American brunette with the damp eyes and long thick lashes of Bambi, was flicking through a stream of selfies – her launch party 'options'. I couldn't see the details but each photo glowed with the tell-tale warmth of an Instagram filter – Mayfair or Nashville?

'You must be Megan' she said eventually, managing to smile and sheet me with ice all at the same time.

'Call me Meg' I said, apparently frozen to the spot.

'I'm Ashley' she said, proffering a bird-like hand. 'I'm head of P.R. We're planning our London launch party, and I *literally* have nothing to wear.' Moodily she picked at an imaginary mark on her perfect-fit dress. 'It's *totally* a Fashion 911.'

'Oh Ashley' said the youngest – an exact replica of her boss, 'whatever you wear, you'll kill it.'

Ashley smiled at her mini-me. 'Isn't she sweet?' she said, flicking her blow-dried mane.

I nodded, still rooted to the spot.

'Oh, where are my manners?' she said, pulling out the chair next to her, giving me a smile that only stretched so far. 'Don't be shy' she said, pulling it out further still. How big did she think I was?

I sat down heavily, the leather padding making a loud squishing sound as the tubular frame sunk several inches closer to the floor. I busied myself arranging my colour-coded files, waiting for the heat in my cheeks to subside.

'Megan,' she said, leaning in conspiratorially, 'you must've been on a few big nights out, with all those awards you've won. Who do you wear?' The look on her face said she thought she knew the answer.

I paused, trying to formulate some witty retort but by the time I'd got a line out – something lame about my Marchesa gowns always getting stuck in Customs – she'd moved on. 'Is this a vintage find?' she asked, rubbing the sleeve of my dress between two bony fingers, suspiciously. 'How clever of you.'

'That's right' I said, knowing that a five-year-old jersey dress from Jigsaw probably didn't count but seemingly unable to snap back. Why hadn't I bought a new dress? Even Becks had told me to treat myself – to give me a lift on my first day. I'd argued that Max wanted me for my smarts not my wardrobe and there was no point trying to compete with these girls on that score – which was clearly correct, but there was a still a threshold beneath which it was not sensible to fall. I wished my head was clearer. I hadn't slept the previous night; my brain had been chasing down rabbit holes. What would my office be like? Would I make friends? Was Shine really the answer? Was it too big a stretch? Should I have gone somewhere more obvious like Mars? And the most crucial question of all, now that I was face to face with the three skinniest girls I'd ever met, why had I spent the last month eating?

I busied myself rummaging in my handbag, wishing I could hide all of me in there – eventually emerging with a biro and a brand new notebook. The notebook featured a garish Ganesh, sporting pink trousers trimmed in tinsel. It triggered an exchange of looks that rippled down the table like an optical Mexican wave. Becks had given it to me as a good luck gift. I loved it for being so her, but now I found myself wishing for something more sophisticated – something bound in duck egg blue leather – like Ashley's.

She turned pointedly to me again, ignoring the notebook in favour of another humiliation. 'Talking about weight loss … have you met our Yoga Director, Jed?'

I wasn't taking that one lying down; I'd done my research. He was one of the hottest teachers in the world – in every sense of the word. He had over three hundred thousand Facebook Likes, and about ten pages of search results on Google … in a handstand on a paddleboard in Hawaii, doing the splits on a precarious rock, in a bare-chested backbend on a motorbike. 'Of course I know who he is – I've seen him on YouTube and–'

'Oooh, he's so much better in the flesh,' interrupted Ashley with a knowing smile. 'Isn't he girls?'

Brittany and Whitney nodded as one, her fashion parade coming to attention.

'And he's gonna frickin' love you Megan,' said Ashley giggling.

'Oh, why's that?' I asked, realising as soon as the words were out of my mouth that I'd fallen into another one of her traps.

'Because,' she said, licking her lips, 'he *loves* a challenge.'

'As I can testify,' said Max, suddenly in the room, playfully patting the place that was once a paunch and assuming his position at the head of the table. The placement of his iPhone on the table acted like a courtroom gavel, creating another Mexican wave that rippled up the table, the Catwalk Caterpillar snapping to attention.

He wasted no time, introducing me with a comprehensive list of everything I'd managed to achieve before Graham left, calling me 'an imaginative left-field thinker with strong commercial instincts.' He talked up the Brand Ambassador programme and the student targeted campaigns, but, while I could've listened to him for hours, I was glad he didn't mention the Lakshmi Ladies – something told me door to door selling wouldn't be up these girls' street. His grand finale was Bar 22 – the chocolate packed with twenty two vitamins and minerals we'd marketed as a hangover cure – or rather we'd hinted was a hangover cure with a bunch of metaphors, to get round the Advertising Standards Authority rulebook.

'I can personally vouch for its effectiveness and,' he said, looking at me fondly as if showing off a new possession, 'it made quite a star of its co-creator.'

'So we've heard' said Ashley, looking at me earnestly. Butter wouldn't melt. 'Let me just say, on behalf of all the girls, we are *beyond* excited to be working with you Megan. We're sure you're going to teach us *so* much.'

'Thank you; I am delighted to be here' I said, stiff as a spoon, wondering why I was bowing my head as if addressing royalty.

Without further ado, Ashley launched into her launch party plan, approaching it with a campaign spirit I recognised. I have to admit that, despite the fact that she was clearly a queen bitch, I was impressed. Her planning was military-grade, and the invite list sounded like a night at the Oscars.

'The five hundred guests will arrive between eighteen

hundred and eighteen thirty. They'll all get champagne and, if they're A-List, they'll be met by you,' she said, looking adoringly at Max. 'Then you'll deliver your speech. I suggest we start with the night it all began, the night you met Jed … but please leave out the bit about the cigar bar – so off message!'

'Actually Ashley,' said Max smoothly, 'Meg is going to write it this time.'

I tried to put on an easy smile. I'd composed a lot of speeches in my time, but not many of them had been given an airing.

'Max, are you sure?' said Ashley looking panic stricken. This is a very big deal, if she–'

'Meg will be fine Ashley,' he said firmly, running his oh-so-pretty hands through his oh-so-thick hair.

She raised her eyebrows as far as the Botox would allow and pressed on, outlining plans for an oyster bar, guest makeovers, and Zoffany's book launch – a coffee table tome on Boho-glam that would be accompanied by a 'get the look' app. Ashley sighed heavily. 'Let's hope she manages to sign her own name.'

I stole a glance at Max, taking extreme care not to get stuck. He was wearing a fixed smile; he'd obviously been here before.

Pointedly, Ashley turned to Whitney. 'Don't let her drink, *like ever.*'

Whitney nodded and dutifully wrote 'DON'T LET HER DRINK, LIKE EVER', then underlined the 'ever.'

Zoffany sounded like my kind of girl.

'Anyway, she's just a sidebar,' said Ashley, 'the real star of the show, besides you Max, is Jed.' She told us she'd dropped by rehearsal the other day and he was…' There was a pause as she searched for the language to truly express what she'd seen, '…awesome.'

I stole another sideways glance; he was suppressing a smile at such critical prowess.

I suppressed a smile of my own.

Ashley continued. Jed's Bollywood inspired performance would end with the popping of more corks – which Brittany would stage-manage. Ashley would then lead the mass migration to the bar, where two celebrity DJs would be hosting the decks – names to be confirmed. Would the Catwalk Caterpillar dance around their coordinated handbags?

By the time I'd torn myself away from that little scene, Ashley was onto what she clearly regarded as her showstopper; the goody bag. Whitney dutifully produced a white leather shopper monogrammed with gold lotus flowers. She put it carefully on the table in front of Ashley, momentarily barring her from view. It was very smart, reminding me of Louis Vuitton, rather nicer than the blue cooler bags Con World handed out at trade shows. Ashley got to her feet and began pulling out the goodies.

First was a bottle of Shine's signature fragrance – the spicy jasmine scent that hit me the moment the lift doors opened. She spritzed it over each of us – rather more generously over me – did I smell of Slough? Then she partially unrolled two limited edition white yoga mats, laying them on the table, side-by-side. Both of them had the Shine lotus emblem on the left, embossed in gold. One also had 'Ashley' written in gold two-inch high letters, the other one had a little gold crown on top of the letter 'M'.

'Nice work' he said, giving her a winning smile. Then he gave the one with the M a push and sent it rolling down the table in my direction. 'You have this one Meg,' he said. 'Inspiration for your first class.'

I could see Ashley bridle but, all credit, she rose above, seamlessly moving on to her next trick – flipping the lid on a tiny box. She put the ring, set with a golden lotus flower, on her wedding finger, sashaying her fingers up and down the table as if they were on a red carpet manicam. 'Isn't it fabulous?' she simpered, waving her hand under Max's nose. Dutifully Max agreed that it was, and congratulated her on another great job. She beamed, flexing her fingers to admire the ring again.

It was at this point that I decided to make my mark on the meeting, to demonstrate both my flair for ideas and the commercial acumen that Max had asked of me. I pulled out the first of my files, explaining that, although the night would be pretty much all about the launch, I thought it important to give some thought to customer retention, to what would happen the next day, and the day after that. 'So, I'm thinking about a loyalty card – like Starbucks – something simple, a bit of plastic with rewards based on behaviour.'

'"Starbucks?"' repeated Ashley, charging the word, seemingly eager to understand. 'Tell me Megan, I'm curious. Why would Shine, a super-luxury brand, want to behave like Starbucks?'

I started again, explaining that it wouldn't be tacky, that it would be aspirational and sophisticated – in keeping with our brand values. 'Perhaps Starbucks is a bad example, maybe something more like AmEx Black.'

'Oh, okay, Starbucks was really throwing me off there' she said, putting on a great show of relief. 'Of course I should trust you to know what you're doing, what with all your experience.'

'We could call it "Diamond Shine"' I said, smiling broadly; confident the name was a masterstroke.

'"Diamond Shine"?' She looked conspiratorially at Max, widening those damp eyes and playing with her earlobe. 'Are you sure Megan? It sounds like a dishwasher tablet to me.'

How had I not thought of that? I started to suggest that we could work on naming it together, to come up with something more on-brand, but Max interrupted me, handing me his phone. It was open on a picture of what looked like a designer bracelet with a small screen – in Shine's white and gold signature colours. 'It's all on there,' he said, as proud as if he were presenting his first-born. 'Shine24 will monitor what you eat, what you drink, how well you sleep, *and*, it'll store all your membership data – record which centres you visit, how often you visit, what you spend, where you spend it.'

I took a moment, trying to take it all in; it really was stunning the way it curved and twisted, but all I could think about was how badly I was messing up.

'I love it' said Ashley, misting up with pride. I expected her to spend the next ten minutes waxing lyrical about how good it would look on her wrist at the launch party, or how it would help her lose five non-existent pounds, but instead she spent those minutes stealing my lines. 'So we can use the data to tailor our marketing to the individual' she said. 'It's totally modern and on brand – a really cool way of getting some great targeting data and pulling it through to build consumer loyalty.'

'Exactly, said Max, watching Brittany and Whitney take it in turns to coo over the bracelet's lines, pleading to be first in line when it landed. 'Hashtag "coolest thing *ever*"' concluded Whitney, completely captivated.

Ashley smiled at her indulgently, a mother hen. Then she turned back to me, 'Don't worry about it Megan. Your idea was great; it's just that Max already took care of it.' She rubbed her hands with zealous enthusiasm, motioning towards the files. 'What else you got?'

There was nothing to do but get on with it. I opened another file, marshalling my notes for another forward charge.

'So I'm thinking that Shine should partner with the pink ribbon people,' I said. Surely this would be more up Ashley's street; the pink ribbon brand was an American brand, and the people behind it had worked with plenty of designer brands before. 'The majority of customers are female so it'll be really relevant, plus it'll give everyone a nice warm glow – great for Shine's reputation.'

'You want to paint Shine pink?' asked Ashley, opening her eyes wide in surprise.

'Of course not,' I said, explaining that I was simply recommending a percentage donation for every pound members spent. 'Plus a donation box on reception, one at the business centre, maybe one in the café by the till – additional reminders.'

'I'd never want to knock another woman's personal colour choices' said Ashley, looking meaningfully at the frilly pink Ganesh on my notebook, 'but I'd sure appreciate the opportunity to share our look book, when you've had a chance to settle.'

'It works for Estée Lauder,' I said, wondering how on earth anyone could be so dismissive of a universal symbol of strength, hope and empathy.

'And soup cans and candy and breath mints and grocery stores and Ford Mustangs. Shall I go on?' She looked down the table, rallying her troops.

'Ashley,' I said, hotly, pushing a file towards her, 'the charity has sold over seventy million ribbons, raised millions of dollars for breast cancer, *and* built sales for every single one of its partners.'

'Let me look,' said Max, pulling the file towards him. He gave it a quick flick and then closed it, tapping it approvingly. 'Health and wellbeing is, of course, what we're about, and you're quite right Meg, we *should* give back.' I tried to catch Ashley's eye, to give her the 'I win' look, but I was premature. There was a 'but' coming, and it was a big one. 'But,' said Max, running his fingers through his hair, leaning back in his chair, a man in command, 'I want my own foundation. I'm not interested in partnering someone else. When the time is right – when we've got critical mass, I'll do what the hedge fund boys did over at ARK – those guys raised hundreds of millions – benefitted hundreds of thousands of kids, applying entrepreneurial smarts to philanthropy. That's the way to make a real difference – to raise serious money.'

'We're talking *serious* money Megan,' said Ashley softly, as if soothing a crying child. 'Like Max, our customers think big. They work hard, they play hard, they spend hard. Think £10,000 a ticket gala dinners. Think Kensington Palace. Think serious raffle prizes – Oscar nights, African safaris, a limo covered in Damien Hirst butterflies. Think Kobe beef and black cod. Think Bill Clinton, Bill Gates, George Lucas, Queen Rania, the Duke and Duchess of Cambridge.'

Of course I loved the sound of all that, immediately leaping to a night at the Oscars with Kate Middleton, but I didn't want to let Ashley have the last word, and I honestly didn't see why we couldn't do both. I countered, arguing that partnering a well-known charity would actually help us grow our brand now. 'Some of them, like the pink ribbon people, have huge networks. They could help us spread the word, build awareness. It'd be good for us, and for them.'

But Max was shaking his head. 'I don't have anything against pink ribbons,' he said, 'but the truth is that right now we need to focus on the bottom line. We can't get distracted. We have a lot to do expanding the business, a lot of cost – I need all eyes on footfall, until further notice.'

'Bums on seats,' said Ashley, in her best English accent, looking rather pleased with herself.

'Bums on *mats*,' I said, smiling at Max, hoping that I might, one day, work solely for the foundation, especially if it got me away from Ashley. Of course, he was right – footfall did need to be the priority right now. 'Maybe what we need is a BOGOF.'

'A *what*?' drawled Ashley. She blinked in slow motion and wrinkled her nose, as if she'd smelt something really offensive. 'A"BOGOF"?'

Instead of making light of it, pretending I was having a laugh about the café's tiny portion sizes, or my own need to eat double quantities of everything (which surely they'd have bought), I committed myself to the idea, enthusiastically outlining some of the ways in which the technique had been used by other brands, and detailing the 'bums on mats' financial payback – for Max's benefit. I was just getting on to how it could be used to build footfall (buy one class or spa treatment and bring a friend for free) when Max's phone rang.

As soon as he'd left the room she dropped all pretence. 'Let me straighten this out for you Megan' she said, looking like she was about to bitch-slap me. 'BOGOFs do not go nuclear. BOGOFs do not have a blast-radius. BOGOFs do not have super-fans.'

'I know' I said, trying to return to the footfall argument.

'Do you know what *does* go nuclear Megan?'

'I'm just trying to give you an alternative way of thinking–'

'P.R. goes nuclear. Events go nuclear. Celebrity goes nuclear. Working it goes nuclear. Not pink ribbons. Not BOGOFs. Not plastic loyalty cards disguised as dishwasher tablets.'

I tried to save myself, telling her that of course a 'BOGOF' was just an in-house shorthand – that we might brand it a 'lifestyle rewards programme'. She wasn't listening.

I still believed it was, at heart, a good idea but it turned out all those hours watching *Fashion Police* only enabled me to understand the language, not speak it. 'Honestly Ashley, I get it, I really *do*. Of course the big news is your news – a celeb-packed party for all the press, for everyone to tweet and Instagram it, but we need some solid customer strategies to underpin the gloss.'

'The "gloss"?' queried Ashley. Her expression told me that wasn't the way she saw her job.

'Okay' said Max, suddenly back in the room, a man in a hurry. 'This has been a really useful discussion – a bit of challenge, a healthy debate – but I need to wrap up. Everyone's focus is "bums on mats" but Ashley,' he said, 'you work the party, and Meg, come back re. the loyalty card. It could work as a temporary thing, until the 24.' Hand on the door he turned, 'Oh, and put a box of pink ribbons on reception. Can't do any harm, right Ash?'

'Right,' said Ashley, through gritted teeth.

'Thank you,' I said, 'and the BOGOF?'

'Well, it doesn't sound like the most natural brand fit, but if it gets bums on mats and it can go by another name, I'll take a look.'

'Deal,' I said firmly, trying to look delighted, realising with a sinking feeling that Shine probably didn't have a stationery cupboard.

'Just breathe'

Pebbledash and Privet's offices may only have been a fifteen minute walk away but I felt as if I was crossing continents. The west side of the Commercial Road, the side closest to Shine, catered to the City trade. My favourite place was Verde & Company – an organic grocer with heavy green canopies, crates packed with vegetables and straw baskets showcasing tissue wrapped fruit. Inside, there were giant ham slicers, copper kettles and pralines, truffles and macaroons from the grand-cru of chocolate makers – the Belgian Pierre Marcolini. Something told me it was only a matter of time before I succumbed – perhaps I'd treat myself to one or two on my way back from the meeting, if all went well.

Heading towards the chalky white spire of Christchurch, passing a Methodist chapel and a synagogue, I soon left the cashmere coated bankers and lads with Estuary accents behind. Fournier Street, on the east side of Commercial Road, was cobbled, with cast iron lampposts, and all the merchant houses had the original black railings – though most of the front doors had been done up in Farrow and Ball heritage colours. I found myself following a bizarre assortment of tattooed slackers, old geezer types and lost-looking Japanese girls in platforms and legwarmers – maybe they were searching for Fashion Street, the next road down.

The futuristic tubular steel minaret marked another turn. A deserted pine-panelled 'Gents' Hair Stylists' with faded old photos of sharp partings and side burns, an off licence with just one bottle of beer in the window, and the supermarket BanglaCity – outside of which were piled vast tins of Consumers Pride cooking oil, jealously guarded by a painfully thin boy. A million curry houses claimed to be Brick Lane's 'Curry House of the Year'. Some of them had to go back to ten years to make that claim, but claim it they did.

When I'd found out that I'd be working with Pebbledash & Privet, affectionately known in the trade as P&P, I'd buzzed with anticipation. They'd won three Yellow Pencils in one night at the last Design and Art Direction awards and were hailed across town as the next big thing. They never did pitches – arguing that their creative work was evidence enough, and they'd turned down clients on the grounds they didn't share the same 'creative vision', or because they didn't like them. The rumour was that Con World had been one such client – that P&P had met Pat and decided, five minutes in, that it was never going to happen. So, when I did my little resignation speech, I'd made a big point of telling her I'd be partnering them; she didn't need to know they were only responsible for Shine's local marketing.

Now, given my performance in the P.R. meeting, I was petrified. They might be the hottest agency in town but clearly they did things their way. If I couldn't manage a few P.R. girls how was I going to manage this? The look of it didn't help. It sat at the bottom of an alley, sandwiched between a couple more Indian restaurants. It was an old warehouse, probably built in the sixties, covered in graffiti. I had to excuse my way through a bunch of pale thirty-something men, all of them standing about, smoking. They wore black t-shirts and jeans that barely covered their bums and beer bellies; a brave look on the local art students, but on men old enough to have children? There was only one word for it, 'mutton'.

I tried to settle into a chintz armchair in a library complete with three wall-mounted flying ducks, a grandfather clock, and concrete floor. It was a long way from Con World's advertising monoliths; no low slung sofas or high priestesses of reception here – unless you counted the Graham Norton lookalike who approached the tannoy with all the panache of a seventies trolley-dolly. I waited patiently for 'doors to manual' and a cocktail, but in the event all I got was a cuppa and a Hob Nob from the resident tea lady. I settled in with a copy of *Wired*, looking up occasionally, whenever the clock chimed. Half an hour went by before anyone claimed me. She was my age, clutching a packet of Marlboro Red and smelling of fags.

She managed a lukewarm 'hello' as her eyes swept coldly over my jersey dress and sensible heels. Sensing yet another judgment, I managed a tight 'good afternoon' and did a bit of judging of my own – wasn't she much too old for pigtails and a mini-skirt? And couldn't her insipid face have done with some make up?

She pulled a couple of bottles of water out of the American style fridge and led me upstairs to a room of six young guys lolling on beanbags. They looked as if they'd just graduated from the art school up the road. Nobody got up, though they did manage a collective but low-key 'hiya'. I think I was supposed to sink into the empty beanbag but I gave it the cold shoulder – I wasn't sure I'd ever get out of its purple clutches.

Their ideas were already on display, plastered all over the room. I could tell at a glance that it was a case of creative egos on the rampage. The result was four walls of scattergun ideas, all of them brave and exciting, and none of them on brand. How could they have got it so wrong? I'd read the brief – we needed a few posters in Shine's immediate vicinity, following the lines of Bloomstein Silverday's global campaign, really straightforward stuff.

I waited patiently, until Pigtails had finished her sales pitch. She talked a lot about community, about the need for the brand to unite people around its purpose and values. But instead of Zoffany's 'modern ethnic luxe', we had an Innocent look – all folksy festivals and chatty by-lines. It was a pity Becks' friend Nate couldn't afford it – it would've tripled his business over night.

'I'm sorry,' I said, as gently as I could, 'I can see you've put in a lot of hours, but I'm afraid your work is off brand and–'

I was interrupted by one of the Creatives. In his late twenties, he was probably the oldest. He'd been lolling on a beanbag but had sprung up as soon as I'd said 'sorry' and was now standing in front of me, his arms folded across his chest. He had the white skin of one who rarely sees the light of day, a flat head and sloping nose, a muscular neck and deep-set, almond-shaped eyes. He was an English Bull Terrier. Instinctively, I stepped backwards.

'Sorry, Meg,' he growled, 'where did you say you came from? Confectionery World was it?'

'That's right,' I replied, stealing myself for his bite.

'And how many creative awards has Confectionery World won recently?'

His team straightened up, scenting a fight, a daisy chain of hostility.

'Picture the scene,' I said. 'That Cadbury's ad has just launched and my boss is glowing like some nuclear winter behind her desk, saying, "Call me old-fashioned Meg but a drum-playing gorilla? I really don't get it."'

The Bull Terrier appraised me silently, patently unmoved.

'That's the main reason I left,' I continued, 'I wanted to work somewhere I could be more creative–'

He took another step towards me. 'Let me explain something to you Meg – something you're going to have to get if we're going to work together.'

'Okay,' I said, taking another step backwards.

'P&P believes in two very simple things.' He spoke slowly,

holding up two fingers, the same two fingers I wanted to turn on him. 'One: creativity equals brand fame. Two: brand fame equals sales. I don't suppose they teach you that in Slough.'

He stretched his hands in front of him, cracking his joints, smirking. Self-satisfied prick.

'Your creativity isn't the problem,' I said, trying to take the strain out of my voice, looking in vain for a bit of help from Po-faced Pigtails. Weren't account directors supposed to nurture the client/agency relationship? 'The problem is your execution-led ideas, and your approach to the brand. It's not in keeping with the US work – you need to be thinking Californian goddesses; golden, sculpted, slender.'

The Bull Terrier's hands were on his hips. His chest pumped, the veins on his neck throbbed. 'So, let me get this straight; you – a girl who's spent her entire career peddling clichéd stereotypes now wants P&P, the most awarded agency in town, to peddle clichéd stereotypes on her behalf?'

'I didn't mean it like that.'

'Then what did you mean?'

Off I went, explaining the need to take the California ideal and give it a London twist – something that would make it feel local, but still true to its roots.

But he disagreed – he didn't like the L.A. work at all, thought it was way too glossy. He wanted to write an edgy new campaign. I knew what he meant about the gloss – I seemed to remember saying something about that myself, just yesterday – but that was what Shine was. Gloss. It didn't mean there wasn't anything underneath, obviously Max was testament to that, but it did mean everything had to look, well, glossy.

'You need to stick to the brief,' I said, working hard not to panic at the prospect of going back to Max and telling him I couldn't even pull off a few posters.

'We're not doing it,' he snarled, straining at his leash.

'You have to do it,' I said, 'I'm the client.' God I sounded just like Pat – her way, or the highway.

'We are P&P,' he barked, 'we don't do anything we don't want to do.'

'Well P&P,' I said, snatching up my bag, 'we'll just have to see about that.'

The dignity of my exit was only slightly spoilt by my decision to use the wrong door. I ended up in a walk-in cupboard, facing boxes of fat pencils and reams of A2. Was this to be my destiny? Forever stationery.

I could still hear them laughing as I ran down the stairs and out of the door.

I was steaming up Brick Lane, ready to take out all the curry house waiters for sticking menus in my face, when I bumped into Nate.

He was the last person on earth I wanted to see, but there was no escaping him or his black Labrador. I managed a bit of bright and breezy small talk about the likelihood of rain, until I bent down to stroke Bernard. Something about his quizzical look, the way he seemed to wrinkle his nose in sympathy, brought tears to my eyes.

Wordlessly, Nate coaxed me to my feet, taking me firmly by the arm and walking me in the direction of his place. Reluctantly, Bernard dragged behind, cheated of his walk. I protested too, saying I was really busy, that he must be really busy, but he insisted, and I was in no fit state to argue.

Nate lived in a side road off Commercial Street. It might, technically, still be Spitalfields, but there was no sign of Farrow and Ball gentrification here. His place was in the middle of a row of tall, still grimy, Victorian houses with peeling front doors. It sat between a cheap clothes wholesalers and a women's shelter.

He steered me along the dark hallway with its mosaic walls

of chipped paint, passing the community noticeboard packed with postcards advertising second-hand bikes and flat shares, the 'pay it forward' donations box, the tiny kitchen where they brewed the twiggy tea, and the yoga studio. There was a class in action, or was that inaction? The students looked half asleep.

Bernard followed us up the creaking stairs, moving as slowly as the students, huffing and puffing, his head hanging low, his feet scratching wearily over the floorboards. I knew how he felt. Nate lifted a heavy velvet curtain and we were, at last, in his private rooms, amongst the rafters. The dog shuffled over to the glowing embers of the fire and flopped down gratefully. His chin rested heavily on his paws, his eyebrows raised in surprise, perhaps at finding he was no longer the dog he once was.

Whilst Nate busied himself opening cupboards, I looked around. Everything was well past its 'best before' date. The TV set was a clunky old black box and beneath it lay the infamous stack of worn out DVDs – all of them eighties classics – *When Harry Met Sally, You've Got Mail, Sleepless in Seattle*. Becks often borrowed them for our romcom binges. The rugs were threadbare, the books, amongst them *My Life in Orange* and *The Heart of Yoga*, were tattered. The table, doors and walls were scuffed – especially at dog height, where Bernard had etched permanent reminders of his presence – but the place was cosy, smelling of ground coffee beans, cinnamon and oranges. The kitchen area, at one end of the room, reminded me of an old fashioned sweet shop; the long wooden countertop, the weighing scales beside a stack of mismatched crockery, the jars of spices – the colours of a setting sun.

Everywhere I looked were mementoes of India; a row of brass deities, a scattering of over-sized cushions, and several Tibetan wall hangings depicting ornate Buddhas ascending to the heavens. There were dozens of photos; a young Chrissie with Nate's dad Madoc, Chrissie hugging Nate tight, Madoc polishing an Enfield motorbike, Nate smeared in chocolate. My favourite was the one of the three of them together on the veranda of a Colonial style bungalow – Chrissie resting her head on Madoc's bare chest, her eyes closed, Nate protected in the well of his father's legs. He must've been about three – the picture taken not long before his father died.

Becks had told me the story many times. How her mother had met Nate's mother, a reluctant It-Girl, on the Magic Bus back in the early seventies. The two had done the hippy trail together, Becks' mum returning home after a few months, Chrissie staying on for over a decade, meeting her yoga guru and Madoc. He had been an idealistic young Welsh doctor who'd come to India to work for a charity but his dream of setting up his own clinic had come to an abrupt end when he had a motorbike accident – contracting septicaemia from a seemingly innocuous graze on his leg. His ashes were scattered on the Ganges. Becks said Chrissie never really recovered. A year later, she brought Nate to London, to this house.

He moved me towards an old sofa, offering me a slice of his orange and hazelnut cake, and a hot drink. I'd been dreading the result – another twiggy tea? But I was in for a surprise; this was hot chocolate from the Marcolini counter at Verde & Company. He served it with a flourish – whipping up some real cream and shaving dark chocolate onto the white whirls.

Warming my hands on the mug, I closed my eyes and inhaled, savouring the rich sweetness, feeling it melt the bite in my stomach. Yes, chocolate was back on the agenda.

He flopped down onto the other equally creaky sofa and together we sat – not speaking, just enjoying our sticky cake and hot chocolate, watching the fire – the weather having done that famous English thing, changing seasons overnight.

Eventually, he broke the silence. 'Want to talk about it?'

I spilled everything: starting with the P.R. meeting. How I'd slunk into my bright office, as much a symbol of new beginnings as it was possible for a room to be, and ignored the flowers, the business cards with 'Brand Experience Director' embossed in gold, even the glimpse of the Gherkin, in favour of a full on damage assessment. I'd joined Shine thinking Max would pay attention to me, listen to all my ideas – and there I'd been, hoping he hadn't.

Licking the last of the cream off the teaspoon, I caught sight of my distorted face in its reflection. The surface was as shiny as Ashley's forehead. While I could endlessly repeat the fantasy in which I gave her an overdose of Botox that would paralyse her whole body, I had to admit that in her position, presented with an out-of-town fat bird who talked nothing but Starbucks' loyalty cards, I would've reacted the same way.

I told him how P&P were arrogant, how angry they were with me, how angry I was with them, how I was going to have to go back to Max and tell him that his posters might not happen, how I was never going to amount to anything but 'The BOGOF Girl'.

To my horror, I began to cry.

Hauling himself up and away from the fire, Bernard settled down over my feet, his chin resting on his paws, those troubled eyebrows raised once more.

Nate hunted down some tissues and quietly handed them to me until my sobbing subsided.

'Meg,' he said, leaning forward across the table, speaking softly, 'you've only been there a few days; please don't be so hard on yourself.'

'It's my dream,' I said, blowing my nose, 'a great boss, amazing offices, creative people, glamorous parties, a glimpse of the Gherkin, and I've blown it already.'

'You haven't blown it – you're just having teething problems.'

'But I can't even get the basics right – P&P are probably going to walk out because of me.'

He put his plate down on the table, speaking firmly, looking me in the eye. 'Would that be such a big deal? They sound like a bunch of moody teens.'

'Max would kill me,' I said, taking another tissue, shredding it to pieces.

He smiled. 'Max has entrusted you to do what's right. Don't worry about him.'

'This is my big chance,' I said, staring unseeing at the floor. 'I'm supposed to be re-launching myself, starting afresh, having some fun.'

'So let's work it out. Clearly Ashley is jealous of you—'

I thought of the skinny doe-like creature and snorted with laughter. 'You can't be serious.'

'Deadly. You're beautiful, you're bright and you've obviously got Max's ear – if I'd been there from the start and you'd walked in, I'd be jealous.'

I shook my head in disbelief. Quite cool he thought I was beautiful though.

'And P&P are making judgments because they don't know you.' He leaned back into the sofa and crossed his hands behind his head – clearly in his comfort zone. 'We all start relationships a little scared – it's normal, but you need to get beyond that, get beyond the confrontations, accept people for who they are, get personal.'

I thought I was supposed to be standing up for myself – now I was supposed to accept everything? 'Get personal?' I knew that was his teaching style and I could understand its place on a yoga mat (just about) but what did it have to do with work? What was he on about?

'They don't know you. You don't know them. The rudeness, the confrontations, they're all a defence; she's "the L.A. Bitch," he's "the Bull Terrier" and you're "The BOGOF Girl." You're all clinging to stereotypes; there's no self-expression there for any of you, no freedom. Don't get held hostage to all that crap – help them, turn it around.'

It was weird – he sounded like he might've been to the same workshops as Becks (come to think of it, he probably had) but the way he said everything, so quietly, was so much more appealing. I was surprised at how assured he was – as if he didn't simply believe what he was saying but knew it, knew it from a place deep inside, with absolute faith.

'And how do I do that?' I asked, setting aside the pile of shredded tissues.

'Why don't you start by getting to know Ashley? Find out a bit more about her – where she's from–'

'La La Land.'

'Why she came to London–'

'Because Max asked her to.'

'What she wants out of Shine–'

'Max.'

'What she likes doing–'

'Humiliating me.'

'Ask her what she needs from you, tell her what you need.'

'So I should just toe the line – play Ms. Nice? I'm telling you now Nate – I'm not doing it. When I left Con World I told myself I'd never be a doormat again. I'd rather walk–'

'Whoa,' he said, hands up defensively. 'That's not what I'm saying. I just think you need to get past *what* she's saying to *why* she's saying it, and think about what you've been saying, and why you've been saying it. Is there – for example – a remote possibility that you were competing with her?'

I flushed.

'Listen Meg, you don't have to do anything – of course you don't, but my advice is that you stop reacting to her moves and take it upon yourself to sort it out.'

I paused for a moment, the beginnings of a grin. 'Perhaps I need to get in touch with my own inner Borgia,' I said, launching into a full account of Con World machinations.

He smiled sympathetically but I could tell I was cutting no ice. 'I just don't think it works to play games,' he said, 'especially not for someone like you.'

'Someone like me? You don't even know me.'

'I know enough.'

'Who are you? Yoda?'

'How did you guess?'

'Your ears. Dead giveaway.'

'The pointy bits?'

'The fluffy bits.'

'Hmm, must get Princess Leia onto them,' he said, laughing.

'Tell her to bring her clippers – she has work to do. Meanwhile, back on earth, please be assured I just mean to wise up a little – I'm not going around poisoning people – not unless they *really* annoy me.'

'I just think you should try my advice before you start weaving your dark arts,' he said, cutting us both another slice of cake.

'"Give peace a chance" and all that?'

'Giving peace a chance was John Lennon and he wasn't much into yoga. All I mean is, it's better to keep things simple – keep the energy clean.'

'I get the theory – I just don't know if I want to put it into practice,' I said, running my finger round my plate, picking up stray bits of sponge and icing. 'I don't actually want to get personal with a Bull Terrier – I'd be faking it.'

'And that wouldn't be very yogic.'

'My point entirely – at least poison would be honest.'

We sat in silence for a minute contemplating the options.

I got my answer soon enough.

'Confucius says,' he began, putting on a very fake Chinese accent, '"a journey of a thousand miles begins with a single step."'

'And what's the step?' I asked. 'Walk back to Shine; invite my new mate Ash back here for a slice of cake?'

'Maybe ...'

He must've seen the expression on my face because he moved rapidly on. 'Just give yourself some breathing space first – let things settle.'

I laughed. 'I don't do breathing.'

'Ah,' he said smiling his crooked smile, 'I seem to remember something about that.'

'You noticed?'

'How could I not? You spent the whole of Savasana checking your watch.'

I smiled weakly. 'I had to be somewhere.'

'The pub?'

I nodded, attempting a cheeky grin.

'Between you and me,' he said, lowering his voice conspiratorially, 'I wanted to come with you.'

'Really? You looked perfectly content to me – surrounded by your fans – like bees to honey.'

He laughed awkwardly, and started clearing plates. Was he blushing? 'Anyway Ms. Rogers, you are diverting me from my purpose on this earth; teaching you how to breathe.'

'Seriously Nate, I really don't want to take up any more of your time. I need to get back to work. I've got a lot to do before the weekend–'

'You can spare five minutes,' he said firmly, patting the seat of a chair.

'I really need to get going.'

He patted the chair again, firmer this time.

Reluctantly, I sat.

'Satisfaction guaranteed, or your money back,' he said, placing a chair opposite me, moving in until his knees were almost touching mine.

Keep calm. It's just breathing. You can do this.

'Now shut your eyes and sit up tall,' he said, assuming his yoga teacher voice, the rich baritone, forged on a hundred thousand oms – slow and smooth and mellow. 'Feel your whole body relax.'

He took a long, deep breath.

I watched him carefully, noticing the small furrow between his unkempt eyebrows and how it gave him an air of permanent puzzlement, a bit like Bernard.

'Let your face muscles relax. Completely relax.'

Another long, deep breath.

I began to giggle.

He smiled good-naturedly. 'Giggling is part of the process – accept it and let it go. Just breathe.'

I shut my eyes, trying to focus.

'Everything is already okay. There is nothing to do here. Om.'

It was so much more fun when we were talking.

'Feel the wave of relaxation spreading through your body.'

Wave of panic more like.

'Just listen to the sound of my breath. Nothing to do but relax.'

My hands gripped the sides of the chair. Get me out of here.

'Don't try to control it – just sit quietly. Observe.'

We were too close. Much too close. My knees were trembling with the effort of not touching his. It was like that game I used to play with Becks when we were kids – when you try to pull your fingers apart but they magnetise. Shouldn't he be more aware of these things, being a yoga teacher?

'Your mind is calm – like a lake, deep and still.'

My eyeballs flickered against my eyelids, straining to open.

'The lake is calm, everything is clear, no thoughts are disturbing you.'

It was no good. My eyes popped open. 'I'm sorry Nate, I can't do it. I really need to get back– '

But his hands were already round my wrists, pulling me back to my chair, his eyes still closed.

'Put your hand on my chest.'

He couldn't be serious.

He took my hand and placed it carefully on his chest, taking a deep breath.

'Easy tiger,' he said smiling, 'you're a lover not a fighter – at least in this room.'

I took a deep breath and relaxed my rigid elbow, relaxed my palm, relaxed my fingers, allowing myself to feel the hairs on his chest, spiking up through his old t-shirt.

'That's better. Now feel my breath. Nothing to do here but feel.'

I forced myself to follow the steady beat of his heart, to feel his chest rising and falling, to feel its warmth.

Gently, he took my other hand and placed it on my heart. 'Good. Now breathe with me.'

His hand covered mine like a blanket.

Shakily, I embarked on that first breath, my lungs labouring like an old lady with a Zimmer-frame, unsure I'd ever reach the other side.

'No need to force it, no need to shape it – just let it flow.'

There was more juddering, more wobbling, and then, there it was, a glimpse of the other side. Don't rush. Just breathe. Slowly.

'Now breathe in for five, breathe out for five, in for five, out for five, in for five…'

A lake of stillness.

'Out for five … two, three, four, five … In, two, three, four, five … Continue for five more rounds.'

Reaching the shore; nothing but peace and calm.

'Now hang in the exhale. Suspend your mind; suspend your body, you're in a hammock by the lake, taking in the view.'

And there I was, luxuriating in my hammock, feeling warm and toasty, breathing with my good companion, feeling his hands against mine, his knees against mine – resting gently. Nothing to fear, nothing to hide. Just us, just being, just cosmic bliss.

And then a ripple …

'Two, three, four, five…'

A ripple of … desire? More than a ripple actually – more like a tsunami. I was so unused to feeling anything below the waist it took me a moment to recognize it. Reaching forward and kissing him would be the most natural thing in the world. Perhaps I should just do it. Not think about it. I thought about things too much. But then he was Becks' friend and it might get complicated, and I didn't want that – life was complicated enough. So perhaps not, or perhaps … it was like a current, impossible to resist.

And then he was getting up, getting up so swiftly I wondered if I might actually have tried to kiss him.

'How do you feel?' he asked, gazing down at me from what seemed like a great height.

'I feel good,' I replied, dazed and confused, trying to read his smile. 'I feel better than good – excellent in fact. I feel excellent. Absolutely excellent.' So much for peace and calm. My heart was thumping so loud I was sure he could hear it. 'Thank you,' I added, not sure where to look.

'You are very welcome Ms. Rogers,' he said, moving quickly towards the kitchen counter, clearing away our cups.

'Perhaps we could do it again sometime,' I said as I took in, as if for the first time, the unintentional Tintin quiff of tufted brown hair, the lived-in creases round his eyes, the long lashes, the faded *Teach Your Children Well* t-shirt –the t-shirt my hand had been resting on just a moment before.

'Sure,' he said flatly, turning on the tap, squirting a dollop of washing up liquid onto a sponge. 'But the idea was to give you the tools to practice on your own – you really don't need me.'

'I'm sure I could do with some more coaching,' I replied weakly.

'You'll be fine,' he said, putting on his Marigolds.

'You could be my "Breathing Butler".'

'Your *what*?' He looked totally stumped.

'Oh, it's just something the luxury hotels are doing these days – "Bath Butlers", "Tan Butlers" … it's all part of the personal service. I just thought maybe, what with all your talk of getting personal … oh never mind.' I trailed off, cursing myself. 'It doesn't matter.' I focused on gathering my things, putting on my coat. 'How's business?' I asked, wondering why I'd embarked on another question when it was quite clear he wanted me the hell out of there.

He hesitated and mumbled something about it being too soon to tell.

'"Too soon to tell" what?'

'I'm sure Shine will do us good,' he continued, in a voice that didn't sound like him – too determined, too forced.

'That's right – Spitalfields will be the new "OM District" – a destination for all things yoga,' I said, laughing, making light – he really didn't have anything to worry about. 'It's great because we appeal to totally different people.'

'You noticed?' He smiled ruefully, vigorously scrubbing a pan.

'It's all about market segmentation,' I said, confident, reassuring.

'"Market segmentation"?' He wrinkled his nose, the furrow deepening.

'It's like this Nate,' I said, assuming the smooth, practiced air of a marketing expert, 'my people wouldn't be able to deal with your place – they'd worry about getting fat from the smell of cake, and your people would hate all those Himalayan pebbles and Tibetan tree bark – they've all been to Tibet for real.'

He smiled, looking a little relieved. 'My people do like small classes, personal attention, the hands-on approach.'

I chuckled easily, though my mind was still on what had just happened. I thought the point of all that breathing was to leave you feeling peaceful and calm, not floundering, all jumbled up inside. 'And my people will always insist on valeted yoga mats and business concierge,' I said, patting Bernard's head, wishing he could pat me back.

Nate picked up another plate, washing it more slowly, apparently lost in thought. I tried but I couldn't make putting on my coat last a moment longer.

'Well, I'll be off then,' I said, heading for the door. 'See you soon.'

'Meg,' he said, returning to the room, 'hang on a minute – let me put some shoes on. I'll see you out–'

But I was out the front door before he could pull off his Marigolds.

'Friends with benefits'

CHAPTER SEVEN

No pink fairy. One Enfield motorbike.

Letting myself in, I put the bottle of wine in the fridge and, following the smell of incense, gently opened the sitting room door.

There was Becks. There was Susie. And there was Nate.

They were lying in a row, on the floor, under blankets and eye pillows.

J.R. the dog was next to them, lying on his tummy, eyebrow cocked in my direction.

Susie peeped at me from under her pink eye pillow. Putting one finger to her lips she tiptoed towards me, pointing towards the kitchen. J.R. followed.

'Play?' she said, less a question than a command.

I fished a juice out of the fridge for her, fed J.R. some scraps, and poured a large glass of wine for me, while I worked out what to do. I was supposed to be having a quick post mortem with Becks on the first few days at Shine, before heading home to Slough; I certainly hadn't been expecting Nate. I still cringed with embarrassment every time I thought about my 'Breathing Butler'.

Out came Yoga Teacher Barbie, complete with pink vest top and turquoise leggings. I'd bought it for Susie last Christmas, a little concerned that Barbie's colonisation of planet yoga might not go down well with my favourite yoga purist, but Becks had shrugged it off with a 'whatever gets her there.'

'Natarajasana,' said Susie, standing the doll on one leg, adjusting an arm so Barbie could catch her other foot behind her head.

'And who's this?' I asked, carefully placing Barbie's Chihuahua pup on the miniature yoga mat.

'Don't do that,' said Susie, quickly moving him out of the way. 'Barbie likes to focus on her mat.' There was a pause in which she appeared to weigh up her options. 'Maybe after "Ustrasana",' she conceded.

'Which is?'

'Camel Pose,' she said, moving Barbie into a kneeling position, adjusting her hands behind her, to meet her heels. 'Watch Aunty Meg!' And there she was, the mirror image, pink t-shirt and turquoise leggings, kneeling on the kitchen floor, hands on heels.

As she moved Barbie through her practice, being sure to show me a live demonstration of each pose, I focused on drinking. By the time Becks and Nate came in, I'd managed to down a full glass.

'Nate!' I said, pouring another while I worked out whether to get up and kiss him. 'What a nice surprise!' He solved the problem, bending down to peck me on the cheek.

'Nice look,' I said, playfully yanking the material on that *Teach Your Children Well* t-shirt.

'Thank you Meg,' he said, backing off as soon as I released my grip, throwing on a sweatshirt. 'Are you good?'

'Still breathing,' I said, waving the bottle at him. 'Drink?'

'I really must get going,' he said, looking pointedly at his watch.

'Stay Uncle Nate!' said Susie, jumping up and down with her Barbie. 'Have a drink with Mum and Megs!'

'I'm sorry sweetheart,' he said, scooping her up, rubbing noses. 'I have a class.'

'But it's late Uncle Nate,' said Susie, pulling back so she could look him square in the eyes.

'An emergency,' he said, untangling himself. 'I just got a text.' He kissed Becks on the cheek, made a start towards me, then changed course. 'Nice to see you Meg,' he said, waving at me from the door, Susie clinging to his leg.

'Well, that was weird,' said Becks, turning slowly back to me, eyes narrowed. 'What happened?'

'Nothing happened,' I said, evenly. 'Nothing at all.' Looking for an escape route I landed on Susie, who in my view was looking very sleepy. I led her upstairs with the promise of a story. When I returned, half an hour later, Becks picked up, exactly where we'd left off. '"Nothing happened"? she said, handing me a large bowl of pasta. 'Seriously?'

I leant in to better inhale the smell of bolognaise sauce – it took me straight back to us as kids, when Becks' mum used to cook it for us. 'He's a nice guy – that's all.'

She slapped her hand against her forehead. 'You don't say.'

'We bumped into each other the other day; I went back to his for a bit and we had a good chat. Delicious, by the way.'

'"A good chat"?'

'Becks, you can stop channelling Kate Winslet in *Enigma*. There's no code to be broken here. Read my lips; nothing happened.' Unfortunately.

She continued to channel the bluestocking cryptanalyst. 'I know you Meg.'

I took a deep breath, putting down my fork, holding up my hands in surrender. 'Okay. Okay. I confess. He gave me some very good advice, and some great cake.'

'How very Famous Five. Did you wash it all down with lashings of ginger pop?'

'Marcolini hot chocolate with whirls of cream actually. Then he taught me how to breathe.'

'Wow. I'd like to have seen that.'

I smiled, good-naturedly. 'I was really struggling but then he did this really cool thing – he put my hand on his chest, and all I had to do was follow his breath.'

'Honestly, you look about thirteen.'

'In a good way?' I laughed, suddenly feeling slightly hysterical.

'You know Meg,' she said, adopting the careful manner of a professional therapist, 'you shouldn't read too much into it; it's very easy to get confused around yoga teachers. It can feel very intimate but really they're just helping you get to know yourself.'

'I know what I felt Becks,' I said, wondering if that was why he backed off.

'He gets it all the time – women hitting on him – women who've not had anyone touch them for a while–'

I was mortified. 'God Becks, you're making me sound like a real saddo.'

'I'm just saying it's been a long time – it would be easy to get a bit over-excited.'

'And now I'm finally waking up, you're telling me not to?'

'Not with Nate.'

'I don't know why not; he's perfect fling material,' I said, laughing a little too heartily. 'He's got a hot bod, and there's absolutely no future in it.'

'Friends with benefits?'

'Exactly.'

'Except that you're not really friends, and believe me, there will be no benefits,' she replied impatiently. 'You certainly don't need another fling gone wrong and neither does Nate, especially with a student.'

'I'm *not* his student.'

'He *was* teaching you to breathe.'

'That doesn't make me his student.'

'It does in that context; even if he had felt something there's no way he would've acted on it.'

'So you admit there may have been something there.'

'I just want what's best for both of you,' she said, polishing off her spaghetti.

I took the empty bowls over to the kitchen counter, ran them under the tap. Maybe she had a point. We might've had a moment but actually he wasn't my type; I probably couldn't have a fling with a man who was into rom coms – *St Elmo's Fire*, *About Last Night*, *The Breakfast Club* – they were a girl thing; a Becks and me thing. I thought about the stack of Blu-Ray DVDs in Max's flat – *Scarface*, *Kill Bill*, *Fight Club* –– they were a proper man's choice.

'I think you're right Becks – I need someone more manly.'

Becks snorted into her wine glass. '"Manly"?! Nate's the manliest man you'll ever meet. Just because he doesn't stride about in a stupid suit all day, just because he likes yoga and cooking, just because he *cares*.'

'Maybe I mean more sophisticated, more worldly?'

This was met by another snort. Apparently, Nate had travelled to more places than I'd done ExCel spreadsheets.

'Maybe I mean more successful,' I said, trailing off, not at all sure what I meant.

'Success is all relative – for your parents it's about the local community, for a doctor it's saving lives, for a yoga teacher it's helping students towards their true nature, for business people it's mostly money.'

'Well, speaking as a business person,' I said, deciding not to rise to the bait, 'I think he could do with some help monetising his assets.'

Becks laughed. '"Monetising his assets"?'

'You know perfectly well what I mean,' I said. 'Making money isn't a crime.'

'I'm listening,' she said, still laughing.

I told her that it was time for him to make some money out of his talent, that he should take what he deserves, and enjoy his life.

'He *does* enjoy his life,' she said stubbornly,

I was not to be put off. 'Take where he lives – it's a golden opportunity to make some money.'

'Really?' She looked unconvinced. 'How so?'

'Well, some of the other houses, just ten minutes walk from him, are stunning; glossy front doors, pretty shutters in heritage colours, miniature trees on doorsteps. He should do up his place – make it like theirs.'

'And their owners are Tracey Emin, Jake Chapman, Gilbert & George, Jeanette Winterson, Chris Ofili,' said Becks, rattling off the list like a Spitalfields tour guide.

I was impressed. 'Seriously? They live there? I should've guessed; all those paintings, all that careful lighting – they look like art galleries–'

'Anyway, it's not his house to do up,' she said, moving over to the window, arms folded.

'I thought his mum left it to him.'

'No – she was a sitting tenant and she was smart – she got succession rights so he could carry it on when she died – he's on one of those fair rent contracts, the ones you can't get anymore–'

'And let me guess … what he saves in rent he spends on discounted community classes–'

'That's right,' she said approvingly.

'So,' I said, 'the landlord won't invest because he's can't make any money, and Nate can't invest because he's got no money – it's such a waste.' I paused a moment, once again visualising Nate and me pouring over heritage paint samples, 'You know, it really could look amazing.'

'Poverty is what saved it,' she said, still staring out of the window, her back resolutely to me. 'If the previous owners had money they'd have ripped out all the original features.'

'It's just that if it looked smarter, he could charge more – and it might bring some new people in. Maybe he should target some of those Shoreditch hipsters, the kind that work at P&P – the kind that drink micro-brewery ale out of jam jars, wear *Dalston is Dead* t-shirts, and grow a moustache every Movember.'

Becks looked like she might be about to throw up.

'You have to follow the money Becks,' I said, recalling Max's phrase, then wishing I hadn't; she was looking decidedly green around the gills. 'Maybe I can help him with his business – that's all I'm saying' I said, wondering if that really was all I was saying.

'*Strictly* business,' said Becks, relaxing a little, pouring herself some more wine. 'And I *am* glad he helped you feel calmer – that asshole at P&P should be put down.'

We settled in, having a good laugh about the Japanese girl who seemed to have lost use of her hand, the way Ashley twirled her pencil with the skill of a majorette, and how it didn't look likely she and I would be dancing round our handbags together any time soon.

Then I told her about my plans to start over. I told her that thanks to Nate, I would be 'getting personal' and that I'd also decided to get on my mat. I told her that the diet would start on Monday and would be accompanied by daily attendance at class, until I'd dropped twenty pounds and two dress sizes – to a size ten. 'As I used to say back at Con World, "packaging is the key agent of brand reappraisal".'

She looked dismayed. 'Why do you want to re-invent yourself? What's wrong with the old Meg Rogers? She's my best friend.'

'I'd prefer to think of myself as the 'New and Improved Meg Rogers,' I replied, tugging at my waistband, squeezing a roll of fat. 'Just look at me, I could be my own BOGOF. It's time to practice what I preach, especially now I'm representing a lifestyle brand.'

This triggered another monologue on images of perfection, which was followed by what Becks termed 'some disturbing revelations' that she was sharing 'in the interests of transparency'. Who did she think she was? Edward Snowden? Then she told me that Shine was attempting to copyright yoga 'as if yoga postures were Kellogg's Cornflakes'.

I explained, as Max had to me, that it was Shine's sequences that he wanted to copyright, not the postures themselves.

'The Indian sages were the only ones who could've owned them,' she said, really enjoying the view from her high horse, 'but they didn't have lawyers back then.'

I tried to break it down – to explain that it was the same at Con World – the same anywhere; companies needed to protect the intellectual property they'd spent years developing. Unfortunately, this took her off on another tangent.

'But this isn't about companies, it's about people – Shine is suing people who teach its sequences and they're going out of business.'

How could it be right that people should steal Shine's sequences, and not give Shine any money? Once more I repeated what Max had said to me. '"If they want to teach our sequences, sequences that are our intellectual property, they must trade as Shine and pay us a percentage."' I understood this completely – when Hinshaw's did a joint promotion with say, a toy manufacturer, we had to pay a royalty to use their brand property. That was the way things worked. Even Con World had dug into the corporate purse for that one.

On she went, arguing that the 'stupid money' the teachers paid Shine for their training should be enough.

I reminded her again that Shine, more specifically '*people* called Max and Jed,' had spent three years perfecting those sequences.

'Not quite the five thousand years that yoga's been around,' she replied, folding her arms and digging into the sofa. 'And I just know it's going to affect Nate.'

'Sorry Becks,' I said, wondering what I'd missed, 'how does Nate even come into this? He's never going to want to teach a Shine sequence.'

That's when it came out – she thought she'd seen a slackening off already. She really had convinced herself it was going to go pear-shaped. I repeated my 'Shine isn't competition' argument, and then I reminded her I was going to help him.

She gave me a look that said she thought I was flattering myself. 'I'm glad you've recovered some of your self-confidence, I really am,' she said, looking anything but glad, 'but do you really think you can stand in the way of Shine?'

'It's all about segmentation,' I replied, reminding her of all my work on chocolate – how some people like nuts and others prefer soft centres. I told her this would turn out to be exactly the same. It was just a question of being sure what you were – nutty or smooth. I was sure I could help him carve out a unique space; it would be straightforward – unlike chocolate, it was hardly a crowded marketplace.

'And how are you going to square all that help with your job at Shine?' she asked. 'You think Max is going to be happy for his Brand Experience Director to help a competitor?'

'I doubt very much that Max has even registered Nate.'

But she wasn't listening. Now she was telling me she had 'a nasty feeling' that Max's sense of ownership might extend beyond sequences, beyond yoga, to actual people.

'There is no way on earth Max wants to control me or anyone else. It's the opposite. He wants to have me fulfil my potential – transform myself.'

'Fulfil your potential? What about the little people's potential?'

'That's not fair Becks,' I snapped, 'you know how much this job means to me, and I guarantee you I'm not getting in anyone's way.'

This was met with a shrug and a long stretch of silence. I was on the point of calling it a night when she suddenly apologised. It was school again. Paperwork. Feckless parents. Wasted kids.

I found myself wondering what Max would say. One thing was for sure, he wouldn't let her sit there, accepting the status quo. He would tell her to make a stand, do what she believed in. So, I came to a decision; I would help her achieve her potential as Max was helping me. My eyes came to rest on her favourite t-shirt, which she was despondently twisting into knots.

'Why don't you write another book?' I said, thinking back to the one she'd been working on a few years back. She'd been doing really well with it, writing about famous revolutionaries who lived off their women; according to her Che Guevara was one of the worst offenders – living not off the wealthy, but off nurses and teachers. But it'd been a case of life imitating art when Susie's dad decided that he'd like to do much the same thing. Becks had binned him and the book around the same time. The Che Guevara t-shirt was the only thing that had survived.

'That dream died a long time ago,' she said, helping herself to more wine.

'A book about life as a teacher,' I explained, not to be put off. 'Start with the day you watched *Dead Poets*, how you'd read every single word of Orwell and Hemingway by the time you were fourteen, how you dreamed of imparting all that knowledge to the adults of tomorrow, and how all your dreams were crushed by a pile of paperwork.'

She wasn't exactly leaping out of her chair. 'What shall we call it, *Death by Ofsted*?'

How was it that Becks, a woman who understood all the subtleties of our great writers could need so much spelling out? Wasn't it time she put all that old campaigning experience to good use? 'Use it to start a revolution – think Jamie Oliver and his school dinner ladies – change the way things get done.'

She continued to throw roadblocks at me – how Susie was

often awake until late, how she rarely had time for the kettle to boil, let alone write a book – but I could tell I'd made her think, especially when she mentioned whistleblowing.

'I guess I could be the Edward Snowden of education,' she said, her smile growing. She talked some more, how she wanted to overcome the existing order like her heroes, Orwell and Hemingway. How she wanted to stand up for kids, and her fellow teachers. 'I'll write it as an exposé,' she said, her eyes bright, 'the truth about teaching in a modern day high school.'

Jamie Oliver. Edward Snowden. Truly, what was the difference? 'I'll drink to that,' I said, emptying what was left of the second bottle into our glasses, wondering if tomorrow really was the best day to start my new regime.

'May the Force be with you'

I arrived early on Monday morning, in time for the seven o'clock class. Brutal. It'd meant getting up at five and I was hungover, but a plan was a plan.

The plan had, as usual, been carefully researched. I'd done my best impression of David Attenborough, meticulously observing the habitat of each studio, weighing up the pros and cons. Yo-Karma placed a lot of emphasis on partner work which, given my track record, was unlikely to be a success. Next along was Studio Jamu, 'inspired by Indonesia's healing sun'. An image of what was apparently the world's longest beach bathed the entire studio in a turquoise haze. One problem was the heat – even outside the door I was breaking into a sweat, my curls frizzing. The other problem was the clothes, or lack thereof – bikinis, basically. The yin-yang shaped portholes of the Chinese studio were pretty, but Yo-Chi wasn't me. All that rhythmic breathing, all that fluid movement, all that rolling of imaginary balls – it was nowhere near as slow as Nate's class but it was still way too slow; I wanted to blast them all with a dose of Meatloaf's *Bat Out of Hell*. In the end, I decided on Yo-Jitsu. 'A fast-flowing blend of yoga and Jujitsu – a fighting warrior sequence that delivers maximum results in minimum time – heating the body, burning fat, building muscle.' 'Minimum time' were the operative words. Forty five minutes ... how bad could it be?

Wishing I'd been able to bottle some of Nate's calm, I exchanged some staff tokens for a small vial of spray-on Meditation Mist, a freshly laundered yoga mat, and two warm fluffy towels. Fully equipped, with lead in my feet, I made my way to the changing room.

The first person I saw was Ashley, naked but for a tiny towel. She was massaging one of her line drawing legs with some heaven-scented moisturizer.

'Mmmm,' I said, seizing a 'get personal' moment. 'You smell nice.'

She looked at me as if I'd just made a move on her – come to think of it, it had sounded a bit Sapphic. Oh god. I blushed, picking up the bottle, intently reading the label. 'I'll have to get me some of this,' I said, reciting the entire ingredients list to avoid having to come up with any words of my own. 'Mandarin, neroli, palmarosa ... essential oils to stimulate the skin ... revitalizing zest of lime.' All of this was met with silence, and then, when she finally finished slathering, 'You're not thinking of doing this class are you Megan?'

'I can't think of any other reason why I'd be here at seven in the morning,' I said brightly. She dropped her eyes, taking in my stomach, butt and thighs. 'Well, I guess you're in the right place,' she replied, picking up the towel that had dropped carelessly to the floor. She might have a textbook Brazilian, but she was totally flat chested.

I turned away, trying to concentrate on getting undressed and into the shower; a pre-requisite of any Shine class. A simple enough task, you'd think, but one that kept me standing for several minutes wrapped in what seemed no bigger than a flannel, trying to work out why there were no shower curtains or discreet wooden doors. I could feel Ashley's eyes burning into me but

I was damned if I was going to ask her for help. It wasn't until I'd had a shower in full view of the entire changing room and was towelling myself dry that I saw another girl flick a cunningly disguised floor operated switch – at which point the glass turned opaque. Thanks for that Ash.

The humiliation continued. Everyone else was rocking Shine's Studio-Ready collection – tight pants, crops or shorts, matched to tiny tanks, bras or vests. It was like landing in a jar of jellybeans – tomato red, sky blue, zesty orange and zingy turquoise – but much less fun; my faded grey t-shirt and baggy black leggings were a long way from the look book. I'd never felt plainer. I tried to tame my runaway hair into a shining ponytail in a vain attempt to have some aspect of my physical self resemble the streamlined silhouette that described every other woman in the whole damn changing room. No joy. I had to settle for scraping it back into a topknot; a topknot from which all those curls immediately launched another desperate bid for freedom.

Trying unsuccessfully not to care, I picked up my mat and my Meditation Mist and made my way to Studio Ki – the Japanese studio. At two thousand square feet, it wasn't the biggest, but it was my favourite for its rice paper shoji screens, hand painted wall mounted scrolls and the Tsukiubai – a wide stone basin in the middle of the room which symbolised purity. Most of all I loved the Tatami mats – despite the rubber back coating that prevented slippage, they smelt of fresh straw.

The room buzzed with excitement – it was like a Wembley Arena crowd waiting for Madonna. Becks and I had been there, celebrating the end of university with tickets to the *Confessions* tour. We'd squeezed each others hand during *Papa Don't Preach* – the news of her pregnancy giving it a whole new meaning. I was glad she wasn't next to me now; she'd have been horrified – she thought yoga should begin in total silence, with at least fifteen minutes of breathing, 'centering' and 'inhabiting the space'.

Everyone was chatting and giggling except Ashley, who was limbering up down at the front – sticking her non-existent bottom in the air as she placed her palms on the floor and went into a full handstand, holding it for several minutes. I headed for the back and tried not to panic. The look was as uniform as the workout wear – the men were muscular, the women were lithe; this was a singular slender and sculpted world. I would've chosen a beginners' class but Jed's thing was that there was always a way of working a pose, no matter where you were at, and that we needed to get inspired by the experienced people down at the front. Inspired was a long way from what I was feeling.

Suddenly the doors swung open and in burst four even more perfectly formed girls, all of them modelling the tiny white shorts. They stood at the door, two on either side, their arms held high, in magician's assistant mode. There was a pause and in jogged Jed. He really was a poster-boy for the brand – all blonde-haired and sun-soaked; glowing with health. The hundred-strong crowd cheered and clapped as he high-fived his way to the front. Jumping on stage, he peeled off his sweatshirt, revealing a vest top emblazoned with a gold lotus and the shortest of shorts. I pulled my t-shirt down over my bum, wishing it were longer. I thought wistfully of Nate, picturing him shambling about in his low-key tracksuit bottoms, wishing he was next to me, keeping me steady.

Jed turned to face us and took a deep bow, soaking up the whoops and hollers – every inch the rock star. He put on his headset microphone, kissed the tiger tooth hanging round his neck and flicked a switch, flooding the room with Van Morrison's *Bright Side of the Road*. We were off.

I tried to start by standing still and taking a large swig of water – surely there was no point in getting dehydrated before I began, but the bottle was immediately removed by one of his assistants whispering fiercely that 'water puts out the fire of the Yo-Jitsu warrior'.

The pace was high energy, high adrenalin. Jed strutted and slinked around the room, persuading us, with all the enthusiasm you'd expect from his L.A. genes, to 'go the extra mile', 'feel the butt cheeks burn' and 'find the extra inch'. It was like being in a never-ending car chase, and just as exhausting. While Ashley's ponytail remained sleek at all times, my curls quickly turned to frizz. I was sweating like a storm trooper. I soaked both fluffy towels, turning ever-deeper shades of red through the ten rounds of sun salutations, wobbling dangerously in Crescent Kick, and nearly crashing into the girl on the next mat with my out-of-control Scissor Sweeps.

Jed worked the room as if he was Mick Jagger, soaking up the energy, spinning it out ten-fold, taunting us, goading us, compelling us into position. We took an all too short break while he used Ashley to demonstrate 'Wheel'. She looked every inch the child gymnast – feet and hands on the floor, her spine in a smooth 180 degree arc. Once he'd perfected the pose, he detailed its many benefits – how it built a strong and supple spine, squeezed out tension, and opened the heart – all of this from his perch – her jutting hipbones.

Just as I was wondering if he'd forgotten where he was, he jumped off and told us to 'mirror' Ashley. I lay flat on my back and placed my hands by my ears as instructed, but I failed at the first hurdle – my arms shuddered like an engine minus petrol, and then they collapsed beneath me. First of all I thought I'd got away with it; last time I looked Jed was standing on someone else's hips, singing along to Cream's *I Feel Free*, but suddenly he was standing right next to me.

He knelt down, speaking softly, telling me to stay on my back, knees bent over my heels, feet parallel, tucked in close to my sit bones. 'Now press your arms and feet into the mat and slowly lift your pelvis off the floor. Push down strongly through the feet and keep your thighs in a straight line with your chest.' Slowly I juddered into position, feeling like a tipper truck shedding its load. 'There you go' he said, admiring me as if I was a perfectly risen soufflé. 'Now' he said, placing his warm hands on my knees, giving them a little squeeze to encourage me back down to earth, 'remember this is "Bridge Pose" – the gentle way to open your heart.'

Giving me a wink, he jumped up, once more in command of the room. 'Okay class, let's forward bend'.

I was amazed to see all the others wrapping their hands round their feet and clasping their wrists. How was that physically possible? The closest I ever got to my feet was reaching for a chocolate on the sofa.

As I struggled to my shins, Jed returned.

'Just breathe,' he whispered in my ear, lowering his chest onto my back.

It was bad enough trying to breathe sitting opposite a man. How the hell was I supposed to do it with one on top of me?

'Let it go Meg. Unfreeze those joints. Release your shoulders. Relax your belly. "May the Force be with you."'

I screamed silently. My rib cage was squashed. I'd lost all feeling in my legs. I was never going to walk again, let alone be a Jedi warrior.

'Just stretch into it. Melt into it. "Yellow mother custard … I am the walrus",' he warbled. Was he going to do the whole bloody song? I was losing the will to live. Finally, the walrus peeled himself off me and lowered himself onto his next rock; the girl beside me. Unlike me, she appeared entirely unaffected, continuing to breathe with the monotony of a metronome.

'Class – you must read Allen Ginsberg,' he announced, following some private train of thought.

Several impossible poses later he leapt onto the stage, mopping his brow and taking a bow, to a round of applause. 'Free form,' he commanded by way of an encore, hitting the button for a laser show that would've put any seventies rock god to shame. Ninety-nine students jumped up and shook their booty to the holiday rhythms of James Taylor's *Mexico*, clapping and shrieking in enthusiastic appreciation as beams of blue, orange and red neon, like *Star Wars* light sabers, targeted their sculpted bodies.

All my neighbours had deserted me, rushing down to the front as the first laser struck – it wasn't just my low-flying kicks that were dangerous. My hair was stuck to my scalp, my clothes were soaked, my face was bright red, and, horror of horrors, I smelled. Now I could see the point of all that Studio-Ready 'advanced fibre technology'. The 'nanoparticles with moisture wicking and anti-microbial shield' that were embedded in every Studio-Ready piece, even the tiniest of shorts.

And there was Ashley, in the midst of it all – performing perfectly controlled Scissor Sweeps to the Mexican beat and still, I was sure, smelling of mandarin and neroli. Unfortunately, my appearance was the least of my problems – my insides were as wobbly as jelly, and I was shaking. I knew it would be challenging but I thought it'd be worth it – that I'd have a road to Damascus conversion, that I'd leave feeling good, walking tall, feeling strong, wanting nothing but pink sushi for breakfast, well on my way to Slender and Sculpted. Instead, I crawled out of the room a shadow of my former self, fixated on a bacon sandwich.

It took a will of iron not to desert the place for the nearest greasy spoon, but somehow, after a long, hot and very private shower, I made it to the café. Feeling like a seasick passenger returning to dry land, I held onto the tray rail for support, forcing myself to order the infamous pink sushi, AKA mashed beetroot. A plan was a plan.

In that plan I would be accompanying Ashley to breakfast, but she was way ahead of me again, having taken only five minutes to shower, moisturise and throw on a perfect little outfit. She'd already taken up residence in the café, and was working her way through a green juice as big as her head, having a seemingly hilarious time with the rest of the Catwalk Caterpillar, undoubtedly at my expense.

I parked myself in a quiet corner – the one furthest from them, and ploughed my way through eight rolls of mashed beetroot (how could two be the standard serving?) as I replayed several of the greatest cat fights of all time; I was Halle Berry versus Sharon Stone in *Catwoman*. Uma Thurman versus Daryl Hannah in *Kill Bill, Vol. 2*. Demi Moore versus Lucy Liu, Drew Barrymore and Cameron Diaz in *Charlie's Angels: Full Throttle*. I was taking down the Catwalk Caterpillar, leaving Ashley and me to slug it out to the bitter end. Yes, I would own her scrawny little ass.

I was just debating whether to wait until she'd left before I went up for seconds, when I caught sight of a famous blonde mane of hair. Could this woman, so familiar from the glossies, really be holding court at the head of the breakfast queue? Was it a mirage? She'd come as Scheherazade, Queen of Persia; wearing a heavily brocaded floor length dress, fully accessorised with tasselled rope sandals, a gauzy headscarf, and a vast mirrored bag big enough to contain an entire bazar.

And then she was gliding towards me, as if on a magic carpet, asking if I was Meg, if she could sit with me. Zoffany was prettier in person, with delicate little features – a button nose, tiny teeth and perfect rosebud lips. There was nothing delicate about that hair though – it was long, thick and ridiculously glossy, a Californian cornfield in the late afternoon sun. Her voice was husky, breathy, soft and sweet, with a trace of a French accent, and she gave off a warm, heady scent – amber mixed with patchouli, gardenia, and creamy men's soap. I hesitated, feeling overawed, and totally unequal to the task; dealing with such glamour would've been unnerving even after a few drinks – at half past eight in the morning? Forget it. But she'd already put down her tray, there was nothing to do but throw myself in.

'Ahh – la belle poupée,' she said, playfully tugging one of my still damp curls, as if it was an old-school doorbell.

I smiled uncertainly, not sure what to say, or do. Eventually, she spoke. Just one word. 'Délicieuse.' What just happened? Had she just called me a delicious puppet? I wondered if I could surreptitiously text Becks for some simultaneous translation. Whenever she came back from one of her trips, there were two things guaranteed: she'd have acquired at least one totally bling religious icon, often with neon coloured moving parts, and she'd be fluent in another language – complete with optional local dialects. I, on the other hand, had never got much further than 'pain au chocolat'.

As I worked on producing a more confident version of my smile, she went on staring. (A French thing?) She did it with the air of an art critic; would she circle the exhibit? 'You know you are a very pretty girl' she said eventually, as if she was confessing one of her darkest secrets. 'You 'ave the look of a young Debra Messing – you know, *Will and Grace*?'

'That's very kind' I said, my heart soaring. Becks liked to say the same thing to me, but I'd always dismissed it as best friend talk.

'Yes' she said, decisively. 'It is so; eyes, nose, *and* mouth, especially the nose – very cute. And your ears ... very Kate Hudson.'

I was happy to take anything of Kate Hudson's – even her ears. 'They're ever so big' I said, giving them a good tug.

'In a good way' she said, as if sticking out ears were one of this year's most coveted accessories. 'You just need help – a little makeover' she said, diving into her bag, emerging a few seconds later with a freshly pressed cotton hanky – the kind my granny used to carry.

'It was my first Yo-Jitsu class' I managed, mopping my face gratefully.

'C'est normal' she said, shrugging, a big Gallic shrug. 'It's tough to start these things.' She reached across the table, her hand cool on mine. 'Ma pauvre chérie. The lightsabers were out? You felt too much "the Force"?'

'The Force was most definitely with me,' I replied, breathing a little easier, responding to her sweetness, 'in fact it was lying on top of me for several minutes.'

She chuckled throatily, a dirty laugh that made me think of late-night bars. Oh for a dry martini – oh for any kind of alcohol actually.

'Eat,' she said firmly, pushing her small bowl of fruit towards me.

'Only on top of a cheesecake,' I replied, pushing the slice of papaya sprinkled with pomegranate seeds back at her, not even tempted. I'd been too long of the opinion that the only place for fruit was in a pudding, a muffin, or, at a push, a smoothie.

'Ahh cheesecake,' she said, with infinite longing – as if cheesecake was the love of her life. 'I am also a fan, but of course it cannot be – not in this lifetime.' She patted her non-existent belly, smiling apologetically, 'We must sacrifice.'

I folded up the hanky, trying to hide the foundation stains on the pretty embroidery. 'Seriously though,' I said, 'is that really all you're having?'

'I 'ave a big lunch,' she replied, a teasing smile creasing the faint lines around her eyes. I had a sudden vision of her in a high-end casino, looking at me over the top of her cards – a winning hand.

'What's on the menu?' I ventured, 'two raspberries and a cherry?'

'Only one raspberry,' she replied, throwing up her hands in mock-horror. 'The cherry is for supper.'

Thank god she could laugh at herself; though I could hear dad saying that she'd have to have a sense of humour to dress like that.

She was explaining that exercise hadn't come naturally to her either. 'I used to be, how you say, a *Gold Dust Woman*.'

'Rehab?' I asked, still not quite believing I was having this conversation.

She shrugged again, 'I was not far away. When I met Jed I was so out of shape the only thing I could lift was my glass.'

'And now you can lift two?'

She chuckled again – bathing me in her glow; it felt so good, I was already a Zoffany addict. I risked a glance at Ashley and the Caterpillar – yep, they were all pretending not to have noticed. Fantastic. I moved closer, besotted by my new best friend, wishing Becks could witness the scene.

'You can trust Jed,' she said, twisting a strand of her hair round a finger. 'He picked me up and turned me round. He'll do the same for you – *certainement*.'

I nodded miserably, confessing that I feared I may not be a natural.

'Then, my darling' she said, leaning forward, that hair of hers swinging across the table, creating a confessional, 'I must share with you all of my secrets.'

'If it's cocaine, I won't do it,' I said, warding her off with the sign of the cross. 'I tried it once, at an ad agency party, and spent the whole night talking to the other girls in the loo.' In truth, it had been a grim affair; after a troubled evening, one of those in which Pat had been lauded by some super-creepy, talentless ad guy, I'd sought refuge with Becks, arriving on her doorstep at one in the morning. She had to sit with me all night, holding me tight to stop me shaking. Zoffany laughed, joking that I just needed more training. 'I've spent a lot of time in the loo,' she said, clearly recalling some fond memories. 'Maybe I should write some short stories – *Tales from the Small Room*?'

'*Mirror Mirror*,' I offered, before diverting the conversation into safer territory. 'So, your first secret is…?'

'Detox.'

I grimaced.

'No caffeine.'

I shook my head. 'No way.'

'No chocolate; absolument.'

I shook my head again, thinking only of Nate's Marcolini swirls.

'Double boiled mushrooms.'

More grimacing.

'And fish maw.'

'Fish what?'

She made a face that said don't go there. 'It has no fat, and it is good for the skin.' There was a pause as she did a mental checklist. 'Did I mention cabbage?'

'I think I'll stick with pink sushi,' I said, pushing my plate away. At least I'd lost my appetite.

Then she told me I'd need some spa treatments.

I agreed, eager to hear her recommendations, imagining she'd advocate the Maharani, but at the top of her list was something called Zero Balancing, which seemed to involve being suspended upside down, supported by nothing but the therapist's feet.

'Sorry – I never fancied life as a bat.'

'You are just hanging out,' she said encouragingly, 'like the womb.'

Perhaps fish maw wasn't so bad after all.

She spent the next twenty minutes talking me through the entire list of detox treatments – each one of them worse than the last – Thai-style colonics, lymphatic drainage, and hose-downs with ice-cold water – which might've been fun, with firemen. In the end, I agreed to go and see Doctor Lily. Chinese medicine seemed to be the least of the evils, and at least I'd get to keep my knickers on.

I asked her whether I really needed to do any exercise if I just stuck to fish maw and Doctor Lily. Wouldn't that be enough?

'Non,' she replied firmly. 'But I will tell you another secret.'

I leaned forward conspiratorially.

'You don't have to love it for it to work. It is simply a necessity.'

'Like brushing your teeth?'

'Exactement. You don't enjoy doing it but it is worth it – you look good, and you feel good. At least, you do afterwards.'

In a funny sort of way, this was a big relief. Becks always went on about how much she loved Nate's classes – the longer the better as far as she was concerned. Not needing to enjoy any of it took the pressure off. It would just be something unpleasant I would do in order to achieve an objective. Suddenly, I felt a little more confident of a successful outcome.

'How long is it going to take?' I asked.

'You must do the detox, you must see Doctor Lily, and you must go to class every day,' she said, wagging her finger sternly, suddenly looking rather strict, 'but if you do you will see a difference in a month.'

A month I could do.

Then she asked how I was settling in. It was time for a couple more confessions.

'Don't be hard on yourself,' she said, her hand returning to mine, bangles cascading down her wrist. 'P&P, Max; pas de problème. He said you gave Ashley a run for her money – that you were very "of the earth, very no nonsense".'

'He said that?'

'But of course, mon anglaise mignonne – this is what you are.'

'Did he mention anything about a BOGOF?'

'Quoi? What is this "BOGOF"?'

Swiftly, I moved on, to Ashley's problem with the pink ribbons.

'Why should she mind, whatever colour they are?' she said, her brow furrowing. 'It's a good cause, non?'

'Exactly,' I said, looking over to Ashley's table. Bambi was shooting daggers in my direction.

Zoffany followed my gaze. 'She was in your class?'

I nodded. 'She's Jed's poster girl.'

'It's her warm up,' said Zoffany, as if this was the maddest thing she'd ever heard.

'You're kidding.'

'Non' she shrugged. 'She does another one after work, and sometimes one at lunchtime too.'

'Does she have a life?'

'She would like mine, but it's not for sale.' She squeezed my hand reassuringly. 'Do not worry Miss Megs. I have plenty of shit on her.'

'Never touching it unless thirsty'

At Hinshaw's, and at Con World, we used to give ad agencies the factory tour to get them immersed in the brand. Deciding that P&P would benefit from our version of the same, I'd asked Zoffany for help. As the creator of Shine's design aesthetic, she'd be the perfect brand ambassador, and, of course, it wouldn't hurt to have my new best friend watching out for me, just in case I walked into another stationery cupboard.

Setting up in a quiet corner of the café, I waited until The P&P Seven had worked their way through the large pile of vanilla bean and blueberry muffins, and double lemon and poppy seed duffins. I'd limited myself to a bowl of fruit. This might've been a mistake, nobody solved the world's problems on a slice of melon, but I was counting on nerves, and Zoffany, to see me through.

Plenty of nerves. No Zoffany.

Taking a deep breath, I assumed my position at the head of the table. 'Thank you for coming, and welcome to Shine.' I paused, clearing my throat ostentatiously, but they continued checking their emails. 'Back in Slough we'd do these tours in disposable hairnets, but at Shine, ever the last word in glamour, it's all about the disposable knickers.'

I paused, waiting for the laughs.

Po-faced Pigtails and the Bull Terrier raised their heads, but only to exchange a look.

'Before we start the tour I just want to say that I'm really sorry – sorry that we got off on the wrong foot. I was three years a slave at Con World, chained to a woman who ran away from ideas with all the commitment of a marathon runner. I left there because I wanted to work with people who embrace the new – people like you.'

The Bull Terrier whispered something to Pigtails. She started to giggle.

'Anyway,' I said, 'I'd like to put last week behind us and get on with making some award-winning posters; posters that will weigh down our shelves with Yellow Pencils. What do you say?'

'I say we need champagne,' said Zoffany, entering in a swirl of musky scent and souk couture: leather headband, embroidered silk kaftan and white patent leather boots that said 'meet me on the starlit terrace at midnight'. Clapping her hands and turning on her heels, towards the atrium, P&P formed an orderly crocodile, following like obedient six year olds. I tagged behind, inhaling her scent as if it was a tranquiliser, my palms still damp.

'Zis,' she said, dialling up the accent as she ran her hand over a coconut wood bench on the pebble walkway, 'I found on an abandoned Vietnamese houseboat. Zis,' she said, picking up the coiled rope beside it, passing it to the Bull Terrier that he might admire its contours, 'is from a fisherman's cottage on Isle de Ré.' The rope made its way down the line as we picked our way amongst the girls in yoga pants, artfully arranged on alpaca rugs and floor cushions. Reaching the shop she turned to face us, 'and zis' she said, caressing a thick circle of leather that doubled as the door handle, 'was handmade by a Cordobán saddle maker for, 'ow you say? … "dominatrice"?'

Everyone nodded as if that was exactly what they expected to hear. The Bull Terrier opened the door for her and set about helping the shop girls open champagne bottles, while Zoffany presided over proceedings, reciting what she described as 'Madame Bollinger's love letter to champagne'. She was right; 'Never touching it unless thirsty' was an excellent personal mantra.

I noticed Pigtails eyeing up a feathered headdress and gave Zoffany a meaningful nod. One of the shop girls unlocked the glass cabinet and Zoffany lowered the headdress into position, making sure it sat just so. Before she knew it Pigtails had received a full makeover.

'You should be on stage,' said Zoffany, leaning in close to apply copious amounts of smoky eye shadow and mascara, bringing out Pigtail's slitty eyes with all the skill of a professional make up artist.

'I can see you now,' I said, eager to follow in the footsteps of my charm guru, 'Night is falling, you're sitting at your piano, your feathers fluttering in the breeze, the Glastonbury crowd singing along.'

'And the right man is falling in love with you,' said Zoffany softly, 'enchanted by your voice, by your presence, by the beautiful woman that you are.'

Pigtails smiled contentedly as if this destiny was no more than an inch from the end of her nose. 'Will you be guest of honour, at the wedding?'

'Of course,' replied Zoffany, smoothing Pigtail's feathers thoughtfully, as I watched from a distance, a reflection in the mirror. It came so naturally to her, why not to me? If only dad had been a French banker, if only mum had owned a florist in a fashionable Parisian arrondissement. I would've edited a glossy magazine, been famous for my signature look: trophy jacket, skinny jeans and heels, for my ability to predict new trends. Or would I? Something told me I'd probably have ended up on a business park off the Périphérique, working le chocolat for a nightmare grande fromage called Patrice.

Following the tinkle of Zoffany's ankle bracelets, we took the stairs to the sixteenth floor. P&P took it in turns to peep through the windows of the Surya studio. Sharp intakes of breath all round. It always reminded me of that Weather Project installation at The Tate: the flaming ball of a setting sun, the vast dark orange light, the black silhouettes of the students – all of them, at this precise moment in time, standing on their heads. There was something of the army about them – row upon row of perfect symmetry, of straight-backed precision, reflected in floor to ceiling mirrors that amplified the effect, stretching to infinity and beyond. Would I ever be a continuation of that line?

Zoffany was only able to tear them away by telling them that the next studio, Dreamtime, was her favourite. We filed in, standing around her in wrapt attention as she explained that Aboriginals view health holistically – keeping body, land and spirit in balance. To symbolise this, she'd imported a tree from Wawu-Karrba – the oldest living rainforest in the world. It stood proudly in the centre of the room, its branches creating a canopy of pretty, circular leaves. 'I love it,' she said, stroking its grey speckled bark. 'The leader of the Kuku Yalanji tribe gave it to me as a parting gift. It is said to heal the spirit of anyone who stands beneath it.'

The Bull Terrier began circling it, rubbing his fingers on the bark and fondling the leaves – was he about to hug it, or Zoffany?

My office was a drive-by. It may have been small but I was excessively proud of my floor to ceiling windows, the latest Mac and wall-mounted flat screen TV, but they turned out to be no big deal to the most happening agency in town.

Zoffany's was a different story. 'Will you tell us about your paintings?' asked Alex, the Tamed Terrier, seeming to pop out of his black polo neck like a nascent Jay Jopling. The vast canvases took up three walls: purple poppies leapt out of the black, a pink lotus flower burst through rich turquoise, a red rose jumped out of watermelon orange.

She walked over to her desk and picked up a heavy perfume bottle, lazily spraying the air with a dry, warm, aromatic scent that reminded me of a campfire on a hot night. She walked into the cloud of vapour as it descended, inhaling deeply, closing her eyes. 'The Dalai Lama asked my friend to paint his private garden. They were a gift.'

She was about to say more, but a strong gust of wind blew out all the candles, sending music through the wind chimes, lifting the gauzy curtains towards the ceiling. She moved to close the windows but six guys rushed gallantly to her rescue; no insouciant lolling. We left the room – Zoffany leading, the agency trailing behind her, as reluctant to leave her nest as freshly hatched chicks.

Max was in his glass-panelled office, boxed in by serious looking men in black suits, as if he was in a minimum-security prison. I'd seen them before and thought they were lawyers, something to do with those copyright issues. I hoped he could still make the lunch. I waved tentatively; I hadn't seen him since the BOGOF meeting. He waved back, mouthing 'help me', which made me smile for the first time that day, a smile that lasted all the way to the business centre. Until, that is, I saw the long queue. I made a mental note to talk to Max about some extra staff. Waiting wasn't a game our members wanted to play.

Seeing the more junior P.R. girls, I asked if they could spare a few minutes to help out. Their faces suggested they considered the task below their pay-grade so, telling the tour party to go on ahead, I went in search of Ashley. Her office was organised chaos; a clothes rail of samples (more launch party 'options'?), endless boxes of scented candles, and several hundred personalised yoga mats, wrapped in gold cellophane, piled against the wall.

'No,' replied Ashley. 'Absolutely not.'

'But we're very busy and it would only be for–'

'I don't care; my girls are not your slaves.'

'I didn't say they were. We just need some–'

'P.R. is the hero department in this company, and we don't do other people's shit, especially yours.'

'I don't have any juniors and–'

'Well that tells you something doesn't it?' She looked round – at the giggling Caterpillar lining up behind her. Were they sharpening their stilettos?

'Ashley, I can't break off the tour to go man a desk–'

'A tour?' she said sharply. 'What kind of tour?'

'It's for the agency,' I said carefully. 'Just a small thing.'

'Gather round girls; news just in. "BOGOF" is now in charge of P.R.'

'It really isn't anything for you to worry about,' I said, trying to move past her, explaining that it was a brand immersion tour – designed to get P&P on track.

'This isn't a chocolate factory Megan,' she said, her girls now blocking the corridor. 'There's a certain finesse to our work–'

'I know,' I said, refusing to be put in a corner, 'that's why I asked Zoffany to lead it–'

'Zoffany? Zoffany! Zoffany couldn't lead her way out of frickin' paper bag.'

I begged to differ. 'Actually she's doing a brilliant job – she's got them eating out of her hand.'

'And I'll bet my last dollar it's all about her. Paused for a few anecdotes, has she?'

'Only one or two–'

'Recited Madame Bollinger's poem has she?'

Conscious that a crowd had gathered behind me, and that the queue for the business concierge service had embarked on a class action stare, I requested, very politely, that we take the discussion into my office.

'What is going on here?' asked Max, barrelling down the corridor, looking like a furious headmaster.

'She started it,' I said, without thinking.

Ashley drew herself up to her full five feet nothing. 'Megan has taken the agency on a tour of the building without P.R. representation. She seems to think she can do our job as well as her own ... which is to say not very–'

'Is that true Meg?'

'Yes,' I said, blushing, 'but Zoffany's been leading it, and doing a great job. I thought, because she's head of–'

'But it's not her job is it?'

'No.' I was looking at my feet.

'Where is the agency now?'

'In the café, with Zoffany.'

'Go and join them; we'll talk later.'

'Yes, sir,' I replied, backing away, longing for the stationery cupboard again.

Zoffany and the agency were sitting cross-legged on floor cushions, passing around the sunny spread I'd ordered in anticipation of a successful morning. I looked at the plates loaded with Lemon Cups and Rainbows in Ribbons – thin slivers of peppers finished with a bow of marigolds – and wanted to throw up.

I took a seat on the periphery and tried to focus. Zoffany was telling a story about late eighties Ibiza. 'Ku was the biggest club in the world back then – seven thousand people. Not many British, or French, but a few Italians, and of course so many Spanish families – one, two, three generations, all together. Fashionistas, popstars, musicians, Polanski, Gaultier ... all of them partying, all of them having fun – no formality. I was home. I spent years there – sleeping all day, clubbing all night ...'

She trailed off as she often did, her eyelids dropping, as if to shade her from scrutiny. The agency waited patiently. Perhaps they were also wishing they could climb inside that mind of hers, spend a few hours accessing memory banks crowded with 'le beau monde' and Balearic beats. It was working for me; hanging out with Freddie Mercury and Grace Jones, Valentino and Moschino, was a much better place than my own head. 'I was an innocent, fresh out of Cheltenham Ladies College. I didn't take any drugs – not even E. I was high on life – always on the dance floor, always looking up at the stars. And then they put a roof on. The next day I took a flight to New York, looking for a new club, a new home. I found it in the powder room.' She looked up and, catching our collectively raised eyebrow, she smiled. Then the smile widened, her whole face radiating like one of those starbursts in a 1950s laundry detergent ad.

There was Max – dressed in an immaculate suit, a few chest hairs curling over the top of his open shirt, barefoot. He was leaning against the doorframe, being handsome. Finally, when he knew he had all eyes on him, he began his slow walk towards us, taking in the scene; Zoffany perched on a leather cube, the agency on floor cushions in a semi-circle, like kids in front of their teacher. Me to one side.

There was a collective swoon as Max kissed her hand.

'Duchess,' he said quietly, 'are you entertaining the troops?'

She inclined her head, her face still aglow.

'She certainly is,' said Alex, now not only tamed but doing his best impression of Nate's Labrador, rolling over to have his tummy tickled.

'We love Shine,' said Pigtails, blushing at Max's peck on the cheek.

Was there a woman on this planet not in love with the man?

'You've been shopping,' said Max, stepping back to admire the headdress, which she was still wearing. 'It suits you.'

She blushed again. Personally, I thought she looked ridiculous but I was supposed to be suspending judgement.

The party fragmented; Max wanted a word with Zoffany. Oh crap. Losing my brand new ally was the last thing I needed. Was he giving her a hard time? I couldn't tell. I looked over at Alex.

He was on his own – it looked like Pigtails was finally doing her job, organising the younger guys. Seizing my chance to get personal, I plumped down on the cushion next to him. I asked him if he had any questions, starting off nice and neutral.

'We definitely need to go again with the work' he said, managing a half smile, 'but I maintain what I said about cliché – I'm not doing airbrushed Californian blondes.'

'No, you're going to make them real blondes, just like me' I said, fake-flicking my mouse-blonde hair. 'That'll really shift some product.'

At least he laughed. 'How is life amongst the beautiful people?' he asked. 'It can't be easy for someone like you – coming from Slough … and everything.'

I plucked the last petal off a marigold bow, feeling my hackles rise, but when I examined his face it seemed to be registering something akin to concern. Seeing Max looking in our direction I decided to give him the benefit of the doubt; the last thing I needed right now was another public bust-up. I took a deep breath and announced that I'd just launched Operation Slender and Sculpted and, with Zoffany's personal guidance, I would drop two dress sizes by Christmas.

'By Christmas?' He looked doubtful.

'I know I'm not exactly the poster girl for Shine, but I *will* lose the weight, and I *will* get that glow. Anyway' I said, reminding myself of the need to get personal, 'it's not just about the way I look. This place goes much deeper than that.'

He raised an eyebrow. 'Really? Pray tell.'

'Okay Alex,' I said, digging deep, channelling Nate. 'Let me give it to you straight. I got boxed in and stitched up in my last job – my boss kept me down so she could nick my ideas, and then she turned them to shit. However many I gave her, it didn't matter – it was always going to be *My Life in BOGOFs*. I can totally understand why you didn't take me seriously – I did stay too long and I don't have anything great to show for the last three years, but coming here, meeting Max, changed everything. I've had a pretty shaky start, but I know I can make it matter that I'm in the room.'

'I get how Max could make you feel that way' he said, awkwardly shifting on his cushion, crossing his legs the other way. 'But you're in a unique position with him; I don't think anyone else is after anything that deep. They want to look hot and' he said, stealing another glance at Zoffany, 'they do.'

I have to say I quite enjoyed pointing out that Zoffany was a total mess before she met Max and Jed.

'Ah, "the powder room"' he said, welcoming the opportunity to look again in her direction.

Choosing to feel encouraged, I continued. 'Look at those girls over there. They work in the City – they should be snorting coke in the toilets, but here they are, buzzing on a natural high. And what about those guys? Shouldn't they be slumped over their desks? But no; they're here, having fun. In my experience most corporate people are going through the same stuff – it's all politics and hard graft. I'm sure they're all looking for a way to … what's Max's phrase? … "Be their best self." I'm not saying they're all sorted, but I think they're on their way.'

He still looked unconvinced. 'But you've only been open a few weeks. It seems a bit mad to say they've all transformed themselves already.'

'It doesn't need to take years' I said, thinking of Becks' lengthy meditation sessions. 'There is such a thing as fast track – which is the road these people are used to taking. Anyway you don't need to take my word for it' I said, offering him a fresh marigold bow as a symbol of peace and reconciliation. 'Why don't you to talk to a few of them yourself?' I gave him what I hoped was my most winning smile, which I may have broadened in order to reassure Max, who was walking towards us.

'I don't suppose it could do any harm' said Alex, managing a bow of acceptance.

Max took up position opposite us, sinking onto the floor cushion, expertly marshalling Rainbows in Ribbons onto his chopsticks as he listened to the tail end of my talk. 'Perhaps you'll find they all want the same thing as me,' I concluded, struggling to keep my voice even, remembering that, in all probability, I was about to receive an almighty bollocking. 'Perhaps we all want to relaunch ourselves – change the packaging, and what's underneath.' Thankfully Alex didn't challenge me again. Instead he nodded thoughtfully and scribbled some notes. Then suddenly he was on his feet. Promising to come back to us in a couple of weeks, he joined his troops. They left clutching candles and class timetables, Pigtail's feathers fluttering in the breeze.

I turned back to Max, expecting to have rescued defeat from the jaws of victory.

'Here's to transformation,' was all he said, smiling gently.

'Bal a Versailles ... Shalimar'

A private corner of the club had been cleared – fenced off by an invisible rope of respect. Two velvet wing back chairs and a bottle of champagne were waiting. I could get used to this detox thing. We settled beneath an ironclad chandelier, beside some zigzagging shelves piled with arty books. Silent for a moment, we watched the rain pelting the gently sloping windows, the black beyond broken only by the yellow squares of empty offices. One girl was still at her computer, pulling a late one. I could just make out the grey burlap lining of her cubicle.

Zoffany spoke first, asking for an Operation Slender and Sculpted update.

'It's still a battle but I feel different; I've got more energy and,' I paused for dramatic effect, 'I've lost four pounds in ten days.'

'Salut,' she said, clinking my glass. Tonight her slender, sculpted frame was kitted out in a long tribal print dress. This was accessorised with a raffia bag, orange, pink and green headscarf and several layers of beads – the effect was of a Twenties heroine honoured by an African chief. I'd really dressed up; I didn't want to buy any new clothes until I lost some proper weight but I had managed to dig out a tailored black jacket and a big scarf that looked good, at least I thought so until I saw Zoffany. Once again, I found myself wishing I'd been born glamorous. I asked her where she'd grown up.

She was a child of the Left Bank, dressing up in her mother's Yves Saint Laurent, accessorizing with Dior. 'My mother lived on cigarettes and gin,' she said, spearing an olive. 'She saw affection the same way she saw food – something to be measured out in small doses. Too much would be harmful. But there were the exceptions.' She kicked off her shoes and curled into her chair. 'When she was ready she would smooth down her dress and kneel before me. She would dab a little perfume behind my ears – Bal a Versailles … Shalimar – then she would kiss me gently on both cheeks. She was promising that one day her beauty would be mine.'

'And you didn't believe her?'

'I'm still waiting for the butterfly to hatch,' she said, taking a swig of champagne.

If someone like Zoffany struggled to feel beautiful, there was hope for me. And I did have an advantage; there may have been no Halston, Gucci or Fiorucci in her wardrobe, but my mum had never rationed her love.

Getting ready for a night of ballroom was my favourite ritual. Like Zoffany, I watched mum choose her dress and do her make up, then I'd stand behind her, helping her – just as I'd seen her hairdresser do, pulling all the hair from one side of her head to the back, criss-crossing Bobby pins to keep it smooth, bringing the hair from the other side into a roll, pinning it so the edge of the roll was sharp, no metal to be seen – and then the 'misting', as she called it, with her Elnett hairspray.

It was the charity fundraisers I loved the most, especially when it was mum's turn to chair the Reading branch of the Royal Voluntary Service. Raising money to get old people involved in the local community was part altruism, and part a way to show off her American Smooth. Her favourite dress back then was a long red chiffon number sprinkled with gold beads. I used to try it on when she wasn't home, slipping on her gold sandals, dowsing myself in Mitsouko and trying not to poke myself in the eye with her mascara wand. Once dad caught me in front of the mirror applying the finishing touches, but instead of being cross he'd offered me his arm, walked me downstairs and taught me some steps.

'All that preparation took on a different meaning when daddy died,' Zoffany continued, refilling our glasses.

'What happened?' I asked.

'He was a racing driver. Killed on the track when I was eight. Mummy and I were watching ... Mummy's screams ... I can hear them now.'

She paused, collecting herself. I wanted to scoop her up and hug her, but she looked so fragile she might break.

'It turned out he had gambled away all the money; she had no one to rely on but herself. She had no qualifications so she did what she knew best, she looked after men – became la maîtresse professionnelle.'

I nodded, not really understanding. Was a 'professional mistress' a euphemism for a high-end prostitute?

'She was very good. She had a house in Chelsea, an apartment at the Marbella Club, and a suite at le Bristol, Paris – like the George V but more discreet.' She looked proud now – her face lighting up. 'Mummy was very resourceful – she sent me only to private schools and paid all the fees with cashed-in fur coats, art and jewellery.'

We contemplated the night skyline as I wondered what would've happened if dad had died, had a heart attack over a late tax return – would a pink-feathered boudoir have replaced mum's floristry? Would she have become Southcote's *Belle du Jour*? I shivered, feeling the need to move into different territory. Remembering what she'd said about arriving in New York, about the powder room, I asked her what happened.

'To begin with, it was a riot,' she said, drawing closer. Working as a waitress by day, she'd spend all her tip money in Patricia Field, turning up at the Limelight Disco 2000 in an all-in-one body suit and face paint. Whole nights were lost rolling with DJ Keoki, dancing to psychedelic House. She described the sumo wrestlers, the bondage girls, the go-go dancers, the 'no tourists' door policy in great detail, but the curtain came down when I asked her about the drugs. 'I had a ball,' she said, 'but the party went on a little too long.'

'How long?'

'A decade.'

Yes, that was a long party.

'New York turned into the Bad Apple for me, but when mummy got the diagnosis I came home and straightened myself up.' She talked some more. About the sadness of nursing her mother, and the joy of finding what she was good at. About her love for the Royal College of Art tutor who introduced her to the joy of ethnic luxe. About things taking off for her immediately – when she had the good fortune to work on a Regent's Park Nash Terrace house. About meeting Max four years ago, when she did a job out in Hong Kong.

'What could I do?' She took another sip of wine, shrugged again, looking beyond my shoulder – unseeing. 'We do not choose who we love.'

I took a deep breath, feeling more than a bit envious – I longed to be caught up in the nets of an iridescent love affair, especially one with Max. Unable to help myself, I asked her how it had begun.

She told me that it was inevitable – from day one. There he was, this over-achiever, this self-believer, a man who could turn his hand to anything. 'He was always focused on the task at hand, consumed by his latest passion, and for a while his grande passion was me.'

I nibbled an olive – needing so much more.

'But I knew what kind of a man he is – I am not a fool. He didn't even want to live together. I knew deep down there would be no happy ending and finally, after two years, I broke it.'

'But you still want him?'

The eyelids came down again, a silent answer. She reached for her drink and sank deeper into her chair, as if the cushions might protect her.

I gave her the usual sage advice that women always give one another – the 'you deserve better' speech that we don't listen to ourselves.

She listened politely, then changed the subject, wanting to know why I was single. How did she know? Did I have a sign on my forehead? I had to trawl back to Richard to find a worthy story. Normally, the bit about discovering him in bed with another woman drew gasps of horror, but she just shrugged, giving me a look that said 'c'est la vie.'

'So,' I continued, hoping the next bit of drama would have more impact, 'I threw the CD at him. The corner cut his forehead and there was *a lot* of blood.'

'How satisfying,' she said, downing her glass, still unshaken. Had a professional mistress for a mother made her shockproof, or was it all those years of clubbing? 'Did you find out who she was?'

I felt she was missing the point. 'Just some young slapper who worked in his local' I replied. 'All I could think about was why he'd kept his socks on.'

'Did he always wear them in bed?'

'No.'

'Did you ask him why?'

'Why he kept his socks on?'

'Why he did what he did.'

'What he'd done seemed more important than why he'd done it.'

'And that was the end of it?'

I nodded even though it wasn't true; he'd hung around for a while, sending me texts and drunk-dialling – telling me all about the error of his ways – as if I didn't know, but talking about him made me feel like a gravedigger and I was desperate to get back to Zoffany's love life. As Becks liked to joke, celebrity gossip was my *Mastermind* subject, but although I thought I knew about Max's love life – the models and models-turned-actresses – I'd never read anything about them as a couple.

They'd met when she was doing up a mutual friend's house. The friend was seriously rich, a VC they nicknamed King Kong. 'Max cultivated him the same way he cultivated me and it worked, on both counts. When the time came the VC invested in Shine and before long I was sleeping with Max, introducing him to all my contacts.'

'He used you?'

'Looking back on it, yes, but I was a willing victim. I saw his ambition; I wanted to be part of it. I wanted to help him prove something to that father of his.'

'You met him?'

'We had dinner with his parents when they came out to Hong Kong.' She caught the look on my face. 'Don't get excited – it didn't mean anything. It was just Max's way of deflecting attention away from himself.'

'What was his mother like?'

'As exacting as the father.' Then she told me that he was only seven when his father, dedicated to the family's further advancement, began posting financial news on the kitchen notice board, assigning each of the brothers a point of view to argue over dinner. Every morning Max, the youngest child, would be the first to the board, and every night he'd stand on a chair, making his case.

'Poor Max,' I said. The conversation in my house might've revolved around the price squeeze on accountancy fees and the best time to plant peonies but, when I thought about the alternative, I was glad I'd landed the peonies.

'He was never going to be rich enough,' said Zoffany, 'or glamorous enough.'

'Even with you on his arm?'

'I wasted a lot of time.'

I thought back to my burlap-lined cubicle and nodded.

'So,' I said, gathering myself, 'no one else on the scene?'

'I'm fussy.'

It was very clear that Zoffany would always want the best of everything: clothes, art, men. It seemed to me, without getting too Becks about it, that they were all ways of proving to herself that she was a butterfly, not a caterpillar. Perhaps Max had that same need. Perhaps that was why they'd been drawn to each other, because they both loved the bigger stage, playing out their relationship around the world. They'd worked together in L.A. on the first Shine centre, they'd been together in Vietnam when she'd discovered that coconut wood bench, she'd bought him the bull fight painting at an auction in Seville. Some silver birch chairs, less exotically, were the result of a trip to Scotland. They'd split up there – the truth laid bare by the solid trunks of Abernethy Forest.

'But what about children?' I asked, 'Isn't it worth compromising a little?'

She laughed bitterly. 'I'm forty three – if I'm feeling hot, it's probably a flush.' For once I hadn't done my sums – if she'd been a teenager in Ibiza in the eighties then yes, she'd be into her forties by now, but she looked so much younger.

'Botox,' she said.

'Really?'

'Twice a year. I went with the P.R. girls last time. We got a group discount.'

I'd guessed Ashley had a Botox season ticket but I hadn't realised the others were in on it. I'd thought that they looked like mannequins because of their uniform ponytails and perfect-fit dresses. I examined Zoffany with renewed interest, wondering if her firm jaw line was natural, or the result of some fancy needlework.

'You should come with us,' she said. 'We only go to the top guy.'

'But I'm only twenty nine.'

'That's old in Botox years,' she assured me. 'You should start in your early twenties, before the lines get too deep.'

'Do you really think I need it?'

She studied my face quizzically, coming too close, blanketing me with alcohol fumes.

'A bit, around your eyes.' She was so matter of fact.

'But they're laughter lines. I quite like—'

'And a bit of Restalyne. You don't want to look like a marionette.'

Detecting the first stirrings of a huff, she backtracked. 'I'm sorry – I forget you're our newbie' she said, emptying the remains of the bottle into our glasses. 'Focus on the exercise and the diet. Forget the Botox, for now.'

'Thanks' I said, softening – wondering if maybe she was right. She was the expert after all. 'Anyway, I can't see Ashley sharing her beauty secrets with me.'

'Oh, don't you worry about that – she'll behave.'

I looked at her expectantly. This seemed a good moment to have her dish the dirt.

'Let's just say, she knows I could get her arrested.'

'Seriously? "Arrested"? What did she do?'

'She hacked my voicemail.'

'You're kidding?'

'This was a while back – when I was still with Max. She was obsessed with him – wanted to know what was going on between us.'

'She must've been pretty desperate,' I said, thrilled that Little Miss Bambi was a psycho. 'How did you find out?'

'Because the stupid bitch zapped some of my saved messages.'

'And does Max know what she did?'

'No and I plan to keep it that way.'

'But you could have her sent to prison,' I said, picturing the scene; Ashley receiving the guilty verdict – cuffs, no make up, an orange jumpsuit. That would make an interesting selfie.

'Believe me,' she said, running her hand through her hair like a villainous Bond girl, 'she's worth more to me this way.'

'More valuable alive,' I mused, my eyes narrowing, relishing the drama.

She speared the last of the olives, suddenly pushing the conversation into new territory. 'Max said you wanted to talk to me about the shop?'

Feeling like a kid forcibly parted from her favourite toy, I explained that I'd gone down there looking for something that would make me feel a little more at home in class.

'I'm not saying we have to stock size eighteen,' I explained, 'but I am a fourteen and there was literally *nothing* – nothing for wearing in class or for going out – except a feathered headdress.'

'But Operation Slender and Sculpted is going so well – you'll be there soon.'

I contemplated the pizza heading towards the next table; olives weren't my idea of dinner, even if they were 'stuffed' with anchovies. 'Yes, but I'm sure there are a few members who aren't a size double zero – don't you want to help them buy?'

Zoffany proved resistant. 'We're not Marks and Spencer; we don't stock everything in every size – it would be the wrong message.'

'But what about the launch party?' I said, trying not to sound whiny. 'I really wanted to wear something Shine.'

'Oh ma belle poupée,' she said, pretending to wave a wand over me, '"you shall go to the ball."'

Then she told me she'd dress me herself, and do my make up.

'Really?' I said, grinning from ear to ear. 'You'd do that for me?' What did she have in mind? Colour? Style? Designer? Would I have 'options'?

She laughed, telling me 'the only option is the right option.' She said she would make some calls, that 'all would be revealed.'

'But you must continue to work hard,' she said, wagging her finger at me, suddenly looking as strict as Becks.

I was about to remonstrate, to tell her I was working harder than ever before, when I realised she meant I needed to lose more weight. That was fine, I was already committed.

'And make sure you see Doctor Lily.'

'It's just a question of time Zoffany–'

'And see Clive.'

I told her I'd been planning a trip to Shine's own blow dry bar.

'Non,' she said, putting down her wine glass, 'Clive.'

Buoyed up by the excitement of a dress bearing a serious stamp of approval, a trip to the London home of Californian hair, and by a lot of champagne on an empty stomach, I decided to pitch my fair trade idea. I told her that all those obi belts, the tribal jewellery and feather headdresses were a natural fit. 'The genius,' I said, 'is fair trade sits really well with the whole transformation thing. Picture the poster; "Shine: transforming lives, near and far".' I explained, perhaps in a little too much detail, how the system had worked at Hinshaw's. How it wasn't just about helping farmers get a fair price for their produce, but also about teaching them how to increase their productivity.

She asked a few questions but the effort of thinking about money seemed to exhaust her, as if her battery had died. Then I mentioned the Hinshaw's twinning scheme. 'My twin was Balinese,' I said, finding a photo of Komang Suardana in his favourite tropical print shirt, and another of I Wayan and I Made, back when they were ten and eleven. They were squeezing the ripe pods of a cocoa tree, beaming and proud.

'They're beautiful,' she said, looking wistfully at the image as I described my pinboard covered in their postcards, their five mile walk to school, and how they never took off those Manchester United baseball caps – the ones I'd sent my first year at Hinshaw's.

'And then Con World cancelled everything,' I said, remembering the awful Sykpe call, with the whole family gathered around I Wayan's computer.

'Where are they now?' she asked, handing my phone back.

I produced more photos, of Komang Suardana in a new tropical print shirt on the veranda of his small guesthouse. Of I Wayan standing tall on the steps of his college, and of I Made with his girlfriend. She was giggling, trying to hide her face behind a textbook, a giant ice cream sundae with two spoons in front of them.

'So what do you think?' I asked, finally grinding to a halt. 'Will you come and see Max with me? Make it happen for all the I Wayans and I Mades?' I raised my hands in prayer, knowing that I'd stand a much better chance of success with her by my side. Maybe it was a genuine desire to improve the farmers' lot, and maybe it was more the prospect of morphing into Angelina Jolie but, whatever it was, it worked.

'Bien sûre' she said, with a happy shrug.

I managed to pass through Liverpool Street station without caving into my craving for a Cornish pasty but the consequence of a night on champagne and olives was a king-size hangover. I met Becks in Reading for a restorative coffee the following morning, before I settled into a weekend of work.

She talked with measured enthusiasm about the Edward Snowden slash Jamie Oliver book idea – saying she was scoping out a structure and there didn't seem to be any shortage of material, but my attempts to get under the surface were rebuffed with a 'too soon to tell'. I knew better than to push her – she'd always liked to keep things pretty close to her chest. She hadn't told me she was pregnant until she was five months gone – letting me go on and on about my plans to score an office within sight of the Gherkin.

That morning she was far more interested in hearing about 'Shiny World'. Needless to say the phone hacking horrified her – it was 'an affront to civil liberties' for which 'Ashley should be arrested', and so on, but she was off that subject as soon as I mentioned the launch party. She insisted that I run through the guest list twice – unable to believe that I would be spending a night living in the party pages of *Grazia*.

'I wanted you to come too,' I told her, dreading this part of the conversation.

'But?'

I'd gone over and over it but no matter how I framed it, it still boiled down to asking Max if I could invite my best friend to a party. I was keen to present myself as a woman of the world, not a ten year old. '"But"' I said, 'I need to be a hundred percent focused on the task at hand. This is their biggest night of the year, and the biggest night of my life. I can't screw anything up.'

'I understand,' she said, slowly stirring the remains of her cappuccino. She paused a moment, then looked up brightly. 'What are you going to wear? How about your mum's sparkly red dancing dress? You always looked so beautiful in that.'

'The thing is Becks,' I said, as kindly as I could, 'I'm going to have to step it up a gear – Zoffany is going to style me, and send me to Clive.'

'Who is Clive?'

'Her hairstylist, in Mayfair.'

'How much is that going to cost?' she asked, pushing back from the table.

I must've looked completely blank; I'd been so carried away with the prospect of California hair, I hadn't considered the price.

'And what about the dress? You may be pretty, and a "Brand Experience Director", but you aren't a celeb – no designer is giving it to you for free.'

I played it down, not wanting to look a fool, telling her Zoffany was pulling in some freebies, but inside I was in a total panic. Just what had I let myself in for? A designer dress would cost thousands, maybe tens of thousands, and Zoffany was hardly one to be tempered by reality.

Attempting to park the issue of my imminent economic demise, toying with texting Zoffany from the loo – 'ABORT MISSION!' – I pulled out the box of scented candles I'd snaffled. This distracted her for a while; it was a very big box. Then I mentioned that Zoffany thought I needed Botox.

She was not amused. There followed a diatribe on the importance of self-acceptance, and a recommendation that I stand in front of a mirror reciting 'I love myself' three times a day.

'She apologised afterwards,' I said. 'I'm not sure she was entirely serious and she'd had a lot to drink. We both had.'

'Hmmm.'

'She thinks that if we change the externals – our face, our clothes, our body shape, then we change the internals too – we change our experience of ourselves.'

'Bollocks,' she said. 'This is everything that worries me about your place. Change happens from the inside. End of.'

I laughed. 'You know Becks, I'm not so sure. I'm drawing the line at Botox, at least for now, but you and I have both bought shoes because they made us feel better. What's wrong with that?'

'Nothing,' said Becks, 'if you live on Planet Zoffany and can afford a lot of shoes.'

'Ze tree berk is from Tibet'

I felt like I was at the centre of a Catherine Wheel – one which might spin off the wall and into Ashley. I ran around London for her – picking up from the printers, collecting for the goody bags – telling myself it was worth some atonement if it got us back on track. Yes, I could comfort myself with Zoffany's nuclear-grade revelation, but that was her weapon not mine, and meanwhile I had to work with the girl. There were no two ways about it; I'd been the one at fault over the agency tour and I'd been lucky there hadn't been any further comeback. Ever the enlightened employer, Max had called us both in and told us, in no uncertain terms, that we were both good at our jobs, and that we needed to make it work. I'd felt about five years old but it could've been so much worse. Now I was determined; failure was most definitely not an option.

Zoffany also had me on last minute missions. Her ever-changing set designs had ranged from 'a magical odyssey through dreamscapes with explosions of colour shine, feathers, ribbons and sequins' to an Arabian night of sand dunes, belly dancers and torch-lit Bedouin tents. I don't think I was the only one glad when she pronounced that Shine City would 'come as itself', resplendent in our signature white and gold. Once she'd decided on this (several days late), I got to work. My contributions were a fancy dress booth, complete with golden feather boas and white camisoles, and a scheme called 'Tweet your Feet', in which guest toenails would be anointed with miniature golden lotus flowers, our pedicam capturing the moment for the Twitterverse. The fancy dress booth was 'too boho', the pedicam 'too last year' for Ashley. I maintained an air of studied neutrality while Zoffany told her to 'suck it up'.

My new best friend had found me a Grecian inspired white and gold dress with plenty of forgiving folds and drapes. It was also mid-calf-length, for which I was grateful – my nickname at school had been 'Sausage Legs' (until Becks got wind of it and force-fed the perpetrator a raw one). Zoffany loved it so much she'd ordered a few more for the shop – in sizes twelve and fourteen – a small victory. The up and coming fashion designer, delighted to get his first break, had given her mine for free. Financial crisis averted.

The night of the party, we got dressed together in her office. I managed by hiding behind a jade green screen that she'd picked up in a Macau brothel. By the time I emerged, rigid in Spanx, wishing I'd started the fruit-only fast more than forty-eight hours ago, she was transformed into a South American tribeswoman – dressed for a black tie Spirit Weaver Gathering. The white-feathered wisp of a dress showcased that killer bod, and she'd accessorised with heavily beaded bangles, a primitive looking necklace, and a pair of feather earrings that I'd last seen in the shop. I felt a little under-dressed, until she did my makeup – giving me those smoky eyes, extending the black eyeliner into an upwards sweep that gave me a Christine Keeler look. I stared into the mirror, unable to quite believe what I was seeing; ancient Greece meets sixties London. Who knew it could work?

Zoffany smiled at me, squeezing my hand. 'Showtime?'

'"Showtime",' I replied, checking my reflection for the last time, noting that my curls were already ominously damp – about five minutes from frizzing. In the end, Clive had been out of the country and we'd both had to make do with the Shine blow dry bar. I was fine with that – I loved my Grecian ringlets, but Zoffany had fussed over them, telling the girl she'd used too much oil. She made her wash it and style it again while Ashley glared at me in the mirror – looking as if she might turn carnivorous.

Officially, Ashley had stationed me upstairs in reception, 'joking' that I should be sure not to hide the box of pink ribbons by standing in front of them. Unofficially, Zoffany had stationed me outside. I stood to the side, making sure I was out of Ashley's eye line, shivering with anticipation as I caught sight of the fleet of Toyota Prius causing a tailback all the way up Bishopsgate. The crowd behind the ropes jostled for position, craning their necks, holding their mobiles high – waiting to grab a celebrity selfie, whilst I soaked it all up on the other side of the red rope, pretending the crowd was there for me.

The first of the celebrities emerged from their cars, like rare orchids from a greenhouse. They blinked in the flash of cameras, trailing gowns, twisting and turning as both paparazzi and crowd shouted their names. I was no use to anyone; all that stardust had me rooted to the spot. The Catwalk Caterpillar, however, was moving with precision, clipboards in hand, microphone headsets on, every gesture as sharp as their stilettos, every word as slick as their ponytails. Of course, Ashley's pale gold dress was a little shorter, her ponytail a little higher, her microphone a lot bigger.

They marshalled the glittering classes toward the lifts. The bell-girls, uniformly tanned, wore special editions of the tiny white shorts – embroidered with a golden lotus flower on the left cheek. The whole thing was as closely choreographed as a ballet, and just as beautiful. I watched as the steel plates zip-locked shut, and the famous names ascended, pointing in admiration at the life-size, gold-tusked elephant – also made entirely of gold lotus flowers – that had taken up temporary residence amongst the Tibetan tree bark below.

There were princess gowns dipped in diamonds, ruched bodices worthy of Helen of Troy, retro eighties-style froth and flounce on some of the younger girls, and tailored columns in ice-white, there was even a 'gold-digger dress' as my mum would call it – sparkling and slashed – down to the navel and up to the top of the thigh, held together in the middle by a large diamond. There was one girl in particular – the supermodel Galina. I felt like David Attenborough all over again; here I was, observing a different species. She might have had two arms, two legs, one head – but that was where any resemblance to me ended. While other dresses had zips and buttons, seams and corsets, to hold their wearers in position, hers was no more than a piece of fabric draped from an embellished collar. The soft golden silk contoured the S of her back, accentuating her light tan, ending mid-thigh on the slenderest of legs, legs that seemed to be weightless – so long and limber that I wondered how the pages of a magazine contained her – was she always a gatefold?

I was so absorbed I completely forgot to keep an eye on Ashley. Creeping up behind me, practically spitting in my ear, she hissed for me to – wait for it – 'move that fat ass!' I took a deep breath, smiled sweetly and moved my 'fat ass' back to reception, fortuitously sharing the private service lift with a trolley of champagne.

By seven o'clock, right on schedule, five hundred guests had been given their first glass, and everyone was playing out their best version of themselves; performances which were captured on the bank of screens behind us, along with live tweets from the social media team, #ShineBigNight. I circled the room, trying to put Ashley out of mind, mentally handing out the awards for 'Best Actress in a Leading Smile' and 'Best Animation in a Crowded Room'. Even the waiters were winners, circling with canapés, returning to the kitchen with golden platters displayed aloft, like Wimbledon finalists.

It was time for Max's speech. He'd been surprisingly nervous that afternoon, writing and re-writing it, calling me in and sending me away, but here he was, melting into it like butter in a hot pan. I watched Ashley in action, adjusting his miniature lotus flower buttonhole, expertly prising him away from a coterie of women, all of them winners in their individual categories – Make Up, Costume Design, Visual Effects. He ignored the podium completely, preferring to leap onto the welcome desk and talk from there, walking up and down the length of it, his own catwalk.

'Honourable ladies, and fellow gentlemen – I want to get personal.'

This was met with whoops from the women.

He smiled, soaking it up. I looked on enviously; I could rehearse for months but I would never attain his ease. 'It's no secret that my journey – from City desk to yoga mat – was a long one, and that I continue to enjoy certain forms of self-medication. Nothing wrong with that – yoga, after all, is a question of balance, but I know one thing – that Shine will, wherever you've come from, and wherever you're heading, transform you.' He raised his glass and took a sip, pausing as everyone followed suit. 'We all want to get fit right?'

Cheers.

'We all want to look hot right?'

More cheers.

'But at Shine we go deeper, much deeper. On every Shine mat, in every Shine centre, in every Shine city, every hour of the Shine day, every day of the Shine week, every month of the Shine year, we transform ourselves. It's this transformation, this desire to step out of the way of our best self, that is the real measure of our success. Who here wants a slice of that?'

Everyone's hand shot up – a room full of celebrity swots. I scanned the crowd for Alex, the Tamed Terrier. The returning nod told me that the campaign idea was signed and sealed. I looked forward to its delivery.

'Now, where's my lady in gold?'

Galina took one step and landed at Max's side.

'All of you will know Galina from the pages of *Vogue*, but I've known her since the beginning, since she walked into our first centre, aged sixteen, and asked for a job. Instead I gave her a free lifetime membership, and an introduction to IMG. How many covers now Galina?'

'Fourteen,' she giggled, 'this year.'

I hadn't been sure about her initially; it'd seemed to me that Galina's transformation had little to do with Shine. Despite her impoverished beginnings, there was no way the world would've ignored a six foot glamazon with cheekbones chopped from the Urals, but watching her up there, I had to agree with Max: she was the right decision.

The next girl was all my idea. Annie was a New York designer whose Yo-Chi practice had inspired her flowing evening gowns – now worn by the younger royals.

'Ladies and gentlemen, please welcome Laxmi.'

Laxmi jumped onto Max's catwalk, mesmerising the crowd with some full on Bollywood moves – rolling her pelvis and shoulders, flicking her hair and hips, vamping it up for her hero – a role Max had apparently just taken up.

I sidled over to Ashley; she appeared almost as transfixed as him.

I whispered fiercely in her ear, conscious that I might be spitting. 'What happened to my dress designer?'

'Oh,' she said, 'didn't anyone tell you?'

'No, Ashley, they didn't. Perhaps because telling me was *your* job.'

'Like you were supposed to tell me about the agency immersion you mean?'

'That was a genuine mistake.'

'And so was this Meg. No agenda, honest.' She opened her eyes wide – the picture of innocence, batting those stupidly long eyelashes. 'I totally thought Max would've mentioned it – being as how you're so close and all.'

'How long has she been a member? How has Shine transformed her life?'

'Over-thinking as usual Meg. Laxmi is hot and Annie is, well, not.'

'What are you talking about? She's a perfectly attractive woman.'

'She might be to you, but to us she's a horseface.'

'"A horseface?" She's practically royalty.'

'I rest my case. Anyway Max wants to wet everyone's appetite for Jed's Bollywood show.'

Wet his own appetite more like, the guy was practically drooling.

I was tempted to say more but she'd turned away, talking intently into her headset, probably to herself.

I scanned the crowd for Zoffany, desperate to have a good bitch, but she was on the move, in Max's direction. Please tell me she wasn't going to attempt a jump; she'd never make it. I'd promised myself I'd keep an eye on her, that I'd watch her back just as she'd watched mine, knowing Ashley would've secretly told Whitney not to bother keeping her sober, hoping it would sabotage her performance. Thankfully, Max came to the rescue, jumping down, taking her hand and leading her firmly towards the podium.

She stayed the right side of sobriety for her 'son et lumiere' show in which shimmering white and gold spotlights, showcasing the lotus pond, the bamboo garden, the Himalayan pebbles, were synchronised with her design narrative. She soaked up the applause like a flower soaking up rain; that pretty voice of hers huskier, more breathy, more French for the occasion. 'Ze tree berk is from Tibet – I am 'oping zat ze Dalai Lama will curme and bless it.' Given Max's views on Buddha, I didn't think there was much chance of that.

I stuck by her side for the book signing. I opened her books to the title page and passed them to her one by one, but I was also mistaking her glass for mine, knocking it back so she wouldn't – such was my dedication. Making her wellbeing my responsibility enabled me to drop anchor for a while, to ride out the stormy waters of Hurricane Ashley. I began to recover, smiling to myself as I watched Alex and Pigtails walk away from Zoffany's table clutching a copy each, discussing 'sculptural organics' and 'interior couture'. Would P&P get a makeover? I thought it time they chucked out their chintz.

Feeling I'd got the gist of the Bollywood show, I went to help tidy up the shop. There was practically nothing left; every obi belt had gone, every tribal necklace, all the Indian jewellery. By the time I'd rehung the last of the dresses, the twelves and fourteens, Ashley was herding everyone back to the champagne bar.

Max was thanking 'the ever-gorgeous Zoffany for her design inspiration and of course, the peerless Ashley and her indefatigable team.'

I stole a glance at Ashley. I thought 'peerless' was pretty good, but clearly she'd been hoping for more. Ha. I was just about to head in Zoffany's direction when Max said my name.

'And, of course, our very own Meg. You've been here six short weeks and already you've made yourself indispensable. On behalf of the whole team, thank you.'

He jumped down off his catwalk and headed my way, bearing down on me with the biggest bouquet of flowers I had ever seen. 'You look beautiful,' he said, kissing me gently on the cheek, looking at me as if he really meant it. 'Keep up the good work.' I must admit I hammed it up a bit, receiving both flowers and compliment as if I'd just won Best Actress in a Leading Role.

Ashley waited until the social circles had reformed and then she was stalking across the floor towards me, trailing her bouquet behind her.

'I hope you're happy,' she said, trying to see over the top of my flowers.

I clutched them a little tighter, stroked a few petals. And breathe.

'We've been working on this party for the best part of a year, and you come waltzing in here with all your "Yes Max", "No Max", "three bags frickin' full Max–"'

'I'm not trying to take anything away from you Ashley. I'm just doing my job.'

'And your job includes standing out front and scaring off Hollywood's finest? I bet they thought they'd taken a wrong turn and ended up on the fat farm–'

'I didn't get in anyone's way–'

'With an ass like that how could you not?'

I bridled. 'Don't talk to me like that' I said stiffly, wondering why I was channelling Pat of all people.

'Listen up, fat girl' she said, jabbing her scrawny finger at me. 'This is my event – mine – and I am not having it messed up by some little, or not so little, chick from Slough.'

And suddenly blood was rushing to my head, my veins pulsing. I knew what it was to be the Bull Terrier. 'Listen, you flat-chested bitch. I'm not messing anything up; I've made a massive contribution to this event and you know it. I'm sorry if I've got in the way of your scheming little plans, but I can't help the fact that he likes me–'

'You might be able to pull the wool over his eyes with your numbers and your tell-it-like-it-is talk, but I've got *your* number missy. I know who you are and I know what you want, and one thing's for sure – he'd lay his goddamn cleaner before he'd lay you.'

'Really? Well, if you're such a big deal why hasn't he made a move on you? How long have you known each other? Three years?'

She lent in towards me, so close I could feel her breath on my skin. 'This is not your world Meg. I'll have you out of here by Christmas. For sure.'

'Not if I get you out first,' I replied, eye to eye.

'Bring it on girlfriend.' She turned on her Louboutin heels, striding into the crowd, shedding petals in her wake.

I wanted to yank her back and pummel her to the ground, and perhaps I would've done if I hadn't seen Max out of the corner of my eye. He'd commandeered a corner of the bar, and Laxmi. I watched them as if in slow motion; his hand on the small of her back, his lips at her ear, his cheek brushing hers. I could feel the heat from the other end of the room. What must it feel like to be that girl?

By the time I prised my eyes from the scene, Zoffany was in a state of lock-down. She was at the other end of the bar, an empty glass before her. I swooped down, picked her up and steered her to the safety of the ladies.

We sat in front of the mirror, beside a box of tissues.

'It's just when I see him with other women,' she sobbed, 'it brings it all back.'

I squeezed her shoulder, wishing I had a blanket I could wrap her in. I'd never been very good at dispensing advice – always feeling self-conscious, thinking I'd say something wrong, but I had to try. I gave her one of mum's favourite lines. 'Maybe you should talk to him? Tell him how you feel?'

At least this question provoked a spluttering laugh. 'Max doesn't do feelings.'

Finding myself wondering if Max might get in touch with

that side of things with the right woman, I busied myself with the practical, wetting a cloth to sooth her swollen eyes and clean her mascara-stained cheeks.

When I was done, she peered into the mirror and, with the air of a swan-song ballerina, pronounced herself 'old'. This provoked another round of sobs. I tried to console her, telling her she was gorgeous, but it was like filling up a bottomless well – no matter how much reassurance I poured on her, she needed more, and to be honest, in that light, with those tears, she did look her age. I wrung out the cloth, focusing on wiping her cheeks, helping her re-apply her make up in silence. What could I say? Max wasn't going to change. She didn't want to change.

A gaggle of models burst through the door, lighting up the room with their evening bags and glittering eye shadow. They didn't stick around, instead disappearing en masse into two cubicles, leaving a trail of scent and cigarettes. We could hear them giggling and sniffing. Zoffany stared at the mirror, looking as if she was seeing her own ghost.

'At least you didn't join them,' I said, nudging her, playfully.

She picked up her evening bag. 'I need to go home.'

Waving her taxi off, I lingered outside for a few minutes, putting off the moment of return – not sure who I'd talk to, or where I'd settle. I leaned against a steel girder, relishing the night air, and the smell of cigarette smoke. Turning, I saw a small circular glow, illuminating some unmistakable feathers. Pigtails stepped forward out of the doorway and offered me a cigarette – a peace offering? We stood there in silence, smoking like a couple of Indians, cupping our ciggies with both hands, inhaling to the pits of our lungs, warming ourselves against the night air. I hadn't had one since university, and it felt good.

By the time I'd moved back indoors, Max had moved away from the bar. He was now at the centre of a tight circle, tucked away in the far corner. I could see Laxmi on one side, Galina on the other, Ashley next to Galina. The rest had their backs to me. It was one of those old Hollywood scenes, an unguarded moment at a post-Oscars *Vanity Fair* party, until Ashley got up and started on the selfies, shooting them all from above, and from the right, even when it was awkward. She must've decided it was her best side.

Just as I was working out how I was going to reach in and pull her out (probably by the hair), Jed jumped up, bursting onto the dance floor like a bullet, arm in arm with Ashley and Galina. He saw me and mouthed for me to join them but I didn't want to do anything with our Head of P.R. but slap her.

I plopped onto a bar stool and ordered two neat vodkas, knocking them back in quick succession as I watched Ashley murder Jed's American Smooth. Gratifyingly, she was a terrible dancer, as sexy as a wooden spoon. Stirring my third vodka, I found myself wishing Becks was there. Zoffany would have given me an invite, no problem but, to my shame, I hadn't asked her. I'd thought she might cause a scene. She might've told Zoffany what she thought of her 'Outside In' theory, threatened Ashley with the cops, or informed Max that yoga could not be copyrighted. Now I wished she was there precisely because she would have caused a scene – she'd have slapped Ashley so hard her head would've spun.

One thing was certain; if she'd been there I wouldn't have been sitting alone at the bar. We'd have flushed Ashley down the loo and come back to rock the dance floor, shaking and shimmying our way through my carefully choreographed routine – the one we'd honed over the years, the one that forgave Becks' jerky arms, foolish legs and other eccentric moves – one part *Don't Blame it on the Boogie*, one part Uma Thurman in Jack Rabbit Slim's twist contest, one part a spirited young Madonna, jigabooing to *Holiday*, about to hit it big.

I'd just decided to call it a night when there was a tap on my shoulder. Jed was by my side and there was no sign of the bitch from hell. 'Shall we?' he asked, bowing deeply. He took my hand and led me onto the floor and suddenly there we were, just the two of us, dancing to *More Than a Woman;* Jed in a white suit, trading his rubbery Jagger for a silky Travolta, and me in my one-shouldered Grecian number, twirling beneath the glitter ball, lighting up the floor with our *Night Fever* feet. Any concerns I might've had that he would take this opportunity to throw me into a u-bend wheel and jump on my hipbones were short-lived. He held me as if I was his leading lady, dancing in the old fashioned-way, cheek-to-cheek, toe-to-toe, and I focused only on him, just as my dad had taught me to do in our sitting room, everything else a blur. I just hoped that somewhere in the blur was Ashley; that she was watching a real American Smooth, perfectly executed by a fat bird from Slough.

'Practice and all is coming'

I decided I should pay Nate a visit. I wanted to reassure him that I wasn't one of those silly girls who fell for her yoga teacher. If I wanted a fling, and I was increasingly of the mind that this would be a very good idea, to mark the official start of my new life, I would take my pleasure elsewhere.

I'd noticed quite a few Ekatman blow-ins getting the Shine tour – a new invention scripted by Ashley and delivered by a word-perfect Whitney. A few of them, the polo-necked poets and visibility-jacketed cyclists, left shaking their heads. But others stuck around. I recognised four of his people from the class I went to years ago. They'd seemed much more interested in Nate than his yoga, giggling to themselves at the back of the class, egging each other on to go and speak to him afterwards. They'd initially been shocked by the prices, but then they'd found out about the loyalty card and the BOGOFs, sorry the 'lifestyle rewards programme', and talked themselves into signing up on the spot.

I was clear – my first loyalty was to Shine but I needed to do what I could to nip his problem in the bud. Why not kill two birds with one stone? Reassure him that I wasn't a psycho-bunny, and give him some ways of keeping his people happy before more mats rolled in our direction. I would position myself as a straight-talking businesswoman – a marketing expert with some useful skills – skills he should be using. I would be well informed, utterly charming, and totally disinterested in him as a sexual being.

I found him up a ladder, repairing Ekatman's wooden shutters. Bernard sat patiently, at the bottom rung.

'That looks like hard work,' I shouted, shivering in the cold October air, trying not to stare at his rather nice bum. 'Want a break?'

He was keen to make me another one of his whipped cream hot chocolates, give me a slice of his fresh-baked cake. I was sorely tempted; it was lunchtime and my tummy was already rumbling, but Operation Slender and Sculpted was still on track – my resolve renewed by Max's 'beautiful' compliment, which I'd replayed more than once.

'Just a few more pounds,' I said, patting my tummy as we reached the attic, wishing the place didn't smell so good. What was it this time? Toffee? Pecans?

He considered me carefully, looking unconvinced. 'We don't all have to be stick insects.'

'Honestly Nate, I'm doing it for me. I want to feel fitter … better in myself.'

Reluctantly, he put the lid back on the tin. 'Well, if you're sure.'

Bernard took up position in front of the fire, lowered his chin onto the warm hearth, and closed his eyes.

We followed him, settling down opposite each other. It felt good to be back.

'Nate,' I said, launching straight in, 'I'm here to say thank you.'

He raised an eyebrow. The gesture reminded me of Bernard, making me smile.

'I've been putting your "get personal" advice into practice and I want you to know it's working – P&P are my new best friends and together we've come up with a great idea.' He didn't need to know about the part played by Zoffany.

'And you didn't poison anyone?'

I laughed. 'My only weapons were aromatherapy candles.'

He smiled and shrugged. 'What is it they say? "An enemy is a friend you don't yet know".'

Did he have a book entitled *Yogic Thoughts for the Day*? If he didn't he should write one; hippies all over the world would love it – though they'd probably borrow it from the library and he'd remain penniless.

'The only remaining problem is Ashley, the P.R. girl. I can't imagine ever getting to know her, or wanting to get to know her.'

'It can't be easy being her; a single American woman in London. We get a few here, the daughters of people my mum knew in Goa, and they're often lonely – they find us Brits a pretty impenetrable lot. Why don't you take her out for a drink? Show her the sights?'

'I'd rather stick pins in my eyes.'

'You need to keep working at it – as yoga guru Pattabhi Jois used to say, "Practice and all is coming".'

'Do you have that t-shirt?'

'I do. I buy in bulk from *ThirdEyeTees.com*.'

I mumbled something about giving it a try, knowing it would never happen, thinking it was time for my punch line. 'Anyway Yoda, it's my turn to "get personal" with you.'

He smiled nervously, instinctively reaching for Bernard. The dog pushed his nose into Nate's palm, closed his eyes.

I took a sip of twiggy tea wishing I'd asked for Builders, or something stronger, realising that I'd been so excited by the thought of helping Nate that I hadn't given much thought to how I might deliver my wisdom. 'I've got some ideas for you–'

'Great,' he exclaimed, rubbing his hands enthusiastically. 'Let's hear them.'

'They're based on my own experience, and remember, they come from my heart.'

He nodded expectantly.

'There's no easy way to say this Nate but, um, I find Ekatman a bit faded round the edges – a bit down-at-heel.'

'Down-at-heel?' He blinked slowly, like the shutter of an old camera.

'I think you should throw away the dried up old soap, replace all the yoga mats–'

'Are you saying it's not clean?'

'No, not at all,' I said quickly. 'It's always scrubbed to perfection – but the towels are threadbare, the mugs are chipped, the walls need some fresh paint, it's a little off-putting–'

'I'd love to update everything,' he said, studiously taking a breath, 'but do you know how much it costs to replace fifty yoga mats?'

'Sometimes you have to speculate to accumulate,' I said, not wanting to dwell on the thousands Shine spent on mats.

'"Speculate to accumulate"?' he said, trying out the phrase as if hearing it for the first time.

'I get it; first and foremost you're a yoga teacher. That means you measure yourself in how many people you help, not how much you make,' I said, silently thanking Becks for her insight, 'but you're also trying to run a business and you need to make money to survive – there's no shame in admitting that.'

He looked as though there might be.

'And more money would enable you to spread the word.'

'Word of mouth spreads naturally if you're good,' he said, now a little grouchy.

This was proving harder than expected. 'Yes, but sometimes it needs a helping hand.'

He looked unconvinced but I pressed on, carefully announcing that I'd had an idea.

'Shoot,' he said, cautiously shifting forward on the creaky sofa.

'Well, you're a community yoga centre so why don't you ask the community to help you out? Some of your students seem like arty types – perhaps they could revamp your signage, paint murals on your walls, design some beautiful rugs. Why not make a feature of your quirkiness? Perhaps you could have a painting party–'

'I don't need charity,' he replied huffily, leaning back, folding his arms across his chest.

God, he was proud, and more than a little touchy; definitely not as yogic as I'd thought – which was something of a relief actually. 'I'm not saying that you do – but in the same way you help *them* out with half-price community classes, I'm sure they could help *you* out – mate's rates, you know – that kind of thing.'

Now he was staring at the floor.

I battled on. 'Look at it this way, if you don't make some changes now it'll cost you more in the long run.'

'How do you mean?'

'People will start to leave – look elsewhere.'

'But everyone who's been coming here for years loves the hands-on approach, the personal touch, that it's all a bit homespun – they don't want manicures or valeted yoga mats.'

'Don't they?'

'No, they don't.'

'Actually' I said, unable to tell him the whole truth, 'I've seen a couple of your people picking up our timetables.'

'My people?' His body started to sag, mirroring the sofa's upholstery, but then he gathered himself, shaking it off. 'No Meg – there's no way my people would be seduced by all that; they'd be as repelled as me'.

I decided not to rise to that one; the poor guy was obviously in shock, and in denial. If Becks had noticed a slackening off, he must've done too. I told him that I was sorry, that I didn't think they were his regulars, but that it would be as well to put some strategies in place that would avert any issues further down the line. I was seriously regretting coming here; half an hour ago he'd been whistling up that ladder, now he was hardly breathing. Perhaps I should place his hand on my chest, have him follow the steady beat of my heart, feel my chest rising and falling … No. No. No! Step away! It was entirely his fault – for wearing that Lovin' Spoonful t-shirt. It wasn't the graphic – a childish illustration of the band without any faces. It wasn't the 'Karma Sutra Records' logo that sat just above his heart. It was what lay beneath, again.

'Nate,' I said gently, 'it's like that these days. People see a lifestyle and they want to buy into it. They walk in somewhere like Shine and it's light and airy, it's got lotus flowers and Tibetan tree bark, it's got a global perspective – they see a different version of themselves, and they want to live that dream. The fact is–'

He was irritated now, leaning forward, his voice tight. '"The fact is"' he said, making bunny ears over my words, 'Ekatman is not "a lifestyle" – it's my *life*, my life's work–'

'I know that, I just–'

He cut me off, looking really cross. 'I'm keeping mum's legacy alive – bringing real yoga to real people, making it available to everyone – not just people who can afford it. It's not something I can actively sell – people believe in me, or not.'

'But that's perfect Nate!' I said. 'My old boss Graham used to say that if you know who you are, and what you believe in, then creating a relationship is effortless. You don't need to "sell". You don't need to change anything about yourself – you just need to dress it up differently. Do some cosmetic stuff to the studio and engage with your community – create a proper website, get a Facebook page, start tweeting, maybe even change your name.' I lived in hope.

'I hate all that social networking stuff,' he said, wearily, 'and we've had this name since forever. I don't want to change it now – isn't that a big rule of branding? "Protect your equity". I'm sure I read that somewhere.'

I tried to keep my voice measured, 'It is usually, unless the name has too much baggage.' Seeing the look on his face, I quickly changed tack, 'but we don't need to go there – I'm sure it's still got plenty of "equity". All I'm saying is that now might be the time to plug into the modern world, get wired, make sure you don't get left behind.'

Walking over to the window, he thrust his hands in his pockets and stared out over the rooftops – towards Christchurch's chalky spire, just visible in the distance.

Silence.

I gave it a few minutes, and then I tried again, a different approach. 'Becks tells me your mother was a free spirit. Surely she wouldn't have wanted you chained to the old ways – she'd have wanted you to make Ekatman your own. Isn't that the whole point of yoga? To be free?' I stopped, feeling quite the Yoda.

It didn't work. I could feel his heels digging in from where I was sitting. He told me, in no uncertain terms, that I was missing the point. 'I do feel free – I feel free to keep it the way it is; I don't want to "get wired", and I don't want to change.'

Again there was a silence, longer this time.

'Perhaps you should do some research,' I suggested carefully. 'Find out what your people want, run some focus groups.'

He looked doubtful. 'Focus groups? Aren't they for politicians? For working out how to manipulate voters?'

I explained that they were for finding out people's motivations, and for working out how best to engage with those motivations. 'I wish I could run them for you but...' I felt suddenly cold, realising that I was walking in the shadows of conflicting loyalties; on the one hand I'd used his 'get personal' advice to write a speech that'd won Max new fans, and on the other I was actively advising him on ways to retain his people.

He looked gloomily out of the window. 'Don't worry; I understand–'

'A focus group is just like a chat except it's structured to make sure you cover the issues,' I continued, brightly. 'You could run one yourself.'

He shrugged.

'If it was my project I might start by asking them what they like about yoga, what they like about Ekatman, ask them if there's anything they don't like, where else they'd consider going. Then I might show them your Brand Vision, ask for their reactions.'

'My "Brand Vision"?'

'Yes, your Vision for Ekatman; the change you want to see in the world – the reason you exist.'

'But I *am* the change I want to see in the world' he said, his colour rising. 'Why can't I just get on with being it? Why do I have to start dressing it up in some phoney "Brand Vision"? Why do I have to talk about it at all?'

'Because quietly being something is not enough anymore Nate' I said. 'When people have options you have to be prepared to make a stand, to grow a community around your values, to shout ... louder than everyone else.'

He sighed and reached for the dog, stroked him under the chin. 'I like to think of Ekatman as "the road home" – home being the place you're most yourself, the place where you're content, happy with who you are, and what you have.'

I clapped, enthusiastically. 'See, you don't actually need a focus group. "The road home" is brilliant. That could be the start point for your Vision, and all the stuff you've talked about before, about personal attention, working with your students over time, that's your Mission.'

'"Mission"?'

'Mission and Vision are two different things. Your Vision is how you see your customer's future, where you're trying to get them. Your Mission is the nuts and bolts, how you're going to help them get there.'

'And will announcing my "Vision" and "Mission" help me get my people back?' He couldn't have sounded less excited.

'Of course,' I said, though I wasn't so sure. Con World had taught me one thing; given a choice between being content with what they have and a bar of chocolate, most people would choose chocolate.

'Zee dragons are 'orny'

CHAPTER THIRTEEN

'Two things smell of tuna and only one of them is fish! Ha ha!'

I didn't know where to look; the woman was old enough to be my grandmother. She had a pure white bob and wore very sensible shoes.

'Laughter makes the poo come faster,' she said, by way of explanation, still chortling, nudging me in the ribs. 'Squeeze diaphragm,' she said, making a helpful downwards motion.

She looked at me again and shook her head, seeming to accept her fate. 'You are tight ass.'

It made a change from fat ass.

Doctor Lily was nicknamed Kung Poo and her many devotees, led by Zoffany, raved about her unconventional methods. Much to Becks' disgust, I'd emptied my home crisp drawer of mini poppadum and tortilla chips, refilling it with soy nuts and seeds – anti-ageing superfoods that were my insurance policy against Botox. My body had forgotten, if it ever knew, how to digest such things; it craved pizza or pasta or chocolate, or a combination of all three. The result had been severe constipation, terrible wind, and a headache that'd lasted a week. The only cure was going to bed at nine – not a long-term strategy, given that my working day lasted well past ten.

Doctor Lily diagnosed me according to the Five Elements, a system in which the body is a reflection of the natural world.

'You are 'Metal.' Goals and deadlines rule your world, structure and discipline. You need – how you say? Loose up! Get life!'

Obediently, I lay on her treatment table while she clinked glasses behind me. Drinking couldn't be in the Traditional Chinese Medicine Handbook, could it?

Explaining that she was drawing out 'Wind-Cold', she used heat to create a vacuum so the glasses stuck to my skin. 'Release toxin, clear blockage, make energy and va va voom! Hanky panky! Naughty girl!'

She stood back to admire her work, 'You! Dinosaur!'

I craned my neck and groaned. 'Stegosaurus.'

'See! Humour back already!' she said, cackling with delight. 'Miracle cure!'

Each session left me with a souvenir – a neat line of red circles. When someone in the changing room asked me what'd happened, I told her it was an African tribal decoration, from Shine's resident witch doctor. She'd nodded and asked how long I'd waited for an appointment.

The treatment worked, no instant 'hanky panky', but certainly the kind of high I'd normally associate with mainlining chocolate. Keen to know more, I borrowed one of Doctor Lily's tomes. I stayed up all night, captivated by stories of ancient Chinese sages escaping the stuffy privations of court to inhabit a world of bamboo groves and snow-capped mountains. The energies, which shifted in tune with the seasons, were named after the five elements; 'Wood is for the spring equinox, Fire for the blooming brightness of the summer solstice, Earth for the sweet ripeness of late summer, Metal for the contractions of autumn, Water for the vast stillness of a winter's night.'

The sages saw these same elements in the rhythms of each passing day, and in the human body, visible in a person's constitution, character, colouring and habits. Disharmony, the dominance of one or more elements, could be treated with diet, heat, acupressure points, herbs, colour and aromatherapy. I thought I'd better leave Doctor Lily to administer herbs and heat, but I found myself wondering if we could give the Studio-Ready line a performance boost. Maybe we could package it with tiny vials of aromatherapy oil that would balance the mood of the wearer according to their element. And maybe we could create a collection of post-practice, elements-inspired clothes that would continue the mood-balancing, and cover my bum. As the sun rose over Slough, I named my idea 'Elements'.

I discussed it with Zoffany that morning after Yo-Jitsu. Jed had moved me up to the Intermediate class just when I was getting to the end of the practice without turning puce, or needing a second towel. He'd warned me against the seductive pleasure of the plateau, quoting one of his irritating catchphrases; 'stretch the muscles, and the mind will follow.' I'd nodded and sighed and resisted the urge to follow my mind in the opposite direction.

He'd been on particularly energetic form that morning and, once more, I was feeling distinctly wobbly by the time I got to breakfast. Doctor Lily had suggested I sprinkle the troublesome nuts and seeds on my morning bowl of fruit salad, but that day the effort of holding the packet steady proved too much and they scattered all over the table, enough to last a budgerigar a week. Was I pushing myself too hard? Maybe, but it was worth it; I was getting into my size twelve dresses.

'Something like this?' said Zoffany, taking my pen, immediately sketching a floaty, bat-winged top on the back of a café menu. She rummaged in her capacious handbag for a long time, finally pulling out a piece of silk. 'Chinese dynasty, with a modern twist' she pronounced, smoothing it out on the table. 'From a tradeshow in Paris.'

I picked it up, gently stroking the fabric, so soft it felt warm, admiring the delicate embroidery and watercolour print. It reminded me of mum's cherry blossoms after the rain. I seized the moment to tell Zoffany about Threads of Hope – a fair trade organisation working in the mountains of Yunnan. Becks had shown me their website, thinking she might order a couple of their cushions. To my eyes, they looked really pretty – Mandarin ducks for love, pomegranates for fertility, and peonies for riches. I found the website on my phone and passed it over.

She squinted at the screen, wrinkling her nose. 'I'm not sure,' she said, not bothering to scroll through, putting the phone down. 'I need to see it, to feel it, to smell it, to know. It must be just so.'

I sent them an email, asking for some samples.

Doctor Lily's tome was definitely to her taste though and, for a bit of fun, we played around with the remedies for ourselves, and everyone we worked with. I found Metal a little dispiriting. Apparently, with my tendency 'to put virtue before pleasure', I'd need to wear white and grey, and my little vial should contain essence of rosemary and sage, which made me feel about as glamorous as a leg of roast lamb.

Zoffany, always the woman I wanted to be, should wear red, and spritz herself with the warming aromas of orange, clove, cardamom and frankincense. This, according to the book, would complement her pleasure in the senses whilst countering her constant lateness, though in my view she'd need these in industrial quantities if she were ever to turn up on time.

'Surely Max is Fire,' said Zoffany, 'like me?'

I shook my head – I'd already made up my mind. 'He's challenging and clear-sighted, so he's Wood.'

'Maybe you're right,' she said grabbing the book. '"Wood is impatient". What's the cure?'

'I prescribe cooling geranium, lemongrass and peppermint.'

'And what scent would make him fall in love with me again?'

'Oh Zoffany,' I said, covering her hand with mine, giving it a squeeze, 'I think you tried them all.'

Her face a picture of grey skies, I moved on to Jed. 'I think that easy-going nature makes him Earth.'

'Well,' she said, beginning a smile, 'at least all those golden chrysanthemums will go with his hair.'

'What about Ashley?' I asked, spearing a piece of sushi with a chopstick.

'Her issues are beyond the remit of scent or colours,' said Zoffany, closing the book.

Max's schedule was packed but mentioning that we had a potential money spinning idea was like saying 'Open Sesame' in front of a thieves' cave. We were in his diary the very next day. We agreed to park the Threads of Hope conversation until we had the samples, the priority being to get the idea sold in.

Zoffany and I ended up pulling an all-nighter. To save running up and down the corridor, I decamped to her office. She spent a lot of time pouring over her favourite photographers' websites – Robert Sturman, Karen Yeomans, Jorell Jones, but she seemed to take most inspiration from *Yoga Style*. I'd pulled it off her heaving shelves and immediately fallen in love with the look – a homage to gossamer-weight cover-ups. This, I told her, was what I wanted. I watched enviously as her hand glided across the page, effortlessly fusing that ethereal style with the strong lines of the Studio-Ready collection.

The rest of the time she spent on her knees, going through the contents of her mahogany traveller's chest; Moroccan rose oil, Indian sandalwood, French lavender, row upon row of miniature bottles, like a Victorian explorer's collection of butterflies. Occasionally, she'd give me one to sniff, reviving my ability to focus on price points and sales forecasts. 'Each to her own and all that,' she said, reassuring me that once Max had bought the concept, there'd be plenty of time for me to get creative.

But then I had an idea that couldn't find expression in a spreadsheet. 'Zoffany,' I said slowly, not sure how she'd respond, 'what if we made a pocket in each piece of clothing, big enough for a tiny swatch of fabric that could be soaked in the oil? Body heat would warm the oil, releasing the scent slowly, so the wearer would get the benefit as they practiced.'

'It's a great idea,' she said, in a voice more measured than effusive. 'Just two issues; the oil would stain the clothes and the swatch would spoil the line.'

I thought for a moment and then I remembered Becks giving up smoking when she got pregnant. 'Forget the pockets. Let's use aromatherapy patches, like nicotine patches. We can sell them in packs, impregnated with oil in measured doses, and people can put them straight onto their skin.'

For a moment, I thought she was going to reject the idea, but then she took up her pencil and sketched a vintage tin, the kind you might find in Nate's kitchen, and then she drew a cutaway to show its contents – ten sachets, stacked like upmarket teabags, two in each element's colours. As her hand moved across the page, I felt full of pride, like an editor watching her first edition come off the press.

Zoffany and I decided that the best preparation for a tough meeting would be a tough class. Max announced that he'd join us. We'd discuss Elements afterwards, over breakfast.

Meetings with handsome yoga mughals were, by now, almost in my comfort zone, Yo-Jitsu classes were definitely not. Although my practice had improved I was still a long way from bendy and, while I now wore a regulation pair of Studio-Ready yoga pants, I was still too embarrassed about my bum to wear anything other than a very long t-shirt. Thankfully, Max seemed as impervious to me, as to everyone else. He pushed his tailbone to the sky in 'Down Dog', strengthened his legs without locking his knees in 'Front Snap Kick', tucked his chin into his shoulder for a smooth 'Forward Roll', all the while sounding like he had a tank of air in his lungs. I could hear him from the back of the class; breathing from the depth of his diaphragm, keeping the rhythm – scuba diving on his mat.

He'd come a long way since the day he met Jed in a Santa Monica cigar bar. Zoffany had told me all about it. Max's client had arrived fresh from a yoga class, bringing his instructor with him. At first Max had dismissed Jed as a flake, but they'd bonded over several whiskies and Jed had suggested a bet; that he could hook Max in just one yoga session – the forfeit? The most expensive bottle of whisky in the place. Impressed by his confidence – the bottle cost over a thousand dollars – Max agreed. The day after the class Max couriered two bottles to Jed.

Now his only issue was flexibility; watching him attempt that upside down Wheel pose, the one demonstrated by Ashley in my first class, I was amazed, and comforted, to see that instead of curving into a graceful arch his spine remained almost flat. 'Once more with feeling,' said Jed, immediately by his side. 'Come back down, hold onto my ankles, and lift yourself from there.' Max's grip turned the skin on Jed's tanned ankles white, but our yoga master didn't flinch. 'And breathe,' he said, gently placing his hands under Max's shoulder blades, raising him up. Somehow his imperfections only seemed to render the whole more perfect; the slight wobble of his bottom and his soft belly throwing the muscles that surrounded them into sharp relief. It was nigh on impossible to banish lustful thoughts. Although I don't think I lost track as many times as Zoffany, I was guilty of being several beats behind, and my 'Reverse Twist Punch Attack' was a total disaster – even when I thought of Ashley.

It wasn't until we arrived in the cool down section that I achieved some equilibrium, remembering to breathe and relax. By the time Jed lay on top of me in seated forward bend (he always remembered me for that one), I was back on an even keel, almost enjoying the experience of being flattened by a twelve stone man.

Settling down for final relaxation, the ten minutes I was supposed to spend meditating on my human potential, I found myself worrying about the meeting. I'd tried broaching the subject at about four this morning, expecting an open discussion, but Zoffany had done her disappearing act, telling me that she was 'over him', that she'd moved on, that I should forget about it. I didn't get it – one minute she was asking me for love potions, the next she was denying all feelings. I understood that she might be embarrassed at how much she'd told me but I was really disappointed – she'd opened the door to her inner life, asked me to share in her despair, and here she was shutting it in my face. I tried to comfort myself with the thought that although the Shine loo was a very nice loo, I didn't want to find myself there again, metaphorically or otherwise, at our next big night. A bit of distance might be a good thing.

By the time Zoffany and I arrived in the boardroom, Max was already there, washing down a plate of melon with lashings of green algae, or at least that's what it looked like. We'd had a bit of a debate about who should make the initial presentation but in the end she'd won because a) she was head of design b) she had the Max relationship and c) she was an impressive speaker, as proven by her 'son et lumiere' performance. It seemed the right decision; while I slogged my way through more pineapple than one person should have to encounter in their lifetime, she walked those boards as if she'd been born to the stage.

'Ere we 'ave you Max,' she announced, dialling up the accent once again, placing the Wood mood board in front of him – an intricately carved teahouse in a peach blossom meadow, an ornate wooden temple in a flourishing lilac grove, and a vast palace in a lush bamboo forest. She stood behind him, resting a hand on his shoulder, allowing her hair to brush his face. So much for moving on.

'Wood is yang in character' she said, bending to adjust the board, 'very purposeful, strong yet flexible.'

Funny; I was sure she'd been watching him in class.

'You are generous, idealistic, creative, outgoing, but you have a social conscience – you think big, and you make a difference.'

Max attempted a modest nod.

'Wood is ruled by Jupiter – you are, 'ow you say, "god's lightning bolt" – unexpected, powerful, luminous.'

Any concern that she might be laying it on a bit thick was soon quashed; 'basking in it' was the phrase that came to mind.

'Can you zee yourself?' she asked, tracing her hand lovingly over the teahouse encircled by peach blossom. 'It's like you my love … always surrounded by beautiful zings.'

He opened his hands in a gesture that said, 'What's a man to do?'

'And zis is *my* element,' she said, placing the second board next to the first; the one with the lava flow that looked like a curved brush stroke, the gold leaf runway hair, and the fire breathing dragons. According to Chinese history these dragons were very auspicious, bestowing health, wealth and longevity; lucky Zoffany.

'Zee 'ere' she said, holding up the picture, 'zee dragons are 'orny.'

'I think you mean *horned* Zoffany,' I said, quickly coming to her rescue.

'Quoi?' she looked totally confused, poor lamb.

'Let Zoffany's dragons be "'orny",' smiled Max indulgently.

'And this 'ere is Meg,' she said, presenting Metal and all its associations, running her finger over the sample of intricate brocade – fine silver leaves entwined with pearl petals, pointing out her favourite pictures – the space age silver eyeshadow, the reflection of the moon on the water, the soft grey silk camisole.

'Beautiful isn't she?' She smiled across the table at me, an irresistible smile, bringing me back into the fold.

'Beautiful,' said Max, giving me a disappointingly friendly wink.

Perhaps intuiting that the other two elements were a little less fascinating, not being relevant to anyone in the room, Zoffany dwelt less on Earth's yellow dragons and golden chrysanthemums, or the black tortoises and snow-capped mountains of Water.

'Now for ze clothes' she said, unzipping the second large black art bag with some ceremony. I gathered up the mood boards, placing them carefully on the ridged ledge running the length of the wall, feeling like a lioness guarding her cubs, fiercely proud and protective.

'I want to launch with a capsule collection – five elements, five designs' said Zoffany, lovingly placing the first pencil sketch in front of Max. She'd illustrated her muse wearing the floaty top in Natarajasana, or Dancer's Pose, her extended arm showing off the bat-wing sleeve. It was still my favourite, although she'd paired it with the Studio-Ready bikini bottoms, the ones they wore in the heat of Studio Jamu. Not a look that was likely to happen for me.

Max seemed taken with the silk chiffon boat-neck top; the sheer fabric gathered in by over-sized velvet ribbons looping round and round to create a cinched-in waist, tying at the back in a large bow. Zoffany had drawn her model in Wheel Pose, the ribbons curling on the floor. I loved it too, but it fell a long way short of the knicker line. The streamlined tunic with drawstring neck was the only one she'd been happy to make longer. 'It's a question of balance' she'd said, sketching a line that just about covered the bum.

As they batted back and forth on fabrics and colours, I decided to make my presence felt. 'Max' I said, 'you'll have noticed that we've styled each piece with the Studio-Ready line.' He nodded, in a manner that suggested he thought this was pretty bloody obvious. '*I* suggested it to Zoffany to encourage cross-selling – you know, buy a sheer tunic and then ... guess what ... you need a little vest top to go underneath.'

'I wanted everything to be a little bit see-through' said Zoffany sweetly, ramping up the husky voice while, at the same time, giving me a 'keep quiet' look. 'Because, of course, none of our members really want to cover anything up.'

In retrospect I should've asserted myself more but I couldn't get past the stupidity of my Studio-Ready comment, so I just blushed and shut up. I thought I'd get another chance at the end of her presentation, which didn't seem that far away. To be honest I didn't like either of the other two designs and I was sure Max wouldn't either – they didn't really fit with the overall idea. She'd seemed to agree, but suggested we throw them in and see what Max made of them.

She'd used Trikonasana or Triangle Pose to show off the silky soft low-rise harem pants, which she'd styled with a tribal belly chain and a Studio-Ready bra-top. Not really my thing but minus the chain and top I could repurpose them as super-glam pyjamas. The final piece was a skin-tight dress with bell sleeves and a puddle train, spun from ultra-fine cashmere. She'd sketched the model in a seated twist, to show off the criss-crossed, v-shaped back.

'For you?' said Max, smiling, tracing the lines with his index finger.

'Just one' said Zoffany, holding up a finger, giggling like a fifteen year old.

'*I'm* not entirely sure about this dress' I said, determined to have the debate. '*My* starting point was a cover-up collection – I don't feel it meets the brief–'

But Max was waving his hand dismissively. 'It's perfect' he said, looking again at Zoffany. 'There's nothing to cover-up here.'

'But the idea was a cover-up collection' I said, trying not to whine. 'That was the point. I really don't think it works–'

'I think Zoffany's taken cover-up to a new level, don't you?' he said, still smiling at her.

While I sat stock still, save the constant juddering of my foot, a mix of anger and nerves, he got up. He walked the length of the wall, peering intently at each mood board, hands behind his back – like Prince Charles inspecting the troops, then he returned to the table and gave each design another once over. I tried to catch Zoffany's eye, but she was leaning against the window, nonchalantly playing with her beads.

Finally, he looked up. 'Let's do it,' he said, breaking into a smile, directed at Zoffany.

'Not too hippy for you?' I managed, remembering my concern that he might find the healing undercurrent overpowering, the look a little too romantic.

'I have one question,' he said, by way of an answer. '"Wood is impatient." Are you sure?'

I held up a vial of cooling geranium, lemongrass and peppermint. 'Don't worry; a couple of sniffs of this and you'll be radiating love and peace all day.'

He smiled indulgently, clearly thinking I was a complete moron, and then he picked up the sketch of the tins with the patches. 'Love this – very original.'

He was looking at Zoffany again.

I waited for her to give me the credit, but she'd moved back to the table and busied herself with some uncharacteristic note taking. I'd have to do it myself. '*My* idea was to make little pockets but then Zoffany pointed out the oil might stain the clothes and, of course, the material might spoil the line, so that's when the patches came into–'

'No question' he said, interrupting me, looking approvingly in her direction yet again. 'The patches are exactly right.'

I looked at Zoffany, still hoping she might come clean, but the grande dame had taken her final bow.

Then he was grilling me on the financials and there was no way back. He didn't want to go through my colour coded files, he just wanted to fire questions. He wanted to know what it would cost and what kind of volumes we'd sell, and then he wanted to know what the profit margin would be and how quickly we could deliver. Biting down on the suggestion that he take a big whiff of lemongrass and peppermint, I gathered myself. Despite the acid coursing through my veins, I answered everything he threw at me.

'Just make sure you get it in-store quick,' he said, folding his napkin and picking up his iPhone, checking his messages as he headed for the door, 'And do something for men.'

The door shut and we were alone. I wasn't going to let her get away with it. I stood, my hands on the boardroom table, my heart racing. 'I don't believe you just did that.'

'He loved it,' she said. 'What's the big deal?'

'You took credit for the whole thing, even my patches! How could you?'

She didn't answer. She focused on loading boards and sketches into art bags, disappearing into that stupid hair of hers.

'You should apologise.'

'So let me get this straight' she said, finally looking up. 'You came to me with the beginnings of an idea and I made it happen. Now, what do you want me to do? Go and tell him it was all down to you?'

'Yes,' I said, noting that her English was back on track, no trace of an accent.

'We're not in kindergarten Meg. We don't display work with our names on it.' She paused a moment, thinking. 'Actually, that's not a bad idea – I'll tag the entire collection, the silver brocade, the dragons, every damn golden chrysanthemum, and you can put your name on the patches. Shall I write you a sticky label, or do you think you can manage that yourself?'

'But you're the designer; it's your job to come up with golden chrysanthemums,' I said, trying to keep from shouting. 'The whole Elements idea was my idea, *my* creative breakthrough, and I wanted him to know that, like you want him to know when you come up with ideas.'

'"Your creative breakthrough"? Please. We'd be stuck with a few oil-soaked t-shirts if it was down to you.'

'Your own "creative breakthrough" wasn't so hot Zoffany; I could've copied all those designs in that *Yoga Style* book and got the same result.'

'And everything would've ended up knee length and baggy,' she said, picking up her art bags and heading for the door. 'Not very Shine. Would you not agree, our lovely Brand Experience Director?' And with that she left.

I sank heavily into a chair and rubbed my aching temples, trying to soothe the compression around my eyes. No two ways about it; she'd used me, just like Pat had used me. If I wasn't careful I'd end up chained to her desk for the next three years, passed over yet again. Had I learnt nothing since I floated amongst those ceiling tiles?

It was then that I made the decision. It was time to become a woman of the world, to grow up, to trust no one, no matter how golden her chrysanthemums.

'In the kill zone'

I didn't notice, until I was half way across his office, that Ashley was perched on Max's desk, leaning towards him like an angle poise lamp. Lazily, she twisted to face me – her skirt no more than a belt, her ankle boots swinging like pendulums.

'Will Ashley be joining us?' I said, addressing Max.

Without saying a word, Ashley slowly unravelled those legs, her nose scenting the ceiling as she stalked towards the door. I stared straight ahead, my eye on the prize.

Max got up and, shaking himself down, closed the window. He did this before any meeting, claiming the noise distracted him, saying he could only focus on one thing at a time. Perhaps he thought this little routine would put his audience at ease, assuring them that he was, despite so much perfection, only human. Then he cracked open a Diet Coke, the second part of his routine; it always made me smile – a starter pistol on a racetrack.

I was as pumped as an athlete on her blocks, despite the late hour. The first item on the agenda was P&P's campaign. I began, not without a little pride, with the idea – members' transformational stories using the line '#shine @Shine'.

I told him that the campaign was flexible, that it would allow us to push specific classes and treatments. That it could go way beyond the original local posters brief. That it'd work in the weekend sections of *The Sunday Times*, *The New York Times*, *The Los Angeles Times* and, of course, *Condé Naste Traveller* and *Vogue*. That we'd create brand buzz with flat screen billboards, and online buzz via our social media. We'd ask our members to tell the world how they'd changed, to detail the difference Shine had made, and we'd give rewards for the best posts. I made sure that I owned it all – I wasn't leaving anything to chance any more; not after the Zoffany stitch-up.

'This is a big idea Meg,' he said, studying the mocked-up billboards in Times Square, Sunset Plaza and Piccadilly Circus.

I placed three more boards face down on the table in front of me, like a croupier laying out a deck of cards.

Each one featured someone who'd transformed since they joined Shine. We'd had to cheat it slightly – Shine had only been open in London for three months so Alex had found a couple of members who'd recently returned from the US where they'd been regulars. Becks had, of course, picked up on the time issue – she'd harrumphed and said if the ads went up they'd be 'guilty' of suggesting profound change could happen really fast. In her view, anything that quick would be 'superficial and temporary'. She could say what she liked. What had already happened to me was living proof of Shine's power – every day my Yo-Jitsu warrior grew a little fiercer, except during Bull Terrier face-offs.

'You want a yellow pencil – you sell this work,' he'd said, zipping up the bag, handing it over with a look that had made my warrior quiver. I was hoping that Max would find the stories so engaging he'd get over the fact that P&P's campaign candidates were mainly trading down, not up.

'This is Alex's favourite,' I said, turning up the first board.

Max studied the sunny smiles on the war-torn kids, and sighed, shaking his head.

'John's ex-City,' I said quickly, 'and this is the estate gang he mentors. He wants them to understand numbers so they can be traders, not crooks.'

He laughed. 'Most people would say there isn't a difference.'

'They opened for business last week – they've got a designer reworking old clothes, and they're selling them on–'

'All very noble, but the public doesn't want to hear about do-good City boys. It's still baying for blood.'

'Isn't it worth doing, even if we only use it to target City people?'

'They come anyway,' he said, turning John face down. 'Because of me.'

The next two went the same way.

'Selling tulips on a market stall? A bit lame.'

'Dog sanctuary; nice idea, but she's a total moose.'

He reached for his mobile. 'Let me give you a few names.'

I reached for my notepad.

'Talk to Kate. She was a second-rate investment banker with a weight problem until she joined Central Park South.'

'But I thought you said the public didn't want to hear about City people?'

'Girls are different. Everyone knows they get a hard time on the Mile; they're under-paid versus men, they're treated like bimbos–'

'And eighty percent of our members are women,' I said, wondering if the ex-City girl might also be very cute.

'And we'll use Shonda Lear – she was a model in L.A.' His face softened. 'She retired when she hit thirty but I'm sure she wouldn't mind getting in front of the camera for me.'

'And we'll use Bob. I met him in the bar a couple of months back. He'd been creatively blocked for two years, but he painted his first canvas after three months of Yo-Chi and now he's the Second Coming. He's a charismatic guy – good looking, great physique.'

There was a pause – I waited.

'Almost as handsome as me.'

I said I'd pass the names back to P&P, wondering if I could just phone them in. Being in the same room as the Terrier didn't seem like a spectacular idea.

Then I showed Max the photographer's portfolio, a thick file documenting day-to-day life in the face of disaster. There were Japanese earthquake victims doing their laundry in the river, American and Iraqi soldiers sharing a bag of crisps, a young boy playing with a discarded bike tire in the rubble of an Afghani village.

Pretty soon, I was crossing out his name.

'A war photographer is a really dumb idea,' he said slinging the book across the table. 'We need fashion photography.'

'I already told them that,' I said quickly, recalling the sneer on the Terrier's face when I suggested we use Jorell Jones.

'And?'

'They won't countenance any alternatives. "This is where you need balls Meg" were, I think, Alex's exact words.'

'Then it's very simple.'

'It is?'

'Take P&P off the job.'

'Off the job?' I blinked, wrong-footed – how were we already at endgame?

'Yes, just get rid of them. If they want to let it all fall apart over a battle-worn photographer that's their look out.'

'But we haven't got time to brief it out again – not if we want to make our deadlines.' I tried to keep my voice level, but I could feel the panic rising. 'Maybe Bloomstein Silverday could sort it? I can fly out to L.A. if you like – make it happen.' (My dedication knew no bounds.)

'Forget Bloomstein,' he said waving his hand dismissively. 'We'll take it in-house – do the campaign ourselves, from here.'

'In-house?' I stared at him stupidly, reminding him that we didn't have a communications department of our own.

'We do now.'

'We do?'

'Yes. You and Zoffany.'

Caught between wanting to scream with delight, and with horror, I managed a nod.

He ploughed on, trying to read my luke-warm reaction. 'She's had a new lease of life with you. You're great together; she's yin to your yang' he said, smiling good-naturedly as I wished he'd given me yin. 'I know how much effort you put in, and what it takes to work with Zoffany – but what a result; it was superb.'

'"It *was* superb",' I said, making an on-the-spot decision not to tell him that his dream team was in crisis. Zoffany and I would have to work it out: there was no way I was passing up the chance to run my own ad agency.

'Though we can't just take P&P's idea,' I said, 'they could claim copyright.'

'But you told that Creative guy about re-launching yourself; it was all coming from you. Remember?'

'I did,' I said, trying to keep a steady hand on the tiller, 'but maybe that's not the point. They built on my idea, made it all about real people.'

'But you suggested the "real people" research – you told him to talk to our members. They'd never have done that without you; they're far too arrogant, and even with your "factory tour" they still managed to screw it up.'

The man had a point.

'So all we need do is threaten to tell *Campaign* that the great P&P nicked your idea.' He grinned at the thought of it, 'and if that fails we'll get my lawyers in.' He took off his jacket and rolled up his sleeves, 'Okay, what's next?'

This was the point at which I'd planned to pitch fair trade for Elements, but with an ad campaign to put together there was no way I'd have time to run around remote Chinese villages sourcing product. Fortunately, I'd prepared a quick-fire back-up plan, in case the Threads of Hope samples didn't work out. I told him that there was a Chinese manufacturer who could deliver the order on schedule, using something they called 'computer-generated, hand-guided embroidery.' Zoffany had initially road-blocked it, but I showed her their work for some big name designers and the barrier had lifted.

I tried, unsuccessfully, not to think about the fact that, if the fair trade reports were correct, these workers slept on the factory floor, and that balancing Wood or Water was a little less pressing than making enough money to eat. I got through it by telling myself it would give us proof of concept – if Elements turned out to be as big as I hoped, well then there'd be no mountain high enough or remote enough for Shine's foundation – we could hire a whole pack of sherpas, do whatever it took to find the finest embroidery in the whole of China. I could see it now; Max, the Duke and Duchess of Cambridge, me, slogging our way to the summit – 'venture philanthropists' one and all.

Keen to celebrate my progress, Max busied himself opening a bottle. I walked over to the window, drawn towards the lights on the distant cranes, luminous yellow in the gathering darkness. This view always made me feel plugged in, as if I too hummed with electricity. I asked him the identity of the men in black suits, the ones who'd been boxing him in these past weeks. Were they lawyers?

'P&P aren't the only ones ripping off our ideas; if people want to teach our sequences, they'll bloody well have to pay for it.'

'Are the lawyers optimistic?'

'It's just a matter of time.'

There it was again; the certain knowledge that he could deal with anything and anyone. It came from that fine-tuned navigational system, the one that told him which artist to follow, what stock to back.

'One thing's for sure,' he said, pouring the champagne, 'I've worked too hard to let a few yogis from Boca Raton get in my way; they'll soon see who's boss.'

'So you're Gordon Gekko in the "kill zone"?' I joked, getting stuck into the fizz.

'I like lunch too much to be Gekko but yes, I was never going to be content with being an average Joe, plodding along, taking orders, earning £500k a year–'

'There's nothing average about earning £500k a year,' I sniffed, trying not to think about those Chinese workers, mum and dad, Becks, Nate, me, or pretty much anyone else in the entire universe.

'I want to be a player, a deal maker. I want two hundred million.'

I nodded, as if conversations involving hundreds of millions were run of the mill to me. 'So that's it for you – money and power?'

'What else is there?'

'Love?'

He shrugged, moving to dismiss. 'As Gekko might've said, "I've got plenty of other reasons to stop myself jumping out of the window".'

I laughed but the bubbles, which were disappearing fast, persuaded me to push him a bit. 'There must've been someone, once.'

He paused, contemplating his own half empty glass. Eventually, he spoke, carefully, quietly. 'It started as a challenge; she stood there sipping orange juice, totally absorbed in the horses, totally disinterested in me. I just wanted to get her drunk, seduce her.'

'And you were successful?'

'Eventually, but it turned into more.'

It was my turn to speak quietly, feel the familiar stirrings of jealousy, yet again unable to stop myself. 'You fell in love with her?'

'Yes,' he said simply.

There was a longer pause, he appeared to drift.

'She was Australian; but not at all the usual vibe. She was pale skinned and freckly, a redhead in a green dress …'

I followed the direction of his gaze, towards the photograph of a forest that stretched across the opposite wall; it had a magical quality, something to do with the mottled silvery bark shining out of the black space.

'She made me think of school – of blackboards, of chalk, of being good.'

'What happened?'

'I turned out bad.'

I tried to dig deeper but he'd closed down, like a clam. That much I understood; Becks was always telling me that I liked to put myself in a box, one that gave me 'protection from messy emotions'. It'd always seemed a good place to be – until now. I wished I could prise his open.

I managed a respectful silence but then curiosity got the better of me. I wanted the other side of the Zoffany story.

'She's an attractive, talented woman,' he said carefully, 'and I'm not entirely immune to her charms – as you might've noticed, but there's so much baggage, so many insecurities – she needs a lot of propping up.'

I knew that feeling. 'That you don't want to give?'

'I never made a commitment,' he said, pursuing his lips, 'despite what she might say.'

It seemed that Max lived in black and white – women were either good or bad. There was no room for the grey area that was Zoffany.

'It was fine while it lasted – I know she claims I used her but the truth is we helped each other. I gave her a blank canvas at Shine and she opened her address book. That should've been the end of it, but she has a habit of trying to turn a short story into a saga.'

And then he decided to tell me my story. He told me his

terms; I was to say nothing until he'd reached the end. I agreed, trying to ignore the feeling I was signing something away.

'You spent most of your childhood looking out of your window, dreaming of escape. You were a bright child and you studied hard, seeing it as a way out of the suburbs. Hinshaw's was your opportunity to travel the world, to make something of yourself and then, when Lovatt left, you were returned to your perch, where you sat for years. Right so far?'

I nodded, slightly terrified of him; a submarine sweeping for information.

He studied me thoughtfully, as if putting together the final pieces of a jigsaw. 'You looked for your prince most of your life but you looked in all the wrong places; there were boyfriends at university and flings at work but they turned out ordinary, mired by the usual crap. They didn't fit your notion of who you might become.'

I nodded again. I wouldn't have called discovering your boyfriend in bed with someone else ordinary but it was certainly crap, and I definitely deserved better.

He polished off his glass, carefully placing it on the table, seeming to make up his mind about something. He asked me if I'd moved up to town yet.

I told him I hadn't had time to look for anywhere yet, though actually it was money as much as time that was holding me back. I wasn't sure, even on my vastly improved salary, how I was going to afford London without sharing, and I hadn't met anyone I wanted to do that with except, in my wildest dreams, him. That penthouse desk had been the subject of one or two fantasies, beneath the bull and the matador.

Without another word, he picked up my coat and put it around my shoulders, guiding me out of the door. We walked in silence, something in his manner discouraging me from questions. He set a fast pace and we'd soon exchanged the bankers of Bishopsgate for the bhajis of Brick Lane, then we were heading west, toward Leman Street, toward the clock tower that looked like a scaled-down version of Big Ben. I remembered it from the interview. We were going to his flat.

Were my lustful daydreams about to become a reality? I wasn't feeling equal to the task – my knickers were not my best, I was still lumpy in my undies. I smiled sheepishly at the night watchman, knowing he could tell some stories, and they wouldn't involve unshaven legs.

Max ushered me inside the lift, and closed the worn brass gates. Then he pressed the button for the fifth floor – the one below his. Damn it. I focused on the floor – not sure what to say.

And then we were in the corridor, standing opposite three identical oak doors; it looked so like a boutique hotel I expected one of the doors to open just a crack, for a stealthy hand to push out a tray with a half finished Club sandwich, congealed ketchup and soggy fries.

He fished around in his pocket for the keys. 'Welcome to the company flat,' he said, opening the middle door, ushering me in. 'We use it for visiting yoga teachers but you can stay a while, until you find something permanent. No more late trains to Slough, and no more weekends hibernating in the suburbs.' He turned to look at me square on, placing his hands on my shoulders. 'Promise me one thing?'

'Anything Max,' I said, really meaning it.

'Promise me you'll have some fun.'

I gave him a three finger salute; Guide's honour.

And with that he took to the stairs, two steps at a time, leaving me holding the keys.

I dropped my handbag on the kitchen counter, taking in the built-in wine cooler and coffee machine, the white Corian worktop with its array of dazzling appliances, the floor to ceiling windows framing the view of the Gherkin which was blinking in the night sky like a space rocket ready to launch, the neat row of aluminium planters on the balcony, the pristine white sofa facing the wall mounted plasma TV, the painting – a fuchsia pink square over a rectangle of grey that reminded me of Fuzzy Felt, and the neat stack of Zoffany de Gournay books on the glass coffee table. Making a mental note to put them in the nearest cupboard, I moved slowly down the hall, passing the bathroom with the rainforest shower, trailing my hands over the soft grey walls, taking in the fifties photographs of Muscle Beach, Venice – acrobatic women flying through the air, launched by toned men in full swimming trunks. I threw myself onto the over-sized bed and bounced, scattering cushions everywhere. Catching sight of the red glass chandelier directly above me – a Dali-esque version of antlers, I laughed.

'Do I look like a Shine sort of girl?'

★

★

Nothing could disguise the shadows under Becks' eyes, or the weight she'd lost. I made her a cappuccino with froth and extra chocolate sprinkles.

'So, what's with the miracle diet? Shall I alert *Grazia*?'

'Tell them it's called The Ofsted,' she said, explaining that her failure to eat was the result of a series of school inspections. In the end, they'd retained their 'Satisfactory' rating but it'd left her exhausted, and frustrated.

The only fun she'd had was the shoes I bought her. 'A parent's evening wasn't an ideal maiden voyage for a pair of three-inch heels but I decided to hell with it – it was worth it just to see the parents' faces.'

I forced a smile, trying not to think about the outing they would've had at the launch party. Concentrating on stirring my coffee, I steered the conversation into safer territory.

I asked her how her book was going. She was wearing her Che Guevara t-shirt, which I thought was promising, though I suspected it might be more in protest at my 'bourgeois building'. It was probably the first time this flat had entertained a communist revolutionary.

Becks nodded, running her finger round the rim of her cup and licking her chops. 'I'm thinking of re-imagining Che's life – what would happen if he'd been around in 2008 and led a peoples' revolution against the banks.'

'You could title it *Che Credit Crunch*.'

At least that raised a smile.

'Actually,' she said, taking a deep breath, 'I've been working on it every night.'

I studied my friend carefully – she really did look terrible. I spoke gently. 'I know you're a brilliant writer and a born whistle blower, but is it worth it if it's so exhausting?'

'I'm managing,' she said, pursing her lips. She thought for a moment, scraping off the last of the chocolate with her finger. 'The people need to know – the lying, the cheating, the bullying – and that's just the teachers – it's way out of hand.'

'As long as it doesn't run you into the ground,' I said, carefully, offering her more chocolate sprinkles.

'The truth is I'm a bit scared,' she said, pulling nervously at her trusty t-shirt. 'What will happen if I actually pull it off? Worst-case scenario – I'll lose my job and then what happens to Susie? It's not as if her father is going to leap to the rescue.'

'Maybe,' I said, proceeding slowly, thinking back to my original Jamie Oliver suggestion, and to Nate and his 'get personal' advice, 'it should be more about your own life, charting your journey, from *Dead Poets* to *Dead Angry*. All the stuff that drives you mad, all your disappointments, but throwing in some of the good stuff along the way; the reasons you keep doing it – when you reach a kid everyone else has dismissed as unteachable, when a kid tells a joke that makes the whole class laugh, when you get the summer off – all the reasons you keep at it.' This last bit elicited something of a sharp look but I knew I'd got somewhere because she did that disappearing thing; she wasn't like Zoffany who seemed to jet off to another more glamorous planet of the mind, it was like she burrowed down into herself – a place that smelled of earth and twigs.

And then she started poking around in my fridge, which didn't take long as it was pretty much empty. Glad to see she'd got an appetite, I rang for a Brick Lane curry. I ate the salad that came with her biryani whilst eyeing up the poppadoms, but I managed to resist long enough for her to eat them all, which was to say, not long.

'So what about you?' asked Becks, balancing a plate and a full glass of red wine, settling into the whitest sofa in London as I looked on anxiously. 'Mr. Walcott clearly loves you.'

'Honestly Becks, I don't know what would've happened if I'd stayed at Con World. One day, someone would've found me slumped and drooling on my keyboard, my pupils fixed and dilated.'

She smiled. 'And Shine has become a fair trade company?'

'I have a bit more research to do,' I said. News of a Chinese manufacturer who quite probably offended every point in the work conditions rulebook would unleash a tirade from which the evening would never recover.

'So that's a "no"?'

'It's a "not yet",' I said firmly.

She changed the subject. 'And how's life on Planet Zoffany?'

I hesitated. I didn't want to admit that one minute I'd been wiping away her tears, the next she'd hung me out to dry.

'We're Max's dream team,' I said, explaining that, as of last week, Zoffany and I were heading up Shine's in-house ad agency.

'To my power magnate,' she said, raising her glass. 'I can't wait for a ride in your Porsche.'

'By the way,' I said, raising mine, 'I can't say too much, but I can reveal you'll be wearing golden chrysanthemums come Christmas.'

Raising an eyebrow, she put her finger to her lips, swearing secrecy. 'Any Botox yet?' She smiled wryly, peering at my face, checking for signs of immobility.

'No,' I said slowly, 'but I've made a few changes, as you might've noticed.' I got up and gave her a twirl.

Her face hardened, 'Yoga's supposed to help you lose your ego, not pounds.'

'You can talk.'

She paused, as po-faced as P&P's Pigtails, and then she smiled. 'Just kidding, you look great, but please don't lose anymore. Some bodies aren't made to be tiny.'

Sense of humour failure re-occurred less than a minute later, this time in relation to my description of Yo-Jitsu.

'That's not proper yoga,' she said, repeating an earlier theme, polishing off the last of the curry.

'No one's saying it is'

'So why is it *Yo*-Jitsu? Doesn't that say *yo*ga?'

'It says it's something else – yoga fused with Ju-Jitsu. It's a progression, an evolution.'

'Yoga's been around thousands of years; it doesn't need to evolve.'

'But it does. Look at Nate.'

Becks gave me a long look that made me wonder why she ever claimed to fail at classroom discipline.

'I was going to talk to you about that,' she said, quietly.

'I know he's in trouble–'

'"In trouble?" That's like saying the Titanic was in trouble. I went to a workshop this afternoon and there were ten people there–'

'That doesn't sound too bad – it's a small–'

'Last time I went there were double that. You're killing him.'

I felt the familiar pang of guilt; our 'lifestyle rewards programme' had been Shine's most successful promotion, but what could I say? My first loyalty was to Max and he'd been delighted. In fact, he'd given me a small bonus, which I'd already spent in the shop; a large bag, as modelled by Zoffany, had spoken to me. Now, since our argument, it hung unseen in my wardrobe.

I suggested that perhaps he should do a promotion of his own.

'He can't discount like you,' she said, already cross. 'He has to pay his teachers the same, whether there are twenty people in the class or one.'

To my mind, that was a stupid system – at Shine we paid by the number of students. The best teachers could make several hundred pounds a class, the worst didn't last long. I'd thought about suggesting Nate try it our way but I knew how it would go; he'd get shirty, telling me it would 'infringe the principles of equality'. No thanks.

I explained that I felt bad for him but when I tried to help he didn't want to listen.

'We all know how hard it is to take advice when we're in the shit,' said Becks, giving me a meaningful look.

'And that's why I rose above his comments and gave him some especially good advice. I told him to do some research, understand his customers.'

'Apparently his customers want hot showers and pink sushi.'

'Has he done his Brand Vision work yet? That might help.'

She gave me a look that said she thought I was talking marketing bollocks. It was similar to the one I gave her when she talked yoga bollocks.

I tried another approach. 'Maybe he should do a local P.R. event; get out there, tell everyone that he offers something more personal. It might attract more of the right people.'

'There's no money for P.R. That's the point.'

'It doesn't need to cost a fortune – he could do a pop-up at Spitalfields. All those quirky little stalls alongside the smart cafes and designer shops – it's got just the right vibe. He could hand out leaflets, demonstrate his techniques on passers by – get people involved, talk it up on Facebook, invite the local radio station, the local press, take photos, tweet the thing.' I trailed off, uncomfortable in the shadows of those conflicting loyalties.

Becks backed off, seeming to understand, occupied once more with her thoughts. I changed the subject; if I'd given her an idea, I didn't want to know about it.

I'd given Nate a wide berth in the last few weeks; a mix of embarrassment and guilt, but I was in the habit of getting an early morning espresso from a place on Brick Lane that made it just the way I liked it – filthy strong, rich and thick – much better than the anodyne stuff they served in the Shine café. The place was really close to Nate and I decided, one morning, a week or so after Becks had come over, to pick one up for him.

It was seven in the morning and he was already opening his shutters, preparing for the first class of the day. It was funny to watch him. While the local newsagent at the top of the street yanked his shutters, impatient to start making money, Nate did his with the urgency of a snail, not wanting to wake his neighbours. Becks had told me that he was a member of The Slow Movement; an organisation that promoted a gentler pace of life – eating regional, seasonal food, letting children discover the world for themselves rather than so-called 'helicopter parenting', enjoying the journey – not rushing to the destination. She joked that if I'd joined they'd have to create a fast lane. I joked they were less a slow lane than a car park.

It happened just the way I planned it. We stood outside Ekatman, warming our hands on our polystyrene cups, having a little chat over our caffeine fix.

'It was your idea,' he told me, in response to my admiration of his freshly painted windows and shutters. 'You told me to get my students to help, and two days later it was done. So thank you, and I'm sorry.'

'For what?'

'For being so grumpy when you came over.'

'No problem,' I said, 'turns out you're human after all – quite a relief really.'

I was rewarded with one of his smiles. The one that was imprinted on my memory, replayed whenever I needed a lift. Suddenly, I was spilling the beans on my pop-up idea, justifying it on the grounds that I could draw a line – he was a friend, and work was work. Besides, Max was never going to find out.

Nate latched on to it immediately; smiled all over again. When to do it? Where to do it? Who to invite? It was brilliant seeing him so animated – it made all those years of marketing theory worthwhile.

'You know I can't be seen to help you, right?'

'This conversation never happened,' he replied, immediately segueing to plans for his birthday party. It was that Friday night, and he wanted me to come.

I had said yes, but now I was nervous. Becks couldn't make it (something to do with a late night staff meeting) and I was worried it was going to be stacked to the rafters with card-carrying hippies, so I delayed, finding plenty of reasons to stay late in the office.

I could see him from the top of his street. He was hanging off a lamppost with one hand, the other tracing uncertain circles in the night air. Bernard sat beneath him, his head cocked to one side, an eyebrow raised.

'Meg!' he announced, letting go of the lamppost and bearing down on me with open arms. 'Give me a birthday hug.'

I found myself in a headlock, breathing in alcohol fumes and feeling his heat. Wearing a t-shirt was a truly admirable feat; it was mild for November, but it could only have been a few degrees above freezing.

'Come and have some curry.'

'I've still got a few pounds to lose,' I said, patting my stomach, sounding like a complete killjoy.

'It's my mother's recipe,' he protested, 'she got it from our cook in Goa.'

I shook my head politely, pulling on the thick ruff of Bernard's neck as if the dog would restrain me; I didn't want to let myself down. I was meeting Jed at seven the next morning and he'd already warned me that I'd be doing a total detox – no more coffee or alcohol for six weeks. I didn't want to make it trickier by loading up on toxins the night before. But Nate wouldn't take no for an answer. He pushed me inside, stole a passing plate of deep fried appetisers and waved it under my nose. 'Just one samosa, geeeve it to Meg,' he sang, to the tune of *Just One Cornetto*.

I took a samosa to shut him up, nibbling a corner.

He stopped swaying and focused hard, 'Now, have some Chimney Fire.'

So that was how he was keeping warm.

Before I could say 'no' he'd grabbed my hand and dragged me to the makeshift bar, presenting me with a cracked mug of Amaretto, cider and cinnamon, and a huge slice of homemade chocolate cake slathered in icing.

I could feel my resolve softening and, as if having two hands full of temptation tipped the scales, I took a large bite of cake. It was all I could do to stop myself licking my hand. I let Bernard do that for me.

'And there was me thinking you yoga teachers are all about discipline and purity.'

He laughed and grabbed my hand, 'Come – I want to show you something,' he said, yanking me up the stairs – I'd never seen him move so fast.

He opened a tiny door at the top of a narrow staircase I hadn't noticed before. 'Who's up here? Anne Frank?' I asked, gently extricating myself from his clasp, wondering if drinking always made him demonstrative.

And then we were in a tiny garden, a garden on the roof of the world; fairy lights hanging from bare branches, colourful statuettes of Ganesh and Buddha taking the place of garden gnomes, railways sleepers marking out what looked like a vegetable patch.

'Carrots, lettuces, cabbages,' he said, reading my mind, 'and here,' now he was stroking what looked like a dead branch, 'there will be raspberries.'

'And that's Christ Church,' I said, clutching at the bleeding obvious – the white spire looked so much closer in the moonlight.

'You see,' he said, grabbing my hand again, stretching out my fingers, 'you can almost touch it.'

'And there's the minaret,' I said, pointing into the distance, shaking my hand free again, then wishing I hadn't – wishing I was less of a tight ass.

He motioned me towards a wooden bench and a brazier of still warm coals, and pulled a bottle of Amaretto from under the bench, along with a stack of plastic cups that had seen better days. Carefully, he wiped the edges with a cloth.

I took a therapeutic swig, trying to relax into being squashed to the seat edge – wondering whether the invasion of body space was also a consequence of his being pissed as a fart.

We sat in silence for a moment, looking out over the rooftops, at the old tiles and chimney pots thrown together at curious angles, at the glowing neon signs of the curry mile.

'Does Brick Lane remind you of India?' I asked, the Amaretto warming me up.

'Strictly speaking, it's Bangladeshi.'

'Oh,' I said, embarrassed – geography had never been my strong point.

'But,' he said, already topping up my drink, 'the smell is the same.'

'Is that why your mother came here?'

'For the bhajis? No, I think it had more to do with a guy at the Nazrul – we certainly got a lot of free dinners,' he laughed.

'You still miss her?'

'Every day – but I'm glad I came home.'

'Came home?'

'I was out in Byron Bay when she was first diagnosed with cancer. I'd gone out there in the mid nineties, planned to stay a few weeks, study with Jen Norman out in Suffolk Park, but I fell in love–'

'Let me guess – a redhead in a green dress?'

'Sorry?'

'Private joke. And so you stayed?'

'But then she took Sannyas.'

'Sannyas?'

'She became a Sannyasin – a follower of Osho.'

'Oh, Osho.' I knew all about him from Becks. 'He was the guy with all the Rolexes, and the Rolls Royce collection.'

'Yep – used to drive them up and down a specially made road – to give his followers a chance to experience, and overcome, their jealousy.'

'Generous guy.'

'Yeah, it was all very entertaining until Alice re-birthed as Asanga and started on about free love.'

I understood. Richard hadn't re-birthed, but it had amounted to the same thing.

'I could've gone back there after mum died – it's a great place to live – a beach for every day of the week, great markets, loads of yoga, but, believe it or not, you can get bored of perfect sunsets; and I wanted to do something with my life.'

'And now?'

'I still do.'

'Here?'

'I don't know any more,' he said, looking out at the spire. 'Everything is changing. Sometimes I think I should take off somewhere, go backpacking.'

'I think you should stick around,' I said, surprised at the strength of my reaction.

He returned to the bench, a half smile, mumbling that maybe it was time to go back to his roots.

'To India?'

'To Wales, where dad grew up. Open a residential yoga centre – help troubled kids – that kind of thing.'

'Maybe you could take in some of Becks' pupils,' I joked, trying to pull him out of a descending funk.

'Tell me, does Shine have plans to target the prison market? I'm thinking of going after druggies and ex-cons.'

I shook my head, 'We like our criminals successful and rich – the Costa del Sol will be our next move.'

He was smiling again. 'Why don't you do it with me?' he said. 'Be my business brains, my brand guru.'

Ignoring the little flutter in my stomach, I shook my head again, 'I'm flattered but I'm not sure I want to spend the rest of my life with ex-cons, besides I'm happier as an employee – I like to know I'm getting paid at the end of the month.'

'Money's over-rated' he said, twisting his quiff thoughtfully. 'Plus we'd be doing it together, and you'd love Snowdonia.'

I felt pretty much the same way about Snowdonia as I felt about the Himalaya and Machu Picchu. I wasn't going anywhere that required a backpack and I certainly wasn't going anywhere that separated me from London. I'd only just arrived. 'I'm sorry Nate,' I told him, serious now, 'I do Gherkins, not mountains.'

'And I hear you do dancing,' he said, offering me his arm.

'I was expecting *Om Namo Bhagavate!*' I shouted over *Club Tropicana*.

He grinned, performing an unsteady pirouette, taking a bow.

Perhaps it was the relief of being in a crowd, perhaps it was the Amaretto, but I finally relaxed. I had to really; dancing with him meant forgetting grown-up airs and graces. He danced with the abandonment of a five year old – pushing and pulling, twirling and jumping, performing a series of ever more adventurous moves until I had no choice but to join in, or have him risk serious injury. Together, we worked our way through the entire Chic back catalogue – *We Are Family*, *Good Times* and *Le Freak*, the Spice Girls' *Wannabe*, *La Isla Bonita*, and *West End Girls* plus, in a rare foray into the noughties and beyond, Outkast's *Hey Ya!*, *Crazy in Love* and, of course, *Happy* – for this Nate rolled up his trousers and donned a passing hat in imitation of Pharrell Williams. I threw myself into the maelstrom that was the dance floor, and all the time, despite the fact that we looked completely ridiculous, I couldn't stop laughing.

His hands on my shoulders, we headed back to the Chimney Fire for a refill, downed our glasses in one and, like refuelled kids eager for another round of Pass the Parcel, we rushed into a high energy rumba, our hips finding their rhythm in Corner Shop's *Brimful of Asha*, that is, until we were intercepted by a gang of flower-powered girls hell-bent on dragging the birthday boy into their circle.

I found myself beached at the bar with a dreadlocked eco-warrior called Carly. She was exactly the kind of person I'd been dreading but, wanting to please Nate, I determined to make the best of it.

Whilst I tracked his progress out of the corner of my eye, smiling at his thwarted attempts to return to my side, she described, in minute detail, her recent trip to Malaysia, where she'd been working on a story about the rape of local women by loggers. We'd mined the depths of that subject, and I'd agreed to share the story on my Facebook page, when she asked me where I worked.

Suddenly, she was looking at me as if I was a Malaysian logger. Thinking she must've had some sort of bad experience, I suggested she drop by. 'I'm sure we can put it right–'

'Do I look like a Shine sort of girl?'

I shook my head; her dreadlocks would be a first.

'If you think I'd do a class taught by you morons you've got another think coming. Meditation Mist? Valeted mats? This season's yoga pants? Yoga's not a frickin' beauty parade.'

'I know it's not for everyone, but we're bringing new people in, appealing to the stressed–'

She was furious now, her pale face ferocious. 'How can you stand here drinking Nate's drink, eating his cake, flirting with him, knowing he's going under, and it's all down to you?'

'I don't think that's fair,' I said, suddenly feeling hot. 'It's not personal, it's business.'

'You should take a good look in the mirror missy–'

'I've tried to help him – I've told him what to do–'

'Not that Brand Vision crap!'

'It's a very useful tool for working out–'

'Your arse from your elbow.'

'For working out what your brand stands for.'

'Well, we all thought it stood for "absolute bullshit".'

'"We"?'

'Yes, "we" – as in all of us.'

'Nate said that?'

'What is it you're not getting?'

'I thought he was interested … oh, never mind,' I said, watching him dance those same moves, now surrounded by a whole bunch of besotted hippy chicks. The moves that were hilarious a few minutes ago now looked plain old stupid; a tragic sight. I was tempted to get in there, have it out with him – maybe put some of those Yo-Jitsu moves into play, but there was no getting anywhere near him.

I picked up my bag, pushed my way out of the door and ran all the way home – gulping down the chill air, putting out the chimney fire. Standing shaking in my pristine kitchen, I made myself drink five pints of water – as if I could purify myself after all that crap. I couldn't believe Dreadlocks thought we'd been flirting. Seriously? I'd have said we were fooling around, behaving like a couple of kids. Anyway, even if we had been, it wouldn't be happening again. He might be a great cook and entertaining on the dance floor, he might have a great bum and strong arms, a heart-melting smile and a pretty decent chest, but he'd been having a good laugh behind my back. And to think I'd been willing to compromise myself for that loser. Never again. From now on, I'd keep my Brand Visions to myself.

'I haven't always been the god of couture'

CHAPTER SIXTEEN

I met Jed at the office as planned, early the next morning. Thankfully I'd managed to stave off most of the hangover with all that water, nothing that a double espresso couldn't cure. I'd followed up with some extra strong mints – Jed was pretty laidback about a lot of things but coffee wasn't one of them.

There, in the palm of his hand, was a white and gold box. 'Shine24' pledged to monitor my food, my mood, my sleep, my stress, my weight, my places – in short, my every waking move. I humoured him, giving the required squeal of delight, tearing off the cellophane, holding the gold bracelet up to the light, admiring the space age screen, trying, as he snapped it in place, to see it as something other than a prisoner's tagging device.

Then he asked me to follow him. I did – all the way to the top floor, to what I'd always thought was a broom cupboard. He punched in a code while I fiddled with the bracelet. Could it detect caffeine?

'And now Madam,' he said, 'I must kill you.'

There before me was a yoga mat.

'Shine360 meet Guinea Pig,' he said, in a loud whisper, 'Guinea Pig meet Shine360.'

He knelt down beside it, lovingly pointing to the hiding place of each sensor, explaining a team of MIT students had developed it. There followed talk of multiplexing and PCBs – words that didn't seem to mean a whole lot to Jed either but which impressed us both. Apparently the mat would know where my feet were and how my weight was distributed and would send instructions back to the bracelet to correct me, momentarily glowing (with happiness?) when I was in proper alignment.

'Cool huh?'

'Um, very' I said, already feeling anxious.

Then he pointed at an all-in-one white bodysuit on a coat hanger behind the door. Think *Catwoman*.

'And that's also for me?' I asked, wondering how on earth I was going to manage – it looked at least two sizes too small.

'Space-suit up baby' he said firmly, handing me the hanger. As I struggled into it he explained that the high-tech stretch-jersey contained so-called 'pharma-particles' that would react with my body heat to burn fat and boost collagen synthesis, sculpting my tum, bum, and thighs, and reducing cellulite.

Hooray.

Like the mat the suit had built-in sensors. They would exert gentle pressure, telling me where to focus more effort. They would also record my performance in real-time, measuring everything from the physical to the biochemical. All 'key performance indicators' would be sent back to the bracelet, which would create a bespoke, continuously evolving programme to shape and contour my body with 360 degree precision.

'It's a complete product eco-system' he said, now grinning from ear to ear.

'So, the 24 was just the first step?' I said, smiling at the thought that Ashley's midnight Instagram blitz, a million uploads of her bracelet, was already yesterday's news.

'There'll be yearly upgrades. We're already planning the 360DNA – which will tailor the programme to your genetic profile.'

'How wonderful,' I said, knowing no double helix of mine would make the genome look book.

He mistook my sarcasm for disappointment. 'Meg, this 360 can take you way beyond right now. You'll get a download after each session detailing your every move,' he said, 'and it'll tell you how to max your results.'

'More fish maw?'

'Diet is key,' he said, tapping the mat firmly, as if to say 'heel'. I assumed the position.

'But don't worry, no more boring old food diary. It'll thermodynamically record both your calorie consumption and expenditure.' He tapped several buttons on his bracelet screen. It was significantly bigger than mine, reminding me of Bridge Command aboard the Starship Enterprise.

My bracelet flashed in response. 'Level *Three* Yo-Jitsu?'

'It's short,' he said, reaching over to press play.

'More pressure through the heel' said the on-screen Jed as the area beneath my heel gave a red glow in the shape of a lotus flower. I pressed down. The bracelet gave my wrist a gentle congratulatory squeeze while the mat rewarded me with a green glow.

'Strengthen your core' commanded Jed's on-screen doppelganger, my bodysuit exerting gentle pressure on my navel.

'Kick higher,' said Jed, just before my bracelet echoed with the same thing.

Ten minutes in, my vest was so soaked I thought I might short-circuit.

'Did you know Meg', he said, taking in the sight as if appreciating a work of art, 'you're standing on a miracle?'

'Let's hope it works them' I said, through gritted teeth.

'Honey' he said, looking very pleased with himself, 'all you have to do is follow the programme and the algorithms will do the rest. Just remember, no cutting class – not if you want to rock the red carpet in nothing but Swarovski crystals.'

'Not sure I'm ever going to rock Rihanna,' I gasped, signalling for a towel.

'I don't know' he said, playfully checking out my bum.

'What did *Grazia* call it? The "couture body" trend?'

'They were quoting' he said, watching me turn a delicate shade of puce. 'It was Veronique Hyland at *New York Magazine*.'

'So this broom cupboard is your atelier?'

'Exactly' he said, striking a Karl Lagerfeld style pose, elbows crossed. 'Though I'm keeping it humble; I haven't always been the god of couture.'

Although I was now too puffed to speak, I managed to move my eyebrows, in an approximation of surprise and, I hoped, encouragement. Anything to take my mind off what was happening to my body.

He told me that his ma, an aspiring folk musician, made clothes for her neighbours, claiming that Joni Mitchell wrote about a vintage coat of hers in her song *Ladies of the Canyon*. His pa scraped a living designing album covers for bands that never quite made it. 'Most nights they'd be partying back at our house – they'd give me a tambourine to beat it out. I'd fall asleep to the sound of Joni and the smell of dope.'

At that point, I forgave him his taste in seventies rock legends – at least he'd been there, sitting on the steps of the Canyon Country Store cadging cookies off Jackson Browne and Don Henley, or sneaking a peak at David Bowie loading up with Cadbury Flakes and HP Sauce in the aisle marked by a Union Jack. All Nate could do was wear the t-shirt.

He checked my heart rate on his screen and moved on to tales of yoga groupies, sell-out world tours, and life aboard ship. We're not talking *The Love Boat* here – we're talking fifty million dollar yachts. When he was in his twenties, long before he met Max, he'd spend the whole summer at sea – a month in the Caribbean, then the Greek islands, finishing off in the Andaman's.

'There's a certain breed of rich woman for whom a yoga teacher is as essential as this season's bikini,' he chuckled.

I motioned for a second towel.

'Man it was boring,' he exclaimed, slumping against the wall in a mock stupor. 'The biggest challenge was filling the hours without doing their daughters.'

I wiggled my eyebrows.

'Let's just say I'm now both a professional sushi chef and a master cocktail maker,' he said, grinning. 'Though I did get married once. Not my greatest move, but I was young and she was beautiful.'

I yawned, mimicking boredom.

'She turned out to be a loony tune. No amount of positive thinking could make it right. She got the Aspen ski lodge and I kept the beach house.'

'Beach?' I managed.

'Paradise Cove, Malibu. It's kinda a trailer park,' he said, holding my wrist like a doctor taking a pulse, adjusting some settings on my screen. 'Minnie Driver, Pamela Anderson, girls like that.'

Ignoring on-screen Jed's instructions for a moment I did my best impersonation of a *Baywatch* run.

'Aw shucks I hardly noticed,' he said winking, 'I prefer surfing and shit – hanging with Matt McConaughey and–'

'Matthew McConaughey?' I spluttered, wondering if I might be about to have a heart attack.

'Never seen him with his shirt on. Not unless a bunch of us are giving the paps a beat-down. But most of the time, yeah, it's pretty chilled – we're over at Minnie's for Boxing Day brunch, or my place for yard yoga, and the rest of the time we're in the ocean – stealing each other's wave.'

'Sounds brilliant. What are you doing here?'

'Getting you to a point we can leave you in charge.'

I managed another laugh, as best I could with no air left in my lungs.

'You think I'm joking?'

I had such a bad stitch, it was a minute before I could look him in the eye. I was expecting to see him smiling but he was studying me carefully, dead serious.

'Why not?' he said, casual as you like. 'You've got the talent.'

I stood there, smiling stupidly. 'I'm sorry Jed,' I said, wiping myself down, still bright red in the face. 'I don't believe in fairy tales.'

'Honey,' he said, handing me yet another towel, 'I think Max will give it another three years, five max. He'll probably do an IPO, or maybe one of his private equity friends will pick it up. There's a lot of ground between here and there, but just keep your head down, keep doing what you're doing, and know that it can happen.'

My mat lit up with flashing green lotus flowers. Game over.

'Work your body and the rest will follow. Max knows that, and I think you know that too. Meanwhile stay off the double espressos.'

'He's not an option'

Turning off the Kings Road, into Radnor Street, I had to check the address. In place of the anticipated glass cube was a pastel pink townhouse. I knocked uncertainly on the pale grey front door and stood well back, expecting to be turned away by a cross old lady, wondering why she was being disturbed on a Sunday morning. But there was Zoffany, in a floral tea dress and cardigan, all smiles.

She'd been away since the Elements debacle, attending a design expo in Miami – probably scouring for more ideas she could copy. She'd been in touch several times – asking how the detox was going, whether I needed any help with the '(m)ad house' as she'd christened our in-house ad agency. I'd kept my responses short.

She took my coat and led me to the drawing room. Still looking for the glass walls and Tibetan tree bark (perhaps the pink exterior was just a facade), I was glad of a chance to recalibrate. I looked about while she busied herself in the kitchen. Hand painted parakeet wallpaper took the place of Shine's pared down plaster walls, thick Persian rugs replaced the pebble and limestone floors, the sculptural organics had been displaced by antique clocks and elegant china. There were books piled everywhere – vast coffee table hardbacks on the Palais de Versailles, Scottish castles, the

English country house. Suddenly, the white floor cushion moved, morphing into a cat. I tried to stroke it but it just stretched and made its way out of the French windows into the garden.

It might've been the last week in November but it was easy to imagine it at the height of summer; sitting on the Lutyens bench beneath the rose arbour, listening to the small fountain bubbling away, admiring the hollyhocks and delphiniums, honeysuckle coating the air. It reminded me of my grandmother – not in the physical details, she'd lived in the same end of terrace house all her life, working in Darwen's cotton mills and holidaying in Blackpool, but in the grace that filled it.

Zoffany came out with some fresh mint tea, explaining that her mother had lived in the house for years and she'd moved in to care for her in the final stages of her illness. 'It's funny – when she was alive she was always pushing me away; now she's dead we're so much closer. Not changing anything keeps her here, where she belongs.' I smiled politely and concentrated on sipping my tea, knowing that, for me, living amongst my dead mother's china would feed my loneliness as surely as ash feeds roses.

Seeing me shiver she motioned us back inside. She settled into the oldest armchair, I sat on the other side of the fireplace. 'I'm really sorry Meg,' she began, sitting forward, a picture of earnest intent. 'I knew I'd done the wrong thing the moment I left.'

'So why did you do it?' I asked, trying to adopt a measured tone.

For a minute I thought she was going to do another one of her disappearing acts but she managed to pull herself back. 'You have every right to be angry,' she said, purposefully looking me in the eye. 'I'm so very sorry.'

'So why not come clean?'

'But I would lose my job,' she said, retreating into her chair.

'I think that's unlikely' I said, unable to keep the irritation out of my voice, 'since you created the whole Shine thing. Or was Tibetan tree bark someone else's idea too?'

'Max,' she said dramatically, her eyes reddening, 'was talking to other designers. I found out and I panicked. I had to do something. I couldn't bear–'

'Okay Zoffany,' I said cutting her off, determined not to waste any more of my life listening to her shit. 'We won't tell Max.'

'Oh, that's brilliant Meg – thank you so much. You are a star, ma belle–'

But I hadn't finished. 'So here's the deal. Whenever we see him we're going to be joined at the hip – his "dream team" – but behind the scenes, it's going to be a different story. *I'm* going to be running the show.' It was my turn to look her solidly in the eye. 'Agreed?'

'But what if I come up with an idea?' she said, putting down her cup and saucer with a rattle. 'Do I have to run everything by you first?'

'We wouldn't be having this conversation if you were the one coming up with ideas.'

'Fair enough,' she said, bridling a little.

'Of course if you do come up with one … well, at least you know you can trust me to say it's yours.' I picked up my bag; it might've been Sunday but I was keen to get back to the office, and to get a session in on the 360 – the bracelet was already vibrating, giving me the thirty minute warning.

She touched my arm, gently. 'Can I show you something before you leave? Do you have just a little time?'

'Okay,' I said, putting my bag down heavily.

She beckoned for me to follow her across the hallway. 'Shut your eyes,' she said, standing with her back to a set of double doors.

A clicking sound. A sudden breeze.

'Open them now.'

There before me, on an elegant dining table, was a stack of boxes covered in Chinese characters. Zoffany ceremoniously held out a knife and I took it, scouring along the tape and reaching in. I pulled out one, then another, and another, throwing them in the air, and then she was doing the same – until finally all the boxes were empty, the clothes covering the table like a luxurious patchwork quilt. The harem pants embroidered with golden chrysanthemums. The silk-chiffon boat-necked top with the vermillion ribbons. The bat-wings with the blue hummingbirds.

'Jed?' she asked, smiling as she held up the palest of yellow tunic tops, man-sized azure tassels matched by dragons breathing flames up each sleeve.

'Very,' I said, laughing, feeling light-headed with the buzz of success, ignoring the bracelet's tap tap – warning that I was due to start my practice.

We'd already agreed with Max, on a three-way email, that we would use the so-called 'Transformation' shoot to showcase Elements. I'd hoped it would have a launch of its own; an ad campaign shot in the mountains of the Far East, featuring smiling women from Threads of Hope. But we were where we were with the factory, the location of which was the Chinese equivalent of Swindon, and Max had once more pointed out that budgets were not unlimited. As I thought I could sense Zoffany goal-hanging, waiting to kick the ball into the back of the net with a 'we need to do what works Meg,' I'd got in there first, talking up the need for pragmatism, entrepreneurial spirit, and a studio shoot in the wilds of the East End.

'I'm going to need my in-house model for this,' she said, wheeling in a rail with the complete Studio-Ready collection, following up with a pile of shoe and accessory boxes from some very serious designer labels, and a state-of-the-art camera and tripod.

As Zoffany moved up and down the rail, pulling out pieces like Meryl Streep's character in *The Devil Wears Prada*, I dedicated myself to sashaying up and down her dining room, striking poses in the name of Wood, Fire, and Metal, as Madonna blared from the sound system – *Vogue, 4 Minutes, Give It 2 Me*. As I strutted my stuff, Zoffany clicked away, doing her best impression of Jorell Jones – the Cockney fashion photographer who'd be shooting the campaign. 'Nice!' 'Gorgeous!' 'Lovely!' 'You look *amazing*!' East End meets Left Bank.

By the end of the morning we had two out of three looks nailed. Shonda, the model-turned-cupcake-maker would be Fire; going back to the fifties in our Studio Wear three quarter length pants, a pair of sky-high Louboutins (that Zoffany and I were both circling), and the pink peony version of the boat-necked top with the cinched-in waist. Photographed with her cupcakes, all that pastel-coloured icing would be the perfect clash-match for the vermillion ribbons. Bob, who was becoming more famous by the day for his sixties inspired optical art, would be Metal in a black Tom Ford beret, Studio Wear black shorts, and the manned-up version of the tunic – slate grey with a white tiger print and big black tassels. Rope upon rope of vintage silver beads (an heirloom from Zoffany's mother) would complete the picture.

That left Kate, the City-girl-turned-milliner who would be Water. Zoffany spent a long time consulting her stash, eventually handing me, with evident reluctance, the floor length dress. It may have been beautiful, the palest grey-blue cashmere, woven with snow-capped mountains made of lace, but it had always been a dress with her name on it. And anyway, all that clingy wool had me reaching for my coat. I took up the camera and Zoffany, who said the dress reminded her of Stevie Nicks and would look perfect with Kate's signature top hat, did a homage to the 1976 *Rumours* album, arms back, left leg raised, toe pointed, dancing around a tall grandfather clock which we agreed made an excellent Mick Fleetwood substitute.

I looked at the photos over her shoulder as she uploaded them into an email to the production company. All of a sudden

I realised that my legs were looking longer, my torso more toned, my bum more lifted. I asked her to copy me in.

'Yes boss,' she said, tapping away at some very detailed editorial comments. I wondered if this level of Ashley-grade preparation had anything to do with Jorell. She'd spent the pre-production meeting playing the part of famous designer to perfection, taking the art of flirting by videoconference to a new high, but despite her efforts, I wasn't sure his door was open. He gave her plenty of charm, agreeing with pretty much everything she said. But would a fun-loving thirty-year-old (the loose limbs, the inability to sit still reminded me of Will Smith) find a much older woman attractive – even if she was Zoffany de Gournay?

Prior to Chrysanthemum-Gate, I would have asked her for more information – did she genuinely like Jorell, or was this just about making Max jealous? I could imagine the response. 'It never hurts to remind a man what he's missing,' she'd say, stretching like her cat.

Instead, I found myself on the end of a question about my love life. 'What about that guy Nate?' she ventured, pressing a gin and tonic on me. Just the one, I thought, trying to avoid the question, talking instead about my run in with Carly the eco-warrior at his drunken birthday party, and how I took off shortly after she called us Shine people 'morons'.

I expected her to be as incensed as I was but she just laughed. 'I suppose we do take ourselves a bit seriously. By the way, I think I saw him the other day, drawing the shutters of Ekmathingy...'

'Ekatman.'

'That's it – I always forget.'

'How did he look?' I asked, still not wanting to indulge in any girly chat, but loosened by the gin.

'If I've got the right guy, he looked pretty good,' she said giggling, giving me a knowing look. 'Unkempt but cute? Dark hair and broad shoulders? Vintage Stills and Nash t-shirt?'

'That's him. That's his favourite; he wears it all the time.'

She burst out laughing, waggling her finger at me. 'You *do* like him!'

It was my turn to bristle. 'How can I like someone who badmouths everything I stand for? He might be cute but he's not an option.'

'If you say so.'

I ignored the continuing smile; she could think what she liked. I was clear; I was finally on course for the top and no one was going to get in my way – least of all a failing yoga teacher who laughed at me behind my back.

She offered me lunch, thankfully not double boiled mushrooms with fish maw and cabbage, but a very light salad. The gin had made me hungry so I accepted, feeling pretty pleased with the fact that I was limiting myself to one helping, until I witnessed just one lettuce leaf brush Zoffany's lips and fall back to her plate. How did her body manage? Did she get her daily vitamins from the lemon in her gin? Then she looked at her watch, suddenly announcing that I was to take her hair appointment at the Albermarle Street salon. Her treat. Turning her down would be the definition of cutting off my nose to spite my face so I punched a few buttons on the bracelet screen. The broom cupboard could wait.

The salon was everything you'd expect – white walls, white floors, huge bowls of lilies, several private consulting rooms and a lot of Botox – receptionists and clients. I settled into a vast white leather chair and took a moment to bathe in the soft lighting – which, lets face it, would make anyone look good – even the old guy with the Pekinese and pink jumper sitting next to me.

I wasn't at all sure what I wanted but that was okay, Clive did. A stack of foils and several glasses of champagne later, two inches of frayed and fried ends lay on the cutting room floor. I was the proud owner of what he joked would be known as 'The

Meg'. Just off the shoulders, longer at the front, white blonde highlights round my face, honey, caramel and gold graduating through the back, my frizzy corkscrew curls had been tamed into gentle beachy waves.

'The Queen of California,' said Zoffany approvingly, spinning me in my chair.

'"New and improved",' I said, hardly recognising myself.

'I wanted to be with you'

It was pouring with rain, there were no taxis and I was already half an hour late for the shoot. So, when Nate happened to pass by on his trusty Enfield, I flagged him down.

'Jump on,' he said, reaching for his spare helmet. 'I'm really sorry to spoil your new hair.'

I'd always been scared of motorbikes. Remembering his father had died coming off one didn't help but I took the helmet, hitched my skirt up, and climbed aboard.

I soaked up his safety instructions as if my life depended on it but, as we whizzed past the green canopies of Verde & Company, my head pressed against his leather jacket, my knees gripping his thighs, I was surprised at how secure I felt. Relaxed, almost.

We moved at quite a clip, whooshing under the white iron railway bridge that, to me, is Checkpoint Charlie; the border between the towering steel and glass of the City and the East End. Then we were shooting past sari shops, building merchants, fried chicken bars, open all hours supermarkets, massage parlours and ice cream parlours and, in less than ten minutes, we were there.

I directed him under the steel arch and we passed into a cobblestone courtyard framed by Victorian buildings – a labyrinth of studios, workshops and galleries collectively known as Perseverance Works.

Taking my helmet off, hearing my name, I looked up. Jorell, the photographer, was beckoning to me from a balcony. Gone was the fun-loving, cheeky-chappy; he was impatient, gesturing with urgency.

The shoot should have been well under way; starting with Shonda surrounded by her specialty – cupcakes iced in designer logos – blue with a white bow for Tiffany, pastel-coloured crystals for Swarovski, and white with a gold lotus flower for Shine.

I jumped off the bike and handed Nate his helmet, thanking him profusely and promising I'd pop by later in the week, wondering how I was going to navigate the course between fresh gratitude and pent-up hostility.

He passed me my bags and I picked my way across the cobbles and up a spiral staircase, acutely conscious that he was watching me. The wrought iron steps were the crafted, patterned kind and my heel got stuck in one of the holes. As I struggled to free it, my bags fell from my shoulders. Nate bounded up the stairs two at a time. He took the bags and fell in behind me – making a joke about 'the great view'. At least we had a mutual appreciation of each other's bum.

I saw that a crowd had gathered at the far end of the loft, circled round the kitchen counter in silence. Kicking off my shoes, I ran across the room.

Nate followed at a slower pace.

The crowd parted like curtains, bringing me face to face with a crime scene. There, on the Formica counter, alongside the fifties style Coca Cola straw holders and pair of waffle irons, was the villain of the piece. A huge pile of cupcakes. Icing seeped over the edges like a Salvador Dali clock. Time standing still.

I thought back to the pre-production meeting. I'd been so absorbed by Jorell's portfolio – the trademark blurry and over-exposed pictures of biker chicks eating fish and chips on the pier, the bowler-hatted supermodels striding through the forest, the film stars cavorting in the pool at the Château Marmont, that I'd forgotten to ask if he'd ever worked with melting substances before. I'd sent a note with the contract the next day telling them to use HMI or Flash, not Tungsten Red Heads, and to book a huge refrigerator and a million fans. 'You got my note, right?'

The production team shook its head, as one.

I took a deep breath and gathered myself, 'Where's Shonda?'

'Locked in the bathroom crying,' said Jorell. 'Zoffany's trying to talk her out.'

'I'll help,' said Nate quietly, over my shoulder. In my panic, I'd forgotten he was there. He came forward to the table and calmly wrote out a list of ingredients. I read to the runner from the list, instructing him to go to the supermarket up the road for utensils, fondant icing sheets, apricot jam, butter, eggs and sugar. I stopped short at 'edible gold leaf and food dye – vermillion, magenta, etc.' I looked at Nate. 'I'm not sure he's going to find that in Sainsbury's.'

'Any Asian supermarket,' he said, 'if they haven't got any out front, they'll have it out back – Diwali's just finished.'

Giving me an encouraging wink he pretended to don surgical gloves, carefully slicing the icing off the first cupcake.

Instinctively, I went to his side, and together we worked as if in an operating room – him the world-class brain surgeon, me the intern – handing him implements.

'Knife please, Meg,' he'd say, holding out his hand expectantly.
'Tweezers please, Meg.'

The drenched-with-sweat runner returned with bags full of supplies just as we finished dissecting the last cupcake. And then:

'Rolling pin.'

'Piping bag.'

'Nozzle.'

'Crystals.'

His hands were steady, the biting of his lower lip the only

sign of strain. I noticed how he didn't feel the need to speak, how I didn't feel the need to speak – after I'd finished cursing myself. I was certain I'd written the note and stuck it on the signed contract, giving it to one of the business concierge team to bike to Jorell. Had it fallen off? Had it been left in the envelope? Either way, I had to take the blame. I should've followed it up with an email, or a call, or both.

There was a glow about Nate as he worked; a sweetness, a harmony that was as soothing as a piece of music, as if everything came from his centre and returned to his centre. By the time he'd placed the white ribbon on the Tiffany blue icing, I too had moved back to my centre, fluttering less, settling more – quite an achievement, considering.

And then we were done and I was almost sorry.

He gathered up his bag and his helmet, his movements still slow, but deliberate and efficient.

I followed him down the spiral staircase, taking care not to slip on the steps. It was still drizzling.

'Thank you Nate,' I said. 'You truly saved the day.'

He said nothing, simply touching his hand to his heart.

I asked if I could pay him for his time.

He looked horrified and refused point blank. 'Just help me with my Brand Vision,' he said, getting on his bike.

'Let's just forget it,' I snapped.

'What's wrong?'

'Oh, cut the innocent crap. Carly told me what you said – that I'd been talking "brand bollocks", that you'd all had a really good laugh, at my expense.'

'Meg,' he said, gripping my arms so hard they hurt, 'I might not have agreed with everything you said but I never described it as "brand bollocks" and I would never ever laugh at you. Do you understand?'

I shook myself free. 'So why would Carly say you did?'

A dark shadow of realization passed across his face. 'Is that why you left the party without saying "goodbye"? Is that why I haven't seen you in a month?'

I shrugged, staring at the gate.

'She doesn't speak for me, you have to know that. She got the wrong idea about me, got a bit confused.'

I carried on staring at the gate, blushing at the error of my ways. 'Well, looks like I got a bit confused too,' I managed, sounding a little hoarse, forcing myself to look him in the eye.

He was looking at me intently. 'It's my fault. I shouldn't have left you alone with her. I got caught up with … I was trying … I wanted to be with you…'

'You had your people,' I said, embarrassed, not sure where I wanted this to go. 'It was your birthday.'

He took a breath, seeming to start something, then he trailed off again. He shuffled his feet, managing an awkward smile. 'Anyway…'

'Anyway,' I echoed.

There was a silence, and then we both started talking at once. I was going on about the rest of the shoot, not really sure why, and he was on about my P.R. idea. He was doing it and he wanted to talk it through.

I agreed, happily, part of me wishing I could take off with him, leave them to it.

'Please come over,' he said, putting on his helmet. 'Not just to talk P.R. I want to make this right. I'll do some food, perhaps not cupcakes…' And there it was, that smile. 'Any time you like, but let's do it soon. I've missed our little chats. Actually,' he said, wiping a smear of icing from my nose, 'I've missed you.'

And with that he was gone.

I stood rubbing my nose as I watched him pass through the gates, turning right onto the Hackney Road. I wanted to run after him, to make it right, right there and then, but there was no time to dwell, only time to clear up and get back on task. We were seriously behind schedule.

By the time I'd climbed back up the stairs, the shoot was in full swing and Shonda was doing what she did best; looking like a cover girl. She wore the silk chiffon boat-necked top and Studio Wear three quarter pants with great aplomb – in combination with her curled out hair and cinched-in waist she was a gorgeous parody of the fifties housewife.

'Are you ladies ready for some adventure?' asked Jed, shaking off his coat, jogging across the room.

I was very clear on that point. 'I think we've had enough for one morning—'

'I'm thinking of a balancing pose,' he said, ignoring me, cranking up the music (Bill Haley's *Rock Around the Clock*). 'Darlin',' he said, addressing himself to Shonda, 'do me a Tree.'

Shonda jumped off the Formica counter and struck the pose, standing on one leg, stretching her palms overhead, pressing them together into prayer position.

It was time to step in. 'Aren't you forgetting something Jed?'

'What's that?' Lord love him, he looked totally blank.

'The cupcakes?'

He giggled good-naturedly. 'Oops.'

There was no way of incorporating the cupcakes into the pose, so Jed arranged her on the work surface in Lotus Pose, her Louboutins resting on her thighs, the red soles matching the Formica and the ribbons. She stretched out her palms, Indian Goddess style, and I plopped a cupcake on each of them.

'Good girl,' I said, winking at her, arranging a few more beside her so that more of Nate's handiwork could be seen.

Bob might've had a great looking body and be in full artistic flow but, like Max, he struggled with flexibility. Jed kept it simple. He arranged him in a gentle seated twist, a guitar and sheet music by his side, looking back at a half-finished canvas – a pose that showed off his strong jaw line, the turn of his torso, his muscular back and arms and, of course, the slate grey tunic, complete with tassels and beads. There was no need to gild the lily. Snap, snap, snap and Bob was done.

As Zoffany didn't do food she filled her lunch break teaching Jorell some yoga.

'Let's do Natarajasana,' she said, pulling him off his chair as excitable as a kid on a sugar-high, garlanding him with the beads and slapping the Tom Ford beret on his head. 'You can be Bob.'

She positioned him the correct distance from the canvas, stretching his right arm in front of him, handing him the paintbrush, helping him stand on one leg, bending the other leg at the knee, introducing his free hand to his big toe, but he managed only a couple of strokes before losing his balance and crashing to the floor.

She helped him get up (looking like she'd rather join him on the floor) and tried again, this time attempting to get him into Tree Pose.

There was palpable relief on his face when the doorbell rang.

Zoffany clutched my arm.

I followed her gaze.

Kate, the City-girl-turned-milliner, had arrived.

The weight problem was back.

'Just a minute,' said Zoffany, disappearing out the door in a flash of red.

She returned a full hour later – a velvet riding jacket draped carefully over one arm, a Peter Jones bag in her hand.

'Follow me,' she said, sweeping into the dressing room.

'Everything off,' she said, addressing Kate. 'Except your bra and knickers.'

'Now get down there,' she said, motioning for me to get on my hands and knees. Opening the bag she passed me a pair of extra-strength, full-length Spanks.

I held them in position.

'Step in' she ordered Kate, offering her a shoulder.

'And roll' she said to me, gesturing several yanking movements.

Oh, the glamour of it all.

Kate didn't seem to care. She chatted happily on, even when my head was less than an inch from her knickers. She was bigger than I'd been when I joined Shine and yet she seemed to be revelling in the absurdity of it all – totally unselfconscious.

Zoffany manhandled the dress over Kate's head and pushed up her boobs with a distinct lack of ceremony. The result was still so much tighter than intended, but at least the lines were smooth and the riding jacket covered all the right bits.

Finally, Zoffany pinned in place the top hat, which could easily pass for an old-school riding hat – especially when she added the black veil and scarf she'd also retrieved from her mother's wardrobe. I wished they could talk; they must've seen some action in the hands of 'la maîtresse professionnelle.'

At this point Jorell knocked and, without waiting for an answer, walked in. 'Who looks a billion bucks?' he asked, grinning from ear to ear.

'I do,' said Kate, launching herself into his arms. For a terrible moment, I thought he was going to drop her, but he righted himself just in time, turning the stumble into a twirl that had them both in hysterics.

'Let's do this thing,' said Zoffany, spitting a hairpin into the sink.

We trooped down the spiral staircase and, right on cue, the sun broke through the rain clouds. Jorell shot Kate on the still wet cobbles, cycling past the artists' studios in the riding jacket, her veil and scarf blustering in the breeze. It was a modern take on an old scene – of riding to hounds, the studio's shaggy dog running alongside her. Amazingly, given our luck that day, it behaved itself – running backwards and forwards on cue, encouraged by the biscuits Kate trailed from her long sleeves. I noticed that she saved a few for herself.

Of course, it was the chemistry between Kate and Jorell that made those pictures. The best was the one of her standing up on the pedals, one hand on the handlebar, the other pointing towards Jorell as if she couldn't wait to get where she was going. The look on her face was one of unbridled joy, but it reminded me of the mirror image on Zoffany's face. I told Jorell we had to use the other one – Kate on the bike, feet off the pedals, hands in prayer position. 'It's *Shine,*' I said, by way of explanation. 'It has to have a yoga theme.'

Zoffany had planned to spend the wrap party in Jorell's arms. She'd chosen to hold it at Shoreditch House, not in the cosy sitting room where we'd had that drink back in October, but in the bar. I loved the New York style warehouse windows, the copper-wrapped counter-top and the turquoise leather sofa, which had witnessed many of her finer moments. Like the night she ended up with a seventies rock star, only to make the untimely discovery he had a nineteen year old at home – and she wasn't his daughter.

She put on a good show, emerging from the dressing room as Frida Kahlo, her hair put up in braids, woven with flowers, working a long pink skirt and Lariat necklace nestled in a plunging neckline, her trademark smoky make-up a useful disguise for those puffy eyes. I followed in one of her cast-offs – a gypsy style dress whose many folds covered up the fact that we were still two different sizes.

We plied everyone with drinks, including ourselves, congratulating the photographic team on a job well done, everyone speaking a little too loudly. I think we were all trying to ignore the ravishing Jorell was giving Kate at the bar.

Ashley chose that moment to make her entrance – her face

freshly primed, her Catwalk Caterpillar in tow. They wore matching micro minis and towering heels, all the better to survey the scene – Ashley's were a little higher, presumably so she'd be first to spot the best looking, richest guy in the room.

She spent a few minutes with Jorell, admiring the pictures on his laptop and then, to my surprise, she made her way over and congratulated me.

'Thank you,' I said. 'Didn't think I'd screw up did you?'

'I thought you might've been a little out of your depth,' she replied, pleasantly.

'This isn't amateur night Ashley.'

'I heard there were some initial problems.'

'Which we fixed,' I said firmly.

'Looks like I underestimated you,' was all she'd said, turning on those heels, her Caterpillar tucking in behind.

Watching her work the room, her vapid features arranged in a placid smile, her hair held in a top-knot by a small bow, her pin-head swivelling as if automated, she looked more show poodle than doe, but she was a show poodle with teeth – what was she up to? I found Zoffany, hoping to discuss, but she wasn't in the zone. Jorell and Kate had moved from the bar to a quiet corner, squishing up on an old leather chair that, though large, was clearly meant for one.

'How can he prefer her to me?' she asked, more than once, blinking in disbelief.

Because she's happy?

Because she's ten years younger?

Because she hasn't got 'DESPERATE' stamped on her forehead?

I said none of these things. I poured her another drink and pointed her in the direction of Jorell's First Assistant, who'd been giving her the eye all day.

I circulated for a while, making sure everyone (especially me) had plenty to drink, but my thoughts soon turned to Nate.

Everyone had asked me where he was – 'the guy who saved the day'. Of course, I wanted to invite him to the party but, knowing Ashley would be putting in an appearance, I couldn't risk her finding out who he was. She'd tell Max in a heartbeat. But now I was standing alone at the bar, nursing my fourth solitary glass, I found myself needing to thank him again, in person, that night.

'I thought you might like some champagne,' I said, leaning against the doorframe, waving a jeroboam at him.

'How thoughtful,' he said, taking the bottle and motioning me inside, running his hand through his hair, checking in with his quiff as if it would tell him what to think.

'You're in pyjamas,' I said, throwing myself on the sofa, dislodging Bernard. 'You look cute.'

'Marks and Spencer's own,' he said, taking a turn.

'I like Marks and Spencer's,' I said, watching him prise the cork, surprised at his expertise. 'Nearly took a job there, did I tell you that?'

'Once or twice,' he said, handing me a glass – not quite as full as I would've liked.

'Didn't like their knickers though.' I looked at him through hazy eyes, taking a large gulp.

'On so little the world turns,' he said, thoughtfully pointing his fingers under his chin; Yoda.

'Just think Nate,' I said, pushing his untouched glass towards him, 'if I'd taken that job I might've been really happy and I might never have gone to Shine, and then … I might never have got to know you.'

He looked towards his DVD collection. '*Sliding Doors*; Gwyneth–'

'Let me guess. Nineteen eighty two or three?' It had to be – all his rom coms were from the early eighties.

'Nineteen ninety eight actually; Gwyneth Paltrow as Helen Quilley – gets fired, takes a tube and–'

'It's a bit like us isn't it?' I said, extending my arm along the back of the sofa – seductively?

'Like us? How's that?'

'If your dad hadn't died, your mum wouldn't have come back here and you wouldn't have met me.'

'Very true,' he said. 'All paths have led us to this moment.'

We were going to be reading from *Yogic Thoughts for the Day* if I waited any longer. 'Yoda,' I said, pouring myself some more champagne, 'I need some fun.'

'Pray,' he said, putting on his best wise face, pulling on his ears, 'how may I be of service?'

I gave him my best, most alluring look, narrowing my eyes and pouting slightly.

He got up decisively, picking up his bike keys. 'Let's go see the Thames Barrier – have you ever seen it at night? It's really beautiful–'

'No Nate,' I cut in, wondering why this wasn't going to plan. 'I definitely don't want to see the Thames Barrier – and besides, as I have already observed, you're wearing pyjamas.'

'And your point is?'

'Nate,' I said, attempting to look him in the eye, my vision blurring. 'My point is, I want some *fun.*'

'"Fun"?' he said, bemused.

'*Fun.* The kind of *fun* that comes with no strings attached.'

'Ah,' he said, looking nervous, at last reaching for his champagne glass, 'so this is a booty call.'

'Might be, if you want it to be,' I hitched up one of my gypsy skirts, attempting another coquettish pout.

'I prefer my women to remember my name in the morning.'

'How very old fashioned.'

'That's me,' he said, holding up his hands in a gesture of mock surrender, 'just call me Tom.'

'"Tom"?' I really wasn't getting him tonight.

'Tom Hanks.'

'Oh.' Still not getting it; he was much more fun when he was drunk.

'As in Meg Ryan, as in rom coms, as in "old fashioned".'

I took another gulp of champagne, thinking maybe I should just jump him, and then the room started to spin.

'I think I need the–' I said, my hand over my mouth, lunging instead for the bathroom.

'You're worth it'

'Vindication at last,' said Max, pulling the letter from his jacket pocket, waving it triumphantly. 'Those Boca Raton yogis are dead and buried; barred from teaching any Shine sequence and barred from selling our merchandise – they can't profit in any way from our name, and if they come with fifty metres I can have them arrested.'

'I take it the judge ruled in your favour,' I said, glugging from a can of Diet Coke, watching him pace up and down. I'd woken up in Nate's bed, my head cracking, and my phone beeping. Max had fifteen minutes and he wanted a meeting. Padding through to the sitting room, I found Nate on the sofa, curled up around Bernard, the shadows of the lattice shutters covering them like a quilt. Gingerly, I grabbed my boots and coat and tiptoed, fast as I could, down those creaking stairs.

'Now no one can take my work away from me. No one.'

I understood the need to defend his copyright, and I knew my need for acknowledgement all too well, but surely, as mum likes to say, 'an elephant doesn't need a bell'. Perhaps, I thought, attempting to get in touch with my inner Becks – it had something to do with his childhood; with all that standing on a kitchen chair making his case.

Next he embarked on a review of everything he'd achieved with Shine, and everything he planned:

'Six billion turnover...'

'Sixteen hundred centres...'

'Sixty million members...'

I let his words wash over me as I waited for the painkillers to take effect, wishing they could also erase the memory of the night before ... "the kind of "*fun*" that comes with no strings attached ..." What had I been thinking? How would I ever face him again? I wondered if he'd woken up yet and wished I'd left him a note, though I wasn't quite sure what it would've said – 'thank you for holding my hair and rubbing my back. It was just what I had in mind – though perhaps not as I leant over your toilet?'

'Meg!'

Max was looking at me expectantly. 'How did it go yesterday?'

Hauling myself back into the room, I pulled my laptop out of my bag, my vision still blurry. 'Let me show you some pictures.'

'I gather there was quite a drama.'

I tried, unsuccessfully, to read his face. How the heck could he know anything about yesterday? He'd just got off the red-eye. No one but Zoffany knew the identity of the mystery surgeon, had she had another swing of the pendulum and got me fired?

'Jed tells me you were a star – well done.'

Still not quite sure what he'd been told, I smiled and said something non-committal about it being nothing. 'All in the line of duty Max. No problem.'

He turned my laptop towards him, 'now show me your triumph.'

As Max admired Shonda and her cupcakes, I took the opportunity to fall once more into the pit of my stomach ... the hitching of skirts, the coquettish pout, the draped arm ... no, no, no.

'Are you alright Meg?'

He was offering me another Diet Coke.

'Sorry – heavy night.'

'Looks like you deserved it,' he said, clicking rapidly

through the photos, stopping to admire Bob's canvas, and the guitar by his side.

'Would you like to have been a rock star Max?' I asked, trying to distract myself from the continuing stabs of mortification.

'Absolutely,' he replied, 'Mick Jagger.'

'Isn't that Jed's job?'

'I do it much better,' he said, curling over his bottom lip in a very passable impression of Sir Mick.

He stood over Kate's pictures for a long time, saying nothing. With the help of Zoffany's clever styling and the soft light of a grey December day, the riding jacket provided excellent disguise; she was as slender and sculpted as they come.

'She looks good,' he said, a knowing smile surfacing, 'and I hear she was a big hit with our photographer.'

I made a mental note never to tell Jed anything that might be held against me.

'I hope you had fun too Meg,' he said, giving me a knowing grin.

I attempted a blank look. 'I don't know what you mean.'

'You're wearing Zoffany's dress. I can only assume you didn't go home last night.'

'I stayed at hers,' I said, wondering how he remembered a dress from several years ago.

'Really?' he said. 'You got here quickly.'

Shit.

'I was rather hoping you'd started following my very strict instruction.'

'I am having fun, but not in that way – not yet – I'm an old fashioned girl.' I attempted a mock-flirtatious look, but my mascara-laden eyelashes, from the Zoffany de Gournay look-book, simply stuck together. I pretended I had a twitch, and rubbed furiously.

I was going to tell him how Zoffany saved Kate's bacon – credit where credit's due – but he was already on to the next item on his agenda, wanting to know who we'd lined up for the US shoot.

'Here we have the next Jennifer Aniston,' I said, opening another file, finding the Californian blonde. 'She went straight from a Shine class to the leading role in next year's biggest TV show.'

'Very nice,' he said, taking time to fully absorb the dossier.

'And this guy's a New York musician who's just signed to Sony with a woman he met in class – she was on her mat singing along to Eric Clapton and the next day they recorded their first track.'

Max gave him a more cursory glance.

'And this one owns a hotel.' I handed him a picture of a striking woman posing outside a renovated warehouse. 'It was a huge risk buying in such a run-down part of town but she conquered her fear with Yo-Jitsu classes.'

'And our born again warrior made millions?'

'Exactly.'

'Excellent work Meg,' he beamed, flicking back to the Californian blonde.

I began to pack up, all I wanted to do was go home, wash last night out of my hair, but he had other plans.

'Meg,' he said, cracking open another Diet Coke, suddenly serious, 'I need to talk to you.'

Oh god – maybe he had heard about Nate after all.

'There's no need to look so worried. You may have got off to a shaky start with some people but now you're humming. Elements is flying. Membership numbers are up, and *you*. Well, look at you. You've transformed yourself, in every sense of the word.'

'Well, thank you. I've been working hard–'

'Jed loves you, Zoffany is doing great work with you and, don't tell them I told you,' he said, leaning across the table, 'but I even heard the P.R. girls talking up the loyalty programme.'

I was stunned. 'Ashley?'

He shook his head. 'She hasn't cracked yet, but the rest of them are unofficial members of the Meg Rogers Fan Club.'

He took a long hard swig from the can. 'So, I've got some news for you.'

I arranged myself in a state of composed neutrality. I still struggled to hope for good news from a boss.

'I'm taking you to L.A.'

I stared at him, not understanding.

'Come on Meg, where are you today?'

'I'm sorry – I don't think I should drink for a while.'

'Perhaps not,' he said, laughing, pushing another Diet Coke across the table.

'Thank you,' I said, pulling myself together, dutifully opening the can. 'Do you want me to cover the shoot? I'd be happy to take it on.'

'No, leave that to Zoffany. Your job is to help launch the 360. I want the three of us – you, me and Jed – to show the beautiful people how it's done. We're having the party at Shine Beverly Hills. We'll showcase the mat and the bodysuit and you'll be our poster girl. You can give your account of the training; how tough it was, how much weight you lost, what you gained. What do you say?'

I hesitated. 'Do you think I'm ready?'

He moved me over to the window and stood behind me, his hands on my shoulders. We stared at our reflections in the gloom; the sharp lines of his suit, the puffed sleeves of my walk-of-shame gypsy dress.

His voice softened, moved towards my ear. 'If you weren't staff I'd have put you in the campaign.'

'Still several pounds to go,' I said, pulling at my waistband, not quite so desperate to go home now.

'One or two,' he said, his hands still on my shoulders.

'Five – to be precise,' I whispered, enjoying another fleeting fantasy in which we were photographed for *The Spiritual Rich List* in exactly this pose.

'So,' he said, moving abruptly away, commandeering a chair,

swivelling in mock-seriousness, 'assuming you do lose those precious pounds, are you up for it?'

I was. Very much so. Just one question. 'Does Ashley know?'

'I'll tell her today.'

I wished I could be a fly on the wall for that one.

'I want you to soak up our centres and L.A. so that when we go to Asia you'll have context, you'll know what works, where we're heading.'

I had Nate to thank for understanding that there was a relationship between California and Delhi. He'd heard a Radio Four programme on the subject and couldn't believe what was happening; it was a long way from the India he remembered. 'Ah yes,' I said, seizing my chance, 'all those Indian Institute of Technology grads – they went to Google and Apple and now they're back home demanding gated communities with swimming pools and Californian style spas.'

'Exactly,' he replied, grinning.

Asia. Not Nate's Asia. Not Becks' Asia. My Asia. Five stars all the way. My mind drifted – Mumbai, Singapore, Hong Kong, the colours, the heat, the shopping, the spas – all in the name of research. Was Jed right? Perhaps I really did have a chance at the top.

I was desperate to ask more questions but Max was already looking at his watch, putting on his jacket, tapping his pockets, equipping himself for the day ahead. 'We'll only be in the Hills a couple of nights so we'll stay at the Beverly Wilshire – it's seven hundred bucks a night but screw it; it's a great hotel, it's Christmas and, in the words of a famous campaign, "you're worth it".'

I smiled, feeling like all those Californian goddesses rolled into one.

He was at the door now. 'I'm off tomorrow – going to see the folks, and then on to Paradise with Jed, so I'll see you there.

Camilla will organise your tickets. In the meantime, have a good Christmas, and,' he said, walking over to the window to peck me on the cheek, 'keep having fun.'

With that, he left. I sat in Max's chair, tilting it as far as it would go, and closed my eyes. The roof garden of Shine Beverly Hills, the scent of Californian oranges mixing with a salty sea breeze, warm sunshine on my shoulders, the tinkling of crystal in my ears, me at the centre of it all – taking to the stage, Max smiling up at me. Ashley at the back, eating her words.

I decided to take Nate a present; a Pierre Marcolini hamper would thank him for the shoot, say sorry for riding his china bus, and give me the perfect excuse to say what I needed to say, without having to stay too long to say it.

The queue at Verde & Co was long, full of Christmas shoppers stocking up on ham and pâté, but I was perfectly happy drinking in the smell of chocolate and tangerines, at least I was until Ashley joined the line, directly behind me.

I took a deep breath and turned to face her – determined to spread a little peace and goodwill. It helped that I felt I could afford to – it was the day after the Max meeting so she'd know by now that I was to be the star of the L.A. show, and that I'd won our little bet. I could be magnanimous in victory. Plus, some 'get personal' progress would be something positive to tell Nate.

'Ashley,' I announced, launching in, my voice seeming to boom around the tiny shop, 'it's nearly Christmas. Since neither of us has succeeded in driving the other out, isn't it time we kissed and made up, or at least just made up?'

Initially, she tried to ignore me, even though I was standing right there in front of her. There was a long pause in which she read and re-read the label on a box of mulled wine sachets.

'Don't you find it exhausting?' I prompted.

'I am a little over it,' she conceded at last, with a little wrinkle of the nose.

'What do you say, shall we start again?'

She appeared to give it serious consideration, transferring weight from one foot to the other, weighing up her options. 'I guess–'

But I couldn't let it ride, could I? 'And since I'm coming to L.A–'

'Wait. You're coming to L.A.?'

'Yes, I'm–'

'You're screwing him aren't you?'

'Screwing who?' I asked, for a moment dangerously disoriented.

'Max. You're screwing him. That's why he's invited you on this little trip – so you can screw–'

'Ashley,' I said, drawing myself up to my full five feet five inches – a full three inches taller than her, 'even you must've noticed that I've lost nearly twenty pounds in the last three months. I was the 360 guinea pig–'

'You?' Her jaw dropped.

'That's right, me. And now Max has asked me to be his poster girl for the launch.'

'The "poster girl"?'

'Yes, I'm sorry you had to hear it from me but–'

'The "poster girl"?'

She threw her head back and laughed. 'That's the biggest pile of crap–'

'If you don't believe me–'

'Only in this dumb ass, bad teeth country could you be "a poster girl" for anything.'

'It was Max's idea, and I don't have bad teeth!'

She took a step back, pretending to give me the critical eye. 'No Meg, there's no way you're going to pull this off. Not in L.A. Not in front of *my* people.' With that, she turned on her heels and was gone.

Crossing 'get personal' progress off the list of positive things to tell Nate, I carried the hamper over to Ekatman. In between cursing her I rehearsed what I'd say to him. I thought I'd start with how sorry I was for turning up drunk and disorderly, for embarrassing him, and myself, but then I'd say something like 'well anyway, you'll be glad to know I'm going to be out of your hair for a while.'

Hopefully, he'd look upset.

Then I'd tell him that Max was taking me to L.A. 'as the poster girl for a revolution in fitness.'

There'd be a pause while he took in the news, he'd ask a few questions about the revolution, and then I'd tell him that actually there was more to it than that – that it'd 'become apparent' (good grown-up words) that I was being groomed as Max's successor. 'That's right Nate; he really likes my Brand Vision – loves it in fact.'

'What's that? When am I going? Boxing Day. That's right. Soon. Camilla is handling all the details.'

'No, I'm afraid not. I definitely can't do dinner before I leave.'

'When I get back? I don't know. Let's see how it goes. Max might need me to go to Asia right away.'

There would be another pause, and then he'd tell me it was cool, that he was happy for me, but it would be really obvious that he wasn't. We'd hug, one of his special hugs, then I'd leave, and he'd stare after me, all the way down the street, already plotting how he was going to win me back.

Then, after all that, no one was there. I had to content myself with leaving the hamper next door, at the women's shelter. I pulled a photo out of my bag – one that Max hadn't seen. The Second Assistant had taken it and popped it in with all the official photos; it was Nate and I hard at work over the cupcakes – him piping the icing, a look of great concentration on his face, me standing by his side, holding out a handful of Swarovski crystals. I scribbled 'Sorry about last night! Off to California on business! Happy Christmas! See you next year!' on the back and signed it, adding a kiss. Then I'd wished I hadn't added so many exclamation marks, or the kiss but, as I only had one print, I couldn't change my mind.

Not sure what to do with myself, I headed for Spitalfields Market. Time for some Christmas shopping. Something for mum (always a heavily scented bather). Something for dad (another pair of gardening gloves?). I wandered around soaking up the atmosphere – picking my way through throngs of Japanese girls wearing platforms, mini-skirts and multi-coloured tights, hair dyed red. I stopped for a juice at one of the cafés overlooking the stalls, watching waiters shuttling backwards and forwards with just-baked friands, muffins and paninis. I inhaled deeply, trying to content myself with the smell.

Then I spotted Ashley, again.

I watched her browse a couple of stalls, picking up union jack cushions and an old Guinness poster but, perhaps bored by the lack of designer labels, she was soon heading out. Thank god. I waited until the coast was clear and headed towards the smell of lavender, thinking a soap stall might lie that way, and that's when I spotted the film crew. A Japanese presenter providing an excited commentary to a cameraman. It took me a while to work my way to where I could see what was happening.

He was helping an old man bend forwards, beneath a homespun banner that read 'Ekatman – the road home – #YogaHood'.

'Just breathe and let go,' said Nate, rubbing the old man's back (clearly he was something of an expert in that area), soothing and coaxing.

The old man was responding. His progress might've been measured in millimetres but it was progress, his head hanging like a ripe fruit. He rested just beyond his knees for a while, and then he came slowly back up – placing one vertebra on top of the other, until he was vertical and smiling.

'You really released something there son,' he said, rummaging in his pocket for some money before Nate stopped him, placing a hand on his arm, shaking his head.

'Another volunteer?' asked Nate, moving hopefully towards to his audience.

A middle-aged woman emerged, rubbing her neck and complaining of shopper's elbow. Once again, the healing hands went to work. I remembered my breathing lesson – how that quiet space felt; luxuriating in my hammock overlooking the lake.

I watched, transfixed. When he'd mentioned it at the shoot, less than forty eight hours ago, I hadn't picked up it was happening so soon, but here it was. He'd done it – put his Brand Vision into action, and then some. He stood at the centre of it all, surrounded by his people, all of them entranced. There must've been a hundred people there – solid numbers of the obligatory lefties of course, but lots of smart shop girls, hip office workers, creative types, and even a few well-heeled locals of the Farrow and Ball variety.

I could have watched him for hours. That smile, that quiet presence, that glow, but I had to move on – emotionally and, rather more pressingly, physically. The last thing I wanted was for him to see me, to ask me to step forward, to get caught on camera beneath his Ekatman placard. So when Bernard started huffing and puffing towards me, dead set on his target, I turned on my heels, and ran – not looking back until I hit Leman Street, a getaway worthy of Steve McQueen.

'The Gucci'd up guru'

'I love you Aunty Meg,' said, Susie, giving me a big hug before she climbed into her dad's car. She sat back, adjusting her tiara, and I passed her the new fairy wings – pink, in the shape of a butterfly – which she folded on her lap.

We waved her off, taking a moment as the car rounded the corner. It'd always been part of the deal, that she would spend half of Christmas Day with her dad, but Becks had never got used to it, and nor had I.

'Let's walk,' I said, offering her my arm.

Becks and I could've navigated the park blindfold. We played here as children, sledging when it snowed, cooling off in the pond during high summer, playing hide and seek in the wood in all weathers. As teenagers, we spread our blankets and sunbathed. I provided the magazines and led the celebrity gossip; she led the chatting up of passing boys. In recent years, we'd stuck to our favourite bench at the top of the hill. Together we sat, snuggling for warmth. Under my jumper I was wearing the soft grey bat-wing top embroidered with pearl moons on water. She was in leggings topped by harem pants and tribal belly chain (a relic from one of those trips to India). Golden chrysanthemums and azure hummingbirds peeped out from under her coat, glinting in the afternoon sun. We watched our breath making small vanishing clouds, the sound of crows circling overhead. Becks threw J.R. a stick and off he went, bounding enthusiastically in the wrong direction, barking excitedly.

'There is good news,' she said, after a while.

I smiled at her smile. 'Your book?'

'I'm already half way done.'

'Bury the headline,' I said, playfully punching her. 'That's bloody brilliant.'

She fanned herself, mock-modest. 'And do you know the best bit?'

I shook my head.

'I might have an agent.'

'Seriously?', I said, quietly picking up my jaw from the ground.

'I've started a blog – anonymously of course – and this guy's got in touch – said he knows a publisher looking for the next Max Pemberton and he wants to represent me.'

'Max Pemberton? Who's he? I thought you were the next Jamie Oliver.'

She explained that he wrote a book about his first year as an idealistic young doctor – how he went into medicine to save lives, and soon realised he was spending his whole time filling in NHS forms instead of learning the really crucial stuff – like how to work out whether someone was dead.

'And this agent sees parallels?'

'Well,' said Becks laughing, 'I haven't had to call a coroner yet, but yes – the dream of making a difference, the paperwork getting in the way of the important stuff – that's my story too.'

'What about the money? Has this agent mentioned anything about that?' It was all very well and good but she still needed to pay the bills. From what I gathered, only the big celebrity names made anything decent, most authors would earn more on the Tesco checkout.

'I wouldn't be giving up the day job; Max Pemberton is a

practicing doctor *and* he has a newspaper column. His is in *The Telegraph*, but,' she added quickly, 'obviously I'd write for *The Guardian*'.

'Just don't get carried away before it's happened,' I said, not wanting to see her disappointed.

This was met with silence. When she next spoke, there was an edge to her voice. 'Talking of getting "carried away",' she said, giving my bracelet a not-so-playful-tug, 'how's the "1984"? I see Big Brother's still watching you.'

This had been the theme of all our post 24 conversations, usually followed by a '*real* yoga teaches us to listen to our inner voice, not a machine' lecture. Today was no exception. Clearly there was no point telling her about the 360, and anyway, sharing a secret with someone having an Edward Snowden slash Max Pemberton moment was definitely asking for trouble. I'd passed off the trip to L.A. as a big party for the 24.

I didn't want to rub her nose in the Club Class flight and the five star hotel, so I focused on the hilarity of Ashley's accusation – that I was screwing Max. I was sure that would raise a laugh but instead she wagged her finger and told me to make sure I stayed away from him. She remained tight-lipped when I assured her, several times over, that this was a business trip and, I felt sure, the gateway to a big promotion.

'At least you haven't had any Botox yet' she said, hurling another stick at J.R.

In actual fact, I had idly thought that perhaps, given my trip to L.A., a preliminary shoot-up might be in order but, in the end, Max's flattery had given me the only glow I needed. I shook my head, trying to restore her sense of humour with some tales from Planet Zoffany. Soon, I was spilling the beans on her quest to make Max jealous, the failed attempt on Jorell Jones and the subsequent summit meeting on her looks. In a lapse of concentration I'd allowed myself to get stuck with her in the loo. She'd spent the next fifteen minutes pulling up the skin on her 'saggy jaw line', weighing up the advantages of a half face-lift. I thought she was joking until she pulled a leaflet out of her handbag, pointing at the 'no woman can look good after forty without a little help' quote from 'Harley Street's leading cosmetic surgeon.' I tried arguing that he was clearly touting for business but she'd swallowed it hook, line and sinker. A consultation was in the diary.

She was as interested in all that as she was in a new set of Ofsted guidelines. 'You know Nate asked Carly to leave?' she said, watching J.R. chase an imaginary rabbit down a hole.

'I thought leaving was what she did? Isn't she a photo-journalist, traveling the world in search of the dispossessed?'

'They had a big row – something to do with you I believe.'

'Me?'

'Wasn't she rude to you the night of his birthday party?'

'She did do some serious shit-stirring, but I'm not sure it was a fireable offence. She was off-duty and I think we were all pretty pissed.' I wanted to be fair, and frankly I'd moved on – there'd been a lot of water under the bridge since that night.

'Well, apparently it'd been building for a while. She'd been bossy with him and aggressive with his students and he realised it was costing him business, plus her fancying him got in the way of things.'

It certainly did.

'He needs a good woman,' said Becks thoughtfully.

'He's a good man,' was all I could think of to say.

She took a breath, 'I have to ask you something.'

Oh god. Had Nate told her about my attempted fling? 'He's a lovely guy Becks; he's kind and caring and funny and, as we've discussed,' I paused a moment, distracted by the memory of those pyjamas, 'he's sexy, in his own way. But I need someone a bit more...'

'It's okay Meg, we both know it wouldn't work.' There was a

long pause in which I tried, unsuccessfully, to read her face. 'He's far too good for you,' she said, only half joking. 'No, I want to know why you ran away from the pop-up?'

'You were there?'

'You didn't see me?'

'There were a lot of people and that camera, and that stupid cow Ashley was knocking about–'

'You should've stuck around – given him a bit of support. You wouldn't be on your way to L.A. if he hadn't saved your shoot.'

I thought it was a bit much to give him all the credit but I let that slide. 'I *am* really grateful to him but I couldn't be seen supporting a competitor. Max would fire me if he found out.'

'Anyway,' I said, finding no sign she understood, 'did it work? It looked like it was working.'

She relaxed a little. 'It was great; he really pulled it together. He got the local press involved, and then we had a stroke of luck with that Japanese film crew who happened to be there, and we emailed a clip with #YogaHood to some yoga bloggers – *Yoga Dork,* Waylon at *Elephant Journal,* Roseanne at *It's All Yoga Baby*, Bob Weisenberg – the *Yoga Demystified* guy, and that hashtag ended up trending on Twitter, @Ekatman attached.'

'Whose idea was that?'

'Nate's. He realised that he's all about community and so are the millions of the yogis already on Twitter and Facebook. Now he's tweeting with #YogaHood ten times a day. Plus, he's set up an Ekatman Facebook page and it's already got a ton of Likes and loads of people using that hashtag. He's really going for it.'

'Impressive – but it won't be enough, and nothing will be, not unless he can morph into Max.'

This was met with a serious harrumph.

'I'm serious Becks. Max went into the market knowing he'd need over a thousand centres to make it work financially. Nate can't do that – he doesn't have the resources.'

'Evidently.' Losing patience, she got up, dusted herself off and stalked down the hill, at some speed. I followed at her heel, dragging J.R with me.

'I know he's not stupid,' I said to the back of her head as I yanked J.R.'s lead. 'He's just not hard-headed enough for business.'

'Perhaps not,' conceded Becks, 'after all, he cancelled a class to help his competitor out.'

'No he didn't,' I said, 'he left in time to get back for it.'

'That was the second class you idiot. There was one before it, which he cancelled because you, his competitor, needed help. He was supposed to be going to his first ever private, teaching this loaded City woman – "getting commercial".'

That stopped me in my tracks. 'But Becks, he didn't tell me that. I would never have let him do that to help me.'

'Wouldn't you Meg?' she said, turning to face me. 'It seems to me you're prepared to do whatever it takes these days. Don't you have any conscience? Nate's ability to run a business has nothing to do with his problems. Nothing can compete with Shine. I read about the Gucci'd up guru's so-called victory in the American courts. I wouldn't be surprised if he's put every single small studio out of business by the end of next year. How can you live with yourself?'

It was time for her to wise up, to get with the programme. 'You have to offer what the marketplace wants Becks; it's the law of natural selection.'

'Natural selection?' she snapped, her face reddening. 'Once upon a time, you chained yourself to a tree to stop them chopping it down, now look at you.'

Why bring that up? I wasn't eighteen any more, and anyway that'd been a one off. One of the girls from the Body Shop had organised it and I'd gone along with it for the sake of the team. 'Becks,' I said, 'I'm in *business* and people in business have to defend their intellectual property. It's their responsibility to themselves and the people who've invested in them.'

'Shine is responsible – responsible for mowing down businesses left, right and centre. It's a bulldozer and you're the one at the wheel.' She turned her back on me and charged off across the road shouting, at anyone that would listen, that I was 'just part of the system'.

'I've been part of the system for a long time,' I yelled back, not caring that people were staring at us.

'Not true!' She stopped again, hands on hips, her voice shaking. 'You were your own person, even when you were at Con World and I used to really admire you for that. Now it's all about you and your quest to be a double zero power magnate, it's all about you and Zoffany de Gournay and Max. So go to L.A. Shoot Botox, eat raw carrots, be slender and sculpted. I'm sure you'll have a really good time. It's your kind of place, full of self-obsessed people who don't give a shit who they hurt to get what they want, and,' she said, opening her front door, jerking J.R. into the house, 'don't come crying to me when it all goes wrong.'

She slammed the door in my face.

'Run This Town'

Max looked relatively sprightly in a cornflower blue linen shirt, but Jed's broad shoulders had the cowed look of one for whom existence is endurance.

I winced. 'Good time?'

Max fixed on the bellboy loading their luggage onto a birdcage trolley and smiled through tight lips. 'What happens in Malibu stays in Malibu.'

Jed concentrated on tossing the valet the keys to his Corvette. They landed a little short.

Max peered at me over his sunglasses. 'You look remarkably perky.'

I'd had a smile on my face ever since I landed, despite the hour-long wait for my luggage, a hangover, and jet lag. Not that it was the picture-perfect place I'd imagined. A long time fan of *Short Cuts*, I expected Tom Waits to be my cab driver, Lily Tomlin to be my waitress, and Tim Robbins to give me a police escort into town – his yappy dog riding pillion. Instead, what I got was a mash-up. Alongside the palm trees on the road from the airport were revolving oil dredges that looked like small, rusting dinosaurs. Alongside the surgically enhanced yummy mummies breezing by in their hybrid SUVs, their kids buckled deep in the rear seats, were Mexican workers squeezed ten in a car, or waiting exhausted at bus stops. Alongside the skyscraper banks sat one hundred percent organic Obama-supporting farmers' markets. Alongside the glamorous super-homes were homeless drunks. Everything was larger than life, hyper-real and hyper-gripping. I'd never felt more alive.

'Enjoy the flight?' asked Max, downing his espresso in one gulp, his hand trembling slightly.

I admitted to an extended session at the moodily lit on-board bar. 'I sat beneath a mirrored glitter ball sipping Laurent-Perrier in my black onesie, chatting with a self-styled "Jetrosexual" and a chirpy steward from Essex who had a way with maraschino cherries.'

'How very Virgin,' said Max, looking pleased. The story prompted him to recount some of his wilder nights in L.A, including meeting Jed at the cigar bar.

'You didn't pay any attention until I told you that yoga men were babe magnets,' teased Jed, somewhat revived. 'And that every class had one man for every twenty women.'

'Actually it was when you told me yoga was a sixty billion dollar industry,' laughed Max.

They went on to describe the all-nighter that followed; how they hammered the neon bars of Sunset Strip, weaving the Corvette ever upwards, along the serpentine roads of Laurel Canyon, the scent of eucalyptus in their nostrils, the howl of coyotes haunting the still air, the city lights laid out below like infinite landing strips. It was a night that became day with a restorative class back at Paradise Cove – the class that cost Max that whisky bet.

'You were so stiff,' said Jed, 'so English, so uptight.'

'It seemed like a long way to my knees,' said Max, laughing. 'Still does, some days.'

'But something changed for you that morning,' prompted Jed.

'It certainly did – I became the proud owner of ten of your DVDs.'

Jed blessed us with that easy Canyon wide smile. 'And then I got the call. "I'm doing yoga spas. You want to be rich"?'

'And you said–'

'I already am.'

'No,' you said, "Let me think about it–"'

'And one minute later you rang me back.'

'Ten minutes – I'm sure I left it ten.'

I smiled as they tumbled over each other, until I thought of how I'd left it with Becks. These days it was just one argument after another and, as far as I was concerned, far from being 'self-obsessed', I'd done plenty to help her and Nate. In fact, I'd put my own job in jeopardy. I wondered more than once, on that flight over, if we were done. It happened like that sometimes. It would be sad, after so many years, and I wasn't sure I could live without seeing Susie again, but perhaps it was inevitable – we were two very different people, with no meeting place.

'Why not re-locate head office right here?' I said, squeezing my hands together in fervent prayer. 'I'll buy a little heritage bungalow with a deck and a palm tree…'

Jed enclosed my hands in his. 'You can hang with us down at Paradise; you, me and Matt McConaughey.'

'Maybe one day,' said Max, smiling like an indulgent father.

He adjusted his shades again, trying to block out more light, and asked me if I'd had time to visit either of the centres. I'd headed down to Shine Santa Monica just as soon as I'd been able to tear myself away from my Juliet balcony (and view of the Hollywood Hills).

'I struck very lucky; the six o'clock show was led by Sal.'

Jed looked concerned. 'He left his machine gun at the door?'

'It was fantastic,' I gushed, still buzzing at the memory of being adjusted by a man who'd lived a revved-up version of *West Side Story*, while there in front of me, stretching out beyond a white marble statue of the Virgin Mary, crashed the ocean, blue with tufted crests of white. I'd known I was in for a ride the moment he walked into the room, to the tune of Jay Z's *Run This Town*. 'We did Crab Claws to Public Enemy *Fight the Power*, Back Hammers to Dr. Dre and Snoop Dog's *Nuthin But a 'G' Thing* and we finished up with Grandmaster Flash and *The Message*.' I paused for breath. 'You know what?'

'What?' they chorused.

'I think Sal would be a big hit in London. We should make a big deal of how he lived next door to an Uzi-toting crack cocaine head, how he got chin-checked by a Blood – our City people would love it – all that gang warfare and adrenaline.'

'Do you think so?' asked Jed, doubtful. 'I'm not sure bandannas are very EC2.'

'Yeah, perhaps we should make him the new Fitness Director,' said Max, slapping Jed on the back. 'Let's rev it up a bit. Leave Eric Clapton and James Taylor behind, along with Jed. He's so last year. What do you say Meg?'

I laughed uncomfortably, pushing away the reminder of Zoffany, focusing instead on the envious glances of the women at nearby tables as Max and Jed bantered on.

I thought they'd want to check in with Ashley, to take a look at the Beverly Hills preparations, but apparently that was tomorrow's concern; right then Max had a more pressing assignation.

'Jed,' he said decisively, turning to his brother in arms, 'here's the deal. You get some sleep. Meg and I get the Corvette.'

'Sun stroked and grizzled'

The Corvette was red. The sky was blue. There was ocean. There were palm trees. Two guys in tinsel trimmed Father Christmas hats. Young Mums jogging with three wheel prams. Bare-chested surfer dudes waiting for their ride, arms round their boards.

'If I was living here,' said Max, returning my smile, 'I'd go into the hills – get a place on Mulholland Drive with a view across the valley.' No surprises there. It was the same reason that, back in London, he drove a four by four; to survey the territory, to know the whole picture, ahead of everyone else.

We were meeting a realtor. She was standing outside waiting for us, looking at her watch, a deep South glamour puss in her mid fifties. She took a moment to appraise Max, who clearly met with her full approval, and then she turned her attention to me, taking a little longer to inspect my shift dress and courts.

We followed her to the front of the building, which she presented with a theatrical flourish of the hand. We stretched our necks, took a few paces back, absorbing what looked like a precarious pile of pastel pink wedding cakes, placed by a cook who'd been at the sherry. A wooden balcony wrapped each tier like cake trim, and each window was framed by a series of neat crests, like piped fondant icing. I could've sworn the house smelt of sugar, but perhaps it came from the nearby candyfloss stall. I took several photos, certain that Nate, King of Icing, would love it.

I was equally certain that it wasn't right for Shine. Venice Beach may have been free of cars, buses and trucks but the long track, which apparently stretched all the way to Malibu, was full of guitar-playing roller-skaters, and Hare Krishnas enthusiastically banging drums and chanting their namesake mantra. Definitely 'ethnic' but certainly not 'luxe'.

'Let's walk,' commanded Sally-Anne, unfazed by the sudden influx of orange robes, gamely leading the way along what she called 'The Speedway'. We followed her and the Hare Krishnas south, past the signs advertising tarot readings and palmistry, the stall selling cartoon boobs and six pack t-shirts, the body piercing parlour, the side tables heaving with cheap trinkets, watched over by henna-haired girls, the wild haired woman with her gaudy paintings, and the 'Venice Beach Freakshow'.

We stood for a moment, watching an old man in a trilby hat getting jiggy to the sound of the Jackson Five, circled by a group of young women who were getting jiggy with him. The jiggy women had drawn their own crowd – surfer types who were sitting outside the No Hassle Discount Pipe Shop enjoying the show. I caught one of them staring at me – a bare-chested guy in dungarees. He murmured an appreciative comment that made me smile and I was still smiling when we passed a sign for a tanning salon on which a stone Buddha had fallen asleep.

We walked up and down side streets that smelt of dope, past stalls selling sunglasses and footballs, buckets and spades, the paraphernalia you would find in any English seaside town, and several cafés named after infamous revolutionaries. I inspected the menu boards, liking the sound of Peasant Onion Pancakes and People's Potstickers. I took a photo – just in case I ever spoke to Becks again.

Then Max announced that he had 'a good feeling' about the area. I was amazed; I couldn't think of anyone less likely to feel an affinity with Mao's Kitchen. 'Isn't it a bit down at heel?' I said carefully. 'A bit scuffed round the edges? Didn't I hear that the canal is full of needles?'

'You're out of date honey,' said Sally-Anne, in her deep Southern drawl. She explained that the beach area was still kinda 'sun stroked and grizzled' but down by the canal and along Abbot Kinney, it was 'rich hip'. She claimed that the surviving artists, 'buddies of Dennis Hopper', kept multi-million dollar lofts there, and there were lots of media types. Apparently, Chiat Day, the US equivalent of P&P, was minutes away. I imagined meeting rooms packed with Bull Terriers and Po-faced Pigtails and shuddered.

I looked around me, at a crazy woman re-arranging the bedding in her supermarket trolley, at a man wearing a sailor's cap sitting in a bath painted with flames, at the graffiti that covered every spare bit of wall. She had to be kidding.

'I'm sorry Max but I don't get it – it's just like Brighton. It's everyone else's funky beach town but to me it's drug addicts, dogs on strings, kiss-me-quick t-shirts and too many tourists.'

Max laughed, 'But that's a good thing – if the property prices move anything like Brighton's we'll do just fine.'

'There's still room for the savvy investor,' reassured Sally-Anne, touching Max lightly on the arm. 'And, of course,' she added, moving in for the kill, 'we're home to more celebrities than Beverly Hills.' She reeled off a list of names that included Julia Roberts, Angelica Huston, Viggo Mortensen, Robert Downey Junior, and even,' she said, pausing for dramatic effect, 'Matt Groening.'

Max clapped his hands decisively. 'C'mon Meg. Good enough for *The Simpsons*, good enough for us.'

'The area isn't on-brand,' I repeated crossly, squinting in the sun. 'We're sophisticated, not quirky, and the house is totally wrong for us; Shine is glass and steel, clean lines and big windows.'

'Let's not worry about that right now,' said Max quickly,

nodding at our realtor. 'I'm sure Sally-Anne and I can work something out.'

She nodded and smirked, probably working out how she was going to spend her commission. 'Would you like to see inside?' she asked, fishing around in her handbag, blissfully unaware she was in the palm of a professional player.

We emerged an hour later. I shook Sally-Anne's hand and watched as Max slowly walked her to her two-seater. Now play-acting the role of Prince Consort, much like he did with Zoffany, he opened the car door, holding her bag as she folded herself expertly into the seat, leaning in to whisper in her ear. I watched her smile – not the tight-lipped version she'd given me an hour ago, but the kind that suggested late-night hospitality.

He returned to me, looking thoughtful. 'Let's walk a while,' he said, draping a lazy arm over my shoulder, steering me in the direction of a gathering crowd.

We joined them, a curious combination of locals, muscle men and camera-toting tourists, all of us transfixed by the tired sun's descent into the ocean; a hazy burnt orange meeting thick slate grey. He squeezed me again, tighter this time, and pointed at the chain of nose-to-tail bicycles.

'Look,' he said, 'it's an avant garde necklace. How very Venice.'

I laughed, my mood was mellowing, but not to the point where I could, in any way, relax. 'Max,' I said, trying to keep the edge out of my voice, 'what's going on?'

Silently, he turned me round, so we were both looking at the wedding cake. There was no doubt; it was the standout building in the row and it'd been no less quirky inside – all that pretty clapboard, the sloping ceilings, the wooden floors. It was so much more Nate than Max; I could see it now – the henna-dreadlocked receptionists, the Mao's Kitchen concession, the slow classes for care-worn Hare Krishnas.

'Look at it Meg, what do you see?'

'A wedding cake,' I replied, wishing he'd hurry up and get to the point.

'Of course, wedding cakes are not to my taste, as you know Meg, but I see something different.'

'What's that?'

'Glass.'

'Wait a minute,' I said, disentangling myself. 'You want to knock it down?'

'Yes,' he said, laughing. 'Why would I keep that old thing? Imagine a giant cube with floor to ceiling sunsets. It'd be breath-taking.'

I stared at him open-mouthed.

'This area needs redevelopment, no doubt about that, but once they get rid of the tat, move the bag ladies on, it'll be great – just like the rest of Venice. Go take a look if you don't believe me. Walk up Abbot Kinney, see the canal, do the galleries. It's just as the fragrant Sally-Anne said.'

'But isn't this a heritage site? Wouldn't the house have a preservation order?' It wasn't to my taste but I was suddenly feeling protective. 'And wouldn't there be years of red tape before we could get anything moving?'

'If they let Frank Gehry build a bird box on top of a house, then a glass cube will sail through. The thought of millions of dollars pouring in will have them dropping their objections faster than a whore's drawers.'

'With as much integrity,' I said bitterly.

'You said it yourself; the place is a pit. What's the problem?'

Max took my silence as acquiescence, reminding me he had the best lawyers money could buy. 'We can't afford to stand still Meg,' he said, digging his hands deep into his pockets. 'I met with one of my VC guys last week and he was threatening to pull his money and invest in The Black Eagle if we didn't move up a level.' This was the latest tallest building in the City, said to have several high-speed scenic lifts, a gym, a sky bar and a roof terrace restaurant. Given Max's addiction to heights, I was amazed we hadn't already relocated.

'I want to commission some new architects,' he said decisively, 'and I want to try out some different designers–'

'I thought you were happy with Zoffany, now that we're working together?'

'"Only dead fish swim with the tide" and all that.'

'You're not a fish Max,' I said, 'and nor is she.'

'Very true Meg, but I *am* over Tibetan tree bark.'

'I love Tibetan tree bark. It's so Shine,' I said. 'Give her another chance; ask her to come up with some new ideas. She's pretty keen to evolve.'

'Meg,' said Max, turning to face me square on, 'why are you defending her? She stole your idea, for Christ's sake.'

'How do you know that?' I said, staring at him, wide eyed.

'She told me – gave me the big confession, said she'd made a big mistake – that you deserved all the credit, that she was really sorry.'

'That's true, strictly speaking,' I told him, plunging into some serious guilt. 'I came up with the original idea and the patches, but a lot of those touches – the fabrics, the embroidery, the things that make Elements truly special – are Zoffany's.'

I was dismissed with a lecture on the importance of keeping friendship and business separate – that it could interfere with judgment.

Had he forgotten his best friend Jed? The two of them could end each other's sentences. And wasn't sleeping with your Design Director a bit more problematic than sharing the odd lettuce leaf?

I was on the point of trying to say something when, all of a sudden, he suggested dinner. He gave me his jacket, suggesting that we go round the corner, to a little restaurant he knew.

Of course, Chaya Venice was perfect; a chic and elegant room full of good-looking, laid-back people living the L.A. dream. We were given a banquette at the far end of the room, the restaurant equivalent of the Presidential Suite, and we sat in easy silence, soaking up the room and, to my infinite satisfaction, the obvious approval of our fellow diners, until our Slingchi Martinis arrived.

'A toast,' said Max, picking up his glass. 'To Meg, my right hand woman. May she always have a point of view.'

'And a toast to Max. May he always hear my point of view, and then do the opposite.'

It was his turn to laugh.

The waiter returned with the menus. I tried to concentrate but the jet lag was getting to me, it was three a.m. UK time, and the simple act of choosing food was too much. Max came to my rescue, ordering a variety of small but perfectly formed dishes from the sashimi and sushi menu. I smiled to myself, thinking of how far I'd come since Becks had shown me that Shine article and I'd baulked at pink sushi. Now raw fish was pretty much all I ate, though I'd yet to love fish maw.

The Wakame Seaweed Salad and Tuna Tataki arrived and Max announced that he wanted to discuss Asia.

'But we've only just got to L.A.,' I said, 'don't you want to discuss Venice?'

'Oh,' he said. 'I thought we'd already done that. I just need to talk to Sally-Anne, get the price halved.'

'Halved?' I nearly choked on my seaweed. 'How are you going to persuade her into that?'

He took a long sip of his cocktail. 'How well do you know Shanghai?'

I shook my head, admiring the segue.

'Well,' he said, spreading his hands wide on the table, as if stretching his fingers indicated advancement, 'it's a city on steroids – forget "a New York minute", these days it's "a Shanghai minute".'

He explained that twenty years ago there was just the old Shanghai, the Puxing district, built by the British to house the banks. Now there was the new Shanghai. It was built on reclaimed swampland, on the other side of the Huangpu River, and already home to more than a thousand skyscrapers.

'They love Western brands,' I said, remembering some preliminary work I'd done for Con World on marketing chocolate to the Chinese, and the argument with Pat about the likely appeal of a chocolate-loving gorilla. 'Rolex, Chanel, even Barbie, they're all there.'

'There's a rumour that Bazu's got another round of funding and the smart money's on China. So, it's very simple, we need to get in there first; Shanghai or Beijing, or both.'

I nodded, hoping to approximate the look of someone who was regularly asked to choose between two Chinese cities.

He even had buildings in mind; Beijing's Fortune Plaza, and The Shanghai Tower – the second tallest skyscraper in the world after the Burj Khalifa, apparently. 'It's stunning – all glass, a twisting triangle – you'll love it.'

'I'm coming? Seriously?' I could get used to dinners like this.

'Yes and to India too – it'll be our Grand Tour.'

'"*The Max and Meg Show*"?'

'Exactly. I'll get some t-shirts printed,' he said, stirring the twizzler in his cocktail, churning the ice, looking at me warmly. 'I'll be very interested to see what you think of Ganga.'

'The river?' Did he expect me to take a dip? Becks had done it and even she'd found those polluted waters a challenge – the need to get out alive outweighing the desire to cleanse her soul.

He smiled indulgently, explaining that Ganga was an old friend from Harrow who was thinking of turning his palace into a hotel, just like his fellow maharajahs at the Samode and the Rambagh, and he wanted Shine to open a franchise, taking care of all the spa treatments and yoga.

The gang of three – Zoffany, Max and Jed – had gone out there to do a recce and fallen in love with its decaying grandeur. 'There are ten rooms stuffed with tigers and panthers.'

'Dead or alive?'

'Very dead – probably related to the five rooms of daggers and pistols.'

'Not Zoffany's thing?'

'Zoffany was perfectly happy. She spent three days roller-skating down the corridors with Ganga, and she loved the Durbar room, where his father conducted his court business. She sat behind the lattice-work shutters, pretending to be the maharani.'

Of course she did. 'And Jed?'

'Jed spent all his time outside, driving around the overgrown golf course and polo park in the maharajah's old Roller, playing cricket with monkeys at the rotting nets, sunbathing in the shadow of ivy clad marble nymphs.'

Then he was describing the party Ganga held in their honour – '*The Beautiful and the Damned.*'

'If I tell you that the dining room chandelier was bigger than the biggest one at Buckingham Palace you'll get some idea of the scale. Ganga's great grandfather tested whether the ceiling would take the chandelier's weight by hauling up his favourite elephant.'

Rajasthan's great and good, wearing the Cartier and Van Cleef jewellery their grandparents had bought in Europe back in the twenties and thirties, sat at a table bearing a hundred place settings. 'Jed and I had definitely drunk too much by the time we sat down to eat; there was a two hundred and fifty foot train that carried food from the kitchen to the dining hall and around the table; we managed to short-circuit its control panel, sloshing gravy and a puree of peas all over the guests. Everyone saw the funny side of it and we climbed on the table and we danced, and danced, and danced. I ended up getting rather friendly with a maharani…' He paused a moment, savouring the memory. 'She told me that Cole Porter wrote *"Let's Misbehave"* for her great grandmother and, well, let's just say the maharani had her genes.'

'I hope Zoffany got friendly with Ganga,' I said. No one likes to see their ex flirting, especially when the object of their affection is a beautiful princess.

'She was furious,' he said. 'She left in the morning, got a taxi all the way to Delhi and took a First Class flight back to London. Then she sent me the bill.' He finished his cocktail and ordered us both another one. 'Anyway,' he continued, 'we'll go and decide how to position it, maybe as a weekend retreat, a Jaipur Babington House. Then we'll fly down to Mumbai, then Bangalore and Chennai, take a look around, get a feel for the customer base.' He picked up his iPhone and scrolled down, looking for an email. 'Ganga is free the second week of February. So am I.' He looked up. 'Does that work for you?'

As if I had anything better planned.

More urgent, in my opinion, was the small matter of the 360 launch.

'Do you want to hear my speech?' I asked, feeling suddenly nervous as I pulled the crumpled sheets of paper out of my bag. I'd been hoping I might get a chance to rehearse.

He waved his hand dismissively. 'No, I trust you, and don't worry – you'll have an autocue. Now then,' he said, leaning forward, lowering his voice, 'much more importantly, what are you wearing?'

I told him I planned on something from Elements, that we should showcase the collection – maybe the bat-wing top and the three-quarter pants.

He looked at me as if I'd announced I was wearing sackcloth and ashes. 'This is going to be a big night, you need something special.'

'Elements is special, special to me anyway.'

He shook his head. 'Haven't you got anything else?'

'I've got another dress,' I suggested, 'it's a bit like the one I'm wearing but I've got some heels, and I could jazz it up with jewellery.'

He put his glass down and reached slowly across the table, fixing a strand of hair behind my ear, brushing my cheek with his fingers, cupping my chin with his hand, as if he was a butler adjusting a place setting.

And then this: 'I'll buy you a proper dress,' he said smiling gently, his eyes meeting mine.

'Okay,' I said, sounding squeaky, 'if you insist.'

I watched his hands return to the table, seemingly unaware of the momentous journey they'd undertaken.

Blushing, I looked down, fixing on those perfect crescent moon nails of his.

He asked me to meet him at midday. I wasn't sure I would ever be ready, especially with Max as my audience, a man who misbehaved with maharanis.

'Now show 'eem'

I had travelled to the other side of the world, to the City of Dreams, only to be met by a nightmare. There she was, clipping along the pavement, lifting her knees a little too high, staring straight ahead of her. Did Ashley always think she was on a catwalk?

Like Shine Santa Monica, Shine Beverly Hills was a bright white rectangle opposite high-end boutiques. Max had obviously decided to make up what it lacked in height with length; it stretched a whole block, gleaming in the December sunshine. Our signature white and gold banners fluttered in the breeze, echoing the fluttering in my stomach.

She was utterly business-like, laying out the ground-rules, explaining that the red carpet would be rolled out half an hour before showtime, telling me where the paparazzi would stand, where she, Max and Jed would stand, and where I should stand (out of the way). I nodded and concentrated on writing the occasional note, meeting it all with studied neutrality. She wasn't going to spoil my day.

The interior was a longer, thinner version of Bishopsgate. Glass cubes with the signature lotus flowers, birch-pole benches, Tibetan tree bark, alpaca floor cushions. All of a sudden a door opened and a herd of Slender and Sculpteds scampered by. I sheltered against the wall to avoid getting trampled in the rush while Ashley, who'd somehow known to take evasive action, stood by the reception desk, keeping her cool.

We followed in their wake; Ashley marching ahead, iPad clutched to her flat chest, while I sneaked peaks into a couple of comfortingly familiar studios. Jamu, complete with tropical beach wallpaper and Studio-Ready bikinis. Yo-Chi's yin-yang shaped portholes and imaginary ball rolling. I found it reassuring, knowing that, wherever I was in the world, I'd get the same experience. Becks didn't see it the same way; her favourite nickname for us was 'McShine'. Total rubbish. Every centre had a twist, something unique that reflected the local neighbourhood. Since Beverly Hills was all about pampering, all the finishes were extra polished, the floor cushions extra soft, even the lighting was extra low, to the point where everyone looked like a movie star. Maybe they were, but I wasn't going to give Ashley the satisfaction of gawping. I'd be back later to do that.

I followed her onto the roof, momentarily dazzled by the bright white cabanas and day beds beside the infinity pool. Two Mexicans were using orange paddles to guide in the last palm tree, the finishing touch on a ten strong line-up. Another pair was fixing the spotlights in place – a bit of a challenge in the bright morning light. Several more were on the floor of the empty pool, giving the tiles that made up the giant golden lotus flower an extra polish. I followed Ashley from one group to the next – trying to make up for Shine's Imperious Mistress of the iPad with some serious smiling.

Ashley talked me through the night's programme from memory, taking care to explain that I mustn't exceed the ten minutes allotted to my speech.

'That's really important Meg, as Max and Jed are the real stars of the show.'

I nodded and, shielding my notepad from view, slowly

wrote the word 'bitch'. Then I underlined it, and looked up, smiling some more.

She showed me where I would sit, where I would stand and where the autocue would be, and then she took my memory stick. On it was the photomontage, a sequence of 'before' photos that would run on the screen behind me as I talked about my transformation from a size fourteen fatty to a svelte size ten. Yes, I'd made it – dropping twenty-four pounds in three months, four pounds more than Max when he transformed himself.

'Okay, we're done' she said, putting the stick in her bag. 'Just one thing though.'

'What's that?' I was in a hurry to get going, to get ready for my assignation with Max.

'I think Max will be super interested–'

She stopped suddenly; I followed her gaze. There was Jed, blinking in the sunlight, dressed in white linen trousers and a matching shirt, which billowed as he strode towards us. He looked rather better than yesterday.

'Ladies,' he said, putting an arm round each of us. 'Are we ready for our big night?'

We played along with it for a minute, each of us in our corner.

I managed to peel off first, pretending I was late for a massage I'd already had. 'Sorry Ashley,' I said, picking up my bag, already half way to the stairs, 'what were you saying? Max will be very interested to know what?'

'Oh, don't worry,' she said, with a funny little smile. 'It can wait.'

Max was sitting in reception behind a newspaper, wearing shades and another blue shirt, this one matching the hydrangeas beside him.

Strangely, I felt very calm. I'd spent the early hours indulging in juvenile fantasies, touching what he'd touched, finally swapping my nightie for my space-suit around four in the morning. It would be going too far to call the 360 my friend but we were at peace, and only needing one towel for Level Three Yo-Jitsu was pretty cool. I'd followed up with an anti-jetlag Rejuvenation massage, a facial and a pedicure and then, inspired by Max's hands, I had a manicure. I was rather proud of the result – I'd waved gratuitously to at least three waiters at breakfast.

'Meg,' he said, rising to his feet and kissing my hand with such dramatic flair I wished I'd been wearing white gloves. 'Shall we?' He guided me across the marble floor, his hand on the small of my back. The gesture reminded me of that time I watched him in the bar with Laxmi (whatever happened to her?).

Off we set, arm in arm, down Rodeo Drive, the street with the cleanest pavements, shiniest windows and freshest white paint, where even the Chihuahuas wore diamonds.

Max approached shopping the way he approached everything else in life – with great focus. We marched straight past Louis Vuitton's double-breasted white marble storefront, the pretty wrought iron balconies of Van Cleef & Arpels, the burnished bronze of Harry Winston, the black and white angles of YSL (that somehow looked like a perfume box), and the glistening mannequins at Miu Miu.

Left to my own devices, I would have missed Prada. The fifty foot aluminium box that overhung the entrance had the feel of a burka, and its shop windows were set into the pavement. I peered inside. A mannequin was resting inside a glass bauble like a ship in a bottle, her ankles demurely crossed. She was engrossed in a book as if she'd slipped downstairs for a rest, to hide from all that public display. Part of me wished I could join her.

But again I felt Max's hand, gently persuading me inside, past Belle Époque alcoves and cloche-hatted mannequins. He led me up the stairs as if leading a blind person, from rail to rail, dress to dress, holding them against me, mostly putting them back, occasionally giving them to a sales assistant. I found myself standing completely still, as if I too was a mannequin. By the time I reached the dressing rooms, there must've been ten dresses for me to try and I was so nervous my hands were shaking. What if they made my bum look big, or my chest look small? What if I tore something?

I tried to concentrate on Elisabetta, the assistant. She was a compact woman, dressed in a plain but impeccably cut suit.

''Ere,' she said, pointing a stiletto at the floor switch, 'you can switch the glass from see through to not.'

I nodded; I knew all about that one.

'Use the screen to order' she said, pointing to a series of icons. 'Shoes, belts, whatever you want; it's all 'ere.'

The size six dresses fitted me (even if they were an American six and therefore a UK ten) but they were all so skimpy – like something Galina would wear. I started with the ones that offered the most coverage but Max simply shook his head and the assistants, lined up behind him, followed his lead. Everything else was even more revealing, sexier, not my thing.

I sat on the stool, my head in my hands, wondering why I agreed to this. I understood that surrender to the higher power of Prada, and Max, was supposed to be part of its appeal but I was too much of a control freak to be good at it.

There was a knock at the door.

'Are you decent?' asked Max.

Before I had time to reply, he was in the changing room, presenting me with a silvery-gold flapper girl number. It had a Twenties style dropped waist, tiny sleeves and a sweetheart neckline. I clutched it to my heart, praying it would fit.

'Try it with these,' he said, tapping away on the touch screen like a seasoned pro, pulling up a pair of gold Mary Janes and a glinting clutch.

I'd never have picked out any of it for myself but when Elisabetta arrived with the boxes I could see that it would work.

She helped me pin my hair into an approximation of a Twenties bob and provided a supportive shoulder while I stepped into the shoes.

'There Signorina,' she said handing me the clutch and stepping backwards, 'look.'

I appraised myself carefully in the mirror and the plasma screen and only then did I allow myself a smile.

She gave me a gentle prod from behind the curtain, as a mother might encourage a stage-struck child. 'Now show 'eem.'

I took a step out from behind the screen and waited.

'Well Miss Megan,' said Max, slowly putting down his newspaper, 'it would appear that you've arrived.'

I spent the rest of the afternoon in my hotel room, having my hair and make-up done. Max organised it for me; he wanted to complete the picture of a Twenties heroine. Lydia told me she often worked with stars in awards season and I believed her. She worked my hair into a series of authentic pleats and waves, securing it all with a Twenties style clip which was almost as big as the ones modelled by the Chihuahuas. Max had sent it over in a blue velvet Harry Winston box with the message:

> *'For Miss Megan,*
> *Respectfully,*
> *Your Mr. Walcott.'*

'That's so romantic,' said Lydia as she placed the clip in my hair. 'You guys been together long?'

'Oh, it's not like that,' I said firmly. 'It's a business relationship – we have an important presentation tonight and he just wants me to look my best.'

'I've met a lot of men, but I never met one who'd shop with a woman he wasn't interested in.'

'Then you've never met Max,' I said, briskly removing the gown and brushing myself down, hardly daring to hope she was right.

'Whatever you say "Miss Megan",' she replied, smiling to herself.

'Actress. Model. Whatever.'

I read my speech for the final time, took one last look in the mirror, at the immaculate creation that had taken up residence in my body, and walked down the corridor to the lift, moving slowly so as not to disturb her.

The doors opened and I crossed the marble lobby, sensing heads turning as I walked. Max looked up just as two men parted the way, their eyes following me with the kind of appreciation I'd only ever seen in black and white Italian films. By the time I reached him, I was smiling broadly, unable to contain this new woman a moment longer.

'Miss Megan,' he proclaimed, kissing my hand again.

'Mr. Walcott,' I replied.

Eventually, he stopped staring, collecting enough of himself to offer me his arm.

It was a warm evening and the streets were busy. Avoiding the large Russians laden with shopping bags and the bum-bagged tourists taking photographs, we took to the side streets. Strolling alongside cashmere-enriched couples on their way to an early supper, I pretended we were also a couple, smiling with complicity at the other women. Max spoke quietly, asking me how I was feeling, assuring me, as only a Southern gentlemen could, that 'Miss Megan' looked 'mighty fine'.

We were on the corner when it happened. He turned me towards him, placing his hands lightly on my shoulders, drawing me in, searching my face as if it might reveal the answer to life's biggest questions.

I smiled uncertainly, not sure what was happening.

Then, he kissed me.

I'll spare you the details – it'll sound too Mills & Boon. Let's just say that it was textbook; a perfect ten.

We rounded the corner bathed in flashbulbs. His hand, once more on the small of my back, was firmer this time, possessive?

I still treasure the look of complete disbelief on Ashley's face as she seemed to intuit what had happened. Jed seemed also to understand, though he'd turned away before I could interpret the shadow that passed across his face. I looked at Max, it was the first time I'd ever seen him look bashful, but he took my hand and kept on smiling, leading me up the three steps and into the party. Ashley followed, ordering us to the roof, hissing that I was late.

Stepping out onto the roof terrace, I was in my own private Idaho, breathing in the warm scent of Californian oranges, craning my neck at those spotlit palm trees, their fronds dusting the sky. The whole place was aglow – the candles, the jewels, the glass baubles clinking in the pool like champagne flutes. Max by my side.

Ashley broke my reverie, propelling us through the crowd, somehow contriving to hand Max a glass of champagne and not me. She dumped me unceremoniously at the side of the stage, with the guy from MIT, and waved Max up the steps. He walked towards the lectern, carefully rolling up his sleeves. To the unpracticed eye, he must've looked utterly at ease, but I knew the man and I knew that gesture. I'd seen it a few times – at the London launch party when he was waiting to greet the guests, and the night he told me about the girl who made him want to be good.

'You know,' he said, placing his hands on the sides of the lectern, settling, 'it's almost four years to the day since I took a bet from Jed – that he could hook me on yoga in just one class. It was a bet I was happy to lose even though it cost me some rather expensive whisky.'

Whoops and hollers, just like London.

'Yoga, Jed tells me, is a science, a discipline that must be practiced daily in order to achieve results, but how scientific can we be when our tools are so primitive? A sticky mat, even if it's the Ferrari of mats, is just a mat. It set us thinking; what would be the big leap forward, what would be Yoga 3.0? And that's the question we put to MIT.'

Jed joined Max at the lectern, taking a brief bow before the two of them introduced the 360, detailing the night they came up with the idea (at Jed's place in Paradise Cove) and moving through the various stages of its development – all the frustrations, all the triumphs. I knew the script by heart, having written most of it.

Ashley made sure she got her moment, of course, tottering onto the stage in towering heels and the shortest of skirts, unveiling the body-suited mannequin on the 360 mat with a dramatic sweep of white silk drapes, gathering them to her like the train of a wedding dress. 'Always the bridesmaid,' I wanted to heckle.

As the MIT guy circled the mat, describing its technical features, Max turned to me with a nod and a wink. I smiled back, imagining the moment when I would have him to myself again, now intent on finishing what we started.

Then Max announced that he was 'very proud' to introduce 'Miss Megan Rogers, the first 360 transformation'.

Perhaps sensing my nerves, he offered me his hand, guiding me gently towards the lectern. I smiled and looked into the crowd, making eye contact just as I'd been taught to do on all those Con World presentation skills courses, and then I looked towards the autocue.

It was there, but it was blank. I searched desperately for Ashley, eventually spotting her at the back, smirking. I looked at Max and at Jed, and then I looked again at the crowd. Five hundred beautiful faces looked back at me, expectant. I thought of the piece of paper I'd left folded up on my dressing table, and realised it was time once more, as Becks would say, to 'stick or twist'.

I took a deep breath and plunged in. I began by describing where I'd started. 'Here's me as a very authentic pre-Raphaelite at an Old Masters Christmas party, and this is one my dad took; our dog Orwell might have been big but my bum was, I think you'll agree, bigger.'

Polite chuckles all round.

I clicked to the next picture, ready to work my way through a few more carefully selected shots. Although I had to look big – that was the point – I'd made sure the camera angles were good. The description I was aiming for was 'lush' or, perhaps, 'blooming' but the next picture was neither of those words.

There were gasps from the crowd, and a cracking guffaw from Ashley.

She must've taken it in the changing room on the very first day I went to a Yo-Jitsu class. Where had she concealed the bloody camera? One thing was for sure – it wasn't in her cleavage. It was horrendous; shot from below, my stomach bulged over my knickers, and my thighs looked like Verde & Co's giant hams, served up with a large helping of cellulite.

What to do? I couldn't risk another click of the mouse. Who knew how many more pictures she'd loaded. There was only one thing for it – the truth. I didn't hold back. I walked them through every step of my journey. I described the corporate takeover that left me for dead, meeting Max and being resuscitated, the way I huffed and puffed through that first class, the panic I felt when Jed had first lain on top of me, the launch of Operation Slender and Sculpted, the sessions with Doctor Lily, the hours on the

360, right through to the moment we hit Prada. I gave them every bead of sweat, every puce face, every raw emotion, every low, and every high except, of course, the kiss. By the end of it, I was practically crying. 'And that, Ladies and Gentlemen, was the moment I became a different sort of woman, the woman you see before you now.'

I looked out at the sea of faces. Ashley looked as if she might be about to throw up, but everyone else was dabbing their eyes, and clapping enthusiastically and then Max was on his feet, leaping up the steps and raising my hand like a triumphant boxer, picking me up and twirling me round so all I could do was wave and laugh. I remember the world spinning around, tilting on its axis, Max and me at the centre of it all.

I was quite unprepared for the interrogation that followed. Looking back, it was entirely predictable; they were the beautiful people of L.A. – anything they could do to stay one step ahead would be met with forensic levels of attention. Exactly how many pounds had I lost? Exactly how long had it taken? Exactly what had I eaten on a Tuesday? On a Wednesday? And it was no good waffling on in that classic good-humoured, self-deprecating English way; they wanted answers and they wanted them quick – it was like *Mastermind* on steroids.

Of course, Ashley should've been by my side, fielding questions and marshalling the unruly crowds, but she was nowhere to be seen. She was probably sticking pins in a voodoo dolly wearing a flapper dress. I ended up stuck between the mannequin and whichever guest had succeeded in elbowing their way to the front. In different circumstances, I would've been thrilled to meet the models, actors, and actresses that kept this town humming, but I just wanted Max.

The podium gave me a pretty clear view of the terrace but all I could see was a blur of guests and white-jacketed waiters bearing more champagne. It wasn't until I'd satisfied the last interrogator that I escaped. I scored myself a glass and, failing to find him, I went in search of the loo.

I remember what happened next as I might a car crash; in slow motion.

Ashley and her funny little smile as she watched me in the mirror, applying my lipstick.

The chink of the baubles in the pool.

The billowing cabana curtains caught up in a sudden gust of wind.

The smell of Max's aftershave – citrus and sandalwood.

The stricken look on Jed's face.

Max leaning in. Her neck. Her dress.

Tracing his fingers down her spine.

Seeing me. His awful blankness. A stranger.

I remember turning on my heels and running down the stairs. Running and running, stopping only to throw those oh-so-pretty Mary Janes in a bin. Running into the hotel lobby. The cornflower blue hydrangeas. Coming to a halt at a lift which stubbornly refused to arrive.

Desperately, I jabbed the button, over and over again, trying to ignore the large Indian family that had appeared beside me, the children staring at me with frightened eyes, the mother and several aunties attempting to shield them from the crazy barefoot lady.

I backed away, finding myself locked in someone's arms. Could it be him – desperate to make amends? I twisted, only to meet disappointment. It was Jed.

I allowed him to steer me towards the bar. My feet were filthy, my eyes were red, my nose was dribbling with snot, and I didn't care.

He settled me in a quiet corner and ordered us both a large glass of whisky. 'We kissed,' I said, hiding my feet under a cushion, retreating into the sofa, the retreat of a complete fool.

'It was written all over your face,' he said gently, dabbing away the smeared mascara with a napkin and some water.

'I'm guessing this isn't the first time you've had to clean up his mess.'

'No,' he said, looking seriously downcast.

'Who was she this time?' I asked, taking the proffered tissue, blowing my nose loudly.

'Actress. Model. Whatever.' He wrapped his jacket around my shoulders, coaxing hair out of my eyes. 'No one special. They never are.'

'What about the Australian woman? The redhead? She was special, wasn't she?' Masochistic but I had to know.

'Max told you about her?' He looked really surprised. 'He *never* talks about her – not to anyone.'

'What happened?'

'They were engaged, until she found him in bed with someone else. It was a cocaine fuelled fling, completely meaningless, so stupid.'

Richard had tried a similar 'meaningless' yarn but he was wrong – he'd thrown me away for five pints of lager – what he'd done was full of meaning.

'She couldn't forgive him?'

'No,' said Jed simply, downing his glass and ordering two more. 'She went back to Melbourne.'

'And that was that?'

'And that was that. But you know, sometimes I wonder if Shine is his Taj Mahal – a way of saying that he loves her still, that he's still clean, that he's created something good out of something bad.'

That one stopped me in my tracks – the romance of it; everything poor Zoffany longed for, and me. 'Where is she now?'

'Married to someone else.'

'Good for her,' I said, dully, wishing I'd done the same post Richard, instead of locking myself in an iron-clad box.

'Don't take it personally Meg; he's never going to change.'

I took another slug of whisky. There was no escaping it; Max had played me. He'd invited me to L.A. to prove that Shine could work for anyone, even a size fourteen girl who'd spent the best part of her twenties a slave in Slough. He wanted to make sure that I played the part so he kissed me just before I went on stage, to make sure I sparkled. Knowing this, remembering how I stood on that stage soaking up the sun and all its stars, I felt nothing but disgust. I'd been so happy to expose myself for a few moments of fame, I hadn't stopped to question any of it – not for a minute. I really was a complete moron.

'If you want my advice,' said Jed, not waiting for a 'yes', 'I think you should see this as an opportunity.'

'"An opportunity"?' He had to be kidding.

'He likes you, so use that. Sit at his feet. Take lessons from the master. Learn. Learn. Learn. Soak it all up until the sell off, then you'll be ready to show the new guys who you are.' He took hold of my hand, squeezing it tight. I could feel more advice coming. I wasn't sure I wanted to hear it. 'And Meg,' he said, looking me squarely in the eye, 'I want you to enjoy your new powers of seduction, enjoy the dinners and the parties, enjoy China and India, just make sure you never kiss him again.'

'"Kiss him"?' I cut in, horrified. I didn't know how I was going to deal with bumping into him, with meetings, let alone with kissing the man.

'Promise?'

'Promise,' I said, clinking his glass.

'If you want to flirt you can always do it with me' he said, polishing off his whisky. 'As long as you're not using me to get to Matthew McConaughey.'

'As if,' I said, managing a smile.

'Peace-up'

I stared unsmiling out of the window, feeling hungover. I was impatient to be gone, but I was also determined to do one good thing before I left – find somewhere to stick Max's stupid glass cube.

The taxi inched forward, and finally the reason for the delay became apparent. The road was clogged with gawkers hanging out of car windows, staring at the view.

An orange modernist cube sat alongside a prim and proper Colonial bungalow, a mock Tudor pile nestled up to an authentic Spanish hacienda, a long glass bungalow dazzled in the morning sun. It might've been a historical mash-up but it was a multi-million dollar historical mash-up.

'It's ideal,' I said, excited enough to share the news with my driver, Dino. 'My boss can buy the "rich-hip" bollocks bungalow and extend up – he'll get a couple of hundred germ-free mats in there.'

'You noticed anything honey?' Dino chortled, mopping the back of his neck with a large handkerchief.

'What's that?'

'The canal. How are you planning on getting your people across? By gondola?'

'Isn't there a bridge?'

'Not for cars – just for people and movies. Ever seen *Valentine's Day*?'

I shook my head; it sounded like one for Nate.

We drove on in silence, soon arriving at Abbot Kinney Boulevard, a few blocks away. This was more like it – a straight, wide road, perhaps a mile long, lined with the ubiquitous palm trees. I asked Dino to drop me off, the better to take it all in. The sanitised version of an old school Venice skate shop. The board announcing twenty five dollars a shot coffee. The white-floored, white-walled, designer shoe emporium that looked just like the Shine shop. All it needed was a bit of Tibetan tree bark.

I'd been walking for about five minutes, past several more boutiques and a couple of glistening office buildings, when I came upon a large plot ripe for development. It was a huge space, perfect for Shine, sandwiched between an elite design agency and a top dollar architect's practice. Max wouldn't have far to come, glass cubes seemed to be the house specialty. I took a photo of the realtor's board – not Sally-Anne's, thank god – and then I took a few more of the surrounding area, happily concluding that Abbot Kinney was Shine's spiritual homeland, and even happier that there were no heritage buildings for us to knock down, or any small yoga studios to put out of business.

I'd drifted five blocks further south, where the shops were a little less polished, the offices a little grittier, when I caught the scent – the warm, spicy smell of freshly baked gingerbread, of molasses and cloves.

Then I saw it.

'The Yoga Project.'

A hundred feet down, on the left hand side, beneath a smart black canopy.

There was a verdant, vertical garden on the side of the building, a mix of vines, ferns and herbs and, out front, a pavement display board advertising the day's specials. Alongside the seasonal soup, twice-baked goats cheese soufflé and the gingerbread, there was a hangover-banishing mantra and an illustration of a headache-banishing mudra which looked a bit like the okay sign; thumb and index finger touching, other fingers stretched out. I took a quick photo; I'd try them both later.

Inside, the walls were exposed bricks, the woodwork that soft Farrow and Ball style heritage green, the floors great big chalk stone tiles. The straw baskets piled high with organic produce – oranges and strawberries, carrots and radishes – reminded me of Verde & Co, so did the staff with their smart folded over black aprons and vintage-style Yoga Project t-shirts. The only difference was that these guys were seriously buff – were they all yoga teachers?

The class timetable was chalked on the giant blackboard above the counter. 'Geek-out' for the stiff-necked, 'Back-down' for spinal problems, and 'Sugar-hit' – a rebalancing class for recovering chocoholics. The forty five minute 'Peace-up' class was the one that caught my eye. Although I did consider myself a recovering chocoholic, what I needed most in that moment was a bit of peace; something slow, a place to breathe. I bought a pair of yoga pants and went upstairs.

The studio was small but smart – loft style. There was more exposed brickwork, floor to ceiling windows, and a wooden floor. Although the view wasn't great, facing onto the road, it was actually good to see real life out there – cars, buses and trucks rumbling by, a bunch of kids gathered around a storyteller in the bookstore opposite, office workers eating lunch at their desks. Somehow the ordinariness made a nice change from Shine's grand vistas – the palm trees of Beverly Hills, the endless ocean of Santa Monica, even the Gherkin.

Light streamed in, soaking the laughing Buddha and my nine classmates in sunshine. There were one or two surfer dudes but mainly it was well-dressed locals, creative industry freelancers, hip office workers, on-trend shop girls – Californian versions of Nate's pop-up customers.

I was surprised to see the teacher, Ryan, already sitting at the front of the room. At Shine, the teachers always waited for everyone to take their place before they made their entrance, rock-star style, but then I remembered there'd been none of that with Nate – he always sat there chatting to his students, waiting for everyone to arrive and settle.

Though he didn't share Nate's good looks, Ryan gave a welcoming smile almost as heart-warming, bowing to all of us with another Nate-ism, a 'Namaste'. Becks had explained it to me, translating it as 'the spirit in me bows to the spirit in you'. At the time, I dismissed it as mumbo jumbo, but now, here in this room, it seemed right. I bowed back and meant it, already feeling a bit better.

Ryan managed to combine Jed's laid-back Californian positivity with Nate's sincerity, putting it together in a package that said: 'Guys, I know what you're going through but relax, I'll get you to the other side.' My classmates certainly appeared to think so. The whole room seemed to sigh with relief.

Asking us to come to our hands and knees, he warmed us up. Unlike Yo-Jitsu, where we slammed straight into sun salutations, we started with so-called Cat and Dog, curving our spines up and down on the breath to the earthy sound of Nina Simone.

Then we slinked along the mat into Sphinx Pose, raising ourselves on our elbows, releasing our neck and shoulders, then into Down Dog, 'walking our dog', padding our feet up and down, stretching our hamstrings, tailbones to the sky, Bon Iver floating through the studio.

Only then were we ready for sun salutations. The flowing sequence was also done on the breath, the movements gentle and the pace measured – the polar opposite of Yo-Jitsu with all its jerky kicks and leaping about. It felt great 'to relax into it, soft but strong' instead of worrying about toppling my next-door neighbour. Rather than sweating into a towel, which still happened despite my new found fitness, I found myself feeling warm inside, as if someone had switched the heating on in my belly; the yoga equivalent of toast.

Maybe it was his sequencing. While Yo-Jitsu often felt like a mixed-up mash-up, Ryan's poses melted into each other like a hot knife through butter. Maybe it was the music (we were on The Cinematic Orchestra's *To Build A Home*). Maybe it was his adjustments, the way his hands seemed to read our bodies, coaxing us deeper. Maybe it was his voice; a soft mellow drawl. Whatever it was, we were all there in that class, with him and with each other, feeling the warmth.

Not that it was airy-fairy. Ryan had a sense of humour. He called the head-to-toe pose 'Pedicur-asana'. Reaching up and pressing down was the 'Cafetière Pose'. Stretching up, wiggling our fingers, was the 'Harvesting Sauvignon Pose'. He made us feel good about ourselves – acknowledging us for squeezing some peace into our busy day, asking us to take a slice of it out into the world, suggesting a 'Prana Colada' on the beach if all else failed.

He taught twists with the same level of care, the same attention to breath, an attention that again reminded me of Nate. Instinctively, he knelt behind me, his hands softening my shoulders, sinking my shoulder blades, slowly rotating my head and body, opening my heart. He stayed with me for several breaths, using each one to lift and twist me a little deeper into the pose, so that by the end I could comfortably see the blankets and bolsters piled at the back of the room.

Finally, we came to a cross-legged position for something called 'Alternate Nostril Breathing'. I had a vague recollection of it from Nate's class all those years ago, but this was different. Instead of getting confused over which finger should cover which nostril and giving up in frustration, I stuck with it. I covered my right nostril as I inhaled through the left, held my breath for a few counts, then covered the left and exhaled through the right. On we went, through several cycles, for several minutes. Shine's Yo-Jitsu classes always left me feeling even more frenetic and buzzy, but this class had, as advertised, taken me to a peaceful place. By the time we finished, I was the most clear and calm I'd ever been. Getting a blanket for final relaxation, I found myself patiently waiting my turn. For once in my life, I was truly in touch with Becks' favourite concept: 'the big pool of cosmic bliss that is the universe.'

Afterwards, I went back downstairs, buying a box of chocolate chip and peanut butter cookies for Susie and a hot chocolate, whipped with Nate-style cream whirls, for me. I chose a seat at the long wooden table that ran the length of the wall. Alongside the neighbourhood noticeboard featuring vegetarian apartment shares, Reiki healers and a 'Project Africa' update (it seemed that Ryan was just back from Nairobi where he'd been training teachers in the Yoga Project way) there was a pay it forward donations box and a 'give one, take one' bookshelf. But there were also branded yoga mats, bolsters and foam blocks, several CDs with the same titles as the classes and one featuring five minute mudras, mantras and breathing exercises, a small range of fair trade yoga pants and vests made from bamboo, and many baskets of organic home-baked bread, farm-sourced eggs and vertically-grown herbs.

The guys in black aprons were doing a brisk trade – no one was spending the kind of money they did at Shine but it seemed as if everyone was buying something – vegetables for dinner, cakes for the office, bolsters, books, or blocks for themselves.

If Shine opened here would these people, currently fans of small classes, individual attention, paying it forward and giving it back, also turn out to prefer valeted yoga mats and the 360? Some of them might, but this place was as smart and polished as it was deep and meaningful. The mats might not be valeted (you were encouraged to bring your own), but the Black Aprons were hot, the studio immaculate and Ryan's all-seeing eye was more than a match for any 360 device.

Contemplating my hot chocolate, I realised that this was exactly what Nate should do. He could keep his noticeboard and donations box, train some teachers in Africa, or India, but he could also give cookery classes, sell his own cakes, do a DVD, even launch his own clothes line – perhaps Zoffany could help, or perhaps I could, now I knew a thing or two about chrysanthemums. A place that made money and gave back – it was perfect. I could see it so clearly – a thriving centre, Bernard curled up at the centre of it all. From what I'd seen at his pop-up, the way he treated the man with the bad back, the woman with shopper's elbow, Nate was a natural at this yoga as therapy thing. Of course, he'd have to cut the length of his classes in half and learn to speed up, perhaps create some hip playlists, but his teaching style wasn't far off Ryan's. It wouldn't be that much of a stretch.

But would he do it? For all his wisdom, young Yoda could be a stubborn stick-in-the-mud. Of course, cutting his class length in half would enable him to double the number of people to whom he could show the 'road home' but there was no getting away from it: installing a café, getting the produce sorted, having clothes made, would cost a small fortune. And Nate, for all his pop-ups and fresh paintwork, had never announced that his 'road home' would be a toll road.

Perhaps I could do more; stop going on about Visions and Missions and get down to brass tacks, help him write a business plan, go see the bank with him. But was I up to it? My judgement had been seriously lacking recently. I'd gone over to Nate's house pissed as a fart and he'd been decent and honourable, offering to take me for a spin – to the Thames Barrier. What could've been more magical? More romantic? More fun? And what had I said? I'd said 'no thanks'. I'd had some stupid idea of how things should be, and when he didn't want to do it my way, I got the hump and thrown up all over his bathroom.

I might take the piss out of him and his rom coms but at least he didn't think he lived in one. I, on the other hand, had been starring in my own version of *Pretty Woman*, staying at the Beverly Wilshire, buying a dress on Rodeo Drive. Who did I think I was? Julia Roberts? And what did that say about me? Wasn't she a hooker before Richard Gere installed her in the penthouse? How did I imagine it would end? With Max climbing up the fire escape, a rose between his teeth?

What to do? I had no idea. All I wanted was dreary old England and my own bed.

'Niche or Nietzsche?'

The pink fairy was on her yoga mat, padding her feet in Down Dog as J.R. looked on.

I held out the box of cookies, shaking it gently.

'Thank you Aunty Meg,' she said, breaking out of position to give me a quick hug. 'Can we have them later?'

'Of course,' I said, leaving the box on the TV, out of J.R.'s reach and mine.

I was in serious need of a sugar hit; I'd spent the night tossing and turning at thirty thousand feet. Becks, on the other hand, looked fantastic. She was a bit more dressed up than usual (new skirt?) and she had an air of confidence, a lightness, as if an albatross had been lifted from her shoulders. I wanted to know everything but first of all I needed to make amends.

Stroking J.R., who had trotted ahead of me to the kitchen, I talked her through my adventures in La La Land, exposing the dark underbelly of my *Pretty Woman* saga; the dress, the kiss, the speech, the 'actress, model, whatever'. She needed to hear the whole truth, and so did I.

'At least Julia Roberts was working her way up the pole; I was on a one-way ticket down. You should've seen me on that stage. I might as well have been doing lap dances.'

She shrugged and dunked a biscuit in her tea, seemingly unmoved. 'You were confused, that's all.'

'"Confused"?' I stared at her in disbelief. 'Is that all you've got?'

She shrugged again, sweeping some biscuit crumbs off the table, straight into J.R.'s gaping jaws.

'I think "self-obsessed bitch" would be more accurate.'

'I didn't know where my friend had gone,' she said evenly. 'The one who cared about other people more than she cared about herself.'

'I am really, really sorry,' I said, starting on a long speech about the error of my ways.

'Just don't pull a stunt like that again' she said, reaching for her laptop. 'Now, have you seen my blog?'

She turned the screen to face me, open on her latest post. It was an announcement that her agent would be submitting her synopsis and the first few chapters to five publishers – 'five!' – after the Christmas break.

I flicked through a few more posts – the whole thing looked great. She even had a nom de plume – Cam Will – after Camila Batmanghelidjh, the founder of Kid's Company, and Emma Willard, who turned out to be a trailblazing nineteenth century American educator. My best friend also had several hundred followers.

'If you ever need any social media advice I'd be happy to help you out,' she said, explaining that Nate had worked on the strategy with her.

'And how is Nate's business?' I asked, not sure I could bear the answer.

Her face changed, clouding over. 'It's picked up, but it's nowhere near good enough to please his bank manager.'

I leapt in, eager to spill the beans on my idea, the one that was going to save him, if only he'd follow the money. 'It's all about niche marketing–'

'Niche or Nietzsche?'

I pulled out the Yoga Project leaflet, talking her through the mudras for headaches and mantras for hangovers and how I thought Nate could adapt the yoga as therapy idea to work for him. This triggered the beginnings of a huff. Thank god, my old friend was back.

'But that's what Nate's always done. His yoga tradition is all about healing. His mother studied with a guru who studied with Tirumalai Krishnamacharya. He went through a few incarnations but in the end he was all about using yoga therapeutically, to improve people's health, emotional balance and mental clarity.'

'So that's perfect then,' I said, wondering why she always sounded like a textbook when she talked yoga. 'He just needs to package it differently, and maybe speed the whole thing up a bit.'

Becks looked as if that might be more of an issue than I'd imagined. Keen to reassure her, I told her that it had really worked. 'You know, Yo-Jitsu was never my thing – I stuck with it for the sake of Operation Slender and Sculpted but I never left that class feeling happy. But by the end of this class, I felt different – more like my old self.'

'Hallelujah,' she said, waving her palms in the manner of a gospel singer. 'So now Yoga Therapy's your thing?'

'It was perfect for me Becks – not too slow and not too fast – it was all about keeping moving and doing it on the breath.'

She looked puzzled. 'Wait; they took a Vinyasa Flow class and called it "Yoga Therapy"? Yoga Therapy's slow, it's personalised, it's tackling real health issues – it's all about the student teacher relationship.'

'Does it really matter Becks?' I said, silently wishing I'd asked Ryan more questions. 'The important thing is that it worked and it might help Nate.'

'I guess anything's an improvement on so-called "Yo-Jitsu",' she said, grudgingly, 'but I don't know how into speeding up he's going to be.'

'I would've thought "Sugar-hit" would be right up his street,' I said, explaining the class's rationale, my tummy rumbling at the thought of one of his cakes.

She smiled good naturedly, but it was clear she thought Nate should be sticking to Tiramisu Krishna-thingy. She changed the subject, asking what was next for Reading's own '*Pretty Woman*'.

I wasn't going to mention the idea of leaving Shine to work with Nate. I'd had time to reflect and it really was a non-starter – probably born of too much 'Peace-up'.

'Well, since Yo-Jitsu is no longer to my taste, I've been thinking about taking some time out,' I said, trying to gauge her reaction to a fledgling plan. 'What do you think? Maybe now you're about to be a mega-star author you won't need your backpack for a while? I could do your ashram trail, climb Machu Picchu, try to work out who I am and what I want.' It wasn't such a bad idea really.

'I know who you are, and you aren't that,' said Becks, snapping a biscuit in two.

Well, that was a relief.

'The *last* thing you should do is leave the country.'

I raised the back of my hand, placing it on her forehead. 'Are you feeling alright?'

She brushed it away. 'Don't throw the baby out with the bathwater' she said, stuffing the remaining biscuits back in the tin. 'I think you should keep at it.'

'But I snogged my boss,' I wailed, freshly appalled at the prospect of returning to Leman Street and to work. 'Page one, rule one; do not snog your boss.'

'Don't make it mean anything – he didn't.'

'Who *are* you?' I asked, clear I wasn't the only one who'd had a personality transplant.

'I'm you Meg. You decided what you wanted and you made it happen. Now I'm making it happen for me and I'm giving you back your own advice. You're going to get in there and do what you set out to do. Are we clear?'

'I don't know Becks—'

'Don't be stupid. You've got a golden opportunity to change the place from the inside. Challenge the Gucci'd up guru. Start playing some games, have a bit of fun with him. Do it on behalf of all those people he's screwed over. You can stop him firing Zoffany and destroying Venice, you can launch that fair trade programme, train hundreds of African yoga teachers, commission Threads of Hope, get rid of Ashley.'

'You mean, payback time?'

'"Payback time",' she said, narrowing her eyes mafia style.

'A few changes'

It was the kind of morning that gets darker with every passing hour. Max was slouched against the window, contemplating hordes of workers bearing down on their destinations.

'Good morning,' I announced, bright and breezy, happy to puncture his bubble. 'You wanted to see me?'

'I thought we should talk,' he replied, peeling himself away from the glass, squaring his shoulders so that by the time he faced me he'd assembled the old guard.

'Don't worry about it Max' I said, holding up both hands, attempting a papal style benediction. 'It was a moment. It felt right and then it didn't. No big deal.'

'So you're okay?' he said, looking as if he'd just been given the all clear from a biopsy. 'We can move on?'

'Absolutely,' I said, enjoying myself. 'After all, you "moved on" that same night, didn't you?'

'Oh Meg, I've missed you,' said Max, smiling with relief. 'Shall we go to The Wolsey one night, like I promised?'

It was a question I was no longer interested in answering. 'The moment has passed,' I snapped.

'Whatever you say, Meg,' was what followed, though I got the distinct impression he wanted to say something else. He took a moment, turning towards the window, staring into the gloom.

'Either way, I'll be giving you more responsibility before too long and, let me assure you, you won't have to sleep with me to get it.'

'Well, Max,' I replied, channelling an Ashley flat-line, 'that's good to know.'

He turned towards me, studying me thoughtfully.

I allowed him a moment, and then I told him I didn't think we should do Venice.

'Did you find some competition? Is bloody Bazu opening?'

'It's not that,' I said carefully. The last thing I wanted was to alert him to The Yoga Project, just ten minutes away. Knowing him he'd take precisely half that time to launch a heat-seeking missile on the vertical garden. 'It's destroying that wedding-cake of a house, that's what bothers me. It really is something special.'

'I appreciate your angelic ways but you know that isn't how the world works. Anyway,' he said, 'I met Sally-Anne after you left and the deal is done.'

I managed a half-smile. 'You must've worked very hard to get a deal like that.'

'Let's get to it,' he said, returning to his desk, shifting some papers, 'we have a more pressing concern. Bazu's VCs have injected a load of cash, and he's rolling out throughout Asia – starting with, you guessed it, the Shanghai Tower and the Fortune Plaza.'

'Oh crap,' I said, realising that his earlier sombre mood probably had more to do with losing those buildings than dealing with me.

'Quite. Which means we need all hands on deck – I'm going after more cash so we can take his heartland – blitz New York, upstate too, but we need to sort Asia, find some new buildings pronto. Can you get on the case?'

'Of course, and I'll talk to Zoffany' I said, pointedly. 'She'll know what's new.'

Max was on the point of saying something when his phone beeped.

'It's one of my VC mates,' said Max, reading the text. 'He says there's a new player in town – "Barre Yoga" – they're going into The Black Eagle up the road.' He scrolled down, reading out snippets, getting more irate. '"Barre Yoga is the last word in luxury" … "the vision of principle ballerina Marina Burdukovsky" … "plié your way to long and lean" … "in partnership with the world's most successful yogapreneur" … "Bazu" … Jesus Christ.' He threw his phone across the table, then he picked it up and punched numbers urgently.

'Well if that's all they're doing,' I said, 'it a very limited offer. Maybe it's not so bad–'

'Okay Meg,' said Max, motioning me from the room.

I returned to my office, sinking into my chair. I sat for a long time, not moving, staring out of the window into the shadows. I tried giving myself the pep talk – the one that Jed had given me. Here was my big chance – to become Max's right hand woman, to demonstrate I had what it took. And yet, I felt about as powerful as the brass lamps on the pub over the road – a victory of form over function.

I made a start on China but by mid afternoon I'd made little progress. Maybe a class would help. I'd forced myself to go to Yo-Jitsu the day I got back to London but it all seemed so fast and furious and I'd left feeling much the same way. Jed had my bracelet reports synced to his mobile but, thankfully, he hadn't noticed the lack of activity (rumour had it he'd been distracted by the Californian blonde on the latest shoot).

I wanted to feel like I did at the Yoga Project, clear and calm, at one with the YogaHood but Shine didn't have anything like Peace-up. The class that came closest was probably Yo-Chi. Perhaps a bit of imaginary ball rolling and some wind chimes would raise my spirits.

I picked up my workout bag and set off down the corridor. The place was strangely deserted, a lot of people taking an extended break into the second week of January. Usually there would be a buzz around Ashley's office, the Catwalk Caterpillar comparing selfies or showing off another fashion freebie. Today, the lights were on but there was no one home. She must've gone to Yo-Jitsu; her Studio Wear bag, a customised white leather number with Ashley in gold down the side, was missing.

I stuck my head round the door, wondering if I should leave her a note asking for a meeting, have it out with her once and for all. That's when I saw her phone, lying on her desk. Of course, it was password protected. I tried her birthday first (how could I forget the day the whole corridor partied without me?) but that was wrong. Then I remembered that Americans reverse the month and the date. Again, no joy. Then I tried Max's birthday. Hey presto, I was in. I stood behind her desk with my back to the door, occasionally glancing in the mirror above her chair for any sign of passing traffic, while I found my way to her photos.

No surprises in her 'Me' album; Ashley doing the splits in front of the Hollywood sign, Ashley arching into a perfect wheel on the Walk of Fame. 'BOGOF', the album, was the next one down. My finger trembled as I tapped it. There were tons of photos, all of them taken in those first few weeks. Coming out of yoga, my t-shirt soaked, my hair stuck to my scalp. Beetroot-faced in the café queue. Leaning over Max's desk, my backside in the air. They went on and on, grid after grid of shots from below – chins, boobs, tummy rolls and thighs. What to do? I couldn't delete them without her finding out I'd accessed her phone, and anyway they'd be backed up on her iMac or a thousand other places. She probably had a safe house somewhere with stacks of servers, all of them dedicated to preserving my posterior for posterity. I closed the album and placed it back on the table, exactly where it'd been.

Then I noticed the desk drawer was slightly open. Out it glided – silently, with only a little help from me. Checking again to make sure no one was passing, I shuffled through her papers. There was a print out of an email seeming to promise a lifetime's supply of designer handbags in return for the Shine mailing list, an invite to a night at the Chiltern Firehouse, a handwritten note from Max thanking her for her work on launch night, signed with a kiss. The sight of it made me feel slightly sick, but at least it didn't say 'Your Mr. Walcott.'

I shuffled through more papers. There were more invites, more freebies, more junkets, but nothing I could do anything with. I was just about to give up when I saw it. There, almost at the bottom of the pile, was my long lost Post-it note, the one instructing Jorell's people to use HMI or Flash, and not to forget the fans and fridge. I stared at it in disbelief. How many nights had I lain awake wondering what'd happened? How the hell had she got hold of it? I thought carefully, retracing my steps back to the moment I gave the paperwork to the Business Concierge girls, asking them to courier it. Ashley must have a mole in there somewhere. Either that or she'd intercepted it herself. Deciding to park that question for later I took a photo and carefully closed the drawer.

I got a cab straight over to Zoffany's.

'Let me get you a drink,' she said. I nodded; we were both going to need one.

I shifted the cat off the chair and tried to relax, noting the half full tea chests dotting the room.

She returned a minute later, with one glass.

'Detoxing?' I asked, taking a thirsty gulp.

'I'm making a few changes,' she said smiling, running her hands through her hair. 'Let me tell you–'

'I've got something to tell you first,' I said, interrupting her, desperate to get it off my chest.

'Go on,' she said carefully.

'I kissed Max.'

She turned away, towards the French windows.

I rattled on for a while. How I felt like such a hypocrite after the hard time I gave her for passing off Elements as her own work. How this was so much worse. How it was against my personal code of conduct. How it was really important to me to be honest with her. How I wanted her forgiveness, but I'd understand if she couldn't give it.

She remained at the window, her shoulders shaking, seeming to cover her face with her hands. Was she crying? I felt terrible.

'I thought we were friends Meg.'

'Zoffie I'm so sorry–'

'It's "Zoffie" now is it?'

'It was over before it even began. He took me to Prada and I looked in the mirror and I thought I was someone different. I got confused, and then, after it happened, I felt like such a fool and–'

'Enough,' cried Zoffany, turning round, breaking her cover, laughing. 'I can't put you through this agony.'

'You don't care Zoffany? Really?'

'You were naïve and lonely, so eager to impress. He played with you, he seduced you, and then he got bored. Sorry to be brutal but that's the way it is with him. End of story.'

I nodded, sickened once more by the memory.

'Tell me – did he take you to Chaya?'

It turned out Max had taken her years ago, when they'd first started talking about Shine. They'd sat in the banquette at the back drinking Slingchi Martinis and he'd fed her Tuna Tataki with his chopsticks. She'd got her inspiration for the Elements hummingbirds from the painting on the ceiling.

A horrible thought occurred to me. 'I think he took our estate agent there too – when he was trading sex for property.'

'What a zero.'

'A double zero.'

I could've gone on for hours, but she didn't want to dwell on Max a moment longer. 'So, I have news,' she said, pouring me another glass.

'A man?' I said, trying to look enthusiastic. Would he be too married, or too single?

'I met Hans last year, at a trade show,' she said, settling back, tucking her legs under her gypsy skirts. 'We exchanged business cards and some emails.' She sipped her tea thoughtfully, silent for a moment. I waited for the familiar retreat but it didn't come. She put her cup and saucer down gently and carried on. 'Then, when I was on the New York shoot, he rang to tell me he'd been commissioned to convert a SoHo loft and the owner wanted alpaca cushions and Tibetan tree bark. Was I interested?'

It could only have been a few weeks but she was clearly besotted with him, recounting his architectural vision with awe-struck wonder; how he was putting the wooden rainwater tank on the roof to good use by installing a master bathroom beneath it. 'Outside, it'll look like something out of *Blade Runner* but inside, with the steel girders, it'll feel like a twenty first century cathedral.'

'So what now? Will you cover New York in Tibetan tree bark?'

'More likely Balinese tree bark,' she said, unable to keep the grin off her face. 'Hans wants a place to warm his bones away from the New York freeze. We're going to travel the back roads by bicycle, look for a property, a traditional house.'

She was already excited about a place she'd seen online; it was a mile inland, in a valley dotted with coconut groves. 'It's really romantic – on the outskirts of a large village, opposite a white washed temple, but it's been neglected for decades, and the garden is so overgrown it's like a jungle. I can't wait to get stuck in but Hans says I should take it easy for a while, give myself a break. He says the first thing he's going to do is set me up on a sun lounger in the shade of a banyan tree, with a pile of books and a highball of coconut juice.'

I smiled at this image, which spoke so easily of love.

'Yes, he does,' she said softly, more to herself than to me. I waited for the long list of considerations and complexities that would surely follow, leaving her with a face like Eeyore. There were none.

'It's actually quite a big house,' she said, her face a glowing sunset.

'With plenty of room for?'

'Exactly,' said Zoffany. 'A whole row of Manchester United baseball caps.'

I smiled again, imagining Zoffany on her sun lounger, platting her adopted daughter's hair, the two of them about to get a drenching from her sons' water pistols.

She lowered her voice conspiratorially. 'You know Meg, I cancelled that Harley Street appointment.' At this admission, I knew that she was, finally, happy.

'Talking of Botox,' I said, preparing for my next confession.

Zoffany sighed. 'Further incidents?'

I told her about the autocue and then I handed her my phone – open on my freshly created 'Bitch' album, explaining how I'd managed to get my hands on such incontrovertible evidence, how I'd be presenting it to Max.

I waited expectantly for the round of applause, kudos for the risks I'd taken, but Zoffany was shaking her head, telling me that Shine wasn't good for me. That I should get out while I still could, while I was still 'Meg the Lovely'.

'As opposed to?' Honestly, she was making me sound like a monster, like I'd gone to the dark side. It wasn't like I'd planned it or anything.

'All I'm saying is this behaviour isn't you. When I told you Ashley had hacked my phone, you were horrified. Now, you've done it yourself.'

'You can't compare what I did to phone hacking,' I replied hotly, realising that maybe she could.

'You can be sure Max will sell Shine, and if he gives you shares, you'll be rich,' said Zoffany, speaking with calm self-assurance, without hiding behind either hair, or accent. 'But you'll have to put in a lot more time before you see any of that money, and you'll still be working for him. Is that really what you want?'

I told her I'd thought it all through. 'I can stomach it – I'm going to be learning from a master, and I can use the Asia trip to secure fair trade deals, and recruit the people we'll need out there – find some poor kids – train them up as teachers and beauticians.'

But while she listened patiently, this strategy clearly wasn't cutting any ice. She told me I was more than capable of running my own business, that I didn't need to spend years sitting at Max's feet, that the only way to make things happen the way I wanted them to happen was to do them myself. 'You know all you need to know. Just start off small and take it from there – build it slowly, and stay true to who you are. And if that's a bit scary perhaps you could do something with the equally lovely Nate?' At this she wiggled her eyebrows suggestively, a gesture that me laugh.

'Actually I do have a plan for him,' I said, telling her about The Yoga Project. How, just like Nate, they had 'pay it forward' donation boxes and hot chocolate whirls, but they also had a vertical garden, exposed brickwork, Geek-out and Peace-up, branded bolsters and (chrysanthemum-free) yoga pants.

'Follow your heart Meg,' she said, smiling to herself as she refilled my glass. 'I'm following mine.'

'Just one problem'

CHAPTER TWENTY-EIGHT

He was sitting alone in the yoga studio, his back hunched, staring into space.

'Nate,' I said gently.

He turned, his eyes taking a moment to focus. He was holding a framed photo of his mum – the one of her standing beside her teacher. She was beaming and rosy in a pink and gold sari, hands in prayer position, several inches taller than him. He was in a blue lungi and pressed short-sleeved shirt, a pen sticking out of his top pocket.

I didn't need to ask what was wrong; the mats were laid out ready for the next morning's class, half the number there'd been my first time.

'I stopped by Shine,' he said heavily. 'I wanted to see you, to thank you for the hamper, but they said you were in L.A.'

I waited.

'I liked that big blow-up picture of you in the café, your eyes all lit up, like a child at the fairground,' he said.

'Thank you,' I said, flatly.

'Max was there and this tiny dark haired girl was standing there gazing at him as if he was the second coming. I thought it might be your mate Ashley.'

'What did you think of the place? Not to your taste?'

'The coffee certainly wasn't.'

Was that a small glimmer of a smile?

'But I made myself sit down and take it all in, and finally I understood – the economics of a place like this don't work – you need branding, products, lots of centres.'

I shrugged, wishing I could feel happy that he'd finally got it.

Attempting another smile, he carefully returned his mum's picture to the wall, placing her above the giant Ganesh, the one he garlanded with fresh marigolds every week, the one he liked to touch before class.

I couldn't think of anything else to say, eventually managing a bumbling something or other about being sad, for both him and his mum.

He shook his head. 'Don't be. This place never made any proper money – even in the nineties when her guru came over. She was about as good at business as me, giving away free classes, letting people stay for nothing, handing out loans to teachers which they never repaid.'

I thought I might cry. He seemed so bereft – like she'd only just died.

He stood before Ganesh a long time, apparently lost in thought. Eventually, he touched the elephant's forehead, seeming to make some sort of peace with himself.

'I've thought a lot about what you said,' he said, 'and you were right. Mum *was* a free spirit. She'd never have wanted me to feel stuck here. It's time to move on.'

'Nate,' I said, 'what if I had a *really* good idea? One that doesn't involve Brand Visions.'

Announcing that he could listen better on a full stomach, he led me slowly upstairs, sitting me down on that old sofa by the fire, shooing Bernard out of the way. The sorry old thing heaved himself to his feet, gave my hand a quick lick and, seemingly exhausted by the effort, flopped back down, his legs splayed out, his chin on the floor.

Nate gave me a bowl of vegetable curry and sank into the opposite sofa. I ate every scrap and agreed to another helping. Then I picked a cupcake from the very large pile. 'No designer logos?' I said, peeling back its paper skirt, biting into the moist yellow icing and light lemon sponge.

'Strictly own label' he said, without enthusiasm.

I helped myself to a second, noticing that the picture I'd left for him, of us on the day of the shoot, had joined the ranks of photographs jumbled on the ledge behind him. It'd been framed and sat between the one of his mother hugging him tight on the veranda and the one of him in the well of his father's legs, smeared in chocolate.

Then I noticed the heap of mail on the table, including, on top of the pile, a rather official looking letter like the ones from lawyers I often saw on Max's desk.

I poked it cautiously, as if it might bite. 'What's that?'

'That's why I can move on, get that place in Snowdonia. The landlord wants me out, a hundred grand to go.'

'That's brilliant,' I said, trying to keep the squeak of desperation out of my voice. 'But my idea means you can stay in London – and make money.'

'It doesn't involve my body does it?' he said, attempting a smile.

'About that,' I began, once more forgetting my carefully rehearsed lines, 'I meant to say … I'm so sorry about all that … all that business … before I went to L.A … it was really stupid of me … I should never …'

At last he seemed to brighten up, a bit. 'You're right. It was disgraceful behaviour turning up like that, waving a bottle of champagne, demanding "fun", what kind of a woman are you?'

'A brazen hussy,' I replied.

'Well, you brazen hussy,' he said, attempting to rise to it, 'any time you need someone to hold your hair while you throw up, you call me and only me. Clear?'

I promised I would, aching to say more – how I wished I'd said 'yes' to the bike ride, how I wished I'd seen the Thames Barrier at night, how I wished I hadn't gotten in the way of myself yet again, but I told him instead about The Yoga Project.

I handed over the leaflet, enthusiastically describing the giant blackboard listing a ton of yoga therapies. 'There were mudras for headaches and mantras for hangovers, and it made me think of your pop-up – you'd be great at it. Plus, it would be a niche market for you. Therapy really isn't Max's thing.'

'Sounds interesting,' he said, sitting forward, picking up his newly acquired smart phone. Pretty soon, he was telling me how many Facebook likes The Yoga Project had, and how many Twitter followers. Then he was on their website, flicking through the pages with the air of a professional critic as I struggled to come to terms with fresh evidence of Nate the digital native.

'Interesting but lightweight,' he concluded eventually, putting down his phone. 'I want to do things that make a *real* difference. I want to use yoga to treat depression and addiction, not hangovers.'

'Hmm,' I said, pulling a large file out of my bag, handing it over. 'You're a real fun guy.'

'You can talk,' he replied, taking hold of it, feeling the weight.

'I'm not saying you shouldn't do the serious stuff – all I'm saying is you should offer the quick fix stuff too – it'll help you spread the word, and you'll get more people in – like you did with your pop-up thing.'

He began leafing through the file – a complete analysis of the US yoga as therapy market. It showed some pretty startling growth rates – fuelled by an increasing recognition, amongst the medical profession, that the drugs don't work, and clinical studies that proved its effectiveness. I sat and watched him in silence, soaking up the sunshine that was pouring through the windows, trying to accept the instant return of my potbelly, waiting for him to tell me what a genius idea it was.

At last, he looked up. 'Just one problem.'

'Shoot.'

'I'm not, generally speaking, a quick fix sort of guy.'

'True,' I said, 'but maybe you could learn to speed up a bit, move with the times?'

He didn't look quite as horrified as Becks had been at this idea.

'Maybe even mix it up with a bit of Vinyasa Flow?' I suggested, explaining how 'Peace-up' had left me feeling united with all beings, in touch with the '#YogaHood'.

He shrugged. 'I guess I could manage that – if it unites you with all beings.'

Encouraged, I told him about Ryan's playlist. Again, I found myself pushing against an open door. Pretending to read from his imaginary *Yogic Thoughts for the Day*, he quoted a Mr B.K.S. Iyengar – 'the rhythm of the body, the melody of the mind, the harmony of the soul create the symphony of life.' Then he told me he'd started compiling his own soundtracks. Unfortunately, on probing, they had more in common with Becks' playlists; more Krishna Das and Deva Premal than Bon Iver or Nina Simone, but no matter. He was interested, and that I could work with.

'I've definitely found my yoga,' I said happily. 'I just need you to teach it.'

'What about your tracking device?' he said, pointing at my bracelet. 'Won't they find out you've gone over to the other side?'

'It would have to be a secret yoga project,' I conceded. 'At least for the time being.'

'But even if I was to speed up a bit from time to time, do the music, do the quick fixes … I mean, the Spitalfields thing was okay but I'd need lots of stressed-out people to make it work.'

'Plenty of them in London,' I said. I explained where The Yoga

Project was, and how I could maybe help him find a mixed area, one that had plenty of his stock-in-trade idealists and dreamers but also lots of freelancers, office workers, and on-trend shop girls, all eager to escape the rat race for an hour. 'We could find somewhere a bit cheaper, somewhere up and coming, and that way we could invest some money in a bit of paint and polish as well as the deep and meaningful.' To my surprise, he didn't disagree. In fact, he thought it'd be a great strategy, if only he wanted to stay in London.

'I'm over it,' he said. 'I want to do a residential thing, like I said, in Snowdonia. Have people come and stay for a month, get proper help.'

Was he ever going to get off this Snowdonia thing? Why couldn't he see that it wouldn't work – who would want to go to sheep-dipped Wales? Not me, and I was pretty sure his druggies and ex-cons wouldn't either. He might as well rip up that cheque.

I pulled out another leaflet – this one would surely put him off. 'I wasn't going to show you this but perhaps, if you're hell-bent on Snowdonia, you should do an "eco boot camp".'

'Which is code for?'

'A hut in the middle of nowhere, no electricity, no hot water, no phone, no mini bar, no telly.'

'That would be great for ex-cons,' he said. 'All that fresh air, team spirit, cook-ups over an open fire—'

'Actually, I was thinking more about celebrities.'

'Really? Don't they prefer Shine?'

'Mostly, but it's a big thing in L.A. I think they like struggling in the wilderness occasionally – makes them feel real.' I read out the Californian camp's timetable feeling slightly sick; '"Four a.m. wake-up call"... "hot water and a squeeze of lemon" ... "yoga" ... "six hour silent hike" ... "stick of carrot" ... "gym"... "massage" ... "more yoga" ... "meditation" ... "stick of celery" ... "bed".'

I handed over the leaflet, watching in horror as he happily absorbed pictures of exhausted-looking women standing on rocks, their fists in the air, triumphant. Suddenly, his jaw dropped. '$4,000? A *week*?'

'Ah yes, the price of carrots.'

'"Revel in luxurious simplicity, commune with nature."' He looked up. 'Do you do huts?'

'Nope.'

'Or communal bathrooms?'

'Nope.'

'Or four a.m. starts?'

I tried a smile. 'Not unless I have a triple espresso in my hand.'

'Come on Meg, what do you say? Let's do it together. It'll be fun.'

I listened to myself sounding prim and distant – as if I was in a meeting with someone I'd never met before. 'I thought about it a lot when I was in L.A. and the quick fix London thing seemed like something we could both get into, but an eco boot-camp in Snowdonia?' I shook my head. 'No thanks Nate; I need to live in the city. I need glamour, fun, action.'

He raised his eyebrows suggestively at this last announcement.

'Not that kind,' I said, no longer sure what kind I meant. He was so handsome, so rooted, so kind, and his cupcakes were so good, but ... But what?

He was off, pacing up and down the room, suddenly full of enthusiasm. 'Fine – if you really don't want to do Snowdonia then we'll go somewhere else.' He picked up that picture of him on the veranda with his mum and dad. 'What about Goa? We could do an Indian eco-camp – that would be much more laidback; we could buy some land, dig a pool, get some Rajasthani tents – we'll call it "The Barefoot Project".'

Several minutes later, following a stream of consciousness regarding the logistics of Indian planning permission, he came back down to rest. He knelt in front of me, squeezing my hands, looking ever more earnest. 'What do you say Meg?'

My stomach lurched. I looked at the floor.

'What's the matter? You don't do tents? Rajasthani tents are *very* luxurious.'

I thought of Ganga's palace, of roller-skating down corridors, of dancing on tables, of sitting behind the latticework shutters pretending to be the maharani, and shook my head, still staring at the floor.

He lifted my chin, staring at me intently. 'So tell me what you want and let's do it.'

Keep breathing. What did I want? Wasn't *this* what I wanted? Wasn't this what I'd longed for, from all those miles away?

'You do your thing,' I found myself saying as I extricated my hands, suddenly needing to get back to the office, even though it was nine at night, 'and I'll do mine. I'm about to do a big tour of Asia – Beijing, Shanghai, Delhi, Mumbai, Bangalore and Chennai. It's really important I stay focused, it's big stuff.'

I gathered my things, looking up to see him grinning from ear to ear. 'What Nate? What's so funny?'

'It's just you always get so serious when you talk Shine, or Max, it's not very you.'

'What's the matter?' I said. 'You don't think my work is as serious as yours?'

'Meg, I didn't mean to offend you,' he said, looking alarmed, following me to the door.

'You watch,' I said, one hand on the bannister. I couldn't believe I was talking like this but I was like an engine stuck at full throttle. 'I'm about to persuade Max into fair trade and, with the amount of business Shine does, we can make a real difference to a serious number of people.'

'I know that,' he said, running down the stairs after me. 'And it's great–'

I cut him off with a slam of the door, not at all sure what I was running from, or towards.

'Let's get something straight'

I got word a couple of weeks later. Becks told me, over a bottle of wine, Ekatman would be closing, almost thirty years to the day after it opened. Nate would be marking the occasion with some close friends and a few drinks. She said he'd made a special point of inviting me. 'Tell him "thank you but no",' I'd said. 'He needs to focus on his future, and I need to focus on mine.' I had expected another lecture on loyalty but she'd said she understood – that '"payback" requires care and attention'.

Although the appeal of roller-skating down the maharajah's corridors had dimmed, I was absolutely determined to be that force for good I kept going on about. I'd accumulated several fat files on potential fair trade suppliers, and I'd already set up meetings with several of them. Bhakti House was an anti-sweatshop centre for Indian women whose families had been hit by alcoholism or violence. I thought they could supplement the maharajah's weavers, who would surely struggle to keep up with the burgeoning demand for our cushions, especially with the growth trajectory Max was now on. Threads of Hope, the Chinese fair trade organisation working to preserve the traditional handicrafts of the Yunnan, would work for the next Elements collection – of that I was sure. It'd taken a while but the samples had been worth the wait – hummingbirds and butterflies darting over sleeves, lotus flowers sprouting over satin panelling. Zoffany had got out her magnifying glass to show me the soft, loose twists (apparently a sure sign of hand embroidery), pronouncing her verdict with just one word. 'Fabulous.'

All I needed now was Max's go ahead.

I scheduled a meeting for late in the day, hoping that the high-octane performance that normally characterised his mornings would've mellowed into something more pliable. I prepared a discussion document, summarising the social benefits in a paragraph, spending many more on the financial payback that would come with all the positive P.R.

He was sitting at his desk, staring at the photograph of the silver barked forest that stretched across the opposite wall, unusually silent. I took a few moments; arranging my files, making sure I had at least two working pens and plenty of paper for note-taking.

'It's official,' he said, snapping the ring pull on his Diet Coke, looking grave. 'Zoffany has resigned. She's decided to meld with Hans Melman.'

I tried to feign surprise, not sure I succeeded. 'You must be relieved?'

He shrugged. 'Not really.'

'But it's what you wanted,' I said.

'I guess.'

'Seller's remorse?'

No response.

I tried focusing on something concrete. That usually worked when he was in one of his moods. 'Give her a party? Say goodbye properly – with a bit of style.'

He nodded, without enthusiasm, still lost in the forest. 'I expect she'll want Shoreditch House. Organise it will you? On me.'

I agreed to do it but, struck once more by how much she'd changed, I wondered if she'd really want a big party. I suspected she'd rather slope off without anyone noticing, leave it all behind.

'And there was another interesting revelation.' He was smiling but there was an edge to him, an undercurrent of anger that I couldn't explain.

I raised an eyebrow, carefully.

'She claims that Ashley hacked her voicemail.'

'Max,' I said, speaking slowly and steadily, 'I hate to tell you this but hacking voicemail is not her only problem. Ashley's also been tampering with snail mail.'

Explaining what had happened, I found the photo of my long-lost Post-it note and pushed my phone slowly across the table. I waited for the explosion.

I waited a long time, eventually breaking the silence with a prompt. 'So you're firing her, right?'

'I'll have a chat,' he said, lazily leaning back in his chair, crumpling the Coke can and lobbing it in the bin.

He couldn't be serious. 'But she broke the law, she nearly wrecked the shoot, she sabotaged my speech *and* she made me take a shower in full view of the whole changing room.' He probably didn't need to know that.

All he did was shrug his shoulders. 'I would fire her Meg but, like you, she's very good at her job, and right now – with all this Bazu Barre bullshit – I need all the help I can get.'

I stared at him in disbelief.

'Actually I'm thinking of making her Head of Defence; she can play Dick Cheney to my George Dubya–'

'You're hardly George Bush Max.'

'Okay, bad analogy, but these newly discovered talents might come in very handy one day. Yours too, by the looks of things.'

I arranged my face in a careful smile, but he didn't smile back – he kept looking at me, trying to burrow under my skin. I gave him a copy of the document and began outlining my case but it was hard to concentrate. Eventually I gave up. 'Is there something else Max?'

'You tell me,' he said, his voice tight.

'No,' I replied, 'I just hope Ashley's going to behave herself.' This got no reaction so I went back to the Bhakti House, skipping through the social benefits, dwelling on the money.

He listened for a few minutes as if he was back in an all-too-long Latin class, and then he chucked the document across the desk.

'Let's get something straight. Ganga's weavers have been with his family for hundreds of years. It's what happens with the Indian royals. Workers are handed down from one generation to the next, their skills are inherited as surely as the colour of their eyes, or the shape of their nose. If we de-commission them they'll be out of work, then they'll have to leave for the city and we'll be breaking up families.'

'But I don't want to close them down – demand is way outstripping supply, and anyway surely they aren't reliant on us? Isn't the maharajah is rich from all his land? He can't need to rely on income from a few weavers?'

'Why do you think he wants to turn his palace into a hotel Meg?' he asked tetchily, looking out of the window.

But the way I saw it, he was lucky to have a palace to turn into a hotel. 'The women I'm talking about have nothing. They're homeless and penniless, the victims of rape and alcoholism–'

He interrupted me, already exasperated. 'I thought I hired a businesswoman Meg. If you want to save the world, go work for Oxfam, and please don't start on about Chinese working conditions – there's no way we're closing that factory down.'

'Not closing it down – just diverting the embroidery to some disadvantaged women.'

'And what do you think will happen to the factory workers?'

'They'll work on something else.'

'No Meg, they'll be out on the streets.'

I launched into my 'fair trade will give us competitive edge' argument but it cut no ice. It appeared the bottom line was still in need of everyone's attention. That anything else would be a distraction. He sounded exactly like Pat on the subject of Chocolate Therapy. All he needed was a disbelieving snort, a shake of the head, a snapping shut of his laptop.

He looked at me sharply. 'Is this latest fit of naïve social fervour anything to do with the fact that Ekatman's closing today?'

'I'm just trying to do what's right for Shine.'

'Listen, Meg,' he hissed, 'I've had it with you and your misplaced conscience. First I find out you like nothing better than a cosy little chat with our nearest competitor–'

Ashley.

She must've followed me from Verde & Company to Ekatman. The woman was a fully-fledged stalker, another *Single White Female*.

I tried to pour cold water on the situation, telling him that 'the owner of Ekatman' and I were acquaintances. That I just dropped off a coffee, from time to time.

'Sure you don't give him advice? Tell him how to build a brand?'

Please say that was a lucky guess.

His body was stiff, his face flushed. 'Tell me something Meg. Where did I go wrong? I brought you in. I coached you. I did my best to make you part of our world, and how have you repaid me? By siding with the enemy.'

'"Siding with the enemy"?'

His phone clattered across the desk, landing in front of me. 'How do you explain this?'

I peered at the photo on the screen. There I was, the 'Ekatman – the road home – #YogaHood' placard clearly visible, a few feet away.

I held the phone in my hand for what seemed like an eternity, wishing I could hurl it out of the window, along with Ashley.

I tried telling the truth, knowing it was useless. 'I was just doing my Christmas shopping, buying my mum some bubble bath, and I came across the stall, quite by chance. I saw the placards and I was curious.'

He grabbed the phone out of my hand and flicked to another picture. 'So how do you explain this?'

It was the one of Nate and me on the shoot, him piping, me looking up at him, eyes wide, holding out a handful of crystals.

I stared at it, blinking stupidly.

'And to think I was wondering if I'd made a mistake…'

'"A mistake"?'

'In L.A.,' he mumbled, 'a mistake in L.A.'

Why was he dredging that up again? 'We both thought that was a mistake.'

'No, I'd been thinking that … well, maybe it was a mistake to have gone off with …'

'You don't even remember her name, do you?'

I waited for an answer, but he'd retreated once more into the silver barked forest. I was alone. For once in my life, I felt no need to rush in, to fill up the silence.

Finally, he spoke. 'Meg,' he said, 'I want you make a choice, and I want you to make it now. Who's it going to be? Shine or Ekatman? Me or Nate?'

'Snowdonia? Goa? Tibet?'

I bolted out of Max's office and I ran. I ran and I ran. Down the stairs, out of the revolving doors, past Verde & Company, past the market, past the white spire of Christ Church, towards the grimy bricks and peeling front doors of Nate's street.

I stood outside for several minutes, trying to tally the scene I'd imagined (Nate and a few friends drinking from plastic beakers on a battered old mat) with this one. One in which Paul Simon's *Graceland* boomed through the steamed up windows and shapes danced behind the glass, the fractured colours lighting up the wintry night like jerky magic lanterns.

There was a makeshift poster on the wall, inviting all of Ekatman's students 'past and present' to 'Party-up', to celebrate thirty years of Ekatman with a 'Closing Party, Eighties Style'. Cautiously, I stuck my head round the studio door. Someone channelling Madonna in her *Desperately Seeking Susan* days, complete with hair bow, several ropes of pearls and crucifixes, and fingerless white lace gloves, was spinning the wheels of steel. Becks was in the front row. She was executing a perfect Up Dog to Cyndi Lauper's *Girls Just Wanna Have Fun* – the bubble-gum-pink wig, gold spandex leggings and matching leotard seeming to sing along. There must have been fifty yogis squashed in there, all of them in wigs and legwarmers, all of them smiling as Nate moved amongst them, stretching an arm here, rotating an ankle there, the spinning retro disco ball sweeping the room with strobing beams of red and green light.

Nate's quiff had been blow-dried into a soft wave and he was wearing a white t-shirt with *Choose Life* emblazoned in big black letters across the front. He was also sporting a pair of neon pink shorts that showed of his ass-etts to perfection, especially when he skipped along in imitation of his alter ego, somehow still managing to look manly. He even had a headset microphone – something of a necessity over the sound system, which was now throwing out Wham's *Wake Me Up Before You Go-Go* at full volume. He saw me just as George reached for 'I want to hit that high'. Giving me a big grin, he threw me a pair of baggy orange leggings (a sadhu's leave behind or MC Hammer's?) and indicated, with some very precise hand movements, that I should get on down, on his mat.

What choice did I have? Nodding to Becks, as if gold spandex was her usual thing, I got with the programme. For the first time in my life, I found myself wishing I'd been in a Nate class from the beginning. People were actually sweating – as was I within a couple of minutes. Not that it was a Yo-Jitsu mat-fight. It was fluid and easy, flowing effortlessly from one seemingly inappropriate song to the next as if all the eighties classics had been created for this class. From Culture Club's *Karma Chameleon* to Prince's *Raspberry Beret*, from Duran Duran's *Rio* to Madonna's *Into the Groove*, we moved 'breath and energy through the body' without missing a beat.

And through it all there was a playfulness to him, which I'd seen in private from time to time but which seemed to have finally made its way into the studio. News just in; Yoda had set himself free. He punctuated the standing sequence with a string of very bad jokes. 'Why stay flexible? So you can kick your own ass.' 'What did the plug say to the socket? It's time to get grounded.' 'Live in the moment, unless it's unpleasant – in which case eat cake.' And his instructions were as playful as the wigs. In Down Dog we were told to 'flower the buttocks', in Up Dog to 'shine the collarbones', in Garland Pose to 'relax the earlobes'. Those attempting Scorpion were told to remember that 'a smile is the most advanced yoga pose of all'. I stayed with Locust so I could focus on 'raising the upper eyelashes' along with my knees and ankles.

Even the breath work was a breeze. He kept it simple – two long breaths in, 'ballooning your tummy', then one short exhale, 'misting your mirror'. By the end, when we came to lie down in Corpse Pose, I was so blissed out I managed to relax into the plucking strings of Enya's *Orinoco Flow* – a song I'd OD'd on as a child because mum thought her flowers liked it.

And then we were sitting up, chanting what he called 'A Sea of Oms'. This wasn't something they taught at Shine, but it was easy to get the hang of. Nate divided the room into rows with each one starting their Om at a different point, until wave upon wave hit the shore. By the time we were done, I felt like I was back at The Yoga Project – totally loved up and at one with the YogaHood.

After it was over, we all sat for a while, none of us moving. The Sea of Oms had turned into a Sea of Sniffs. Becks passed me a tissue and I dabbed my eyes as subtly as I could, not feeling it was my place to cry. How was Nate doing? Better than the rest of us by the looks of things – if he'd shed a tear it didn't show. He was smiling, his hands in prayer position at his heart. He rang a small bell and we said a final 'Namaste' bowing to him, and to each other. I, for one, could've sat for hours (well at least a few minutes) contemplating the peace and feeling of connectedness but Nate wasn't in the mood for contemplation. He was thanking us for 'sharing our energy', telling us that the class was a celebration of everything that his mother stood for, 'legwarmers, community, and fun', and that he hoped we would take that feeling with us wherever we went, starting with the dance floor.

I wanted to thank him, to congratulate him, to hug him, but the crowd immediately subsumed him, moving around him like a shoal of fish. I turned to Becks but she had disappeared. Feeling suddenly alone, I went in search of the loo. Changing out of those baggy orange leggings was something of a relief but then, with the sound of Roxette's *It Must've Been Love* booming in the background, it hit me again. It was over. There'd be no more Ekatman. No more Nate.

What had I done to help him? More to the point, what was he going to do now? He was probably leaving for Snowdonia in the morning – charging $4000 for an eco boot camp, or helping ex-cons. Either way, his plans didn't include me. I put the loo seat down, grabbed some more tissues, and buried my head in my hands. He'd been prepared to go anywhere with me, do anything, and what had I done? Rejected it all in favour of that sleaze ball and his stupid maharajah. Yes, yours truly would rather be a buff-bodied, fast-tracking corporate girl, circling the globe eating pink sushi than put down some solid roots with a man who could look manly in a pair of pink shorts *and* bake cake.

Deciding that I needed to get out of there, I dried my eyes, did my best to restore my makeup, and crept towards the door. Hopefully, he'd still be mid-shoal and wouldn't notice me leaving. If I hurried I could get back to the flat, pack my stuff and make the last train for Devon. I could stay with mum and dad for a few days while I decided what to do next with my dumb-assed self.

I was inches from a clean getaway, my hand on the doorknob.

'Not so fast young lady,' he said, covering my hand with his, pulling me back into the studio with a strength that belied that gentle manner, maintaining his grip as he guided me firmly towards the long trestle table piled high with crisps, dips and cocktail sausages, and centre stage a giant bowl of Chimney Fire alongside a massive tiered cake. It reminded me of that house in Venice – a precarious pile of three layers, each trimmed with crests of piped fondant icing. Judging by the uneven edges, Nate had been at the Chimney Fire when he made it. Grabbing a giant ladle, he sloshed what must've been a pint of alcohol into my glass, all the while maintaining his grip.

Whilst I'd been crying in the loo, the studio had been emptied of mats, blocks and props. The picture of his mum and Ganesh had been freshly garlanded in so many ropes of marigolds they were pretty much invisible. The rest of the marigolds hung round the necks of my fellow yogis, which gave the party a Hawaiian air. A blissed-out Becks was right there at the centre of it all, arms akimbo. I made a move towards her, dragging my warden in her direction.

I was expecting us to fall into our carefully choreographed dance routine, but Nate was holding me back and I soon realised why. My services were surplus to requirements. A tall guy, a fop-haired type, was playing Prince to Becks' Sheena Easton. It was a pitch perfect imitation of the *U Got the Look* video. It worked well for both of them; she stood with her feet theatrically astride, her hands on her hips, throwing her head back and to the side, just about in time to the beat, giving the occasional hip shake, while he preened and pranced around her – eating her up with his eyes.

I raised my eyebrows, questioning Nate.

'Her agent,' he confided.

He was the polar opposite of what I'd expect; his chiselled jaw gave him the look of an old Etonian but there was no arguing with it – she looked nineteen again, back on the college dance floor.

'We have him to thank for our drinks,' said Nate, raising his glass.

I raised my glass obediently. 'To?'

'Sebastian,' he said, putting on his poshest accent. 'His grandfather sold his company to Unilever. Made squillions.'

'A thoroughly decent chap?' I said, mimicking his accent, looking on as our Seb played air guitar at Becks' feet.

'A very decent chap,' said Nate, downing the remainder of his tumbler.

I joined him, feeling it heat my entire body, right down to my toes.

'Shall we?' asked Nate, taking hold of my arm.

We really worked it; first a Michael Jackson medley, then Madonna, then Shalimar and S'Express. We made it into the nineties at one point – with some Britney, Destiny's Child and even a bit of Right Said Fred. Guess who was too sexy for his shirt?

'Bit modern for you!' I shouted in his ear, at least an hour later, trying to catch my breath.

'I'm moving with the times,' he said smiling, shamelessly shaking his booty.

And on we went, past midnight, then one, then two, then three. There was no way either of us was going to let each other out of our sights again – even when the conga snaked out of the house and down Brick Lane, even when a coterie of female followers attempted an intervention, even during the speeches and the tears and the group hugs. I was always by his side, my hand in his.

And finally, at four in the morning, after Becks, Seb and the two of us had given Paula Abdul's *Opposites Attract* a good going over, a process that involved several dodgy eighties neck rolls (Becks and me), implausible moonwalks (Nate and Seb), and a Cabbage Patch foursome – the two of us were alone.

Up the stairs we went, one last time, followed by the unmistakable wheeze of an elderly dog.

We sat together, contemplating the rooftops and chimneypots and the white spire, Bernard sandwiched between us, huddling for warmth.

'So, what happened?' he asked, reaching under the bench for his secret stash of Amaretto.

I shrugged – it all seemed so simple now. 'I made a choice.'

I fished around in my bag, emerging with an already battered copy of the brand new *Shine* magazine – the one with the *Relaunching Meg* article which described me as 'plucked from the obscurity of a burlap lined cubicle and deposited in a Rodeo Drive dressing room, emerging to gasps of astonishment, as a beautiful, self-assured young woman.'

I handed it over. 'It came out last week.'

'Well,' he said, holding up the double page spread to the light, 'they got one thing right – you do look beautiful.'

'It's like reading someone else's story,' I said, shaking my head.

'It's a great story,' he said, still looking at the pictures.

'I spent the whole week carrying it around, trying to work out what was wrong and then, just now, when I was in this meeting with Max, I realised what it was. I need to live my own story, be my own person, make a difference on my terms, with people I admire – with people I like, with people who eat cake.'

'Proud of you Yodini,' he said, reluctantly parting with the magazine. 'But you should send Max a thank you note.'

I stared at him, completely baffled. 'Why on earth would I want to do that?'

'It's about acknowledgment.'

'You've lost me there Yoda.'

'Because Shine got you to this place. Whatever form the yoga took – whatever kind of a mash-up it was, it worked. It transformed you – inside and out. You're here now – a different person to the one you used to be.'

'But I stooped pretty low in the process,' I said, explaining my own phone hacking episode, and drawer-raid.

He listened quietly, taking it all in and then, refilling our glasses, he suggested I should also thank Ashley. 'Because all her stirring helped you get to this point – you got to see that Shine, and Max, weren't your story.'

I took a deep breath and sighed, mentally writing both notes, then I found myself wanting to kill Ashley again, so I changed the subject, to the one I really wanted to talk about. 'So what's next for Nate? An ex-con boot-camp eco-lodge half way up a mountain?'

'How did you guess?' He pulled some estate agent details from his pocket, smoothing down the papers.

My heart sank. 'Where is it? Snowdonia? Goa? Tibet?'

'Bruton.'

I'd been there once, years before, on a family holiday through Somerset and Devon. The three of us had laughed at a school called Sexey's, but it wasn't as promising as the name suggested – less sexy, more Church of England. The place had no glamour, fun, or action, and definitely no bright lights. I'd been bored, at the age of twelve.

He seemed to read my thoughts. 'It's changed a lot in the last few years. There's a huge art gallery nearby and an award winning restaurant in a converted chapel right in the centre of town – it's got a bakery, a wine shop, loads of designer tree bark, and they make the perfect espresso.'

'Sounds okay,' I said slowly, unconvinced.

'And they put on lots of events – book clubs, fashion shows, films, even flamenco dancing.' He clicked his fingers, modelling a twig as if it was a rose between his teeth.

I laughed.

'But the best bit is the "demographic profile",' he said, earnest now. 'My extensive consumer research has revealed a mixed area with a weekday population of working families, and a lucrative weekend market of second homers, yummy mummies and creative types. Would you like a full market analysis? I have several files on the subject.'

'Proud of you Yoda,' I said. He really had been listening, and not only that, he'd done something about it – put a plan into action, which was more than I'd managed.

'Whether my customer has a headache, a hangover, or full-on depression, I'll be there.'

'Yoga as therapy?'

'It'll be my own special blend – moving on the breath, music, mudras, meditation and mantras – I'm calling it "Freedom Flow".'

'Your own brand?' I smiled. 'I'm impressed.'

'I have a good teacher.'

I faked modesty, fanning my face. 'So this is really happening?'

'I'm going to see this place tomorrow,' he said, handing me the details. 'I hope it's okay. It's going for a song–'

I took in the Spartan details of the long disused dairy. 'Nothing but a few old milk churns...'

'And lots of worn-out brickwork, plenty of room for improvement.' He paused a moment, pouring me yet more Amaretto. 'You interested?'

I stared at the white spire, at the fairy lights. There'd we'd been ... fifty yogis and me – one YogaHood under a groove. I took a deep breath. It was suddenly very clear to me that the YogaHood needed to extend beyond yoga students and teachers to yoga studios, and that it needed me to make it happen. 'Yoga is a high fixed cost business – the only way to make money is to create a global brand so that's what we're going to do; except in our case it's going to be a yoga alliance – an alliance of independents. We'll create a network of studios and we'll share ideas and programmes, teachers and values, branding and marketing–'

'Brilliant,' said Nate, pulling his laptop from a canvas bag under the bench, opening it on his Facebook page – which I noted had a thousand likes. He shared one of The Yoga Project's posts as he explained that we'd build our community really quickly if we pinned each other's studios, Instagrammed our teachers, retweeted each other, all with the 'YogaHood' hashtag. How this would make the marketing budget go that much further, how this would improve both 'our reach and our engagement'.

I nodded as if these were entirely normal things for him to say and then I told him that we should have our own range of workout clothes, that we should get them embroidered by Threads of Hope, and have Bhakti House make up our floor cushions. Then I told him that we would be good global citizens, training yoga teachers in the developing world, and that all our centres would be rooted in community, teaching local disadvantaged kids the art of freshly baked gingerbread.

'We'll be smart and polished,' said Nate, following his own train of thought, smoothing down his hair, pretending to preen himself. 'We'll wear black aprons and chalk up our daily specials on blackboards.'

I felt the need to remind him that we'd also be deep and meaningful, that we'd help cancer sufferers and alcoholics, the depressed and the dispossessed, but he appeared more interested in Friday night yoga raves, in 'moshing the bhajans pit, glo-sticks at the ready.'

'We'll have vertical gardens and horizontal gardens,' I countered, 'grow our own produce, cook using a few simple ingredients.'

But his shallows knew no bounds. 'A thick glossy cookbook which we can retail for twenty pounds; *Zen and the Art of Cupcakes*,' he said, sitting up tall, looking every inch the yoga mughal.

'Don't forget the 'take one leave one' library Nate. We'll stock it with plenty of copies of *Yoda Yoga: the Art of Breath*.'

'We can do our own app – "a class a day the Yoda way",' he continued, on a roll. 'A pound a pop.'

'Whatever happened to community classes and paying it forward?' I said, laughing. 'Of course, we'll need a mission; getting newbies on the mat – "one small step for yoga, one giant leap for mankind"–'

'"#MakeGoodHappen",' said Nate, sharing a photo of a dancing Becks and Seb on The Yoga Project's page.

'We'll be yogapreneurs,' I said, thinking back to the day when

I first told Becks about Max, never dreaming I'd be one myself one day, that I might even be his competition. Partnering all those existing independents, bringing yoga values to entrepreneurship, rather than City values to yoga, would give us a pretty powerful brand – open, authentic, engaged with the local community. We might even win.

'We'll be billionaires!' said Nate easily, sitting back and enjoying the view. 'Down Dog billionaires.'

'Nate,' I said, giving him a fake stern look, 'you're motivated by your mission more than money, remember? We'll reinvent what "billionaire" means – make it about changing lives – one billion lives.'

'Starting with our own lives? With Bruton?' said Nate, pretending to look chastened.

'I'll be travelling a lot of course – networking – making sure we get the economies of scale we're going to need,' I said, already planning my schedule. 'I'll need to go back to L.A., have a chat with The Yoga Project people – best to start with them. We need to be ethical right from the word go – honest and transparent. Then I can maybe go on to New York, then Canada – see who we might want to partner in Vancouver and Montreal, then Sydney, Melbourne, Perth, Byron Bay, possibly Asia. Do you think Goa Nate? Or should we take a look at Chennai first?'

'I get it,' he said, '"the world is not enough" for Meg Rogers, but Bruton? What about Bruton?'

'I'm seeing yoga house parties,' I said, 'an open kitchen and a well-stocked honesty bar, with plenty of Chimney Fire and that Friday night yoga rave.'

Nate beamed, quoting as if from his new website. '"The studio aesthetic is by Zoffany de Gournay – a world leading interior designer."'

'I think she has other plans,' I said, shaking my head, smiling at the thought.

'But what about our alpaca cushions?'

'Fine,' I said. 'We'll find a South American affiliate and spin our own.'

Then I told him there was just one more small detail we needed to agree.

'The name?'

'That's right – and it can't be Ekatman. Please.'

'Oh, Meg,' he said, putting on my voice, which sounded just a little bit preachy, 'don't you get it? Marketing rule 101: "a brand name must always be memorable".'

'I was thinking maybe "The Yoga House"? Like "Soho House"?'

He shrugged, telling me it was a possibility, of course. Then he told me, with great seriousness, that we needed to consider our partners, and that the name would need to work for a global alliance. 'I'm thinking if we're doing joint branding it should be "The Yoga Project: Bruton" as long as "The Yoga Project: Abbot Kinney" are okay with it.'

'Why wouldn't they be?' I replied, looking forward to that conversation.

'And you're okay with it?' he said, searching my face. 'With Bruton? Definitely?'

I took his hand, feeling its warmth in mine, and then, listening to the simple joy I felt on the back of my neck, in my tummy, between my toes, feeling my heart beating slow and sure, knowing that I was exactly where I wanted to be, and that I would carry this feeling with me as long as I could gaze upon his face, I told him. I told him that there would be more roads to travel (hopefully with a few five star hotels along the way) but that he, Nate, would always be my road home. Then he kissed me, and finally, I knew the true meaning of Ekatman.

Acknowledgments

David, my husband, has been with me from first to last; contributing his formidable EQ to characters and dialogue with insight and patience. Thank you my love.

Thank you to my agent John Noel, editor Alex Hodson, and readers: Jo Prince-White, Lorna Spear, Leah Giorno, Sabine Winkler, Sara Sherriff, Rosie Winston, Heather McColm, Sam Turpin, Mandy Brinkley, Rachel Barke, Jane Worrall.

Mum and my step dad Oliver shared their wit and grammatical wisdom. Nikki Edge, Matt Edge, Paola de Carolis and Annabel Chown kept me on the rails. Yvonne Mascarenhas was the light at the end of the tunnel. Cynthia Mascarenhas, cordon bleu chef, gave me the designer icing and the dash to the Asian supermarket. Rosie Winston and Frances Ruffelle sprinkled their stardust on the best of Shine, and the cover. Duncan Peach, Ben Wallman, and Princess Leah were a galaxy of smarts. Carleton Van Selman nudged me to the title. Paul Schwartzman owns L.A.'s revolving oil dredges, small rusting dinosaurs, and Obama-supporting farmers' markets. Maria Glynn gave me Southcote. Tony Conway wrote most of Zoffany's French. Stephen Rowson taught me Tungsten and Flash lighting. Steve Kelly donated the toast and peanut butter.

I first read about 'celebriyogis' on Yoga Dork. Luke Lewis, editor-in-chief of BuzzFeed UK, wrote 'Twenty Ludicrous Things Said By Yoga Teachers' – including flowering buttocks and shining collarbones. Vinyasa yoga teacher Clara Roberts-Oss wrote the LuluLemon blog post that inspired Ryan's playlist. Jed's tales of home have roots in Michael Walker's *Laurel Canyon* (Faber and Faber, 2006). Model-turned-baker, Lorraine Pascale, inspired Shonda's back story. *New York Magazine* writer Veronique Hyland coined the term 'couture body' and named the gym 'the new atelier' *(Grazia,* 18th May 2015). Thomas Burrow, with an MIT team and industry professionals, developed a high-tech yoga mat that lights up and detects pressure. 'When coupled with an instructional video, Glow can teach yoga nearly as well as an instructor or yoga class.'

Freedom at Midnight by Larry Collins and Dominique Lapierre (Vikas Publishing House PVT Ltd, 1976), Gayatri Devi's *A Princess Remembers* (Rupa & Co, 1995) and *Maharajah* (V&A Publishing, 2009) gave me insight into life in India's royal courts, but I experienced it first hand thanks to Yadavendra Singh, esteemed descendant of the royal family of Samode. His generosity resulted in several nights of unbridled luxury at the beautifully restored Samode Palace, Jaipur. The magnificent Durbar room, where Ganga's father had conducted his court business, Zoffany's place behind the lattice-work shutters, and the idea of a roller-skating maharani come from this experience (although I'd like to reassure the family that I did not try this for real).

About the author

Lucy Edge worked in advertising for many years; spending her days debating whether the Jolly Green Giant should extend his vocabulary beyond 'ho, ho, ho' and her evenings eating M&S ready meals for one. One day she gave it all up in favour of a quest for life's deeper meaning in the yoga schools of India. Her memoir *Yoga School Dropout* records her encounters with Gucci clad gurus, hugging mothers and swoony swamis as she searches, ever more desperately, for mystic Indians, Tantric bliss and a boyfriend. Emails from readers wanting recommendations inspired her to create YogaClicks.com – the place for the global community to find, love and share their yoga. Now married and living in Norfolk, Lucy spends her days making YogaClicks the best of web platforms and her nights writing books. (She is very lucky to have such an understanding husband, as he likes to remind her.) *Down Dog Billionaire* is her first novel.

lucyedge.com

Yoga School Dropout describes a quest that never went entirely to plan, but brave readers didn't let that stop them - they got in touch, wanting recommendations on yoga holidays and classes and teacher training.

So far, so brilliant. Just one problem.

I was sun saluting on a pinhead; I didn't know jack about yoga anywhere except India or London.

Then I had an idea.

I was, in the words of Brody as he stared down the shark called Jaws, 'gonna need a bigger boat'.

A much bigger boat. A crowd-sourced boat.

A place for the global community to find, love and live great yoga – the teachers that inspire us, the centres that welcome us, the holidays that change our lives.

So we found our rock star developer and we built our boat, and David named our boat YogaClicks. And now all it needs is you. Join us!

Lucy

#YogaHood

Printed in Great Britain
by Amazon